BRIARPATCH
TIM PRATT

ChiZine Publications

FIRST EDITION

Briarpatch © 2011 by Tim Pratt
Cover artwork © 2011 by Erik Mohr
Cover design © 2011 by Corey Beep
All Rights Reserved.

LIBRARY AND ARCHIVES CANADA CATALOGUING IN PUBLICATION

Pratt, Tim, 1976-
    Briarpatch / Tim Pratt.

ISBN 978-1-926851-44-0

    I. Title.

PS3616.R38B75 2011   813'.6   C2011-905038-2

CHIZINE PUBLICATIONS
Toronto, Canada
www.chizinepub.com
info@chizinepub.com

Edited and copyedited by Chris Edwards
Proofread by Stephen Michell

For my family, which gives me purpose.

BRIARPATCH
TIM PRATT

"You can skin me, Br'er Fox," Br'er Rabbit said. "Or pluck out my eyes, or pull off my ears, or cook me for stew. Do your worst, but just please don't throw me in that briarpatch."

But Br'er Fox wanted to hurt Br'er Rabbit just as bad as he could, so he caught him by the back legs and flung him right in the middle of the briarpatch. Br'er Rabbit hit the bushes and commenced to twistin' and wailin' until he dropped down in the vines and thorns, and Br'er Fox waited around to see what would happen.

By and by Br'er Fox heard someone call his name and saw, way up on the hill, Br'er Rabbit sitting on a log, laughing fit to bust. Then Br'er Fox knew he'd been tricked.

Br'er Rabbit hollered out, "Born and raised in the briarpatch. I was born and raised in the briarpatch!" Then Br'er Rabbit raced off as quick as could be.

—from "Br'er Rabbit and the Tar Baby" (traditional)

ONE
JUMPERS

BRIDGET JUMPS

1

The night before Bridget walked out of Darrin's life, six months before he watched her climb over the railing of the Golden Gate Bridge and dive headfirst into the water 200 feet below, six months and four seconds before she struck the surface of San Francisco Bay with a force of 15,000 pounds of pressure per square inch, dying instantly from the resulting physical trauma, they had this conversation:

"Remember when you said you wanted to drink wine from the small of my back?" Bridget asked. She stretched out face-down on their bed, naked, a pillow under her chin. Candles burned on the dresser, and tinkling jazz played on the bedside radio.

Darrin trailed his fingertips down the smoothness of her leg, past the little scar she'd acquired trying to break up a dogfight as a child, pausing at the back of her knee, one of the many places she loved to be kissed. "I remember. The first night we slept together." He leaned over and kissed the concavity at the base of her spine, the little cup that hollowed when she lay on her belly. Her skin smelled warm and sweet and like nothing other than Bridget herself.

"That was the sexiest thing I'd ever heard," she said. "I still get fluttery when I think about it."

"Really? I don't remember you reacting much at the time."

"I was probably too fluttery back then. That was, what, two years ago? My flutters are under better control now." She paused, piano and clarinet filling the empty space between sentences. "Why didn't you ever do it?"

Darrin ran his finger in a circle around the little elliptical birthmark between her shoulder blades. "I don't know. Logistics? I could do it now, if you like. I think there's a bottle of shiraz in the kitchen."

"No." She rolled over into him. "Let's just sleep. I like sleeping with you. You're never wiggly or restless. I don't know how you sleep so well."

"Just blessed with good brain chemistry, I guess." He spoke lightly, unwilling to broach the subject of sleepless nights, the principle symptom of Bridget's anxieties and dissatisfactions. So he got up, blew out the candles, climbed into bed, and she curved against him, into him, in the dark. He felt no trepidation, nor did he feel unusually blessed; they'd slept together this way every night for more than a year, since she had moved into his apartment.

In the morning, he woke alone. She'd taken an overnight bag and a few changes of clothes, and most of her things from the bathroom. She'd left her art supplies, the pressed-flower handmade paper, the glue, the linen, the brushes, even her stash of dried hallucinogenic mushrooms; but she'd taken her good red winter coat, the one he'd bought for their ski trip the year before. The missing coat struck him as strange, because it was spring when she walked out, and warm. For a while, he tried to believe she'd taken the coat because it was a gift from him. She hadn't left a note, so he had to take comfort where he could.

Bridget was wearing the red coat when he watched her die. That was a colder day, and it was windy then, up on the bridge.

2

Darrin almost never went into the city anymore, not since losing his lover and his job and his car in one terrible month, so it seemed beyond the range of normal coincidence that he should encounter Bridget for the first time in two seasons on the pedestrian walkway halfway across the Golden Gate Bridge. Had he arrived five minutes sooner, he might have reached her, stopped her, saved her; had he arrived five minutes later, he would not have seen her at all, just the knot of tourists clustered around the guardrail, leaning out, looking at the grey water below. Instead he arrived at 10:17 A.M.—he knew to the minute, because his digital camera had a time-stamp for each photo it took—at the perfect moment to see but not intervene in Bridget's death.

Darrin had not believed in God since he was eight years old, but the fact of his arrival at that moment on that morning was enough, almost, to make him believe in something, some forceful consciousness looking down on events in the world and occasionally manipulating them for reasons of its own.

Darrin had taken a train from Oakland, under the bay, into San Francisco—The City, as everyone called it, as if San Francisco were the Platonic ideal of cityhood, and Oakland a clumsy imitation. Darrin took nothing with him but his wallet, containing a few dollars in cash and his only un-maxed-out credit card, and his best digital camera, the one he'd bought during the last of the good days. He probably should have sold the camera, but he liked to think things were less dire than they were, and taking photos was his current comforting obsession, newest in a long line of passionate diversions that had included brewing his own beer, rock climbing, juggling, Chinese cuisine, designing his own crossword puzzles, and various other mayfly pursuits, each explored deeply, then quickly discarded when he grew bored. For the moment though, taking photos consumed him, and observing the world through the lens provided a distraction from the broken-up mess his life had become. He was going into the city to have lunch with his friend Nicholas in the financial district—where Darrin had once worked himself—and he'd decided to come early and take a few pictures.

It was a day of surpassing clarity, as windy and cool and bright as only a rainless autumn day in San Francisco could be, and he wanted to stand on the Golden Gate Bridge and take pictures of the boats and islands in the bay, the headlands of Marin, and any other people drawn to the morning views. After Bridget left him, after he was fired, after his car was repossessed, Darrin had retreated into himself, into a depression deeper than any of Bridget's had ever been, but one day, a few weeks before, he picked up the camera and decided to take a walk. By forcing him to look at the world again, the camera had saved him . . . or at least arrested his downward spiral. He wasn't happy, but he was, at least, awake.

In that first two minutes on the bridge he photographed the hilly headlands of Marin, the dizzying heights of the suspension towers and the thick support cables, the boats in the bay against the bleak profile of Alcatraz. All were photos he'd seen countless times before, but he'd never taken them himself, and that mattered. Darrin moved along the pedestrian walkway, almost halfway down the bridge, and then stopped when he spotted a familiar-looking woman standing twenty-five feet away, her face in profile.

Bridget.

At least he thought it was Bridget, but in the past months he'd caught so many glimpses of women who looked a little like her, and felt his heart leap up only to fall again when he realized they were strangers, that now he resisted his own recognition. She leaned with her elbows on the rail, looking not out to sea but in toward the bay, her blonde hair blowing around her face— longer than Darrin remembered, but the colour was right: the honeyed hue of the best afternoon light. She wore a coat just like the one he'd bought Bridget, red as an arterial spurt, but that was a common colour. Her cheeks were pink from the wind, her gaze seemingly fixed on some point in the distance. Darrin almost called her name, but then lifted the camera instead, zooming the view to make *sure* it was her, feeling a surge of pre-emptive disappointment in his chest.

Her image rushed toward him in the viewfinder, and yes, it was Bridget, suddenly brought into heartbreaking range. He instinctively pressed the button and took a photo—he didn't do much else these days, and the action was automatic.

Darrin lowered the camera and drew breath to call her name just as she grasped the railing and vaulted nimbly over it, graceful as always—she'd been a gymnast as a teenager, before discovering the joys of alcohol, psychedelic mushrooms, and smoking, all passions she'd retained into adulthood. Darrin didn't shout, stunned by her action, though he didn't believe she intended to jump. Bridget had often been sad, but never suicidal. If anything, she wanted *more* life, profounder experiences, grander passions, greater wonders to behold. She'd talked often about changing her life, but never about ending it.

Bridget steadied herself beyond the guardrail, her footing firm as she held the rail nonchalantly with one hand. Darrin ran toward her, calling her name, but his voice was lost in the wind and the chorus of voices from the tourists, all shouting at Bridget to watch out, to be careful, to come back, some of them starting toward her, to save her from herself. She ignored them all, the expression on her face a sort of determined serenity. Darrin was five steps away, not quite grabbing distance, when she let go and fell, head first, to the bay below.

One of the tourists chanted loudly, as if counting the moments between the flash of lightning and the crack of thunder: "One-one-thousand, two-one-thousand, three-one-thousand, four-one-thousand," and then Bridget hit the bay and disappeared. She looked like nothing so much as a single drop of blood striking the water. Tourists crowded around the railing, surrounding Darrin, pressing him against the rail. One of the small boats on the bay manoeuvred to the place where Bridget had struck, but Darrin knew it was hopeless, too late— she'd hit head first, and she was gone.

The tourists were yelling, and Darrin hated every member of the human race at that moment. Someone spoke calmly to a 911 operator on a cell phone, and Darrin's hatred subsided as suddenly as it had erupted, replaced by a cold aura of shock and disbelief. The woman he'd loved—still loved—the woman who'd hurt him as no one else ever had, was dead, by her own decision. Darrin pushed his way through the massing crowd and stumbled along the walkway, camera dangling forgotten around his neck, looking nowhere, at nothing, not even within.

3

A week after Bridget left him, five months and three weeks before he watched her die, Darrin agreed to go out with his friend Nicholas. He picked Darrin up on a Saturday afternoon, and the enforced joviality began right away. "I never liked that bitch," he said. "You're better off without her."

"Doesn't feel that way." Darrin gazed out the window as Nicholas piloted his gleaming SUV across the bridge into San Francisco.

"You just need some distractions. I'm going to introduce you to this one girl, Echo? She's hot like *fire*. I don't know if she's a keeper, but she'll take your mind off your troubles."

"I appreciate that, but I'm not ready to date anybody yet. It's too soon."

"Suit yourself, but just say the word when you want to meet her. You *will* be ready at some point, bro. You'll bounce back."

Nicholas passed him a flask, and Darrin took a long drink of the bourbon inside—he wasn't much of a drinker, but the veil of inebriation was tempting. He was somewhere between buzzed and drunk by the time Nicholas found parking in a garage a few blocks from the strip club. They ambled down stained and trash-strewn sidewalks, Nicholas guzzling from the flask to catch up with Darrin, now that driving didn't require his sober attention. They'd rented a room in a nearby hotel so they could get as drunk as they pleased. Nicholas entertained hopes of picking up a couple of entrepreneurial strippers to bring back to the room, but Darrin suspected that was mere wishful thinking—and anyway, he was more likely to wind up crying on a stripper's shoulder than enjoying her company.

A humourless bouncer checked their IDs, and as Nicholas paid the cover, Darrin wondered when, exactly, he'd become the sort of guy who went to strip clubs before the sun even went down. His weekends with Bridget had been far more sedate. After they moved in together they'd settled into a comfortable routine, spending most Saturdays and Sundays puttering around the apartment, or they had a late lunch at the Coffee Mill, or caught a matinee at the Grand Lake Theater, or walked to the farmer's market by Lake Merritt. He'd been happy then. Apparently Bridget hadn't been. He should have seen it coming, maybe—she always said she wanted to have adventures, but he'd never been much for spur-of-the-moment road trips or choosing a random direction and going as fast as they could with no destination in mind. Bridget *was* his destination, the one passion he never got bored with, and once she was part of his life all his other time-filling strategies had seemed pointless. He'd drifted away from urban exploring, geocaching, biking, and had become something of a homebody. Maybe she'd gotten sick of his home and his body both—but she could have *talked* to him. Instead, she'd just gone.

Darrin got his hand stamped with a purple blob, and the bored attendant explained that, due to the quirks of San Francisco strip club laws, they didn't serve alcohol in the club with fully-nude dancers. Their considerable cover charge, however, entitled Darrin and Nicholas to move freely between this all-nude club and its sister establishment across the street, where they could get booze, but where the dancers were legally obligated to keep their panties on.

"Let's catch a dance or two," Nicholas said, "then head over to drink a few beers, and just ping-pong back and forth until we can't walk anymore."

Darrin nodded, though he'd never seen Nicholas so drunk he had to stop partying, even in college. Darrin would sip as Nicholas chugged, but he'd still be the one who couldn't stand up at the end of the night, while Nicholas sailed along, just getting louder, more boisterous.

They took seats at the edge of the stage—the club was nearly empty this early in the evening—and watched a young blonde dancer finish her set. Various scantily clad women circulated in the crowd, but Darrin avoided their eyes. He hadn't been close to any woman but Bridget in years, and it felt unfaithful to even contemplate a lap dance.

Nicholas seemed to know what Darrin was thinking—he had a knack for that; it was part of what made him good at office politics—and he slapped him on the back. "Cheer up, bro. You need this. Don't waste another minute thinking about Bridget. I told you I saw her in San Francisco with some Eurotrash-looking fucker. She's already moved on. Hell—she moved *out*."

Darrin winced, and Nicholas had the good grace to look sheepish. "Sorry, man, that was harsh. But I want you to enjoy yourself. Get out of your own head."

If Bridget really had left Darrin for another man, that was almost enough to make him want to fuck someone in pure retaliation. He hated how petty and squalid and insecure this whole situation made him feel. Nicholas passed him a fat roll of one-dollar bills. "They don't like you sitting this close to the action without paying for the privilege, so start throwing some bills around." He leered at a dancer and waved a dollar bill at her, beckoning her closer, and Darrin did his best to ignore her glassy eyes and focus on her more obvious assets.

Two hours and several drinks later Darrin finally felt better, or at least, he felt less; his problems were still there, but they floated in a knot some distance away, easily ignored, like a balloon on a very long string. The club was more crowded then, with additional dancers as well as customers. Nicholas leered cheerfully and catcalled the dancers on stage while Darrin vaguely smiled. Drunkenness had drowned whatever stirrings of libido he might have felt.

"I'm not quite seeing double anymore." Nicholas said. "Let's go back to the land of beer and mere boobies for a while."

A moment later they emerged onto the street, into a world of headlights, parking meters, bright signage, and the silver coin of the moon shining above it all. Halfway across the street to the beer-and-breasts bar, Nicholas grabbed Darrin's arm. A car swerved around them and honked, but Nicholas didn't even flinch, just gripped Darrin's arm and stared across the street. "Motherfucker," he said at length.

Darrin looked around, trying to shake the tendrils of drunkenness from his brain, but the movement only scrambled his visual field, headlights leaving traceries of light in the air, fissures of shadow spreading on the street, and for a moment he caught the briefest glimpse of a high bridge, moon-coloured, delicate and immense, arching over the city and across the sky. Nicholas pulled him toward the opposite curb, and the bridge—was it just a trick of the light? A reflection off the clouds?—disappeared. "There's that motherfucker," Nicholas said, satisfaction mingling with fury in his voice.

Darrin's hindbrain generated little pulses of fear and confusion. Nicholas stalked toward two people leaning against a wall near the topless club. The woman was young, hollow-eyed, blonde hair too stringy and dirty to trigger Darrin's Bridget-recognition sensors. The man was short, thin, black-jacketed, scarf wound around his throat, long-faced and pale in a way that made Darrin think of portraits of dead kings, a face that might be called soulful or dolorous or melancholy, even at rest. "That's the guy I saw Bridget with," Nicholas said, and it was like a splash of chill water on Darrin's brain. He straightened, stared, and stopped, standing by the curb. Nicholas apparently felt no hesitation, existential or practical, and he raised his voice to say, "Hey, I want to talk to you!"

The dirty-blonde turned and walked away on her high heels. The pale man only looked at Nicholas, not even expectant, hands in his pockets.

"You've been fucking around with my friend's girl," Nicholas said, and the man glanced at Darrin for the first time.

"Oh?" His voice held neither challenge nor even, really, curiosity.

"Do you know Bridget?" Darrin took a step forward, sober enough suddenly to ask the next, and only important, question: "Can you tell me where she is?"

"It's not my place to tell you, Darrin," he said, but he was looking at Nicholas.

"You'll tell him all right," Nicholas said, all bearish menace, and Darrin felt a surge of affection for him. He could be crass and unsubtle, but Nicholas was a good friend—he might not *die* for Darrin, but he'd certainly get into a fight for him. Nicholas moved forward, to grab or shove or throttle the man, Darrin never knew. The pale man flicked his wrist, and a long black baton appeared in his hand, matte and telescopic, hidden in a sleeve or pocket in its collapsed state but now opened into three feet of menace. "Stop," he said, and Nicholas did, holding up his hands, saying "It's cool, I just want to talk to you."

"Please." Darrin was unable to keep a note of pleading from his voice. "Can you, would you, at least give her a message? Tell her to call? I need to talk to her. The way she left, without a word, I—"

"She doesn't want to talk to you."

"Please, Mr., ah . . ."

"Plenty," he said, a word that made no sense, until he elaborated, pinned it down as a name: "I'm Ismael Plenty."

"Bridget never mentioned you." Darrin swallowed. "Was she . . . seeing you?"

"She didn't leave you for me, Darrin. She left you for herself, and that's why she'll never come back."

"Please, where is she?" Darrin took another tentative step toward him.

"You *are* tedious." Ismael sounded like he was agreeing with someone. He shook his head, but in exasperation, probably, rather than in answer to Darrin's question.

"You'd better tell him," Nicholas said, and the man merely sighed. Diplomatic channels exhausted, Nicholas lunged, grabbing for the baton. Ismael ducked, squatted, and brought the weapon around in a hard flat arc, slamming it against the back of Nicholas's leg, right in the meaty part of the calf. Nicholas fell backwards with a look of drunken outrage, and Ismael straightened up. He stepped lightly toward Darrin, baton cocked back, and said "Next."

"You *bastard*." Darrin launched himself at Ismael without even thinking. He wasn't a confrontational person by nature, but he wasn't going to back off after his best friend was attacked. Fortunately, his rush took Ismael by surprise, and when they collided, Ismael fell hard—he couldn't have weighed more than 120 pounds, barely more than Bridget—his baton clattering on the sidewalk. Darrin reared back to kick him, and Ismael scuttled away.

"Enough," Ismael said, and ran for the safety of a narrow alleyway. Darrin started to pursue, venturing in a few steps after him, but came to his senses—this could only get uglier if he escalated things, but oh, how he wanted to escalate. He returned to Nicholas, who was rising and wincing. "Fucker," he said. "Did you see which way he went?"

"Yeah, he ran into—" Darrin started to gesture toward the alley, but let his hand fall. There was no alley, just a wall, and Darrin wondered just how drunk he was to hallucinate an escape route where there wasn't one. Where had Ismael really gone? "He . . . just ran off," Darrin finished.

"Hell." Nicholas tugged up his pant-leg, looking at his calf. "It's bruising already. Fucker had an ASP baton, I've seen those at gun shows, the guy who sells blackjacks and brass knuckles has them. He could've broken my goddamn leg."

"You okay?" Darrin helped Nicholas up, letting him lean against him.

"Wish I could've whipped that guy's ass for you." Nicholas's voice was all regret and chagrin, his anger gone along with Ismael.

Darrin nodded. Now that his adrenaline was starting to fade, he didn't feel fear or anger or outrage but simple grey exhaustion. "This didn't turn out to be as much fun as I'd hoped," Darrin said. "I appreciate it, but maybe we should just give tonight up as a loss."

Nicholas stood straighter. "Fuck no. I'm all right, that prick just knocked the wind out of me. I ever see him again I'm gonna shove that baton up his ass and open it *sideways*. Come on, I need some painkiller. Beer will have to do."

"Nicholas, I don't know . . ."

His friend gave him a wounded look. "Don't let this night end with me getting beat up on the street, huh? I'd be a lot happier if the last thing I saw tonight was a great set of tits instead of that fucker Ismael's pasty face." Nicholas grinned, and Darrin let himself laugh.

"All right, you win, one more dance."

"One more *lap* dance, maybe, I haven't even bought you some time in the champagne room yet." Nicholas limped toward the bar, and Darrin paused by the wall where—he could have sworn—the alley had been. Was there a crack, a shadow, a suggestion of a narrow escape? No, nothing at all, and Darrin turned away.

ORVILLE JUMPS, TOO

1

On the Golden Gate Bridge in the morning in October, Orville Troll stood with his hands on the rail looking down at the waters of the bay, and worried about messing things up again. This would be his last endeavour, and he wanted to do it right, if only to prove he was capable of completing one momentous act in his life without failing. He imagined climbing over the guardrail, tangling his legs in the railing or snagging his coat, slipping and cracking his head against metal, knocking himself unconscious and tumbling in a rag-doll pinwheel down to the bay below. Sure, he'd still die, the result would be the same, but he wanted to go wide-eyed and conscious to death, wanted to look up at the sky and watch the world that had so reliably mistreated him for the past thirty years disappear. So he ran through the physical moves in his head, visualization intended to overcome his innate clumsiness, a lifetime of slips and falls having broken his confidence. He would swing first one leg over the rail, then the other, keeping his grip on the rail with his hands. He would turn to face the bay. A deep breath, because a moment like that, a no-turning-back moment, deserved a breath of contemplation. Then he'd release the rail, step forward, and fall, straight as a plumb bob, and dash himself to death on the water below.

Orville wondered if any of the tourists on the bridge would notice him climbing over the rail, if anyone would try to stop him, pull him back from the brink, convince him life was worth living. If so, it would be a first. There were days when Orville looked back almost nostalgically on his junior high days, when he'd been picked on mercilessly, because at least then he'd been part of a social order—he'd had a place. As an adult, he didn't even warrant much in the way of ridicule.

Orville climbed over the railing, careful, careful, because the way you did things *mattered*, and he wanted a proper death, exactly the death he'd chosen.

It was windy on the bridge, fogless, and there were a few boats sailing out on the bay. What would it be like, he wondered, to have the sort of life where you owned a sailboat, with so few cares that you could take advantage of a clear morning to go out on the water? Orville would never have that sort of life, even if he didn't kill himself. Orville was a telemarketer—or had been until yesterday, when he walked out of the job—working from a warehouse in Oakland in an echoing space with dozens of other dead-end men and women, selling newspapers, magazine subscriptions, dietary supplements, or whatever else the script indicated. Orville received plenty of hang-ups, of course, and profanity, and he mumbled through his scripts by rote, feeling his soul atrophy a little more with each day. It barely bothered him, anymore—at work, Orville was a talking zombie.

But yesterday, his last conversation had been different. The computer dialled, someone picked up, Orville asked "Is this Mr. Ismael Plenty?" Upon hearing the affirmative, Orville launched into his spiel. The man at the other end didn't interrupt, or say anything, until Orville was done, but then he began to speak. There was something strange in his voice: a kind of infinite pity. "Is this your life?" he said. "You make these calls?" He then described his own life: Arctic expeditions, overland caravans, desert nights, tense meals with mortal enemies, fortunes found and squandered, lovers, wine, wonder. Orville listened, rapt, the man's voice a low enchantment. And the man said, "My friend Harczos used to say that a small life is worse than no life at all, because a small life commits the singular sin of squandering potential. I have lived, and now, I am ready to die. But you have not lived, and by the sound of your voice, by the rustle of your breath in the receiver, by a dozen tiny tells, I'm sure you never *will* live. And so, I feel compelled to ask: Why do you bother? Why don't you just kill yourself?"

Orville's mouth was dry. "I don't know."

"Come meet me for lunch," the man said, and named a restaurant within walking distance of the warehouse. "We'll talk it over, and figure out your next step."

Orville didn't intend to go, of course. Only crazy people asked to meet with their telemarketers. Orville didn't eat at restaurants anyway, because he had no sense of taste or smell—hadn't since he was a baby, ageusia and anosmia as the result of early head trauma—and so, for him, eating was just taking on fuel, not a pleasure.

But when his supervisor yelled at him a few minutes later—Orville had let a call go through without reading his script or speaking at all—Orville tore off his headset and rushed out of the room, out of the job, out into the street. The sunlight was dazzling and merciless. Orville went to the restaurant, just a little sandwich place with outdoor seating, and a tall, narrow-faced man with dark eyes stood and nodded at him. "You're Orville," he said. "Sit, and talk with me a while."

Orville did. Afterward, he couldn't remember much of what Ismael Plenty said, but every word had somehow carried great weight, and sitting in his presence had been like sinking into a cloud of dense smoke. Ismael had talked of the commonplace terrors of life, Orville remembered that much. He said happiness was an illusion, that corrosion was the nature of the world ; all lives were miserable, differing only in the degree of their misery. "And your life is miserable to a *great* degree," he said. "Isn't it?"

Orville nodded.

"Then I ask again," said Mr. Plenty, leaning in, looking at him seriously, paying attention to him in a way no one ever had before. "Why don't you kill yourself? If you free yourself from this world, a better world might wait for you beyond. And even if it doesn't, wouldn't oblivion be preferable to this?" He stood, threw some bills on the table to pay for his apparently untouched lunch, and said "Ponder that."

Orville pondered. Talking to Mr. Plenty had made it all seem clear, as if the man's aura of fatalism had enveloped Orville, and clung to him even when Ismael himself was gone. Orville went home to his small apartment in a bad part of town, because he had nowhere else to go. He sat up most of that night, flipping through old unsigned yearbooks and sparse photo albums, thinking about his lack of goals or plans, and finally deciding the world would be better off without him—and him without the world. He had, literally, nothing to live or die for, so why not die, since that was easier? He dreaded waking and working in the mornings, and he dreaded coming home to emptiness at night. Weekends were too long and increasingly difficult to fill. He'd lived for thirty years, and had never made love to a woman, never found or lost a fortune, never made a mark nor been noticeably marked himself. Having given life a fair shake, he'd discovered it wasn't really for him, so why *shouldn't* he kill himself? Best advice he'd received in years.

So Orville stood on the far side of the railing, the last barrier between himself and the chance of a clean death. He wondered if it would hurt, and thought not—from this height, death would surely be instantaneous. He took a breath, prepared himself—and then caught a glimpse, from the corner of his eye, of a woman climbing over the rail and, with far less deliberation, jumping off headfirst. Orville watched with a sick weight in his stomach as the blonde woman in the red coat tumbled the impossible distance to the water below. But when she struck, she disappeared, swallowed utterly, no mark of her passing left behind. It wouldn't be so bad, then. He'd just disappear, like she had. He did wish he'd jumped first, since he'd spent most of his life following other people, and he'd wanted this to be something he did on his own.

But it is, he thought. *Everyone gets their own death.*

People shouted, pointed, clustered around the rail, and a sailboat began tacking toward the place where the woman had gone in, but there was no way it would be able to reach her or help.

No one was paying Orville any attention, which was just as well, really. He looked up, into the blue sky, and took a single step off the edge.

He plummeted, feet first, wind screaming past his ears, eyes watering as he watched the bridge above him recede. The sensation of velocity was profound, but it seemed to Orville that he fell for a long time. His life did not pass before his eyes, and he was glad; his life was behind him now, or rather, *above* him, and he was falling out of it with great relief. This wind, this giving in to gravity, this onrushing sprint toward death—this was the feeling of freedom. He had no regrets. He did not believe in heaven, or hell, or reincarnation (life would have been better if he'd had the comfort of such beliefs), but he believed in oblivion, and he looked forward to that dreamless sleep in a state where loneliness did not exist even as a concept.

He looked down at the water, which seemed close and far all at once, with nothing in his field of vision to provide a sense of scale. But he saw something in the water, a luminosity, a pale soft light shining up and out of the bay, a light that seemed not warm, exactly, but rarefied, clean.

Heaven? he wondered, but before hope or incredulity could follow, he hit the water, feet first. The light was all around him, then, but the pain as his ankles shattered and his legs broke was so tremendous it forced consciousness out, blackness closing over him before the waters of the bay could do the same.

2

The first problem was: Orville woke up. He opened his eyes and saw light. But not the soft light that had surrounded him when he hit the waters of the bay, that Heaven-coloured light—this was buzzing fluorescent with too much blue, a cold hospital light.

There was pain in his legs and ankles, but the pain didn't seem important—more a distant curiosity than something of any real importance. There were square acoustic ceiling tiles above his head, just like the ones in the telemarketing pen.

"I'm not dead," he said, and his own voice seemed far away. He didn't expect an answer. But a blonde woman in a red coat—so familiar, but who was she?—leaned into his field of vision and sneered. He wondered if she was a nurse, but only in a sort of perfunctory way, because nurses were the sort of people he expected to see in such circumstances, not because she looked anything like a nurse at all.

She said, "No, you're not dead. You should've jumped headfirst. You jumped like you were trying to survive a sinking ship, feet first, ankles crossed to keep from smashing your crotch to bits on pieces of flotsam." She sighed. "Or so I gather from listening to the doctors. I was already gone by the time you made your leap."

Orville recognized her, and reached out for her, weakly. "I saw you jump. You survived, too."

He couldn't quite touch her. It seemed like he should be able to—her wrist was *there*, his fingers *there*, they should have been occupying congruent space— but there was no physical contact. *The drugs must be messing with my mind*, he thought, and that was his first understanding that he was medicated, on some painkiller that didn't actually kill pain but merely made pain seem trivial.

The blonde woman moved back, out of his field of vision, and turning his head seemed like a Herculean task, so he let her pass from view. Her voice remained, husky and a little echoey, as if she were actually speaking around some corner in a corridor, the sound bouncing toward him through strangely angled acoustics. "Yes, you saw me jump, I guess. But no, I didn't survive. I did it right, head first, mind cleared, straining toward the light like Ismael told me—"

The light, Orville thought with a thrill of recognition; oh, if only he'd fallen into and through that light.

"—but I just died," she finished, bitterness and bile in every syllable. A sigh.

"Well. I didn't *just* die. I came unhinged, halfway between here and there, body gone under the water, and the rest of me, the parts that Ismael taught me to separate and hold apart, those are still here. My spirit, if you want to call it that, left behind."

Orville couldn't follow this, though that name she mentioned, Ismael—he knew that name. But she'd said something else, something his mind seized on more eagerly. He swallowed and said, "I saw the light."

Her face loomed in his vision again, eyes grey and intent. "What did you say?"

"When I jumped. I looked down, and there was the most wonderful light. Like, sometimes on summer afternoons, coming home from work, the sunlight slants in and touches the trees and the buildings and everything gets . . ." He groped for the right word. "Luminous. I saw light like that, in the water, before I—before I didn't die. Why didn't I die?" Orville was distressed, in a far-off sort of way. He wasn't dead. That meant he was still alive, but he didn't have a job, and he was, he suspected, grievously injured. He'd lost his health insurance when he walked out on his job, probably. He wasn't panicked, not through the haze of world-distancing drugs, but the worry was there, like the pain in his lower body, something he'd have to face eventually.

"So you saw the light," she said, but not as if she were talking to him. Her face moved from his field of vision again. "Huh. Maybe that's why I'm . . . huh. Did you ever meet a man named Ismael? Ismael Plenty?"

"I think so." The drugs made remembering difficult. "I think I called him. For my job. He asked why I didn't just kill myself. We met, and talked, we had lunch but he didn't eat anything and neither did I, he just told me to ponder. So I did, and I saw the light." Something occurred to him. "If the light is so wonderful, so much better than even the best life, then why doesn't he just kill himself?"

She laughed, raucous and genuine and bitter all at once. "If only he could. Ismael would've found his way out of the briarpatch and into the land beyond a long time ago, if it were that easy for him. So. Mr.—What's your name, anyway? You didn't have any ID. When you hit the water it tore your clothes half off, and anything you had in your pockets got ripped away. The doctors are calling you Mr. Doe."

"Troll. I'm Orville Troll."

"Seriously? *Troll*? What kind of name is that?"

"My ancestors were Norwegian," Orville said, an oft-repeated answer to an all-too-common question. "When they immigrated, the officials misheard their name, and wrote it as—"

"Right. Anyway, Mr. *Troll*, the reason you didn't die is simple. It's because you're a fuckup. You landed in the water feet-first. You broke every bone in your feet—there are a whole lot of bones in the feet—and shattered the bones in your legs, and did a number on your knees, and snapped a few ribs. What you *didn't* do was incur sudden and fatal head trauma, which you would have, if you'd landed headfirst, like I did. In fact, in a way, I kind of saved your life. There was a boat headed toward the place where I went into the water, trying to rescue me, so they were already nearby when you hit the bay. They pulled you out, got you to shore, and into an ambulance. Big heroes. We're going to make the news, me and you. Two jumpers, one who got rescued, and one who got dead."

"If you're dead, what are you doing here?" Orville suspected it was a stupid question, but then, he'd always been told most of his questions were.

"I'm apparently haunting you. I know. Not the sort of problem you ever expected to have, I bet. Not what I would have wanted, either, but here we are."

"You're a ghost?" Orville said. "How can . . . I don't think I believe in ghosts."

"Maybe I'm not exactly a ghost. But I'm a spirit with no body, so it's close enough. And you're my haunted house—seems I can't stray too far from you. As long as you do what I want, and go where I tell you, we'll get along fine."

"I can't go anywhere," Orville said, regretfully, because this was really a very pretty girl, even if she did think she was dead, and he didn't want to disappoint her. "I think my legs are all messed up."

"That's okay. There's a wheelchair here, and we're going to put you in it before those doctors come back."

"I don't think I should move. I'm hurt bad."

Her face appeared above him again. "Speaking as a dead woman, apparently cursed to haunt a botched suicide named Troll, I don't have much sympathy for you. I've got people to see and answers to get. Upsie-daisy. Into the wheelchair."

Orville didn't quite understand what happened then. He didn't exactly feel her touch him, but somehow he was rising, as if lifted by a strong wind, IVs tugged from his arms, a white fog filling his vision and receding, and soon he was sitting upright, and there was a flash of pain coming up from his legs, like being stung by a bee, and it seemed a harbinger of worse pain to come. The dead woman—what was her name?—was behind him, and the wheelchair was moving forward, through the door, into a white corridor.

Orville thought he should be worried, but the drugs wouldn't let him. And anyway, how likely was it that any of this was even happening? He was probably just in a coma, dreaming, or even drowning to death in the bay, imagining all this. "Where are we going?" he asked.

"Into the briarpatch," she said, and Orville couldn't tell if he heard anticipation or fear in her voice.

ARTURO HAS A SWEET RIDE

1

Darrin stepped off the bus after his long trip back across the bay. During the ride he'd tried to wrap his head around what he'd seen, and he'd passed beyond disbelief into a kind of profound numbness. Bridget was dead. She'd jumped from the bridge. That chapter of his life was now completely closed. He trudged from the bus stop down by the high school on Park Boulevard toward his street, across from the 24-hour grocery store—Bridget had always called it the "grab and stab" or the "loot and shoot" because it seemed like the kind of place that probably got robbed a lot—and up the steep hill, past stucco apartment buildings with white-painted wrought iron gates.

He wondered when he'd see Echo next, what he'd say to her when he did. They had no plans, but she often dropped by unexpectedly. She would hold him, at least, and would offer whatever other comforts he was willing to accept. She didn't like hearing about Bridget, anymore than any lover relished tales of her predecessor, but Echo understood the impact Bridget had made on Darrin's life. She would try to help him get *past* this grief though—she wasn't one for brooding. Those were the things Darrin liked about her: her spontaneity, her honesty, the remarkably short distance that existed between her thoughts and her actions. Those qualities certainly made sex with her wonderful—athletic and ecstatic, anyway, if seldom exactly intimate—but it could make more delicate emotional matters difficult to navigate.

Darrin paused by a car parked a block down from his building. It was painted a bone-coloured off-white, a battered-looking, four-door landshark of a sedan, probably from the '70s, though the chrome grille that seemed to silently snarl and the pop-eyed oversized headlights were more like something from the '50s. The car's back seat was filled with paper, heaped from floorboards nearly to the ceiling, and the passenger seat was similarly piled, papers spilling onto the wide dashboard and encroaching onto the driver's side a bit. Darrin frowned, peering inside. He'd never seen anything like this—was it some kind of gypsy recycling wagon? There were takeout restaurant menus, old tax forms, handwritten letters, torn envelopes, catalogues, advertising circulars, bills, bank statements, cancelled cheques, coffee-stained contracts, and all other manner of paper paraphernalia. There must have been hundreds of thousands of sheets, and hundreds of pounds of paper, and when Darrin stepped back to look, he saw the car was riding low on its axles, fenders weighted halfway down the tires. He walked around the vehicle, its strangeness temporarily distracting him from his more serious concerns. He thumped the trunk, wondering if it was similarly stuffed, and if the car's owner had some sort of deeply arcane filing system, or if it was, as seemed more likely, simply the vehicle of an obsessive crap-hoarder.

Then he noticed the car's name. There was the familiar winged Chrysler logo in the middle of the trunk, and on the far left, in raised silver letters, the name of the model: "Wendigo."

A Chrysler Wendigo? Darrin had never heard of such a thing, but then, he wasn't a car fanatic. Nicholas would know—probably this was some briefly-made and quickly-discontinued model with a tendency to explode in collisions or flip over in high winds. But wasn't "Wendigo" the name of some kind of monster? Something like a Bigfoot, maybe, or . . . hadn't Bridget made him sit through some horror movie set in Canada called *Wendigo*, with a monster made of sticks and trick photography?

He unzipped his bag and removed his camera, turning it on and glancing down at the screen to make sure it was working. This car was practically a piece of folk art, and he wanted to document it, get a shot of the name and some of the interior—you wouldn't be able to read the paper in the photos, so it wasn't really an invasion of privacy, he thought. He sighted through the viewfinder and pressed the button.

"You like my car there, buddy?" The voice was cheerful and touched slightly with a Minnesotan accent, and when Darrin looked up he saw a rotund man of middle age, with a deeply receding hairline, a compensatory walrus moustache, and a reddish nose. He wore an untucked shirt with a loud pattern that looked like it had been generated by a computer program, faded corduroy pants, and sandals held together with duct tape.

"Ah, sorry," Darrin said. "I just, uh, wanted to take a picture of the name, I've never heard of a Wendigo before."

The man slapped the hood of the car with an open palm and said "Yeah, she's an import."

Darrin started to respond—*If it's a Chrysler, how can it be an import?*—but the man was walking toward him, hand extended, saying "Name's Arturo Glassini, pleased to meetcha, and you are?"

Darrin shook with his non-camera-wielding hand and said "Darrin, Darrin Phare." Arturo's handshake was firm and dry.

"You live up in the big ugly Georgian, right?" Arturo said, and Darrin was startled into a laugh, but Arturo was right, the house was ugly, a blocky Georgian house, complete with fake pillars, rendered in shades of tan stucco. "Big place for one guy, you got a family?"

Darrin was suddenly uncomfortable with the thought of revealing the specifics of his life to a total stranger, and one with a car that bespoke a troubled mind besides, but the answer seemed safe enough: "It's not that big, the house is broken up into four apartments, I just rent."

"Ahhh," Arturo said. "I seen you leaving there some mornings." Darrin kept expecting Arturo to smell funny—he looked like he should—but he didn't, except faintly of paper. "Hey, listen, my Wendigo is a sweet ride, I see you taking the bus sometimes, so if you ever need a lift somewhere, let me know. I got nothin' but time."

The offer struck Darrin as genuinely kind, rather than creepy, and he said, "Thanks, that's nice, I really appreciate it." He wondered how Arturo could expect to give anyone a ride, at least without removing several reams of loose paper from his passenger seat, but he didn't say anything. Arturo was obviously eccentric, and probably harmless. He didn't reek of suppressed violent crazy, as some of Darrin's fellow travelers on mass transit occasionally did. Darrin considered himself a pretty good judge of character anyway, and using a camera so much these past months had helped make him more observant.

"You live around here?" Darrin asked.

"Oh, yeah, right by here," Arturo said, motioning vaguely. He raised his hands and took a step back, toward the middle of the street. "Don't let me stop you from takin' your snapshots."

Darrin took a couple of quick shots of the logo and the car's name, mostly to satisfy Arturo. "Well," he said. "I'll see you around."

"Yup," Arturo said. "And that's somethin' to look forward to in this cold old world." He waved as Darrin walked away.

2

Darrin went up the steps to the house, leaning his shoulder against the door to push it open, because the wood always swelled and stuck during the rainy season. He clumped up the narrow stairs to his apartment on the second floor of the big old house. Once upon a time it had been a single-family residence, but some decades ago it had been carved up into apartments, walls erected, rooms partitioned to create space for necessities, and as a result he had a narrow kitchen—far too much of which was taken up by a cranky old water heater—and an enormous bathroom with a shiny black-and-white tiled floor and a tub big enough for two.

Darrin hesitated in the entryway to his office, where his computer sat humming, its enormous flat screen a leftover from his more prosperous days, its hardware once top-of-the-line but now growing ever more obsolete. Part of him wanted to plug in the digital camera and look at that photo of Bridget, the last picture anyone would ever take of her while she was alive. Another part of him wanted to put off the morbid enterprise for as long as possible. He went into the kitchen and sighed at the mess of tea bags, spilled sugar, dollops of honey, and splashes of cream on the counter. Echo had stopped by, apparently, and as always she'd left a little disaster behind. He tidied up the wreckage of her tea, and then noticed the red light flashing on the phone hanging on the wall by the refrigerator. He pressed the button and winced as Nicholas's booming voice emerged: "Hey, fucker, did you forget we were supposed to have lunch today?" His tone was jovial, hiding irritation. "You missed out, the waitress was hot. She had that kinda geeky chunky-glasses-wearing thing you like going on. Give me a call, tell me you didn't get crushed under a train or something, let me know how you're going to make it up to me. Hope you're all right."

Darrin sighed. Another person to tell about Bridget, another person to explain things to, and Nicholas would insist on cheering him up— incapable of letting misery and grief run their courses, he was all about *getting back to normal*, and though he was well-intentioned, Darrin didn't look forward to coping with his sort of therapy.

Darrin was hungry, having missed lunch, so he put together a sandwich and took it back to his desk. No point putting this off—he'd just obsess about it until he looked. He plugged the cable into his camera and waited while the computer imported the latest bunch of photos, about a hundred taken in the past two days. Darrin didn't do much these days *but* walk around and take photos—unless he was hanging out with Echo, who wanted sex more often than he did, and dragged him to bars, and routinely beat him at video games—and as the thumbnail images flickered by during the import process they provided a sort of map of his recent days: there was the long stairway on the way to the lake, flanked by chipped cherub statues , and the crap-covered benches of the bird sanctuary on the far side, and the faded whimsy of the giant metal dandelion sculptures, and the gate of Children's Fairyland, the little fairy-tale theme park, and the marquee of the Grand Lake Theater with its liberal protest signage alongside the names of the latest Oscar-courting melodrama movies, and ranked headstones at the cemetery down past Piedmont Avenue, and the remarkable intersection of half a dozen overpasses and pedestrian walkways criss-crossing above the freeway, whimsical and brute-concrete-functional all at once, and shots of the bay and the Marin headlands. And finally Bridget, in the red coat Darrin had bought for her, leaning against the railing on the Golden Gate Bridge just moments before she jumped, just a flicker across his screen before the computer started downloading the photos of the Wendigo.

Darrin launched his photo software and opened the photo of Bridget. It was a good picture, clear, and he could adjust the colours to make them less saturated, if he could stand to look at her for that long. He leaned forward, elbows on the desk, bringing his face close enough to the screen that she almost dissolved into individual pixels, and there it was, inevitably: he started to cry, tears welling in his eyes, blurring his vision, and he thumped the desk with his fist and sat back in his chair, wiping his cheeks. God damn it, why had she done this? What had driven her to kill herself, how could things be so bad, why hadn't she talked to him? The way Bridget had left him, without a word, without warning, was the great gaping mystery at the centre of his life, the event that had undermined his foundations, and it seemed all his troubles had flowed from that—after she left he lost his job, setting him utterly adrift, with only photography and, more recently Echo, providing distraction. And now Bridget was dead. "She was crazy," he said aloud, but it didn't have the ring of the plausible, not really, though it was as good an explanation as any, and better than no explanation at all. "Only crazy people kill themselves for no good reason." But maybe she'd had a reason. Maybe she'd had a brain tumour, had left to spare him the pain of watching her get sick, and had decided to kill herself to stave off a slow decline. It was a nice fantasy, in a way—it was a fantasy built on the premise that she loved him—but it didn't really fit the available facts. After all, she'd left him *for* someone, for that man who'd beaten up Nicholas outside the strip club—what was his name?

And then Darrin saw something, some*one*, in the photo. There were lots of people in the background, tourists mostly, but there was a familiar figure, half-eclipsed by Bridget's body, but the face was visible over her shoulder, and Darrin jabbed at the keyboard and zoomed in on the man.

Long, lank black hair. Sallow skin. Shadowed eyes and a narrow face, prominent cheekbones, a long nose. It was the man Nicholas had seen Bridget with, the man they'd confronted on the street, the man who'd escaped into an alley that (apparently) didn't even exist.

Plenty. His name was Ismael Plenty, Bridget's lover, probably, and a witness to her suicide. Had he driven her to the bridge? (She'd always hated driving in San Francisco.) Had he helped her plan it, or tried to talk her out of it, or just come along because he got his kicks from watching people die?

Darrin frowned. He would find this man—how many Ismael Plentys could there be in the city? He would find him, and demand an explanation, and this time he'd be prepared, so Ismael couldn't just whip out an ASP baton and refuse to answer any questions. Bridget's abandonment and death would trouble Darrin always, but if he could understand why, he might be able to get past it, eventually. And this way, at least, he'd be doing *something*. Action was the best therapy.

But he couldn't start searching for Ismael yet. He couldn't deal with *anything* yet. He left the apartment and walked the half a block down to Park Boulevard, passing Arturo's paper-jammed car, hurrying through the crosswalk and over to the grab-and-stab. The clerk, a Middle Eastern man Darrin was on friendly-nod-hello terms with, didn't raise an eyebrow when Darrin bought a bottle of vodka and a jug of orange juice, though Darrin didn't think he'd ever bought alcohol there before, his own vices being more of the potato-chips-and-ice-cream variety.

"You hear about the shooting?" the clerk said as he handed Darrin his change, and Darrin shook his head. "Just a few blocks from here, someone got shot. You saw the flier, about the muggings?" Darrin hadn't, so the clerk pulled it down from the window and handed it over. The flyer was blurrily photocopied on yellow paper, produced by some community group Darrin had never heard of, and it warned area residents to beware. "Something like thirty people have been mugged in the past month," the clerk said. "Two men wait in their car late at night, and when they see you heading toward your apartment, they come out and hold you up at gunpoint and take your money. They made one woman take them inside her apartment and they raped her, and last night they shot somebody."

Darrin blinked. He didn't think of his neighbourhood as dangerous not compared to many places in Oakland. It was near the high school, so there were occasional break-ins, petty thefts, cars being stolen for joyrides if they weren't secured against casual theft. There were million-dollar homes in his neighbourhood; it was a nice residential area. In Oakland nice areas nestled right against bad neighbourhoods though, and for muggers, it probably made more sense to rob people in relatively prosperous areas. "Are the police doing anything about it?"

The clerk shrugged. "They say they have more patrols in the area, but I haven't seen any. By the time the police get involved the muggers usually move to a new neighbourhood anyway. Just be careful walking around at night."

"Thanks, I will." Darrin took his bag. Just what he needed. More fear. He'd go home, lock his doors, turn off his phone, and drink screwdrivers all afternoon. And tomorrow morning, assuming he wasn't too hungover, he'd figure out how to find Ismael Plenty, and get answers from him by any means necessary.

ECHO'S GOT A GUN

1

"I know where he was." Ismael Plenty didn't bother opening his eyes. He'd had a terrible headache ever since watching Bridget jump earlier that morning, and no amount of water or caffeine had served to make the pounding go away, so now he lay on the threadbare velvet couch in his front room with his eyes closed, letting the pain inhabit him, letting it strengthen his resolve. "Darrin was at the Golden Gate, watching Bridget jump. That's why he wasn't home when you visited."

"Holy shit," Echo Reins said, her voice closer than before, and Ismael opened his eyes to find her face just inches from his own, her pale green eyes gazing at his face. Her breath smelled of spice tea and honey.

"Do you mind?" Ismael said mildly. "You know I don't like people in my personal space."

Echo belched unselfconsciously into his face, sniffed, and flopped down on the armchair. "How'd he know to go to the bridge today?"

Ismael shrugged. "I don't think he knew, not consciously. It's just further proof that he's a child of the briarpatch, led by impulses he can't understand. Or else it was simply coincidence."

"Coulda been fate," Echo said, but Ismael ignored her, knowing she was just trying to provoke a reaction. *Fate.* He wished there were such a thing as fate. Then he'd be able to believe there might be some sort of *conclusion* in his life, preferably sometime before the heat death of the universe. No, Ismael knew that in this world and any other you had to make your own fate.

"I wonder if this might be enough to push him," Ismael mused, closing his eyes again. "I think he got a glimpse into the briarpatch after I attacked that useful oaf Nicholas—I swear he saw the alley I disappeared into—but if all it took was a cheap surge of adrenaline to send him into the liminal world, he'd be a seasoned traveller by now. I still think despair is the key. He's lost his job, his financial stability, his mobility, and now he's seen his true love take her own life, so if he's not over the edge yet, he's surely teetering."

"How'd that go, anyway?" Echo said. "With blondie's leap, I mean? Did she see the light?"

"I didn't notice a pinprick of light." Ismael massaged his temples. That failure was part of the reason his head hurt. Bridget had been a good prospect, but he'd fucked it up somehow, hadn't prepared her well enough, and as a result she'd probably just died, the way anyone did, without passing into the light of a better world. He might have felt guilty, if the weight of one more pointless death could be felt on his already bloodstained conscience, but as it was, Bridget was just a very small drop in a very large bucket. "No, I think she botched it, poor thing."

"But she was such a good prospect!" Echo said. "At least her death will help spur Darrin to follow his path."

Ismael opened one eye. "Stop it. Don't do that."

Echo looked at him, all wide-eyed innocence, and she really was adorable and fuckable all at once, perky and eager-to-please, but Ismael knew it was all pretence, that the real Echo—if there was such a thing, deep down underneath—was eager to please only herself. "Don't do what?"

"Parrot back something I've said to you before in order to make me think you're intelligent and insightful. I don't forget the things I've told you, Echo. My memory is flawless."

"And that's your greatest tragedy," Echo said, and it was another parrot-trick, turned only slightly mocking by her tone, but he ignored the jab, because giving Echo the satisfaction of annoying him would only encourage her.

"Yes, well," Ismael started. "It's true. Darrin might provide another way, if we can push him, if we can make him run. He might reveal pathways I can't see on my own."

"I dunno if he'll run, but he's still *walking* all the damn time. All he does all day is walk walk walk and snap snap snap, taking pictures of trees and stairs and graffiti and drains."

"He is seeking something," Ismael said, surprised at the touch of hope he heard in his voice. "He is practicing psychogeography, though I doubt he's ever heard the term."

"Psychogeography, huh? What, you mean like trying to read the city's *mind*? I can imagine what's on Oakland's mind."

"It's not urban telepathy, but you're . . . close. Cities have moods, and modes, and people can sense those moods. Everyone is unconsciously shunted along particular paths through the city, appropriate to their class, level of income, race, professional interests. Every individual's personal map represents only a fraction of the real city, with the rest simply unregarded. In a way, there are a thousand unseen cities hidden in every city you think you know, parts of the terrain you never encounter, neighbourhoods you never even notice. Psychogeographers attempt to free themselves from their unconscious constraints of habit and propriety, either playfully or seriously, and engage wholly with the city as it is. They *explore*. Such attention to reality, rather than the imposed mental map everyone carries with them, is good training for the greater acts of exploration I hope Darrin will undertake. With enough wandering, a man of his . . . talents . . . could discover parts of the city no one has seen for *centuries*, pockets of forgotten terrain. And once he's gone that far, it will be trivial to send him one step farther. He may nearly be ready."

"So do we finally get to move on? Not that being a spy and playing girlfriend with Darrin isn't fun, and since he's been walking so much he's even got a nice tight butt, it's just I thought the whole point of me making him a little happy again was so we could make him even *more* sad later. Can I dump him yet?"

"He just saw the love of his life die, so I don't think a simple breakup will be enough of an . . . escalation anymore," Ismael mused. "We need to do something more extreme."

"What do you have in mind?"

"Perhaps something involving Nicholas. He still trusts Nicholas, and a betrayal from that unexpected direction might urge him completely out of this world, and into the briarpatch."

"You mean tell Darrin the real reason he lost his job, or . . ."

Ismael opened both eyes. "I meant something rather more carnal and immediate, actually. Something to shock Darrin. I expect Nicholas will go along with the idea. He'll put up a protest, but I'm sure we can persuade him."

"Heh," Echo said. "I've seen Nicholas look at me. I think I can guarantee he'll go along with it."

"Good girl."

"But it'll cost you."

Ismael knew what she wanted. But he said, "Money's not a problem," hoping perhaps he was wrong, that she was just looking for straightforward remuneration.

"Money's never been a problem for me. That's not what I mean. I want to try another experiment."

"We just *did* this," Ismael said, irritated. "Last week, with gasoline, the backyard still stinks of it."

"I got something new." Echo unzipped the duffel bag at her feet. She withdrew a gleaming chrome-plated pump-action shotgun and pressed the barrel against her cheek. "Isn't it beautiful?"

Ismael shuddered. He didn't like guns. He'd seen too many people taken to pieces by guns, including people he'd cared about, back in the old days, when he still sometimes cared about people in more than the abstract. And self-inflicted gunshot wounds were either too unreliable or too quick a death to be useful for transition to the better world—they didn't provide the crucial moments of contemplation that pills, bridge-jumps, and slit wrists did. "Where did you get that? It looks like a toy."

Echo shrugged. "Boosted a Mercedes last week, and this was in the trunk, in a locked box. Probably belonged to gangbanger royalty or something. I tried it out, but I just shot at a wall in an old house in West Oakland. I want to shoot something *good*."

"So I'll buy you a side of beef. You can blast it to pieces. Blood and meat everywhere. Surely that will be more satisfying than shooting me."

"You need me to drive Darrin over the edge, so you'll do what I want," Echo said, absolutely confident. People almost always did what Echo wanted, but at least Ismael was aware of her manipulations.

"Fine," Ismael said.

"Now?"

"No better time." He heaved himself off the couch. Perhaps this experience would make his headache go away, or at least make him stop thinking about Bridget's failure—his *own* failure. He led the way through the narrow, furniture-crowded hallway, through the essentially empty kitchen, out the back door and down the three low steps to the overgrown weedy backyard. An absurdly high wooden fence screened him from his neighbours, the welcome legacy of some privacy-obsessed former owner. The sun was bright but not hot—the rain hadn't settled in for its six-month stay just yet, but fall was cusping—and Ismael wished he'd remembered to wear dark glasses. He paused by a rusted-through wheelbarrow, gazing at the sagging, spider-filled tool shed, the shredded trampoline, and the broken birdbath with its puddle of black water at the centre. Ismael considered his backyard a metaphor for his life. Parts of it had been nice enough, perhaps, once, but it was all rundown and pathetic now, and there was no telling when or if the debris would ever be carted off to the trash heap.

"Why do you always call these 'experiments'?" Ismael asked, looking ahead but sensing Echo and her shotgun behind him. "It's not as if the results are in doubt."

"But *maybe*," Echo said, with relish, "*maybe* this time it will be different. The shotgun fires lots of little pellets, after all, so *maybe* some of them will strike home, maybe enough of them to do so some real damage."

"If so, I would die," Ismael said.

"Well, yes. Which would be kind of a thrill for both of us, right?"

"Yes." Ismael turned to face her. "I suppose so. Go ahead."

Echo took a stance, legs spread, feet planted firmly, and lifted the shotgun before her, pointed at Ismael's chest. She was very close to him, and by reaching out and leaning forward a bit, Ismael could have stuck his finger in the gun's barrel. She pumped it, grinning, clearly loving the sound of the impeccably working machinery of death. "See you, babe," Echo said, and fired.

Ismael heard the incredibly loud crash of gunfire, and then the world swirled and dipped. He fell in every direction at once as dark and light streaked interchangeably past his eyes, and then he was upright again, leaning against a dirty shelf, and, of course, utterly unharmed. As always, when death or even serious injury seemed imminent, some secret reflex kicked in, shunting him through the briarpatch to safety. A spider scuttled over his hand—probably something poisonous, not that it mattered—and he realized where he was. Ismael kicked at the wooden door, which swung open, and stepped out into his backyard.

Echo stood, shaking her hand vigorously back and forth. It was probably numb from the recoil. "Hey, you didn't go far at all this time."

"Yes," Ismael said. When Echo had attempted to set him on fire the week before, Ismael had fled deep into the briarpatch, and emerged nearly two miles away beneath an overpass, perhaps because there was a chance the fire would fill the whole back yard, making closer re-entry too dangerous? Or was that ascribing thought and consciousness to what he believed was mere mindless instinctual self-preservation? Perhaps the places where he re-emerged were simply random. This time he'd been dumped right back into the baseline world, but other times he'd had to journey for a while in the briarpatch to find his way out again, and there seemed no reason or pattern to the nature of his escapes. He'd had a long time, and many brushes with death, to look for such a pattern, even before Echo came along and started trading attempted murder for her services. "Are you satisfied, now?" he asked her.

"Sure. Want me to call Nicholas and set this up?"

"Not just yet. Go to Darrin, find out how he's doing. Perhaps he's overwrought enough already, and further steps are unnecessary. You don't mind playing the concerned girlfriend, do you?"

"Nah," Echo said. "I like Darrin."

Ismael believed her. Echo was entirely capable of simultaneously liking someone and betraying them. There was no distance between her whims and her actions. She was the most alive and thriving person Ismael had ever known, though she was more like a cancer than a flower. When he'd first met her a year ago, he'd thought she was a good candidate for suicide, but she was wholly immune to despair despite the dire straits she'd been in back then, and seemed oblivious to the influence of Ismael's depressive aura. She had better uses than dying, anyway. She wasn't exactly his Renfield—Nicholas fit *that* description better—nor his Dr. Watson, nor his faithful companion. He wasn't sure there *was* a shorthand to describe his relationship with Echo. She would help him, for as long as he kept her entertained, and she seemed to find him very entertaining. "Go on, then," he said. "And let me know what you think of Darrin's mental state."

Echo blew him a kiss, dropping the shotgun on the ground—she got bored with her toys easily—and strolled around the side of the house toward the gate. Ismael considered picking up the shotgun, but didn't bother. Let it rust.

2

The wheelchair moved, so Orville supposed the dead woman must be pushing him, and his legs moved too as the chair shifted, which caused distant pulses of pain deep in his bones, or what was left of them.

"I'm hurt bad, huh?" he said, throat dry.

"Not as bad as me."

"Wait." Thinking was like swimming through honey, but he tried hard, and things got a little clearer. "If you're dead. A ghost. How can you push me in a wheelchair?"

She sighed, pausing in their forward motion. "I just *can*. I don't know how.

It's not like there's a Frequently Asked Questions file I can refer to here—there's no user guide to being dead. All I know so far is that nobody except you seems to see or hear me, and I can move things around, though it feels weird when I do, and takes a lot of concentration. Unless I really try, I just sort of . . . skim along the surface of things. I don't know if I got any of the other powers that come with the standard ghost package. I tried things out while I was waiting for you to wake up, and I haven't had any luck flying or walking through walls or possessing people or puking ectoplasm, but I think I could handle rattling chains in an attic, snuffing candles at dramatic moments, opening kitchen cabinets, and throwing china plates at a wall. All of which I could have done when I was *alive*, too, so it's a shit deal." The chair started moving again.

"I'm sorry," Orville rasped. "You sound so angry. Maybe being angry is why you can't . . . move on."

"I can't *move on* because I was given shitty directions, and you're damn right I'm angry. I *did* figure out that I can't get too far away from you, for whatever reason—maybe our souls got tangled up when we both jumped, who knows? I tried to leave the hospital a while ago and everything got . . . fuzzy. I started to lose coherence, to forget who I was and what I was supposed to be doing, and I think if I'd pushed on much farther I would have just fallen apart. Worst of all, it *hurt*, like being swarmed by fire ants, which is apparently the only really powerful physical sensation I can experience anymore. The pain went away when I came crawling back to you so it looks like we're stuck together. Which is why I'm taking you on a little trip."

Orville looked around. The hospital corridor just outside his room had been brightly lit, but the woman had guided him down other hallways, and once into what looked like a broom closet, except they'd slid through the chemical-smelling darkness and out the other side into another corridor. Now the chair rolled down a dim hallway, fluorescent lights overhead sputtering, more than half of them burned out. The floors were filthy and slick, and occasionally the wheels made a squelching noise, as if rolling through organic debris. They passed doorways framing darkness, and sounds emerged from some of them—bells, whispers, weeping. "This isn't the hospital," Orville said, and his mind felt clearer than before, and the pain below his waist was more insistent.

"Well. I could argue semantics with you. This *is* the hospital, or maybe a part of the hospital that was never built, except in a place where there was a nuclear war or some *Omega Man* scenario with flesh-eating vampires living in the wreckage. It's sort of like the mad whimsy wing of the hospital."

"You're kidnapping me," Orville said, feeling dumb for not realizing it before, drugs or not. "Take me back! I'm *hurt*!"

"Yes, you're hurt. But I'm not kidnapping you, I'm helping you." Orville tried to twist around to look at her, but moving his head too quickly made everything spin. A sudden stabbing pain in his chest made him gasp—hadn't the woman said something about broken ribs? God, it was like having shards of broken metal inside him. What had he done to himself? What would become of him? He thought of grabbing the wheels, turning the chair around and trying to get back to his room, but there was a sound like distant howling, and the corridor was very dark, and he was lost, and afraid.

Suddenly there were lights again, and the hallway was clean and wide and brightly lit. Everything was chrome and translucent white plastic, and the tiles on the floor cycled in colours, from orange to yellow to green. It was like some spaceship sickbay from an unusually stylish vintage science fiction film.

"This is better," she said. "I was worried there for a minute, when it was so dark. Ismael showed me this place once, when I got hurt on one of our exploring trips, but I wasn't sure I remembered the way."

"Where am I? Who are you? What is this?" Orville was rapidly becoming sober. He felt balanced on a sharp edge, a brief window when he was lucid but not yet overwhelmed by pain. The pain was building, though, like a storm in his body, and he was afraid to let his hands leave the armrests of the wheelchair, afraid of dropping them to his lap and brushing the wreckage that had once been his own ordinary, healthy legs, two things he'd never appreciated before.

"You're in the hospital," she said. "A hospital, anyway. Briarpatch Memorial." The chair rolled around a sharp curve into another corridor. There were signs on the walls, but Orville couldn't read them. The letters were sinuous, not quite Arabic, but closer to that than anything else Orville could think of. "And I'm Bridget. As for what this is . . . I'll explain more once we get your legs taken care off. In the meantime, just relax. You'd planned to be dead this afternoon, so anything else has to be an improvement, right?"

She pulled open a bright blue door with a square window set at eye level, tugging like it weighed a ton, until some mechanism clicked and it locked open. Then she wheeled Orville into the room, which was small, barely big enough for the chair. The walls were studded with coloured crystals, some small, some as big as fists. "Don't worry," she said. "This should only take a minute." A moment later, the door shut behind him with a click.

"Bridget?" he said, but she didn't answer. She was gone, and the tiny room made him feel closed-in and short of breath, claustrophobia starting to wrap its tendrils around him. What was this? A gas chamber? Was she trying to finish the job he'd started on himself?

The crystals on the walls began to pulse and glow, yellows and purples and reds, and then Orville's eyes blurred, or else the room blurred, and his body became a distant and tenuous thing. Phantom sounds rose around him—bird calls, string music—and Orville wondered if he was having a seizure, if the jump had opened lesions on his brain. He'd read about such things, about patients undergoing brain surgery who experienced vivid memories, so real they thought they were reliving past moments , and that was happening now, only these weren't *his* memories. He was making love to a woman, with dusky skin and black hair, and he'd never done that, too ashamed to hire a prostitute and too shy to pursue other channels. Now he was playing basketball with his friends, and he knew their names, knew they played every weekend, knew he wasn't any good at the game but he loved it anyway. Now he was on a ferry, leaning over the bow, looking out at the water, leaving some kind of life behind, heading toward something new. A cascade of experiences he'd never actually experienced washed through him, little snippets of existence, conflicting and mutually exclusive memories fluttering by.

And then it stopped. He was back in the crystal-studded room, in his wheelchair, completely lucid, with no pain in his legs or chest. But, oh, the pain in his heart; the pain of seeing what might-have-been, or could-have-been, or what was only dreamed-of, or desperately-wanted.

The door opened behind him. "C'mon out, Mr. Troll," Bridget said. "You're all fixed up."

Orville rose from the chair, his legs whole again, and he turned to look at Bridget. She was a beautiful woman, but angry, and tired, and, yes, dead. There was no mistaking her for a living person. It was hard to say why. She wasn't waxy, she wasn't translucent; she didn't look dead. He thought it might be because she wasn't breathing consistently, wasn't blinking enough, wasn't producing body heat. He could see her, and hear her, but she seemed shifted halfway out of reality. She was a walking, talking evidence of absence.

"That room . . . what is that room?"

"I don't know how it works. Ismael brought me here when I got hurt, I told you that, and he said it's a place that sort of . . . fishes the probabilities. It doesn't heal you, exactly, it just finds a version of you that never got hurt in the first place, and makes that body the reality—lets the likelihood of health achieve immanence."

Orville pushed the chair out of the little room. "I saw things, but the memories are fading, it's like they were a dream . . . I played basketball, I made love to someone, things I never . . . but I *am* better now." He was in a hospital gown that hung open at the back, and was embarrassed now that the drugs were out of his system. He kept the chair between himself and Bridget. He suddenly sneezed, then sniffed. He could only breathe out of one nostril, and not very well. "Except now I've got a cold. I didn't have that before."

Bridget laughed. "I think it's a decent trade, don't you? New legs in exchange for the sniffles?" She stepped past him and looked into the small room. "I wanted to bring you here to heal you, but I also wanted to try something. If it could make your legs work again, maybe . . ."

"Maybe it can make you alive again?" Orville said. "Bring you a body that never jumped off a bridge?"

"Yeah."

Orville stepped aside and gestured. "Go on in."

Bridget stepped around the chair and into the crystal-lined room, and Orville shut the door gently after her.

He peered in through the high window set in the door, but nothing happened—the lights didn't dim, the crystals didn't glow. After a few moments, Bridget lowered her head, said "Open the door," and emerged from the room. "No good. It doesn't even recognize me as a potential patient."

"I'm sorry," Orville said, awkward as if at a stranger's funeral. "I guess this isn't what you expected death to be like."

"I expected to be basking in the light of the next best thing to heaven by now, not—forgive me—stuck haunting a failed suicide." She balled her hands into fists, and seemed very small and lost in her enormous puffy red coat.

"You talked about the light," Orville said. "I don't really remember, I was on a lot of drugs, but didn't you say something about the light I saw in the water when I jumped? It was—"

Something clattered far off down the curving corridor, a noise like ball bearings falling into a steel pan. Bridget stared at Orville, her eyes wide. "Fuck," she said. "What was that?"

"I've never been here before." Orville took a step back, away from the sound.

"Ismael said this place was uninhabited, like it was a place too implausible to actually support life, but—"

The clattering came again, and this time the noise continued, a sound like marbles rolling down a steel chute, and getting closer.

"Let's get out of here." She set off down the corridor. "I might be dead, but that doesn't mean there aren't still dangers." Orville went after her, his legs operating as well and painlessly as ever—maybe better. He was acutely aware of his bare ass hanging out as he ran, and of the noise, which had now grown to roaring waterfall proportions. Now that he was sober, Orville could see the stranger properties of these hallways, including the ghostly corridors that shimmered in the corners of his vision, disappearing if he looked at them directly. Some of the passageways seemed more tangible than others, and occasionally as he passed these insubstantial side-corridors the air changed, growing hotter or colder or wetter or more dry.

"This way," Bridget said, shouting to be heard over the roar, and she darted hard sideways, disappearing from view, passing through a wall. Orville hoped it wasn't some ghost-trick, hoped he'd be able to follow, and he hurled himself after her. As he turned, he caught a glimpse of the hallway behind him fraying away into threads of silver and darkness, like a rapidly unravelling piece of cloth, and he realized the noise was the sound of the hallway disappearing. Then he was through the wall, back in the half-dark asylum hallways they'd passed through in the wheelchair. He leaned against a wall, and Bridget flung herself at him, hugging him tightly—at least, it seemed she was hugging him tightly, but it was more like standing in a stiff breeze than holding a human being, and it was profoundly dissonant, seeing her clinging to him, but being unable to feel her warmth or weight at all.

He tried to pat her back, but it felt like wind on his palm, and she pulled away.

"I thought you were lost," she said, standing before him. "I thought you were going to die!"

Orville felt absurdly touched. When had anyone ever cared about the possibility that he might be lost before? "No, I'm okay, it's okay."

"What *was* that?"

Orville thought about trying to explain what he'd seen. He'd never been very good with words, descriptions, making himself understood, so he just shook his head and said, "Something terrible. I only got a glimpse , silver and dark, but it was destroying everything ." That was wrong, he knew—it implied there had been a *thing* doing the destroying, when the process of destruction *was* the thing, but before he could try to clarify, Bridget was talking again, almost shouting.

"You have to run faster when shit like that happens, Orville, you can't hang around and look behind you and get a peek, you could *die*. The briarpatch is a dangerous place, you don't even know. If you'd died, I might be stuck haunting this fucking hallway forever. Who knows where your spirit or soul or animus or whatever would go, maybe you already got your ticket to a new golden world and you'll go there when you die, but I'd be stuck with your rotting corpse I bet, here in the ass end of the middle of nowhere, deep in the ugliest brambles of the briarpatch."

Orville didn't even feel disappointment, exactly, though he was a little hurt. Why would a pretty girl, even a dead one, care about him for anything other than pragmatic purposes? "I'm sorry you're stuck haunting me. I'm sorry I didn't die when I jumped."

"Yeah." Bridget turned her back. "Maybe it would've been better for both of us if you had. I'm sure you had good reasons to try to kill yourself. I mean . . . you must have let *everything* go, divorced yourself from all worldly things, if you saw the light."

"You make it sound Zen. It wasn't Zen. It was . . . just being tired. Realizing I didn't have anything to live for, and deciding I was tired of the hassle. But you were a suicide, too. I guess you understand."

Bridget laughed harshly. "I didn't hate my life. I just wanted my life to be better, to be extraordinary, wonderful beyond wonderful. And Ismael told me I could have that—if I left all this behind, gave up everything in my life, and finally gave up my body, I could go to a better place."

"Sounds like a cult. Like those Heaven's Gate people who committed suicide, and thought they'd fly away on a spaceship in a comet."

Bridget sniffed. "Maybe the comet did take them away, the parts of them that transcended their bodies, anyway, but probably not. Most cults are just hobbies for the power-hungry and deluded. Shit, suicide isn't like a magical doorway to the land of milk and honey; you have to *work* for it. Suicide is the last step, it shows willingness to leave the most elemental part of yourself behind, it's like turning a knob and opening a door—but first you have to open up the ten fucking thousand locks on the door, the bolts and chains and padlocks and crossbars. People who think just offing themselves will let them go to planet Xanadu or some other paradise are just lazy, it's cargo cultism, it's mistaking a part for the whole."

"So *your* cult leader knows better, huh?" Orville said, surprised at the contempt in his voice. Bridget had hurt his feelings, which made it easier to be mean to her, even if she had taken him to get his legs fixed. Besides, focusing on his annoyance with her kept him from thinking about the impossible situation he was in, the dark and viscera-stained hallway where they stood. "He's *really* got the keys to enlightenment."

"I'm not sure it counts as a cult when I was the only member. Though I think he might have had cults before, or at least groups of like-minded people—he talked, sometimes, about trying to mass-produce transcendence, giving up the one-on-one mentor thing in favour of teaching groups, trying to save more people all at once. Ismael convinced you, too, Orville, and a lot faster than he did me. Anyway, you saw the light. *That's* the place I was trying to reach. But I must have done it wrong, or Ismael didn't tell me everything I needed to know. I didn't open all the locks on the door, I guess. But you, without even trying, you saw the light. You're like some kind of idiot savant of transcendence."

"Take me out of here," Orville said coldly. "If you have to haunt me, at least haunt me back in my own world."

Bridget shrugged. "You're a briarpatch boy now, Orville. The borders of your world just got a lot more permeable. Once you've seen the light, it's hard to go back to blindness. Ismael taught me to see, a little, but it's so much clearer since I left my body behind. I can see all the bridges and corridors and stairways. I saw you looking around back there, in Briarpatch Memorial, you can see the passages now, too, at least a little. It's going to get harder and harder for you to tell where your world ends and the briarpatch begins. You've only been here once, and you can already see the pathways that lead from one broken fragment of a world to another. Ismael said sometimes trauma can do that—knock the doors of perception right off their hinges. Maybe that's why you can see me. That's lucky. It would be even worse haunting someone who couldn't even hear me talk—not that you'd be my first choice for an eternal companion. But, sure, I'll guide you back. Want to go to the hospital? I mean the normal one?"

Orville shuddered. How would he explain, how would he talk to the doctors? But they hadn't found identification on him, and if he didn't go back to the hospital, maybe they'd never discover his identity. Even if they did find him, his body was the perfect alibi—how could he be the broken man who'd escaped from the hospital, when his legs worked fine? "No," he said. "I want to go home."

"Where's home?"

"North Oakland. Near the MacArthur BART station."

"Nice," Bridget said. "Crackhead adjacent."

"Just how long do you intend to haunt me?" Orville said.

Bridget frowned. "Well, that's the question. Like I said, I didn't get an instruction sheet. Maybe we're stuck together until you die, or maybe I'll have to hang around forever." She shuddered. "I don't want to think about it. I'm a big believer in action over contemplation—of course, that's kind of what got me *into* this mess—but I'm hoping I'm like a standard ghost, the kinds you hear stories about, either a revenant or a returner. Either I'm here to take revenge for wrongs done to me, or I'm here to take care of some unfinished business. Whichever, I know where I need to go."

"Where's that?"

"To see Ismael Plenty, my 'cult leader.' He's going to love you, Orville. You saw the light, but you didn't die. That makes you some kind of rarity, and Ismael loves rarities. He's been alive so long he almost never encounters anything rare anymore." She started down the hallway, stepping around dark puddles, beckoning Orville to follow. "And after he's done marvelling at you, he's going to fix *me*. If we could fish a whole body out of the timestream for you, there must be a way to get me back to life."

Orville wasn't so sure. The existence of one impossible thing hardly proved the existence of every *other* impossible thing. If you saw a unicorn, it wouldn't mean there were also giants, hydra, pegasi, and leprechauns. And dead wasn't the same as hurt. But if trying to save herself kept her from going crazy, he supposed it was all to the good. Having something to work toward probably made her life a lot easier. Orville had never had any purpose at all, and look where that had gotten him.

"Come on, Mr. Troll. I don't like this relationship any better than you do. Let's get you home, and into some outfit that covers up your ass, and then we'll visit Ismael, and see if you and me can get out of each other's hair forever."

This was, Orville thought, at least more interesting than working the phone banks, if also more frightening. He sneezed again, and they walked back into the world he knew.

BRIDGET SEES THE LIGHT

1

Before she was dead:

"But what about love?" Bridget reclined on a pile of mismatched throw pillows in Ismael's living room, looking across at him through a cloud of fragrant smoke from the hookah.

Ismael scratched at a patch of dry skin by his ankle. He took a puff on the pipe, held the smoke, released, and said "What about it?"

Bridget wore a velvet cloak she'd unearthed from some long-forgotten trunk in Ismael's "legacy room." She was always cold, especially now that she'd been to the briarpatch a few times and was subject to the cold drafts of other worlds, which blew through this room in cross-dimensional gusts. Those liminal winds didn't stir the smoke, but both Ismael and Bridget could feel them. They didn't bother Ismael; he'd frozen in the snow during Napoleon's march to Russia. A little draft was nothing.

"Have you ever been in love?" Bridget asked.

"Literally scores of times. And for a long time, yes, I thought love was a gateway to a better world. Then, when I gave up on love, I tried music, and that was closer, and when I gave up on that, I tried opium." He took another hit—just marijuana, not opium, never again. "I lost *years* to opium, convinced myself it would set my spirit free as my body wasted away. But, as you see, I'm still here, body and soul bruised but intact."

"I'm not talking about addiction," Bridget said. "I'm talking about love. I love Darrin. I'm not sure all this . . . the things you've shown me . . . are worth the cost of giving him up."

"If you love Darrin, why do you tell him so many lies?" Ismael wondered why he bothered trying to make Bridget miserable. She was remarkably resistant to his gravity-well of despair, his contagious emotional state—not as resistant as that odd girl named Echo he'd met a while back, but still very much her own woman. More importantly, Bridget wasn't following the path of despair to transcendence—she was driven by something else, a thirst for meaning, a need for her existence to *matter*. Ismael didn't need to drag her down, but needling people was a practice honed to habit over the centuries.

"Darrin wouldn't understand," Bridget said resignedly. "He's . . . happy, or at least content. He's satisfied with his job, his house, me."

"Show me a contented man, and I'll show you a fool or a liar." Ismael wanted to steer the discussion away from Darrin. He had high hopes for Bridget's spiritual development—she was a wonderful prospect for transition—but she was also a way for him to reach Darrin, and manipulate him. Helping others free themselves from the misery of life was all well and good, but in Darrin Ismael saw a possibility to finally free *himself*. Better if Bridget didn't know that, though. She might get . . . protective about her lover.

Bridget shrugged. "Darrin knows I'm not happy, but he doesn't know how deep that goes. He thinks I need to find a job I like, or something instead of just temping. I wish I could be more like him, get excited about the prospect of buying a house, having babies, all that, but it just seems so fucking *ordinary*. I want to be more content, more—"

"Idiotically sheep-like? Bridget, never wish for that. You're an idealist, and I can tell you, for certain, that ideal things exist. You're on your way to a better world. Loving Darrin just holds you back. You must learn to let these unimportant desires go."

"I hate it when you get all Zen."

Ismael sighed. "I'm not Zen. I didn't say you should cultivate a lack of desire. I desire things fiercely. Specifically: Oblivion, or eternal bliss. I want those more than *you've* ever wanted anything, and I've been wanting them since before your great-grandparents were born. I'm just saying you should want the right things. I don't want steaming piles of dog shit, or rotten meat, or a knife in the eye, and those are the only things this world can offer: rot and decay and pain, the cheap and the useless, the hallucinated and the fake. You have to *want* to transcend this lesser world, Bridget, more than you've ever wanted anything, and throw away all your distractions. The only way to get there is by casting all your baggage aside."

"Darrin isn't baggage, he's—"

"He's a nice guy," Ismael said. "Yes. I know. I believe you. So marry him, have his children. Suffer through his mid-life crisis, his inevitable affairs. Have children who will love, despise, and forget you, in that order. Grow old with him. Go on. Be like all the rest for your threescore and ten, eat cheeseburgers and race mountain bikes, take cruises and see museums, and when you're done, die and rot in the ground or burn to ash and be finished. Be eaten by worms and the dark." He gestured toward the door. "If you think that's better than living forever in a place of pure joy, go."

"You know, fuck this, Ismael." Bridget threw her pipe down. "I don't think I even believe in your better world. Yeah, you've shown me crazy shit, but I haven't seen any proof of this magical la-la pie-in-the-sky wonderland you're always going on about. I think you're old and desperate and crazy, and eager to get out of your skin. You believe in this 'better world' the way people believe in God, or salvation, it's something you need to get through the day. That's fine, but I'm not some idiot looking for escape from a shitty job, or to be led around by the nose by my own personal guru. I just want *more* out of life, and I don't mean more of your bullshit!"

"Come, then," Ismael said, rising.

She stared up at him, half-furious, half-curious. "Come where?"

"Into the briarpatch. If you don't believe in the better world, I'll show you."

"I thought the whole point was that you couldn't get to the land of light and honey by walking, couldn't reach it in your skin?"

He shrugged. "I have never found such a direct path, though one may exist, in the vastness of the briarpatch, somewhere. But you don't have to see a bear to know there's a bear nearby—you can look at the footprints, the bark stripped from trees, the dung, the mauled bodies. I can show you the proof of a better world, if not the better world itself."

Slowly, Bridget stood up. Ismael watched the emotions move across her face: doubt, frustration, hope, fear. He'd only taken her into the briarpatch a few times, and she still didn't really understand it—she thought it was shortcuts and novelties, and the vast sprawling strangeness of it all hadn't penetrated fully. Well, this time they were going deep, and she would be made to understand. Maybe that would straighten out her priorities.

"We should take backpacks," Ismael said. "It will take a few hours to get where we're going."

She came along, saying nothing as he packed jerky, water bottles, dried fruit, and a first-aid kit—for her, not him, of course—in a pair of high-end hiking backpacks. As he adjusted the complicated straps on his pack, Ismael mused that more engineering had gone into creating these bags than had gone into the construction of bridges, in the old days. The world did change, was always changing, getting better in some respects— fewer fleas now, less slavery. The world just never got good *enough*.

Ismael opened a closet and gestured at dozens of walking sticks leaning against the walls inside. "Better take one of these."

Bridget peered into the closet and shook her head. "For a guy who disdains worldly things, Ismael, you sure do have an awful lot of shit."

Ismael shrugged. "People give me their possessions, sometimes, just before they take the leap. I never ask for it, but it seems rude to refuse. Even this house was a gift from one of my jumpers. I do have a lot of walking sticks but, well, most of those people took a lot of walks with me. Like we're about to."

Bridget grunted and took a ski pole from the closet, just to be contrary, Ismael supposed. He didn't take a stick. He had his ASP baton if he needed to fend anything off to protect Bridget, and he didn't worry about tripping and falling. He knew every dip and pebble on *this* path, though he didn't have the emotional strength to walk it very often. The despair he felt afterward was too great, and paths in the briarpatch could be treacherous.

He led her down his back steps, through his weedy yard, to the leaning wooden shed, full of dust, dark, and spiders. Pulling open the crooked door, he gestured. "After you."

She shifted her pack and stepped past him, pausing just inside the threshold. "I don't see a way," she said petulantly. Well, that wouldn't last. Ismael considered clubbing her in the back of the head and dragging her into the briarpatch to die or find her own way out. Her disappearance would have the same affect on Darrin as her transition to the light. There was a time when he'd reacted to the insolence of these short-time mortals with that sort of extreme prejudice, but the idea of murder made him tired now. Besides, he liked Bridget, and she would probably come around, once she saw the light.

"Look harder." He touched her on the back of the neck.

She stepped forward, muttering "I see," and vanished into the darkness at the back of the shed, a spot where the back wall might have been, but wasn't, just now.

Ismael followed her into the dark, and through, and out into the light again. They were on an isthmus barely wide enough for the two of them to stand side by side, a natural rock bridge dropping away to chasm on all sides, crushed-seashell soil underfoot. The old wooden shed stood behind them, or else its double did; Ismael was never sure whether liminal objects had doppelgangers here in the briarpatch, or if they inhabited both spaces simultaneously. Maybe "space" was an irrelevant term in this setting. Despite years of curiosity about science and philosophy, Ismael was neither scientist nor philosopher, and his approach to the briarpatch was mostly instinctive. His old friend and travelling companion, the talkative Harczos, had been the one with all the theories about this place, but Ismael hadn't spoken to him in years, since their falling out in the wake of Harczos's last great act of cruelty.

A swinging bridge stretched before them, over the chasm, to some unseen shore on the far side. The bridge was a mishmash of metal and wood, boards that resembled those from the shed, patched here and there with scrap metal (like the shed's tin roof), bits of old lawnmowers (like the one that sat rusting in the shed), with handrails made of chain and rope (like those that hung on the shed's walls).

Bridget put her hand on the rail, hesitated for a moment, and then started walking across.

Ismael shook his head. She was so brave and foolish, walking into the briarpatch ahead of him this way, with no idea where she was going or what waited for her ahead. When she saw the corpse, perhaps she'd let him take the lead.

The bridge barely swung as they crossed, and it didn't produce the sorts of creaks and clanks such a structure should have made. Ismael believed it probably wasn't a bridge at all, certainly not a *built* thing, but was instead a metaphorical bridge made real by their presence, their act of observation.

A few steps ahead of him, at the end of the bridge, he heard Bridget say "What the *fuck*!"

Ismael paused, allowing himself a small smile. "Find something unpleasant?"

"There's a dead body," she said tightly, gripping the rope-and-chain railing with both hands.

"Could you be more specific?" Ismael was enjoying this despite himself. He hardly ever enjoyed anything anymore, but this inevitable confrontation with the memento-mori of his jumpers-to-be always pleased him. They figured out things were serious, when he took them over the bridge behind the woodshed.

"It's . . . it's fucking *mauled*, Ismael."

"But does it have a face?"

Silence. Then: "It can't be. I know what it looks like, but it can't be."

"Are you being cryptic on purpose?" Ismael said; it was a question Bridget often asked him.

"It's me, Ismael. The dead body looks like me."

"Well, step over it and let me off the bridge. I don't want to keep swinging in the wind indefinitely. If it's dead it probably can't hurt you. Now, if you ever bump into a *living* version of yourself, that's a different story. I've never heard of it happening, but if it does, I would advise you to run away, and hope your double does the same."

Bridget did a standing long jump over the corpse. Ismael stepped over calmly. He prodded the dead Bridget-double with his toe. It looked like some animal had torn her up pretty badly. "Sometimes they're burned almost beyond recognition, but the face is always recognizable," he said. "People don't recognize their own arms and legs in isolation, unless they have distinctive scars or tattoos, but they know their own faces."

"What are you talking about?" Bridget stood a few feet away hugging herself, her back to the path that wound through high cliffs of red rock. She was cold again, probably with fear this time.

"The body," Ismael said. "Everyone who crosses this bridge finds their own dead body. If two people come, there are two dead bodies. I've never brought more than two at a time, but if I brought twenty, I'm sure there'd be twenty corpses piled here. That would be hard to get passed."

"So . . . it's just some briarpatch thing?"

"'Just?'" Ismael marvelled at her. She seemed almost calm. "This is your own dead ravaged corpse, Bridget. If you pulled down its pants—well, the shredded remains of its pants—you'd find that same birthmark you have on your leg. I don't know why these cadavers appear, if they're a warning, or a sign that means 'turn back now,' or the briarpatch's idea of a gift, or an apport from some other more or less likely universe, but it's personal, and it's meant for you."

"What's an apport?" She knelt and looked at the body, her head cocked, revulsion replaced by curiosity.

Ismael sighed, and his voice took on a lecturing tone. "Basically? An apport is an object out of place. Sometimes an impossible object in an ordinary place, sometimes an ordinary object in an impossible place. Spiritualist mediums would make flowers and fruit and feathers 'appear' out of nowhere, and claim they were messages from the spirit realm. An apport is anything in a place where it shouldn't be—where it *couldn't* be—with the assumption that it must have come from somewhere . . ." He waved his hands vaguely. "*Outside*. Beyond the ordinary world. Beyond reality as it's generally understood."

"Huh," Bridget said. "So everyone who comes here sees their own dead body?"

"Yes. Sometimes dead from obvious causes, sometimes without a mark on them. Sometimes they're wearing wedding rings when their living counterparts aren't married, and sometimes they're missing fingers or toes or have different piercings or the lack thereof, but they're always recognizable."

"Maybe, if there's an infinity of universes, there are some universes where everyone is already dead, and the bodies come from there."

"Makes as much sense as anything, which means, not much," Ismael said. "This place isn't about science. This is the briarpatch. Everything you think you know is wrong."

"Science is just a way to understand the universe." Bridget stood up, apparently prepared to dismiss the body from her thoughts. She paused. "So where's your corpse, Ismael? Is there no place in all the vast interlocking universes where you're not alive?"

"I don't know." Ismael kicked the corpse in the ribs while she wasn't looking. The kick wasn't very satisfying. "I've never found my own corpse here. Perhaps because I come from the briarpatch. Was born here."

"You gotta have parents to be born, Ismael."

"I may have had parents, though I suspect not. It's impossible to say. My earliest memories are walking the forking paths. I think I just . . . came into being."

Bridget grunted. "Maybe *you're* an apport."

"The idea has occurred to me. We should keep going."

"Lead on." She stepped aside to let him start down the path before her, and Ismael counted that concession as a small victory, at least.

2

The high cliffs went on for some time, and the sky above was a reddish haze, which Ismael checked often for disturbance or thickening. It rained here, sometimes, and it didn't always rain water. He'd packed ponchos in the backpacks for just that reason.

They finally emerged onto a roof in Oakland's Lakeshore district, beside an enormous illuminated sign that said "Grand Lake Theater." The night was clear, the lights of houses on the hills in the distance glimmering like captured stars.

Bridget took a drink of water and glared. "Ismael, this place is only a few miles from your house. Why didn't we *start* over here, and avoid crossing the bridge and walking through dry gulch back there?"

"The briarpatch isn't linear." Ismael gazed at the sparkling comet on the sign. "It matters where you start walking. If we'd started from here, we wouldn't wind up in the same place. It would take much longer to get where we're going. Days, probably." It would have also required trailblazing, which Ismael was reluctant to do. Harczos had been the great explorer, not him. Ismael had been lost wandering for years in some of the uglier corners of the briarpatch, and was reluctant to risk such an ordeal again, so he seldom strayed from the paths he knew well. He gestured, and she followed him *around* the sign, not *behind* it. When they stepped around it, they were someplace else instead, at the top of a long slick spiralling stone ramp, like something from a medieval castle. They descended for a while, then the path levelled, and after a few dozen yards of walking through something like the tunnels in a catacomb, the roof opened up into a dark, strange sky. Bridget craned her neck, staring up at the lights far above, too big to be stars, and finally stopped in the middle of the path. She stood on tiptoe and reached up, extending her ski pole to jab the darkness vigorously, and a few drops of water fell into her upturned face, making her cough and blink.

Ismael scowled. "How did you know poking the sky like that wouldn't bring the whole lake crashing down on us? You have to be careful here, Bridget."

"Lake? The sky is a lake? But there are stars."

"We're under Lake Merritt," he said. "Those 'stars' are just the electric fairy lights strung along the path that circles the lake, and the lights of buildings nearby."

"I don't understand. I thought we were in the briarpatch?"

Ismael nodded. "We are. But we're very close to the world you know as well. Everything isn't 'in' or 'out'—many things are in-between. What is the thickness of a border, and where are you when you stand precisely on that border? When you pause in the threshold of a door, are you in, or out? Is twilight night or day? This is a twilight place. It touches the world you know, it is *adjacent* to that world, but not wholly of it."

Bridget frowned. "I still don't get it. How can there be a place like this, a path with air, under the lake?"

"It's not under the lake, not exactly, not the way you mean. If you swam down into the lake, and dove to the bottom, you wouldn't be able to get here. If

I boosted you up, and managed to get you entirely in the water, though, you'd be able to swim up and out. You just wouldn't be able to get back down here again."

"Something to do with multidimensional space maybe," Bridget muttered.

Ismael was annoyed by her constant need to quantify the mystery, but on some level he could sympathize; the briarpatch was vast and confusing and dangerous, and trying to understand it was one way to create the illusion of control. Next she'd be trying to *map* the briarpatch, which not even Harczos had been mad enough to try."You wouldn't want to swim in that lake anyway," Ismael said. "It's full of duck shit."

"They're geese, mostly. There's a bird sanctuary, with some more exotic birds, but mostly it's geese." Still staring up, she pointed. "Look. There goes a gondola."

Ismael looked. A narrow boat passed slowly through the water above them. "How *romantic*." He made the word sound like a skin disease.

"The gondolas on the lake are made in Italy, I've heard. By real gondola makers."

Ismael wondered how anyone who built a functional gondola could be anything but a "real gondola maker," regardless of their country of origin, but it seemed like a pointless argument to start. Most were.

"Darrin took me for a gondola ride on one of our first dates."

"Hmm," Ismael said. "There's no denying I take you more interesting places."

3

"This is the grove," Ismael said. "We're almost there." He paused outside the wood of towering, pale, faintly luminous trees and sat on a flat rock to have a drink and eat some fruit. One of his earlier prospects, a poet, had called this place the Grove of Poison Delights. She hadn't been a very good poet.

Bridget sat next to him and rooted through her bag, pulling out a wad of jerky, ripping off a chunk with her teeth. She chewed thoughtfully, looking around, looking up at the sky. "No stars. Is this some *really* unlikely universe, then?"

"I think we are far underground," Ismael said. "That is why the trees are so pale, perhaps. This is a vast cavern, with a ceiling and walls so far away we cannot see them." In truth, he wasn't sure this *was* a place in the conventional sense, even a very improbable one. Sometimes he thought this was a sort of boiler room for the universe, a place where incomprehensible but necessary mechanisms hummed and whirred to themselves.

"Wild," Bridget said, and Ismael checked a sigh. She made him so angry sometimes, which was quite an accomplishment, considering how old he was. She claimed to thirst for transcendent experience, and he had taken her to places that only a handful of living humans—or things so near to human as to make no difference, like Ismael himself—had ever seen, and yet she still acted jaded, as if she'd seen it all before. Perhaps she was truly driven by the thirst for new experiences, and whether or not she *had* the new experiences was irrelevant; she was always overlooking the present miracle, trying to catch sight of the next.

"Be careful when we pass through the trees," he said, standing up. "Don't take fruit from the branches, if you see any, and don't try to climb them."

"I haven't climbed a tree since I was a little girl," she said, a hint of wistfulness in her voice.

"I'm not even sure these are trees, exactly." He thought about telling her not to look up, but that would only ensure she *would*, so he'd have to hope the natural human tendency to ignore things above their heads would hold. He kept his own eyes resolutely on the well-worn path as he walked, winding circuitously between the strangely smooth trunks. Up close, the trees looked less like trees and more like oversized models of nerve endings, smooth and wildly branching. Harczos had believed this place was the brain of God, but Ismael was decidedly more secular. The universe was an exceedingly strange place, but if there was any intentionality behind its operations, Ismael had yet to see evidence of such a guiding hand. Harczos had never fully pulled himself out of the medieval mindset, where the world was full of signs of God's plans and fury. Still, they'd been friends for a long time before their falling out, and passing through the grove always gave Ismael a little twinge of emotion, like the phantom ache in a long-ago amputated limb.

The path was not straight, in a visually-comprehensible linear sense at least, but he was loath to stray from it. The fact that there *was* a path that went all the way through the grove was testament that people had passed through successfully by that route, and if he strayed from the path, who knew where he might end up? Ismael's peculiar nature protected him from physical harm—or from death, anyway—but there was no mechanism to keep him from getting lost, which was always a great danger in the briarpatch.

Ismael had gone barely fifty feet into the trees when he realized Bridget wasn't behind him. He turned around, careful to keep his feet on the path, and saw Bridget partway up a tree, eyes fixed straight up, clambering through the branches.

Ismael raced toward her, though that necessitated leaving the path, and climbed up the tree after her, keeping his eyes on the soles of her boots and trying to ignore the kaleidoscopic swirl above her, the hypnotic distance into which the uppermost branches vanished. He grabbed her ankle with both hands and let himself drop off the tree, his weight enough to jerk her out of the branches. He hit the ground, the breath whooshing out of his lungs, and then Bridget fell on top of him. Since the impact wasn't life-threatening, Ismael wasn't transported away. Bridget's boot hit his chest hard enough to make his heart stutter, and then she started kicking and twisting and trying to get away, making little inhuman grunts, and all the time turning her head to stare up, up, up. Ismael climbed up her body the way she'd climbed the tree, finally getting on top of her, rolling her over face down, and pressing her nose into the peculiar gray dirt. He held her for a while until she stopped struggling—not suffocated, but simply in control of her senses once again.

Ismael eased off, but didn't let her up completely. "Are you all right?"

"It was so beautiful," Bridget murmured. "Up above the trees. Is that the light you talked about?"

Ismael snorted. "No, Bridget. That's just . . . well, you know pitcher plants, the carnivorous plants that catch flies? They have an odour that flies find irresistible, and when the flies try to get close to that good smell, they slide in and they're trapped and they die. These trees are pitcher plants, sort of. Those pretty coloured lights are a trick."

Bridget tried to sit up, and Ismael let her. "How do you know?" she demanded. "Maybe if you'd let me climb all the way up, I would've reached that better world you're always talking about!"

"No, Bridget," he said gently. "You would have died, that's all."

"How do you know?"

Ismael sighed. "Because I've been here before. You think I never climbed these trees? You think I never went for the pretty colours like a monkey up a rope, just like you? Of course I did! And when I got to the top—because I didn't have a friend to pull me down—the lights faded, and there was a horrible blackness with rustling all around, and then something uncoiled toward me. I can't explain it better than that, really, I want to say it was like a frog's tongue but frog's tongues aren't that big and they aren't fractal, and it wasn't really anything like a tentacle. It moved at angles, and . . . well. Before it reached me, my self-preservation mechanism kicked in, and I found myself sprawled on my back in the middle of the Utah salt flats, with the worst headache of my life. And

I've had some bad headaches. If whatever's up there wasn't deadly, I wouldn't have been transported away."

Bridget sighed, scuffed at the ground with her heel, started to look up, thought better of it, and determinedly kept her eyes down. "How does your stupid magical teleporting life-support system know when you're about to die, anyway?"

"I don't know," Ismael said, truthfully. "It plays the percentages, I think, examines the probabilities, and when things look too dire, it jerks me away. But I get hurt often enough—like your hiking boot in my solar plexus, I'm going to have such a bruise—that I know it isn't exactly a hair-trigger. Only my imminent demise seems to activate it." Something occurred to him. "Oh, and the other reason I know those colours up there aren't the light from a world of perfect bliss? You can't really remember what was so wonderful about the colours now, can you? The effect has faded, now that you aren't staring at them, right?"

"Yeah," she said cautiously.

"The light I'm taking you to see isn't like that. Once you've seen it once, you remember it forever." He stood, brushing dirt off his pants, and held out a hand to her. "Come on. I'm ready to get out of this place. Just don't look up."

"Wish you'd mentioned that earlier," she said.

"I told you it was dangerous here. If I enumerated every danger we passed, we'd never get anywhere." He thought about warning her about the bears, but they were too complicated to explain, and she would probably argue about them, since they were hard to believe until you *saw* them. He settled for saying "Just be careful. And always expect the worst."

"I always do." She followed him back to the path.

4

After a long trek over rocky terrain, beneath a neutral sky, Ismael and Bridget turned into a sudden narrow corridor of stone and then, there they were: in a ruined courtyard, dry fountains and columns choked with weeds, paving stones cracked and heaved underfoot, a whole broken city stretching out on all sides, and shining on it all from an oval hole in the sky above: the light of a better world.

They both sank to the ground, leaning against the broken lip of a fountain, and even the sharp edges of the stone were like a lover's caress against Ismael's back. Bridget's hand crept out, and Ismael took it in his own, and the light seemed to flow through them, through their touch, into each other, and back out again. Bridget's eyes were wide, her breathing shallow, and she'd never looked more beautiful; by definition nothing looked more beautiful than it did when it was touched by this light. Out in the ordinary world, there was nothing to compare with such illumination, though Ismael was often reminded of it by the sunlight slanting down on late afternoons in Oakland, when the leaves of the trees seemed limned with gold, when the hills appeared lit by some divine luminosity, when the waters of the lake shone like scattered diamonds. But even that light was nothing like this, really; it just *suggested* this light, the way a photograph of the Sistine Chapel ceiling acted as a sort of symbol of the real thing, but couldn't replicate reality's scale and scope and grandeur.

Tears ran down Ismael's cheeks, and he felt utterly at peace, stoned on bliss, but underneath it all, deep down, there was an element of longing, and that element would only intensify when he finally, inevitably left the light.

After a long long time, he took Bridget's hand, and drew her away, and she rose languidly, as if awakening from a sweet dream. She stared at him, reached out, and touched his cheek with her fingertips, and he knew what she was thinking: that he was beautiful. As she was beautiful. As everything, seen by this light, was beautiful.

He led her away, into what remained of a building, a half-collapsed dome roof over them, where they were shielded from the light enough to make concentration and conversation possible.

Bridget just swallowed, and stared at him, and didn't speak, and so Ismael talked, responding to what he thought her questions might be, to what his own had been, long ago, when he first caught sight of that light from another place.

"We can't stay in the light forever," he said, and saw her face fall. "We still have our physical bodies, you see, and eventually they will die. When I first found this place, I stayed for days, and never intended to leave, but I must have been near to dying of thirst, because I was transported into a creek, water flowing right into my mouth, and I wept and wept that day, pounding the creek bottom, hating my body. If you stayed, you would simply waste away." Or be killed by bears, or worse, become one; but that was a whole other story, and not particularly germane just now. "And you wouldn't care, of course, because you'd be here, in the light . . . but when you died, you'd stop being able to experience the light. That's why it's not enough to come here, where the light is filtered, indirect, a pale reflection of a reflection. We have to find the source of the light, the world where it shines directly, and live there. It's possible. I've known people who've gone, I've seen the moment of transition when they leave their bodies and ascend. It can be done."

"What is it? Where is it? What kind of place? Is it . . . heaven?"

Ismael shrugged. "I don't know. The briarpatch leads us to possible worlds, you know, and some of them are more possible than others. That light . . . I think it comes from what truly is the best of all possible worlds. You've seen how the light looks, how it transforms everything out there, if it shone on dogshit the *dogshit* would be beautiful."

"Ismael, let's follow it. Let's go looking for the source of the light!" Her eyes were shining, and Ismael was gratified to see that she was finally impressed, her wall of cynicism finally breached.

"That's like rainbow-chasing, Bridget. The light passes through places that people can't go. There are spots like this, scenic overlooks, where the light can be glimpsed, but I've never found a path to it. And even this light, it's thin and attenuated, there are places where it's brighter—this is just reflected light, I think, the way moonlight is a reflection of sunshine. Can you imagine standing in the undiluted light?"

"You'd just . . . melt away."

"Perhaps," Ismael said. He sat down, looking up at the cracked dome, at the line of shadow against the sky of light. "You know all those stories about creation gods shitting out the universe, expelling stars and planets from their bowels? Did you ever wonder what sort of wonderful things those gods must have *eaten*, to shit *stars*? How wonderful the substance of that devoured world must have been? That's the place we're trying to go. The place where the gods live, or would live, if they lived anywhere."

"I feel like shit right about now," Bridget said.

"I know. That's why I don't come here often. After I leave, everything feels so useless and pointless and ugly. Transcendence withdrawal."

"You know how people who are dying see light at the end of a tunnel?" Bridget said. "'Go toward the light,' all that sort of thing? Do you think . . . they're seeing this light?"

"No," Ismael said, disgusted by the notion. "That light is just the symptom of a dying brain—ugly misfires in the grey matter, the last pulse of electrical sparks. If anyone could get to the world of light, just by dying . . ." He shook his head. "That would be too easy. Getting there is hard. Besides, I've seen people die unprepared, and there is no flash, no portal opening—as far as I can tell they just *die*, their souls go to the same place the brightness goes when a lightbulb burns out—nowhere, into nothingness, back into oblivion. But people who let everything go, who prepare themselves, who loosen the moorings of their spirits . . . they can go into the light. I've seen it, blinding pinpricks in the fabric of the universe. You'll learn to see it, too, once you've spent more time in the briarpatch." He rubbed his eyes. "We should go. The longer we stay, the harder it will be to leave. Anyway, isn't your best-beloved Darrin going to worry about you?"

"Okay," Bridget said. "That light . . . it's like everything else in the world is just set dressing in a play, fake things on a stage. Like the light is the only real thing, like it makes *me* real just by shining on me. I think . . . maybe it's the meaning of life I've been looking for."

"It is, at least, a means for finding such a meaning," Ismael said. "Come. The way back is shorter, at least, and doesn't pass through the grove."

"Can we . . . just for a minute . . . go into the light again?"

Ismael nodded. He'd expected as much. In truth, of course, he wanted to stand in it too, and feel cleansed. When he came here, he was able to forget about the misery of his condition, and he was untroubled by his liver flukes, his eczema, his various non-lethal STDs, and all the parasites he'd picked up over centuries of stumbling through this filthy, disease-pocked world.

They went back into the light and stood near a trio of broken pillars. They didn't hold hands this time, and after a while Ismael drifted away from her, toward a freestanding fragment of wall decorated with ancient bas-relief carvings of animal-headed women; he didn't recognize any of the animals, though, and he supposed the carvings might have been truly representational of the city's former inhabitants. Where had they gone? Had the light started shining on their civilization one day, and doomed them all to a death of bliss and dehydration? Whatever had become of them, there was nothing alive here now, except the bears, and Ismael, and the people he brought. It was possible that other children of the briarpatch, or assorted mad wanderers, passed through from time to time, but Ismael had never encountered them.

There was no wind here, and so Ismael didn't smell the bear coming, and it was almost upon Bridget by the time he noticed. At first, he was struck by the unimaginable majesty of the bear—over 750 pounds and easily seven feet tall if it rose onto its hind legs. In this light it looked like something that should be worshipped as a god. Ismael froze in place, unable to be precisely terrified because of the light's calmative influence, though wariness wormed up from his deeper self. Bears were unpredictable under the best of circumstances, and the light affected them oddly. Sometimes they became blissful. Sometimes they became enraged. This one seemed merely curious. Blue ribbons were woven all over its hair, giving it a cheerful air, but in its face there was no expression Ismael could read.

These creatures weren't usually very dangerous as long as they stayed in bear form. Then they were just animals, wary of people, and this bear was male, with no cubs to defend.

"Bridget," Ismael said. "We should go. Walk toward me."

Bridget ignored him. She'd noticed the bear. "Beautiful," she murmured, and walked toward it, hand outstretched. Ismael wanted to shout at her, but the loud noise might startle the bear and make it notice him. If Ismael was attacked, he'd be wrenched away from here by his body's ultimate defences, and Bridget would be left alone.

The bear sniffed at Bridget, cocking its head. "You're someone's pet, aren't you?" Bridget said, in a faraway voice. "Such pretty ribbons." She stroked the bear's shoulder, and the bear simply stood there, untroubled.

"You shouldn't," Ismael said, trying to rouse himself from his light-stupor, to take action. "Bridget, just move away from it, it's a fucking *bear*, I told you this place is dangerous."

Bridget looked at him, brow wrinkled. "Silly Ismael. He's a nice bear." She stroked the bear again.

And then the bear changed. One moment, it was a grizzly on all fours. The next it was a man, filthy and hairy. Not terribly large, shorter than Bridget and wiry, with blue ribbons tied into his chest hair and pubic hair. Bridget's hand was on his cock, which was erect and brown with dirt. She jerked her hand away, and the bear grunted, grabbing her wrists and forcing her back against the pillar. Bridget stared at the bear, eyes a bit unfocused. "You're not a bear," she said.

Ismael got to his feet, shaking off the peace of the light like a man waking from a heroin nod. He'd been here before, often, and built up something of a resistance—he knew how to pull himself away by now. He reached into his pocket for his baton, snapped it open—every action felt slow as the advance of glaciers—and he advanced on the bear. If he could give the bear a crack across the head while it was in man-form, he might be able to knock it unconscious. Fortunately, the bear seemed utterly bewildered by Bridget's clothes, fumbling with buttons and tugging at fabric. Bridget tried ineffectually to pull herself away, a look of profound confusion on her face.

Just as Ismael cocked his arm back to swing the baton, the bear transformed again, back into grizzly form. Now Bridget was pinned against the wall by 750 pounds of dangerous animal, but at least it didn't have rape on its mind anymore. It wouldn't see Bridget as a sexual partner, but it did see her as a potential meal, and Ismael stopped walking. It was too late. He couldn't fight off a bear with his baton, and Bridget was as good as dead. Being mauled by a bear was hardly a pleasant experience, but here, in the land of light, at least it would be as pleasant as such an experience *could* be.

Having the bear leaning against her, breathing its carrion-and-berries breath into her face, must have been overwhelming, because she simply passed out and slid down the wall. The bear pushed himself back, going down on all fours, and took a swipe at Bridget, claws taking a chunk out of her side. That woke her up, and she screamed briefly, before shock set in, and then went silent. The bear nudged her, took a bite out of her elbow, bit her leg, and then bit at her head. He didn't crack her skull, though bears liked to do that, considering brains a treat; he just tore off a great swath of her scalp and hair, chewed it briefly like a piece of gum, then spat it away. Ismael didn't dare move. If the bear smelled him, or noticed him, it might try to kill him. It might run away too, but there was no telling. If Ismael stood very still, and the bear lost interest before completely devouring Bridget, then all was not lost. So he waited.

After about a minute of pawing at her, the bear lost interest and wandered off, leaving Bridget behind. If it had intended to keep her as a meal for later, it would have scraped dirt over her and left her partially covered to tenderize. It must not have been very hungry.

Ismael hurried to Bridget, checked her pulse, took off his shirt and tried to staunch the bleeding from her head. He consulted his complex mental map of the briarpatch—a place resistant to mapping, where the paths shifted over time and distances varied with the seasons, with the tides, with the weather, with *anything*—and thought maybe it was possible to take her quickly to that strange crystal hospital Harczos had shown him once. Assuming the hospital wasn't so improbable it had already dissolved into a void of unlikelihood. That was really her only hope. Even if she survived her wounds, she'd been bitten by one of the bears in the briarpatch, which meant *she* might eventually transform as well, and go mad in the process. She needed a better body.

Ismael scooped Bridget up tenderly in his arms. In this light, even her wounds were beautiful. She was breathing raggedly, but she was alive. "Come, little Bridget," he murmured. "You're stubborn and sometimes stupid and too contrary by half, but you deserve a better death than this." He carried her away.

DARRIN CATCHES A LIFT

1

After seeing Bridget die that morning, Darrin stayed home for a couple of hours, but then he couldn't stand his apartment anymore, cluttered as it was with so many reminders of his loss, so he gulped the last of his latest drink, grabbed his camera, and went out the back door and down the stairs, jumping over the loose third step from the bottom, almost tripping and stumbling when he hit the ground. He'd only had two screwdrivers, but they'd been more vodka than orange juice, and he hadn't eaten lunch. It was a good thing his car had been repossessed all those months ago—he was in no shape to drive anyway, and self-preservation wasn't high on his priority list at the moment.

The backyard was shared by all the apartments, but was seldom used, though there was a nice brick patio, a barbecue, two posts with dangling chains for a hammock, and a picnic table with benches. Darrin walked around the big redwood growing by the detached garage and out the back gate. He set off down the steep hill toward Park Boulevard with no fixed destination in mind. He'd go down a couple of blocks, he figured, then curve back into the swirl of residential streets, walk by some of the million-dollar houses, and make his way down toward the apartment buildings and liquor stores closer to Lake Merritt. Maybe looking at the water would soothe him. Or maybe it would remind him of walks with Bridget, of their one ridiculously expensive gondola ride, the way she'd always insisted they rush out at the first hint of spring to see the newborn goslings while they were still fuzzy and adorable, before they turned into fat, foul-tempered geese.

As he walked, the light seemed to shift around him, and he glanced skyward, expecting to see clouds moving across the sun, channelling the sunbeams in unexpected directions, but the sky was blue and clear. Still, the light seemed fragmented, as if shining through a lens of broken prisms. He must be drunker than he'd realized. Darrin ducked his head and kept his eyes on the sidewalk, walking over broken beer bottles, past Arturo's paper-stuffed Chrysler Wendigo, past the corner apartment building with the fake castle crenellations on the roof. When he hit Park Boulevard he turned right, down a block of storefronts with signs he couldn't read because they were written in Korean, until he hit the next side street, which sloped back uphill again at an angle. A palm tree flourished here, its giant fronds overhanging the sidewalk and turning it into a sort of tunnel. Darrin ducked in, feeling obscurely comforted by the screen of leaves. And there, just up from the corner, he saw a set of stone steps disappearing into a heavily wooded vacant lot. Darrin went toward the steps, curious, because he'd never noticed them before.

He lifted the camera, thumbed it on, and looked down at the screen. The camera did its trick of making him pay attention and notice details. Weeds grew up through the cracks in the concrete, and weathered stone lions with chipped ears snarled from either side of the broad steps. They must have led up to a house, once upon a time, before the lot was bulldozed and overtaken by bushes and trees. He took shots of the lions (probably shitty shots, he figured, since his compositional sense was currently drowning in OJ and liquor,), and then followed the camera up the steps, just a dozen of them and then trees and darkness. There was the barest suggestion of a path, and Darrin decided to follow it, though he knew it probably just led to a burned-out campfire, a pile of beer bottles and used condoms, a hangout for the homeless or horny teenagers. Still, even the squalid could make for a good photograph, and if Darrin had ever held himself above such ugly things, that time had passed. He stopped looking through the camera to move branches out of his way, and to brush aside ancient spider webs.

There was a surprising variety of trees here. He was no botanist, but he'd walked in Oakland enough to recognize most of the common trees, even if he could only name oak, eucalyptus, redwood, and palm. There were trees here with silver-white bark, and others wound around with black thorns, and others hairy with parasitic vines. He trod fungi underfoot now too, as he went deeper—ghost-white things, some of them as big as footstools, the sort of cartoon mushrooms he hadn't realized existed in real life. The ever-present smells of asphalt and car exhaust, so ordinary on his street that he barely noticed them, were gone now, replaced with a deep-woods scent of earthy rot and riot, vegetable wetness, fungal dust, and something sharp, like a whiff of piss. What light filtered in from above still seemed fractured, slanting in at odd and even contradictory angles, it seemed; but he was no optics specialist, no more than he was a botanist. All he knew these days was anxiety and cameras, and so he lifted the camera to his face again to take some pictures of those mushrooms, trying to get his foot in the frame to provide scale.

The path kept winding, and though he heard running water nearby, he was loath to leave the path for reasons that hovered between superstition and instinct. He knew, intellectually, that there must be houses a few yards away, that if he kept walking this way through the trees he would emerge behind one of those Korean stores, within shouting distance of his own front door, but this place gave the impression of being deep dark woods, and somewhere beneath the booze and his detached observation it unsettled him. There were no beer bottles here, no candy wrappers, no used condoms, though it seemed like an obvious place for teenagers to fuck and bums to drink and crash. It was like a pocket of deep wilderness in the middle of a city.

The path ended at an open pit ten or twelve feet across, with steeply sloping sides of crumbled black earth. An odour like chalk dust and ancient paper rose from the hole, and Darrin looked in vain for some suggestion of a path leading around its perimeter. He went to the edge, wondering if the hole led to the remains of a basement, or if it was a sinkhole. The bottom was deeper than a grave, littered with dead leaves, but Darrin could discern some white structure underneath—a lattice of PVC pipes, maybe? He looked around and picked up a long stick—a fallen sapling, really—and poked around in the hole, expecting the hollow thump of wood against plastic pipe. Instead, the sound was a muted clack, and as he prodded and stirred the leaves he realized the white things were bones. Was this some North American urban version of an elephant graveyard, where deer or skunks came to die? Or maybe it was a pet graveyard of convenience, where families from decades before had tossed their dearly departed cats and dogs?

Then his probing stick flipped over something that was clearly a ribcage, and revealed a skull with a star-shaped hole punched through the middle of its forehead. Not a dog's skull. Or a cat's. Darrin was no anthropologist, but . . . *Could be an ape's skull or something*, he thought, letting his stick fall into the hole among the leaves and bones. His dry mouth made swallowing difficult, and the fuzziness of the alcohol he'd consumed no longer seemed like a pleasant buzz but a dangerous impairment.

"That's a human skull," Darrin said aloud, but if anything, animal or otherwise, heard him, there was no sign. This wasn't just bones in a hole anymore—this was an open grave.

Almost without thinking, Darrin raised the camera, gazed at the digital reproduction of the grisly scene before him, and zoomed in on the broken skull and its bed of leaves. He pressed the button, which gave an artificial but satisfying "click," a little sop to those who'd grown up using non-digital cameras. He was thinking of evidence for the police as he snapped his pictures, but he was also thinking of beauty, and composition, and light levels, and because it was dim under the trees he turned on the flash.

The leaves stirred as he took pictures. Wind? A strange wind, to stir only in a hole. Then the bones clattered and rattled together, and Darrin kept taking pictures, oddly mesmerized, until a great pile of bones and leaves heaved up, like a blanket with a body moving beneath it. Darrin stumbled back, camera thumping against his chest.

A voice rose from the pit, no more human than a lion's roar or an avalanche, but making words: "Fee, fie, foe, fum, I smell blood and shit and come. Make you spatter, make you spurt, make you scream and flinch and hurt." Something rose from the pit, bones and leaves cascading away as it emerged. "Bind your bones into my bed, make a soup bowl from your head, eat your heart and eat your lungs, make a morsel of your tongue."

Giant, Darrin thought, and for just an instant he lifted his camera, wanting to take a picture of whatever monstrous head and shoulders might rise from the pit, but he wasn't *that* drunk, or such a voyeur that he'd watch his own oncoming death. He let the camera fall again, strap pulling at his neck, and raced away from the pit, away from the path. Terror gave him the luxury of not thinking about the words he'd just heard, about the impossibility of giants, let alone a giant in an empty lot a block from his house. So he ran, leaping over those footstool-sized mushrooms, crashing along through low-hanging branches. Noises came from behind him, great stony grindings and cataclysmic thumps as the half-buried thing in the hole dug itself out. The sound was more like that of earth-moving equipment than of anything alive. And still that droning, inhuman voice, chanting words Darrin couldn't make out now. Something whizzed through the air over his head, a spinning blur of white that struck a tree and exploded into fragments. As Darrin pushed himself faster, his side beginning to ache from the exertion, camera bouncing painfully against his breastbone, he realized the thrown weapon had been a long bone of some kind, a recognizable knobby joint lying in his path where it had bounced after impact. The thing behind Darrin was hurling body parts at him.

The ground sloped, up and possibly out, the trees thinning, and Darrin expected to see a familiar street, houses he knew, maybe even his own home; this was the right general direction.

But when he crested the ridge and emerged from the trees, there were no houses, only a road paved with great flat stones, and more trees across the way. There was, however, one familiar thing, which made Darrin pause in his flight, confusion compounded into paralysis.

The Wendigo was parked in front of him, passenger side facing Darrin, and the door was open. A great mound of paper, envelopes, notes, and sheets of musical notation was scattered all around the car, and the bucket seat inside was clear of litter, mostly. Arturo popped out from the driver's side, looking at Darrin across the Wendigo's roof. His balding head glistened with sweat, and his moustache twitched. "Get in," he shouted, slamming the flat of his palm on the Wendigo's roof.

Trees snapped behind him as Darrin sprinted the last few yards to the car, and from Arturo's wide eyes and gaping mouth, Darrin knew the thing from the pit, the creature that slept under a blanket of bones, had cleared the trees too.

Darrin flung himself into the Wendigo, whipped the door shut after him, triggering an avalanche of mounded litter from the back seat, paper cascading down his shoulders, paper cuts nicking his neck, and he had the absurd thought that the Wendigo was a vampire, sampling his blood through tiny slices.

Arturo jumped back into the car as well, revving the engine, but before they could escape, something stepped into the road. But something that size shouldn't have been able to *step*, shouldn't have been able to move at all. It had the proportions of a house rather than an animal, and its body was a mess of dirt, draped with clacking chains of bone, ivory, and fungus, as if the forest back there had decided to rise up and go walking. If it had a head, Darrin couldn't see it, but its chanting drone went on, blood and death and pain, the specifics drowned out by the Wendigo's growling engine. The creature held a tree, a mess of roots and hardened soil at one end. It cocked back the club, clearly intending to smash the Wendigo.

A horrible noise started, and Darrin realized it was his own screaming, mingling with the rising shriek of the Wendigo's engine—the sounds harmonizing.

Arturo didn't scream. He threw the Wendigo into reverse, and they rocketed backward, out of the arc of the swinging tree. But the thing rushed toward them, seeming to approach without any need for a practical method of locomotion, just flying along like a special effect come to life, and Arturo braked abruptly. Darrin stared at him, and Arturo gave him an "A-OK" sign with his fingers. Then he slammed his hand down on the centre of the Wendigo's huge steering wheel, and the car horn sounded.

Detroit had never built a car with a horn like this. No car customizer had ever tricked out his ride to make such a sound. It was an animal's roar, the voice of some alpha-beast that was to lions as lions were to mice, something that ate wolves and picked its teeth with the bones of Komodo dragons, a predator's predator. The sound was so bestial and threatening that every hair on Darrin's neck stood up, gooseflesh covered his arms, and his bowels nearly let go. He was paralyzed, and even though he knew it was the car horn, some trick or recording, his hindbrain was certain it was the cry of the pinnacle of apex predators, and that Darrin was about to be devoured.

The thing—Darrin didn't like to think the word "giant" again, didn't like the word as anything other than maybe an adjective—dropped its weapon and loped away, disappearing into the trees.

After another moment, Arturo took his hand off the horn, but Darrin went on hearing the sound for several seconds, and was sure he'd remember it in dreams forever.

Finally Arturo turned to him and said, "I wasn't sure the horn would work. Some of these things in here don't have ears. I was afraid I'd have to turn the high beams on, and that would've led to a whole lot of other problems, most likely." He put the Wendigo in gear and drove down the paving stones.

All that remained of Darrin's alcoholic buzz was a dry mouth and an aching head. "Arturo," he said, measured, trying to keep his voice steady, but having no choice but to raise it in order to be heard over the Wendigo's engine. "Where are we? Am I going crazy?" Maybe he'd gone mad with grief over seeing Bridget die. That sort of thing happened in books sometimes.

"I saw you was out walkin', thought I'd say hello." Arturo guided the Wendigo around a fallen tree. Though the road looked rough, more cratered than potholed, the ride was smooth; the Wendigo had one hell of a set of shocks.

"Then I saw you take a, ah, side path, you know what I'm sayin', and I'd been that way—this way—*here*—before, and I thought maybe you'd need a ride out pretty soon. I didn't follow you on foot, on account of I don't get around so good in the briarpatch without the Wendigo." He patted the dash affectionately. "I'm not a natural, like you are, so I came after you in the car. Good thing, too. You should know it's dangerous around here. There's worse things'n what you ran into in those woods. God forbid you should run into a bear. Sometimes not even the high beams work on them. One of 'em took a chunk out of the Wendigo's fender one time, and that's the only thing I've ever even seen scratch the paint on this baby."

Darrin tried to seize on something he could understand. Briarpatch? A natural? Bears? He finally said, "Thanks for helping me," though that hardly seemed adequate.

Arturo shrugged. "You and me got things in common. I lost somebody, too. I lost my Marjorie, and you lost your Bridget."

Darrin pressed himself against the car door, away from Arturo. "How do you know about Bridget? Do you work for Ismael?"

"Don't know any Ismael. Is he another briarpatch boy? The way I know about you is, I read about you. Here." Arturo drove with one hand and rummaged in the trash pile with the other, pulling out a torn scrap of paper. He handed it to Darrin, who read, in his own handwriting, things he'd never written down, about Bridget leaving him. He turned it over, but the back side was blank. "What the fuck is this?"

"Oh, you know the briarpatch," Arturo said, cheerful and vague, and Darrin began to realize there was some vast misunderstanding here, some knowledge Arturo assumed they shared. "I think maybe it's a page from a diary you might've written, but never got around to writin'? There used to be more, but I lost it, or the Wendigo ate it, either one. The Wendigo gives me what I need. When I saw them diary pages and then met you, and realized you was the Darrin who signed your name on those diary entries—not every page, but you wrote like letters you couldn't send, to Bridget mostly, and you signed *those*, just like they was regular letters—I knew I was supposed to get to know you."

"Supposed to?" Darrin said, chasing a minor point, unwilling to face the larger mysteries, let alone acknowledge his own ignorance. "What, like God put you in my path? Fate?"

"I don't think there's any such thing as Fate. Not for me, anyway. For me, there's only the Wendigo. And I don't know about God. What happened to my

Marjorie, it's hard to believe in God after that. I ain't seen God, unless God's a ray of light, or the briarpatch itself. Here's our exit." He spun the wheel, and the Wendigo dropped off the edge of the road, landing with a hard thump after seconds of free fall, and suddenly the trees were gone and they were on salt flats, endlessly blank in all directions, but only for an instant. Then the Wendigo was smoothly merging into traffic on Interstate 580, less than two miles from Darrin's home. Darrin looked in the side mirror, but there was no sign of an on-ramp or feeder road they could have come from. They'd just . . . appeared on the highway. *It's like the alley Ismael escaped into, that night with Nicholas*, Darrin thought, and there was a sort of *click* in his head. He'd once seen an alley that didn't properly exist. Today he'd walked into some woods that were simultaneously near his house and nowhere near it at all.

And now, as if it were a sort of rainbow only visible from certain angles, an impossibly high and distant moon-coloured bridge shimmered into visibility high above the freeway, like an overpass for angels. Darrin had seen the same bridge for an instant that night outside the strip club, with Nicholas. He raised his hand and pointed, too breathtaken to speak.

"I know." Arturo leaned forward over the steering wheel and looked up at the bridge. "I've been tryin' to find an on-ramp to that thing for years." The anguish and frustration in his voice were so clear and undisguised that Darrin reached over and patted his shoulder. "Home again," Arturo said, forced joviality in his tone, and drove the Wendigo onto the exit for Park Boulevard. One left and one right turn later he stopped the car in front of Darrin's place. "I'll see you around, friend. And don't be too sad—I know Bridget left you, but maybe she'll come back, right, realize what a good thing she had, you know?"

Darrin stared at him. Arturo clearly knew all sorts of things, but he didn't know everything. "Bridget . . . she's dead. She jumped off a bridge today."

Arturo's face fell. "Oh, I'm awful sorry to hear that, awful sorry. You and me are more alike than I realized."

"Your Marjorie . . . she killed herself?"

"She . . . it was a car thing," Arturo said, looking down, as ambiguous an answer as Darrin could imagine. "Ah, hell, anyway. That explains why you went stumblin' into that nasty part of the woods. The briarpatch is what it is, but it bends around us a little, too, like a plant grows up to the sun and roots grow down to the centre of the Earth. The briarpatch sort of turns us toward misery or wonder, whichever seems to suit us best."

"Right." Darrin opened the car door.

"Better wash your shoes off with bleach," Arturo said. "You might've brought some seeds or spores with you from those woods, and you don't want some of those plants takin' root out here, you know?"

"Thanks." Darrin looked down at his own shoes in a sort of bemused horror. "I'll do that."

"Hey, look," Arturo said. "Before you go. Maybe, if you got a few minutes, I think we should talk. What do you say we go get a beer?"

Darrin opened his mouth to make a polite, reflexive refusal, but the look on Arturo's face was so hopeful that he nodded. "Sure, we can do that."

"Let me park the Wendigo, and we can walk," Arturo said. "I know a place."

DARRIN AND ARTURO SWAP STORIES

1

"There's a bar about five blocks down," Darrin said when they reached the corner of his street and Park Boulevard.

"I know a closer place," Arturo said. "Just across here." He strolled toward the crosswalk, and Darrin followed with trepidation—he'd lived in this neighbourhood for years, walked every street within a few miles, and there were no bars closer than the one he'd mentioned. Not in the normal world, at least.

Arturo reached the far side of the street and continued up the hill, past an apartment complex, and turned down a narrow footpath between apartment buildings, turning sideways to pass through the bushes crowding the pavement. Darrin began to feel hope. Maybe there was some illegal bar run out of a basement apartment; maybe they weren't going back into the strange world he'd stumbled into earlier.

But no. After a few more turnings, down progressively-narrower passageways between high stucco walls, they reached a wider street with cobblestones, and the air there seemed ten degrees cooler than it was everywhere else. Brick buildings lined the cobblestone street, most with their windows barred and their doors secured with chains or closed behind steel gates. Only one door stood open, and Arturo gestured. "This is the place. You'll like it. It's very plausible. I don't like to go too deep without the Wendigo, but places like this, right on the outskirts, I can manage."

Darrin went in, relieved to see a normal tavern of the local-dive variety, with a few stools by the bar, a dusty mirror on the wall behind, one pool table back in a corner, round tables and chairs scattered throughout the room, and a jukebox against the far wall. Curiously, there were no bottles of booze lined up behind the bar, just row upon row of pint glasses on the shelves.

Arturo led the way, and they sat on stools. The bartender eased himself away from the far end of the bar, an area darkened by a deep confluence of shadows, and approached them. He was dressed like a tavern keeper from a Western, with a white shirt and sleeve garters, and he had an impressive array of facial hair, muttonchops converging into a wild beard. His eyes were flat and incurious, and he looked past them rather than at them. "Your pleasure, gents?" His voice was soft and gentle enough for pillow talk. He nodded toward two tap handles, placing his right forefinger on a handle of flaked obsidian, and the other on a handle fashioned from a lump of amber with several bubbles trapped inside.

"Two pints of the amber," Arturo said quickly, and glanced at Darrin. "The, ah, darker stuff isn't really to our taste."

The bartender smiled, then, a flash of teeth in the midst of his beard, and Darrin caught a glimpse of extraordinarily long and pointed canines. As the bartender drew the pints, Darrin leaned away from him, made uncomfortable by the man's teeth. Were they filed down, or . . . ?

He noticed then that the bartender cast no reflection in the long mirror behind the bar, while Arturo and Darrin himself showed up clearly. "Arturo, the mirror—" he began, thinking it had to be some trick. The giant he'd seen in the woods, okay, maybe it had just been some huge wild homeless man, his size magnified in Darrin's mind by panic, but someone with fangs, who didn't appear in a mirror—

"S'okay," Arturo said. "Don't worry about it. There's no danger. It's just . . . one of those things."

The bartender set their pints before them, glasses of golden-bright liquid, like fluid light. "I'll run you a tab." He eased back into the shadows at the end of the bar.

"It's mostly plausible, anyway," Arturo muttered and sipped his beer.

Darrin tried to lift his glass, but his hands were shaking, and he stopped, staring at his trembling fingers. *I think I'm going crazy*, he thought, and it seemed like one of the few sensible thoughts he'd had all day. Seeing Bridget jump like that must have done something to him, set up some nasty resonances in his mind. How else to explain the things he'd seen since? To explain this?

"I think I have to go," Darrin said slowly. "I think I need to find a doctor."

"You're hurt?" Arturo said, worry creasing his forehead.

Darrin frowned. "I think I'm having some kind of an episode. I've been seeing things that aren't real." That was a relief, in a way. He could call his old therapist, and she would help him, refer him to the sort of doctor who could write him a prescription for some wonderful drugs. He and Bridget had been . . . estranged, yes . . . but he was still traumatized, still unravelling from grief at seeing her die. It was painful, but it was an explanation.

"Oh, hell," Arturo said softly. "This is all new to you? I thought you were, you know, a seasoned traveler, that you just stumbled onto the wrong path. But, what, today, this is your first time in the briarpatch?"

"The briarpatch," Darrin repeated. "You said that before."

Arturo nodded. "It's what some people call, ah, the place, or the whole combination of places, the paths and roads and bridges some people can reach from this world. I dunno what it really is. I've heard some people say it's God's maintenance tunnels, or worlds that got half-built and then abandoned, or worlds that might have happened, if things had been a little different." He glanced at the bartender. "Or, you know, a *lot* different. Some places in the briarpatch don't last long, and those are the weirdest places, the ones that aren't very plausible at all, and I've seen some demented shit, lemme tell you, but lots of paths are stable. You can use them to get from one place to another in this world, there are some great shortcuts, but that's not all. The briarpatch . . . there are secrets in there, if you can get in deep enough to find them. Wonderful stuff. Dangerous stuff. But, shit, it's big, and hard to navigate." Arturo went silent, tipping his half-empty pint glass from side to side, watching the beer move around inside. Long speeches didn't seem to suit him.

"I'm leaving," Darrin said abruptly, and stood up. "Thank you for . . . your help, whatever help you gave me, but I have to go."

"Drink your beer," Arturo said. "Please, for me? I gotta pay for it, the least you can do is take a sip. It'll help."

To be polite—it was easy to be polite in an unreal situation, Darrin realized, because courtesy provided structure—he took a sip.

The beer was cold, crisp, a little hoppy, better suited to summer than autumn. But there was something else, not exactly an aftertaste, almost like the mouth-filling vapours from a good sip of cognac, but these vapours filled his mouth and his throat and his chest and the rest of his body, a sort of soothing mist inside him, and he sat back down on the stool, closing his eyes to savour it. His hands stopped shaking. "I . . . that's wonderful beer." Everything seemed less dire now, somehow. He lowered himself back onto the stool.

"There's some places in the briarpatch where you shouldn't drink or eat anythin'." Arturo took another gulp of his own drink, getting the ends of his long moustache damp in the process. "But other places, as long as you pay for what you drink, it's okay, and it can make things seem a little easier."

"Like in fairy tales." Darrin took another sip. The beer just tasted like a beer, now, its extraordinary quality fading into memory, but he felt less disassociated, and the clarity that had followed the first sip remained. "If you eat or drink fairy food, it makes you part of their world, somehow. That kind of thing?" The idea didn't distress him particularly, which, he supposed, was further proof of the drink's effectiveness.

Arturo shrugged. "I picked up a hitchhiker in the briarpatch once—I don't usually do that, but the Wendigo thought it was a good idea—and it was some guy who said he used to be a folklore professor, but he camped out in a fairy ring while he was doing research, and he woke up in the patch. He said all sorts of old legends and myths could be traced back to the briarpatch, and things that came out of it, or disappeared into it. The guy talked my ear off, and I offered to give him a ride back to Minnesota—that's where he was from, just like me—but he said no way, he was still explorin'. He just wanted to borrow some paper because he'd filled up his notebook with notes. Fortunately, in the Wendigo, one thing I've always got plenty of is paper."

Darrin nodded, only half-listening, still processing the things he'd seen. After all, the strange experiences hadn't started today. There was the alley he'd seen Ismael vanish into, and the glimpse of a high, moon-coloured bridge. Hadn't he always suspected there were worlds other than this, pathways and passages that went mostly unnoticed? That's why he'd gotten involved in urban exploration in the first place, prowling through steam tunnels, abandoned factories, and condemned train stations—he was looking for places no one knew about, forgotten places, *magical* places. He'd given up that pursuit because one empty desolation looked much like another, and because he'd found a baseline of contentment in his relationship with Bridget. But the impulse had been there, in his constant shuffling from one temporary passion to another, always looking for the key that would unlock a universe of greater experience. He'd wanted to find a secret world behind the world.

Bridget had felt the same urge, though she'd leaned on drugs more than Darrin ever had. Maybe that's why she'd left him. Darrin had found the end of his rainbow in their relationship, and become excited about the idea of having a family with her, a little house in the country, babies, the whole thing. That was enough of a new world for him. He'd believed it was enough for Bridget, too . . .

but he'd obviously misjudged her. And now she was dead, and in that most proverbial undiscovered country.

"I'm still scared," Darrin said. The fear was distant, not an immediate heart-pounding thing, but a kind of shadow of unease lying across his heart. "The beer helped, but it's still there. I feel like I'm walking on a ledge."

"That's a natural response. But once you learn more, that kind of general fear, it'll become a specific fear of specific things. Like, a useful fear."

Darrin nodded. That made sense. And once this fear passed . . . what would he feel then? Having found entry into a world he'd maybe been half-consciously searching for most of his life?

"So tell me," Arturo said. "How did you and Bridget meet?"

The change of conversational direction surprised Darrin, and he wondered if Arturo was genuinely curious or just trying to set Darrin at ease, take his mind off their present circumstance. "I don't . . . it's not much of a story."

"So long as it's a love story," Arturo said. "There's nothin' in the whole wide world above or below or beyond I love more than a good love story." He grinned his walrus moustache grin, and Darrin couldn't help but smile too. He'd never had a drinking buddy, really. He thought Arturo might be a good one.

"Okay," Darrin said. It was a good love story, at least, as long as he stopped telling it in the right place, which was the case for most love stories, he suspected. "It was like this."

2

"Have you ever heard of geocaching?"

Arturo shook his head, and Darrin nodded, because Arturo didn't seem like the most tech-savvy guy in the world. His universe didn't involve things like geocaching and flash mobs, but Darrin had worked for a tech company—albeit one designed to bring people together in the flesh—and he'd always been an early adopter.

"Well, geocaching is sort of like a high-tech treasure hunt. Basically you get a GPS unit of some kind—a global positioning system, like a handheld navigational tool that talks to satellites and tells you your coordinates, you know what I mean?"

Arturo nodded. "I thought about gettin' one of those for the Wendigo, but it wouldn't work in the briarpatch anyway, so I figured screw it."

"Right. Well, there are people who hide little boxes or canisters around, with treasures in them, and then post the GPS coordinates on the Internet. Other people find the coordinates, and go out to find the cache. Now, it's not like the coordinates are accurate to within inches or anything, so you still have to hunt around for the cache. Once you find it, there's usually a little log book inside, so you can record your name, and when you found it. It's okay to take the little treasures, usually, as long as you leave something just as good or better in its place. Lots of people take digital photos and post them online."

"What kinda treasures?" Arturo asked.

"Usually nothing big. Candy, little toys, stuff like that. I got a bunch of glow-in-the-dark plastic scorpions once, and left a carved wooden frog in its place. Stuff like that. The point isn't the treasure, but the hunt, you know? Some people do this solo, and some do it in groups, and sometimes there are really complicated hunts, where the GPS coordinates just lead you to a hint or a puzzle, and that leads you to another hint, and so on. Sometimes the caches are easy to find, like just hidden next to a rock or something, but other times they're underwater, or forty feet up a tree, or on a roof, stuff like that."

"Sounds fun." Arturo tapped the bar to get the bartender's attention. He glided over and refilled Arturo's glass, but didn't leave this time—he polished glasses with a white rag, and seemed to be listening.

"It can be," Darrin said. "I used to have this group of friends—people I worked with, mostly, I don't see them much anymore—and we'd do geocaching sometimes. There was this really big cache hunt a few years ago, put together by a guy who got rich selling his start-up company, and this time there was a really valuable treasure hidden, to be kept by the first group who found the cache. Nobody knew what the treasure was, exactly, just that it was worth a lot. Four of us got together to look for it, first thing in the morning when the coordinates were posted. The hunt took us all over—it started in San Francisco, with the first clue hidden in the Japanese Tea Garden in Golden Gate Park, buried near the base of this giant stone Buddha they've got there. We knew we weren't the first to find it, because it had been dug up already and re-buried, but the people before us played fair and didn't destroy the clue, and neither did we. It was just a cipher, and we had a guy with us named Rick who did cryptography for fun, so he cracked it in no time. That set of coordinates led us to the old fort by the Golden Gate Bridge . . ." He trailed off. He'd just seen Bridget die this morning, so how could the fact that she was *gone* keep ambushing him like this, taking the wind out of him?

"Go on," Arturo said, and the bartender nodded.

Darrin drained the rest of his beer, and the bartender refilled it for him while Darrin resumed. "Anyway, there was another clue, a jumbled-up word puzzle this time, and I'm good at that sort of thing, so I solved it, and we had to go across to Marin, which took forever in the traffic, and we wound up at this little vineyard, with a stone wall. I thought we'd never find that clue. When we finally did, it was a quote from the Bible, which we didn't have any idea how to interpret. But somebody turned the note over, and someone who'd gotten to the clue before us had written 'Too easy,' and some numbers that looked like coordinates. Turned out later it was the chapter and verse numbers of the quote—I don't even remember it now, something about planting a vineyard but never enjoying its fruit? Nothing any of *us* would have known, but whoever beat us to it had, and had even given us a little help. We didn't feel right using those coordinates, and Joe, who was sort of our leader, thought it must be a trick, but we followed it anyway. That took us back across to the East Bay. By then it was afternoon, and we were getting hungry, and Joe and Rick both decided to quit and get some lunch, since they figured there was no way they'd get to the cache first."

"That's hardly in the spirit of the thing," the bartender said.

Darrin laughed. "Yeah. They got into caring about the treasure, which was stupid, because the company we worked for was pulling in money like crazy—never underestimate the money-making potential of a well-designed social networking site, that's all I have to say. They didn't need the treasure, whatever it was, but they wanted it. My best friend Nicholas was with us, but he'd been lured by the idea of treasure from the start, he never much cared for geocaching or urban exploration or things like that. He said he'd keep going with me if I wanted, but I could tell he just wanted to quit and get a beer or something, so I told him not to worry about it. Back then I had a car, so I wasn't completely stuck. I lost some time in the hunt, but I knew I wouldn't be first to the treasure anyway, I just wanted to figure it out, you know? I followed the coordinates and wound up at that little kiddie amusement park Children's Fairyland, over by Lake Merritt—like, two miles from here."

"It's farther away than that," the bartender said. "And closer, too. But go on."

Darrin felt the hairs on the back of his neck rise, proving he could still be affected by reminders of the uncanny. "Well. Anyway. The whole thing about Children's Fairyland is you can't get in without a child, no unattended adults allowed. I was sort of standing around by the gate, wondering what to do—none of my friends had kids, and even if they had, what was I supposed to do, call and ask if I could borrow their child for a while? The person running the gate saw me and said 'Are you another treasure hunter?' I nodded, and he laughed. 'It's not actually inside. Check over by the dragon's head.' Outside the gate, actually *part* of the gate, there's this giant sculpture of a dragon, and there was a cache buried at the base of the wall. The last clue wasn't even in code, or anything, it said 'Grand Lake Theater, upstairs left screen, third row from the back, centre.' So I hustled over to the theatre, which was just a few blocks away, and bought a ticket to a matinee, and got there just as the movie was starting. There was someone sitting in the seat, a mother flanked by her two little kids—it was some animated movie. So I sat there for 90 minutes, wondering how many other treasure hunters were waiting in the theatre. Finally the credits rolled, and the mother took her kids away, and I went straight for the seat. There was an old cigar box stuck underneath it, the wooden kind with a metal clasp, held onto the seat with duct tape, and when I opened it up, there was a sheet of folded paper inside, a pen, and a little necklace with a silver oak tree pendant. Once the lights came up, I was able to read the paper. It said 'Bridget was here, treasure was plundered, but here's a present for the second-best.' That was the necklace. So I wrote my own name under hers, and a note that said 'Here's a gift for number three,' and put a fifty-dollar-bill in the box. I doubted the necklace was worth that, but I was making good money at the time, so I didn't worry about it. I just put the necklace on and left the theatre, and really did feel like I'd accomplished something. Because, hell, second best isn't bad at all in things like this. I liked the necklace, too, the little tree with silver branches." He touched his throat, where no necklace hung, and felt a brief but deep pang of loss. "I misplaced it, a while ago, I guess. It's too bad. The first thing Bridget ever gave me."

"Wow," Arturo said. "So that was your Bridget?"

Darrin nodded. "I didn't meet her in person for another year. I was in this group doing urban exploring, where you go out and sneak into places, like steam tunnels, old warehouses, condemned hospitals, stuff like that, just for the thrill of going someplace other people don't. One day we were going to the old Amtrak station on 16th Street—there's some awesome architecture there—and there was this beautiful blonde woman." Darrin smiled, just thinking of that first time seeing her, the arresting clarity of her eyes, her upturned nose, the way he'd felt instantly drawn to her. "She was a friend of a friend, and had never gone out with us before. I was leaning over a railing in the Amtrak station, trying to get a good angle to take a photo, and the necklace fell out of my shirt, the little tree dangling. She said 'Hey, where'd you get that necklace?' So I told her about the treasure hunt, and she said 'I'm Bridget, and that was my necklace.'

We got to talking, and it turned out she'd done the whole treasure hunt on her own, with no team. I asked her what the treasure was, and she said it was the biggest diamond ring she'd ever seen. She sold it and had enough money to pay her rent for months, and to buy, and I quote, 'tons of really wonderful drugs.'" He laughed. "She was wild back then, really wild, but so smart, and she never stopped moving, she knew everybody, and it was exhilarating and wonderful and exhausting, just being with her. We hit it off, started going out, she said I made her feel peaceful, I said she made me feel alive, and, well . . . a love story, I guess. Like you asked for." He took a drink, suddenly feeling self-conscious for talking so long. The bartender, seemingly bored now that the story was over, ambled back to his shadowy corner. "So, Arturo. Tell me about your wife . . . was it Marjorie?"

"Yeah, that's her name," Arturo said. "But, nah, I want happy love stories, and it's hard for me to talk about meetin' Marjorie without gettin' all sad, so let me tell you a different love story instead. Let me tell you about how I got my car."

3

"I was workin' in this little town where I grew up, nothin' around really but fields and a couple factories, and I had a pretty good job runnin' this garage. I didn't own the place, but I was the one who came in every day, like the manager, because the owner was getting old. I figured I'd buy him out one day, you know. So the day after Marjorie died, I felt like I had to come in to work anyway, because it was my responsibility, and because I wanted to throw myself into some kinda work so I wouldn't think about things so much. All our friends and relatives thought I was crazy, that I should take a few days off at least, but I convinced them to leave me alone and let me deal with things in my own way. I got into the garage at about 5 a.m., before first light, and the car was sitting there in the lot, big as life. Lots of people would get their cars towed over if they broke down at night, and just leave a note on the windshield tellin' me what was wrong. But there was no note." He tapped the bar again, signalling for another beer, and the bartender returned. Arturo continued. "So I opened the door, and the backseat was just filled up with papers, you've seen it, and while I was standin' there a piece slid off the pile and fell into the driver's seat, just a folded-over sheet of lined paper like from a school notebook. I picked it up, and written in, I swear, my own handwritin', was a note that said 'A man needs a purpose like a car needs a driver.' So I sat down in the front seat of the Wendigo to think about that—"

The bartender dropped the glass he was polishing, but since it was a heavy pint glass it didn't shatter; it just thumped. "You drive the *Wendigo*?" the bartender said, and his voice was less soft now. There was something strange in it, some note Darrin couldn't identify, something between reverence and terror.

Arturo sighed. "Yeah, brother. I drive the Wendigo."

"Drinks are free," the bartender said. "But I need you to leave now."

"Look, buddy, I been comin' here for days, I know I never mentioned the Wendigo before, but I didn't even drive her here, I just walked—"

"Please go," the bartender said, and for the first time his eyes seemed alive.

"Arturo, the mirror," Darrin said, and Arturo looked, seeing what Darrin had. Some form was coalescing in the glass where the bartender's reflection should have been, something hulking and shadowed and fraying at the edges—the reflection of something monstrous, coming into focus.

"Hell," Arturo said, but resignedly. "Thanks for the drinks, pal. I won't come back."

"I would appreciate that."

Arturo and Darrin left, emerging on the trash-littered, desolate street, and they heard the bartender noisily lock the door behind them.

"What was all that about?" Darrin said, following Arturo as he set off down the street.

"Not everybody knows the Wendigo like I do," he said. "I get that reaction sometimes, but I didn't figure a bartender who was part monster himself would care so much." He swayed a little as he walked. "Anyway, I had enough beers. I'm gonna go back to the Wendigo and see if it'll drive out of this neighbourhood yet. It's been parked here for a while, refusin' to go very far at all, and when I found those pages about your Bridget, I figured it had somethin' to do with you. But I brought you back from that dark part of the woods, and got you a drink, and helped you figure out what was goin' on, a little bit, at least. So maybe I did what I gotta do, right?"

"Where will you go?" Darrin asked.

Arturo shrugged. "I go out lookin' for Marjorie most days."

"She died . . . it was a car thing, you said?" They reached the shrubbery-lined path, and the quality of the air changed, and Darrin realized they were back in the world he knew, and out of the almost-plausible world where the bar had been.

"Yeah," Arturo said.

"But . . . you think you can find her, her spirit, or something, in the briarpatch?"

"The briarpatch is a big place. I've seen signs there might be hope, yeah. But, when I've had a little to drink, I wonder. I think about what the Wendigo first said to me—not 'said,' but you know. A man needs a purpose like a car needs a driver. If you're gonna get anywhere in life, you gotta be goin' *towards* somethin'. I'm goin' towards Marjorie. Maybe I'll never find her. Maybe the whole search is just the Wendigo's way of keepin' me from killin' myself. I—" He stopped speaking and winced. "Hell, Darrin, I'm sorry, I shouldn'ta said that, not after Bridget—"

"It's okay," Darrin said. They reached the familiar expanse of Park Boulevard and went across, back to Darrin's street. "If I don't see you again, good luck," Arturo said. "Or, if the Wendigo thinks I'm not done with you yet, then I guess I'll see you sooner. You'll be careful, right?"

"Arturo," Darrin said, hesitant to bring it up. "Do you think . . . I might be able to find Bridget in the briarpatch?"

"You got as good a chance as I do," Arturo said. "I bet you got some questions for her, at least."

"I guess I do."

Arturo stopped beside the Wendigo, which still just looked like a car to Darrin, albeit a strange and enormous one. Arturo patted the car's roof. "Just . . . go in with the right kind of expectations. Dead isn't necessarily gone, not in the briarpatch, but dead *is* changed. You know?"

"I know," Darrin said. "I do know." Looking for Bridget . . . that was a possibility. A strange one, but something to consider. For now, though, he already had a project. Bridget's death wasn't a "car thing," whatever that meant. Her death was an *Ismael* thing. Ismael was very likely the last person to talk to her before she died, he'd probably known she was going to die, had stood there and watched her fall. Before Darrin ventured back into the briarpatch, he wanted to confront Ismael. He was no longer undone by grief—the grief was there, crouching in wait, but for now, he would be able to outrun the curve of grief, and focus on something else. Anger, maybe, or maybe revenge, but he had a purpose. That purpose was finding Ismael Plenty.

ECHO ENQUIRES

1

"Any sign of him?" Echo asked, for the third time in ten minutes. The repetition was pissing Nicholas off, she could tell, even as he tried to hide his annoyance. Needling Nicholas wasn't much of an amusement, but it would do in a pinch.

Nicholas didn't turn around. He sat on a low couch by the windows that looked down on the street, peering out. "No. You sure you heard him head down the back stairs?" He'd asked her that three times too, but it didn't annoy Echo, his attempt to bother her was amusing.

"Yep. Heard the back door close as I opened the front. It squeaks." She was sprawled on the big wine-red couch across from the television. The couch had been nice once, but the cushions were starting to wear, and Darrin was a long way from being able to afford a new one. Echo didn't mind. She'd sat on worse things.

"He just saw his girlfriend die like a few *hours* ago," Nicholas said. "Where the hell did he go?"

Echo yawned. "Probably for a walk. He's all the time walking, he says it helps him think, though I don't know what he thinks about, besides how shitty his life is. Maybe me. I'm fun to think about, I bet." She stretched languidly on the couch. "Want to get to know each other, since we probably have to fuck in a day or two?"

Nicholas finally turned to look at her, his expression one of undisguised disgust. "How is it that Darrin can't see right through you? He's a smart guy, I don't get it. I understand being blinded by pussy, but *shit*."

"I can be very convincing when I need to be, Nicky." She propped her feet on

Darrin's scarred coffee table. "Besides, I'm an honest liar. I've never given a damn about Darrin. What's your excuse? Or have you been planning to screw him over since freshman year?"

"You shut up," Nicholas said, but there was no heat in it. He went back to his vigil.

"No, I'm serious. I know why I'm doing this, but how did Ismael get to you? What did he promise you?"

"He said he'd kill me if I didn't help him," Nicholas said.

Echo burst out laughing, and laughed harder when Nicholas hunched his shoulders and twisted, as if to turn even farther away from her. "What-*ever*," she said. "Ismael doesn't kill people. He just *outlives* them. Seriously, what's on the table for you? Darrin tells me stories about you two, you know, about how you saved his ass by paying his rent for two months when his financial aid got delayed, about how he helped you pass your math classes, about all those drunk and stormy nights you spent together in college. You guys've got history, and you're just pissing on that. I mean, getting the guy *fired* is one thing, at least you could do that in secret, but you didn't say boo when Ismael told you the next step in his little plan, and that's going to be it for you and Darrin—"

"Shut the fuck up, Echo." Nicholas got up off the couch, looming over her, fists clenched at his sides. "You don't get to judge me."

"Ooh, big strong man." She looked up at him, noting the sweat on his forehead, the frown lines that were someday going to be etched permanently on his face. Echo almost never frowned. Her face was one of her weapons, and wrinkles would weaken that. "Going to hit me if I keep mouthing off? You'll be pissing through a *tube* if you try it, and we'll just have to fake part two of Ismael's plan."

The front door rattled. Echo blew Nicholas a kiss, then fixed her face into a well-practiced look of concern. She listened to the thump as Darrin trudged up the stairs, and when he stepped into the doorway—looking like he'd been rolling in dirt and leaves, but hey, we all grieve in our own way—he stared at her blankly for a moment, then at Nicholas, then back at her again. His expression was abstracted, the deeply interior look he got when he was mulling over some project or processing new information.

"Honey," Echo said.

"Bro," Nicholas said.

"Bridget is dead." Darrin turned, abruptly, and walked toward his office.

Echo lifted her eyebrow, and Nicholas made a "go ahead" gesture. She rose, smoothed her skirt (pleated, flannel, the schoolgirl thing, because it pushed Nicholas's buttons, and Echo loved sending mixed signals), and went after Darrin. He sat at his desk, chin in his hands, staring at something on his screen.

"What happened?" She stepped behind him, massaging his shoulders. He was beyond tense—his knots had knots. He smelled a little like beer—that was understandable—and like dirt and leaves, which was weirder, but whatever. The image on the screen was Bridget, standing on the Golden Gate Bridge, leaning over the railing. Echo had never met her, though she'd seen her leaving Ismael's house a few times, while Echo spied on them from across the street. That was back when she just knew Ismael was a weirdo, before she figured out he was even weirder than she could have imagined.

Darrin gradually relaxed, letting himself lean back in the chair. "I don't know. I went out to the bridge, to take some photos, and there she was. Bridget. Before I could say anything to her, she just . . ."

"Fell?" Echo said. Enjoying it, careful not to show it.

"*Jumped*. She jumped."

"That photo is from today?"

He nodded. "Just . . . god, just hours ago."

She stroked his hair. "Oh, Darrin, that's terrible. I had no idea she was so . . . troubled. But you can't blame yourself. It's not your fault—"

"I don't blame myself," he said, more fiercely than she'd heard him say anything, ever, in the three months they'd been together. "I blame him." He clicked his mouse, and the image on the screen zoomed larger, centred on a figure in the background, behind Bridget. A pale man, with lank dark hair.

"Who's that?" Like she didn't know. This *was* interesting.

"His name is Ismael Plenty. Bridget was . . . seeing him. After she left me. Before she left me too, I think."

She was seeing *him*, Echo thought, *but she wasn't* fucking *him. At least, not regularly*. Ismael didn't fuck many people these days, and when he did, it was only when they'd decided to die soon anyway. Ismael was immortal—to the limits of current experimental data, anyway—but that didn't mean he was clean. He probably had weird STDs that had died out during the Middle Ages, still lively in his blood and brain, not doing any permanent damage to him, swimming around confused in his not-quite-normal innards. It was only luck that he didn't have the plague, or smallpox, or some other population-decimating illness. Luck, or the good offices of the briarpatch. He never seemed to contract anything deadly. The briarpatch probably flung him across the world if he tried to stick his cock in someone with anything too dangerous. Maybe that's why he'd never fucked Echo. She didn't have any deadly STDs, but she was dangerous in other ways.

"This guy," Darrin said. "He watched her jump. He came like, like a *spectator*. Or a cheerleader. She never talked about killing herself when she was with me. I think he did something to her. Like, got her into a cult, or something, made her go all Jonestown, all Heaven's Gate, I don't know what."

Getting warmer, Echo thought. Ismael had talked to her about the idea of starting a cult (except he called it a "group of like-minded seekers"), trying to show the light to a bunch of people all at once instead of one at a time, but he was more focused on Darrin as a way to achieve his own goals right now.

"I'm going to get answers, though," Darrin said grimly.

"Oh? How will you do that?"

"I'll look for Ismael. Someone must know him. Bridget couldn't have cut ties with all her friends. I'll start by asking them, and if that doesn't work . . . hell, I'll enhance this photo, I'll put it online, I'll put it on flyers and hang them all over the city, with a headline that says 'Do you know this man?' I'll offer a reward. I'll find him."

Echo leaned down, putting her ear close to his, and whispered: "And what will you do, once you find him?" Darrin talking this way was actually making her kind of hot.

"I'll make him answer me," Darrin said, and there was something dark and sure in his voice, a tempered steel certainty.

Oh, Ismael had fucked up. Echo couldn't wait to see him try to tap dance and chatterbox his way out of this mistake. He'd been working all this time to break Darrin, to push him into the depths of despair and grief and send him stumbling into the briarpatch, where Ismael could follow him . . . and find access to new paths, ones that would open for Darrin. Paths that Ismael hoped might lead to his stupid better world. Instead, he'd let Darrin discover his existence, and given Darrin a mission. Bridget's introduction to the briarpatch had only ever been a tool, a way for Ismael to take her away from Darrin and open his eyes to the broader world beyond, to pathways Ismael couldn't find on his own. But it was a tool that had turned in Ismael's hand. Now *Darrin* was hunting *him*. It was almost funny. No, it *was* funny. Echo remembered her role just in time to stop herself from laughing.

"I'll help you find him," Echo said.

"We both will," Nicholas said from the doorway. "I still owe that Eurotrash fucker a beating from that night at the strip club. We'll find out what he did to Bridget."

"Thank you." Darrin took Echo's hand in his own. "I don't know what I'd do without the two of you."

Poor stupid Darrin, Echo thought. *Nicholas has been screwing you over for months and months. At least when I screw you, you get an orgasm out of the deal.* "But we'll start tomorrow," Echo said. "You should take a shower, Darrin. I'll join you, and try to take your mind off this. And Nicholas will run out and get us some drinks, won't you Nicky?"

He frowned, but nodded. "Sure. I'll get that chocolate stout you like, Darrin. We'll have like . . . a little wake for Bridget, you know? How's that sound?"

"Sounds good," Darrin said. He stood up and embraced Nicholas, briefly, in an awkward one-armed man-hug. "Thanks. Bro."

"No problem." Nicholas hurried away. Echo wondered if he was embarrassed, ashamed, or pleased with his own acting job.

No matter. She had a job of her own, now. She kissed Darrin's cheek, and began to undress him. "Wow, babe. You're filthy."

"I went for a walk. Got a little lost in a patch of trees. Too many drinks I guess." There was something strange in his tone, and he seemed beyond distracted, his mind a thousand miles away, but with everything he'd been through, it was no wonder he was acting weird.

And he had no idea that things were probably only going to get worse.

2

Echo made Ismael kneel and kiss her patent-leather shoes before she'd tell him anything. He performed the act with his usual infinite weariness and dignity, licking from toes to buckle and back again. One of these days she'd make him really abase himself, but she didn't think it would matter. As he liked to tell her, he'd been through several forms of hell—he'd pretended to be a corpse under a pile of dead soldiers, face down in a mud composed of blood and shit; he'd been attacked by dogs at the behest of German soldiers who thought he was a Jew; he'd been chained and staked out in the sun on a salt flat by an ex-lover who'd wrongly believed he was a vampire, and he'd roasted there until he came close enough to death for the briarpatch to save him. Compared to those and a million other miseries, kissing boots or drinking piss or verbally abusing himself was nothing. His patience in the face of her humiliations was annoying, but at least it was a challenge. Life presented few enough of those to her.

When he was done, she flopped down in a beanbag chair and reached for the bong. "So ask," she said.

"Why didn't you stay with Darrin? I didn't expect you until later."

She shrugged. "I blew him in the shower, and hung out for a while. When I left, him and Nicholas were looking at old photo albums and shooting the shit. I told Darrin I had an early shift tomorrow and kissed him goodbye. You know, he never cares if I sleep over? And he fucking tosses and turns when I do stay over. Did he do that with Bridget?"

"She never mentioned," Ismael said. "What did you and Nicholas determine about his emotional state?"

"Well, I think maybe he was *in* the briarpatch, before he came up the stairs. He had dirt and leaves all over him, and one of the knees was torn out of his pants. So either he went into the briarpatch, or he fell down in a park somewhere. Who can say?"

"I see. That's promising. Anything else?"

Echo grinned. "Oh, yeah. You're fucked. You're Darrin's public enemy number only. He got a photo of Bridget right before she jumped, with you in the background, and he's convinced you're some cult recruiter who convinced Bridget to kill herself. It's a crazy idea, but, I mean, he's basically *right*."

"Cults believe they have knowledge of a true revelation, but they do not." Ismael rose from his knees and seating himself on the couch. "But the path I showed Bridget is a true one. It's an important difference. Bridget was not a cultist. She was my student."

"Yeah. You're *sure* you're right. Unlike every other cult in the history of the world."

Ismael ignored the jibe. "What does Darrin intend to do with this knowledge?"

"Hunt you down. He'll do it, too. He's got your photo, and it's not like you're all that inconspicuous. Hell, it'll probably only take him a couple of weeks. The question is, what will *you* do?"

"I always intended to reveal myself to Darrin. In the depths of the briarpatch, I thought—I could step in and save him from some trivial danger, or guide him toward a place of sweet water and fruit, be a mentor to him. That plan was . . . made difficult . . . when he met me outside the strip club."

"Why the fuck did Nicholas point you out to him anyway?" She took a hit off the bong, and the smoke made everything feel lighter.

"He was trying to show initiative." Ismael twisted his mouth. "He didn't believe that Darrin was suffering enough from the loss of Bridget, and he feared that even losing his job wouldn't make Darrin too sad, since he didn't much care for the work. He thought Darrin's suffering would be increased if he believed Bridget had left him for another man. I was the logical choice to blame. Nicholas didn't share this plan with me, of course, and I never told him I intended to introduce myself to Darrin someday. A measure of the blame is mine, I suppose."

"Nicholas is a moron."

"True," Ismael said. "But he is a key to Darrin—someone close to his heart, but corruptible. If I could have made Bridget betray Darrin, I would have, but she would never have agreed. So I seduced her away, and showed her the light instead. She was actually a good candidate for transition. I was sad when her death was only a death, and not a passage to peace forever."

"Yeah, it's a tragedy." Echo stared up at the ceiling, daydreaming. Maybe she could make Ismael lick her asshole. She liked that, and nobody had done it for her in weeks. Ah, the pot was making it hard to focus. She tried. "But what do you do now? What's plan B? Or C?

"If Darrin merely believes I was sleeping with Bridget, that is inconvenient, but not insurmountable. If he believes I convinced Bridget to kill herself . . . it will be difficult to gain his trust." Ismael steepled his fingers and stared off into the middle distance. "Difficult. But I see a possibility. I think we will proceed as planned. I need Darrin to be wholly unsupported, to have the only sure pillars in his life—Nicholas, and, to a certain extent, you—torn away from him. Then he will be able to see the briarpatch more clearly, and new passages will open for him, to lead him out of his torment."

"And maybe he'll find this northwest passage you're always going on about?"

"The overland route. Yes. It is possible." Ismael had that faraway look in his eyes that Echo hated. She wanted people in her presence paying attention to *her*.

"So when do we do the deed?"

"Tomorrow, I think. We must find some pretext to get Darrin out of the house, to allow you and Nicholas time to . . . prepare. Can you arrange that?"

"Easy," Echo said. She already had a good idea how. Ismael wouldn't like it, but she wasn't planning on telling him the details.

ORVILLE TAKES A BITE

1

"Nice place," Bridget said. "Sort of lacks character though."

Orville sat in a swaybacked armchair beside a dusty bookshelf. "Like me, you mean?" he asked, dull and exhausted. This had been the longest day of his life. Bridget had found a path that took them near his apartment, but he'd still had to walk two blocks barefoot in a hospital gown—he was lucky no one had seen him and called the police. He was in his own clothes now, which helped, but only a little.

"Oh, you're a character all right." Bridget wandered through his sparsely-furnished in-law unit of an apartment, peering at the one thumbtacked poster on the wall—a flyer for a play he'd had a bit part in during his one semester at college, before a lack of funds and talent made him give up his dreams of acting. Orville had never really loved drama anyway. What he'd loved was the idea of being someone else.

"I'm starving." Orville stood and walked past Bridget—wondering if he could walk right through her—into his tiny kitchen.

Bridget moaned. "Food. *Food*. Don't even talk to me about food, Troll. I'm never going to taste anything ever again. If I'd passed through into that other world it wouldn't matter, I'd be a god eating light and shitting stars, but here and now all I can think about is a big dish of vanilla ice cream with hot fudge and crushed walnuts. God, it's killing me just thinking about it."

Cry me a river, Orville thought. He hadn't tasted anything since he was six months old and his stepfather threw him headfirst against the fireplace. But he didn't expect to get sympathy from Bridget, so she didn't tell her about his ageusia. She'd just remind him that he was *alive*, and she wasn't, so what did he possibly have to complain about? "In some of the stories about . . . um . . . what you are, I mean, ghosts, I guess . . . you can burn food, and the ghosts can eat it, somehow . . ."

"Good luck burning ice cream," Bridget said, sitting (or appearing to sit) in Orville's chair.

He opened the fridge and peered inside. He hadn't done his shopping this week, since he'd expected to be dead. He sniffled and wiped his runny nose with the back of his hand.

"What're you having?" Bridget asked. "You can at least describe it to me."

He shrugged. "Bologna sandwich, I guess, if the bread isn't mouldy."

"Gross," Bridget said. "Bologna? My mom made me eat that stuff when I was a kid, I can't stand it. How can you eat that crap?"

Well, she'd asked. He took a plastic bag of sliced meat from the shelf and turned toward the counter. "It's cheap, and I can't taste it anyway."

"What're you talking about?"

"I don't have a sense of taste. Or smell."

"You can't smell? I'm dead, Orville, and I can still smell things. What happened to you?"

"Congenital thing. I was born this way." He didn't want to go into the ancient history of violence that was his childhood, the head injury that damaged the parts of his brain that controlled his senses of smell and taste—he was just lucky he hadn't been mentally impaired. "It's not so bad," he went on. "I used to win bets in high school by drinking bong water." He slapped the bologna between a couple of stale slices of bread.

"Jesus, Orville, no wonder you killed yourself. Never had sex, can't taste food, what pleasures of the body *did* you have?"

"I used to jerk off a lot." Orville took a bite of his sandwich.

He sputtered, bits of bread and meat falling out of his mouth. He hadn't tasted food in living memory, and now his mouth was filled with the richness of the meat and the wheatiness of the bread—it was like going from being deaf to hearing a world-class orchestra; like blind eyes suddenly seeing a glorious sunrise. "I can taste this!" he said, and gobbled another bite, wolfing the sandwich down. He didn't have any condiments in the house—why bother with mustard and mayonnaise when he couldn't taste either—and now he desperately wished for some, or for ketchup, or for those spices he'd only ever experienced as burning pain in his mouth. He sniffed, hard, and *almost* smelled something—his sense of smell must be back, too, but with the cold, he hadn't noticed.

Bridget stared at him for a moment, then burst out laughing—not a laugh of contempt this time, but what sounded like genuine delight. "Of course! It was the hospital, Orville! When you swapped bodies, you got one with a head cold, yeah, but you also got one with a sense of *taste!*"

Orville finished the sandwich and started looking around for something else. He'd never seen the appeal of junk food, since both salty and sweet were lost on him, but now he wished desperately for cookies, chips, even the ice cream Bridget had talked about. This was easily the second most amazing thing that had ever happened to him. "I want to eat *everything.*"

"You're scrawny enough that a binge won't hurt you," Bridget said. "Let's hit a nice restaurant, what do you say? I'm a cheap date, and vengeance can wait."

Orville slumped a little at the counter. "I could afford one good meal at a restaurant, maybe, but then I couldn't eat tomorrow. I never had much money, and I thought I'd be dead today, so I didn't plan well. My wallet was in my pocket when I jumped, so I don't even—"

"*Orville.* You've got me, now. Money isn't something you have to worry about anymore."

Orville tore off another slice of bologna and gnawed on it. "What, you can rob banks now? Foretell the winning horse at Golden Gate Fields?"

"Hell, there's no reason to go all the way into the city, Orville," Bridget said. "We'll just catch a bus over to Emeryville. Maybe there are advantages to this ghost thing after all."

"What do you have planned?"

"Well, first, we'll get you an ice cream cone, and then I'll show you, what do you say? I don't have that many pleasures left—at least leave me the anticipation of pleasantly surprising you."

Orville wanted to ask why she was being so nice to him, after her earlier pragmatic disinterest. But then she'd been busy coming to terms with her new and tragic circumstances, so a lack of kindness was certainly understandable. Besides, he was afraid that if he asked why she was being nice to him, she might get angry again. Better to just enjoy her kindness while it lasted. "Okay," Orville said. "A bus, and ice cream, and then whatever your surprise is. But I'm not doing anything illegal."

"Perish the thought. You'll need whatever cash you have available. Don't worry about wiping yourself out financially—you've got to spend money to make money."

2

"But I've never gambled," Orville protested. "My stepfather used to gamble, and it didn't work out so well for him."

"It's only really gambling when there's a chance you'll lose." Bridget eyed his half-eaten strawberry ice cream cone with undisguised avarice. "I already told you, it's a sure thing."

They stood outside the Oaks Card Club in Emeryville, one of the few legal gambling establishments in the area. "What did you want me to play? Texas what-now?"

"Hold'em, Orville, Texas Hold'em. Don't you even watch TV? Poker was a full-blown fad there for a while, but I learned it from my grandmother when I was just a kid, and I was good enough to count on it as a fallback plan when I was running short on rent money. You'll be fine. But you need to stop talking to me—standing here on the sidewalk, licking an ice cream cone, and talking to empty air is going to get you a reputation as a crazy guy, and they don't like crazy guys coming in here. No, damn it, don't even nod, that's only marginally less crazy-looking. Nobody else can see me, as far as we can tell. Well, probably Ismael could, he sees all kinds of shit, but for the most part, I seem to be a total ghost-of-Christmas-present kind of girl. Just blink twice if you get me."

Orville blinked. This was complicated, and he had a fluttering in his stomach that was familiar from college—he'd even gotten stage fright during rehearsals, even during *blocking* rehearsals, and this was the same sort of near-nausea. The ice cream was wonderful, creamy and sweet and delicious—all words that, until an hour ago, had been nothing but abstractions—but he was going to have to throw the rest of it away uneaten, because his stomach was too unsettled. He tossed the ice cream, eliciting a low moan of dismay from Bridget, and went through the door into the building, which wasn't much like the casinos he'd seen in movies—no slot machines, no roulette wheels, just a big room with a sunken section in the middle, bordered by raised walkways and rails. There were twenty or thirty tables in the sunken area, sparsely populated with people playing hands of cards.

Bridget whispered in his ear. "You have to pay rent to the house—that's how they make money, they don't get a cut of the winnings, and you never play against the house, they just charge you for the privilege of playing. We'll find a game and get you settled. Just do what I tell you, when I tell you, and you'll do fine. Normally poker involves a lot of reading your opponents and thinking about percentages, but you've got an edge—I can walk around and see what everybody else is holding."

Orville squirmed a little at that—he wasn't comfortable with the idea of cheating—and Bridget sighed in his ears. "Yeah, it's dishonest, it's despicable, whatever, I'm not going to let you clean anybody out, we're just going to make a decent little pile, okay? Morals are all fine and good up to a point, and that's the point where you get hungry and don't have a place to live."

He didn't argue, but only because he wasn't supposed to talk to her. He'd always tried to be honest. It hadn't gotten him very far in life, admittedly, but at least he hadn't hated himself for being a liar.

"This'll do," Bridget said, and Orville sat down, trying not to show he was trembling, trying to remember if he'd ever played a game other than solitaire since he was a kid.

3

"That was amazing," Orville said when he emerged, four hours later, his pockets considerably heavier than they'd been when he entered.

"I thought it was going to go belly-up when they realized you didn't know how to shuffle," Bridget said, dryly, "But you covered okay with that story about how you shut your hand in a car door and couldn't handle the cards properly."

Orville was proud of that. Improv had never been his strongest skill, but he got by.

"So what now, my wealthy friend?" Bridget said. "The night's all yours."

Orville took a deep breath, and even the exhaust-laden air of San Pablo Avenue seemed sweet to him, because he could smell it—his cold was even getting better. He had nearly a thousand dollars in his pockets, a sound body, and a beautiful (if immaterial) woman by his side. The world, which had only this morning seemed so utterly bereft of possibility, such a closed system of privation and desperation, now seemed alive with opportunity. If his life still lacked any underlying meaning or purpose, at least he could manage to have fun.

He wondered if Bridget was trying to make *sure* he had fun, so he wouldn't try to kill himself again, and ruin her chances of pursuing her own goals. It would explain her kindness to him. He wanted to believe she felt something more for him, but he was willing to enjoy the effects regardless of their causes. "I don't know what I want to do," he said. Having wads of disposable income, and the means to make more, was a new experience for him.

"Well, I'm not ready to call it a night. For one thing, I don't think I can sleep, and for another, no offense, but your place sort of depresses me." She tapped her thumbnail against her teeth, a mannerism Orville had already come to recognize as thinking-behaviour. She snapped her fingers. "Orville. My boy. Let's find you a woman."

And just like that, his gutful of infinite possibilities turned into a bellyful of ice. "Ah, I'm not so good with bars or clubs, I've tried, but I can't hear over the music and I get too drunk and I'm not much of a dancer and I never remember to look for a wedding ring so even if I get up the courage to talk to a woman I—"

"Shh," Bridget said, a long soothing sound, and Orville subsided, hunching his shoulders and walking silently along the sidewalk until he reached a bus stop bench, the kind with an armrest right in the middle to keep people from sleeping on it.

"I'm not sending you into some high-stress meat market situation, Orville. There are other ways. I used to be a dancer." She raised one eyebrow. "You understand what I'm saying? *That* kind of dancer."

Orville understood. And wondered, not for the first time, what she would look like underneath that puffy red coat. If she were still alive to look like anything. Was lusting after a ghost necrophilia?

"When I first moved out here," Bridget said, "I needed to make some money fast, and I danced in a lot of places around the city. I still have friends in that world, and I know a few women of—what's the joke?—negotiable virtue. I wouldn't send you to some woman who gets beat on by a pimp or strung along with drugs, because I'm not that much of a moral relativist, but I know some independent contractors, let's say, who'll be nice to you and won't cheat you. Especially when you tell them you're my cousin from out of town."

"A prostitute?" Orville said, halfway between aghast and fascinated. He'd thought of hiring a hooker, of course—he suspected all urban male virgins of advancing age considered the idea—but the streetwalkers in his neighbourhood terrified him, and he was afraid that if he ever approached one, she *wouldn't* be a prostitute, and would mace him or hit him or stab him. He'd sometimes looked at the ads in the back of the free weekly papers, with their sultry newsprint women promising incall, outcall, and sensual massage, but he was the sort of person who got nervous just calling a restaurant to get some takeout delivered, and so he was sure he wouldn't be able to cope with that kind of transaction.

"Well, my friend Geneva is a dancer, mostly," Bridget said. "She sees a few regular guys, to supplement her income, but she's not out walking the streets every night. She operates on a pretty strict referral basis when it comes to new clients. I'm not saying she's a wounded princess with a hidden heard of gold— she's a pretty hard-headed businesswoman, actually—but she's a pro, and she'll treat you right, if she's available. It's early yet. Let's find a pay phone, if there are any left in the land of cell phones here."

"Ah, I'm not sure . . ."

Bridget regarded him patiently. "It's up to you, Orville. This morning your life sucked so bad you wanted to end it. Tomorrow, I'm asking you to help me find the immortal asshole who steered me toward throwing my *own* life away. But tonight, I want you to take a bite out of life, to have a great time . . . because there's no telling what tomorrow will bring. I'm here to help you any way I can. It's the least I can do. I know you didn't ask to be haunted. So I know a woman, and I might be able to help you have something you've dreamed about. Orville, I'd take you to bed myself, but, well . . ." She spread her hands. "I'm not equipped anymore. But if you're nervous about this, or if it feels wrong—"

"No," Orville said. In a sense, he had nothing to lose. This morning he'd been willing to die, and if things went disastrously wrong, if humiliation befell him, he could always take that ultimate escape again. "I'd like to call your friend."

"All right." Bridget clapped her hands. "Ismael always said sex—good sex, without head games—was almost as good as standing in the light of a better world, and for a while he tried all kinds of tantric things as a path toward transcendence, but it didn't get him any closer to the light than drugs or music had."

"Tantric? What's that?"

"Don't worry," Bridget said. "We'll start off slow."

4

This time, Orville felt flush enough to take a cab, and gave the driver an address in Berkeley.

"She's a grad student," Bridget said. "In her last year. You're lucky she was free to see you tonight."

Orville just nodded, almost imperceptibly, because he didn't want the driver to think he was crazy. The call had been relatively painless—he'd introduced himself as Bridget's cousin, said she'd recommended he seek out Geneva's company, and did she have an opening tonight . . . ? Geneva, very businesslike, said they could meet at a café in Berkeley, introduce themselves, and see what happened.

The cab pulled up to a curb, and Orville paid and got out, Bridget following. He wondered if Bridget really *needed* him to open the door, or if she could just pass through it; wondered how much her ongoing pretensions to physicality were born out of habit, and how much out of fear.

They went into the café, a big place with a tile floor, brick walls, high ceilings, and lots of square tables. "That's her in the corner," Bridget said, pointing. She'd gotten the hang of being confidently invisible. The woman in the corner by the window was dark-haired and dark-eyed, not at all what Orville had expected—he'd imagined a Barbie-doll blonde, for some reason, probably the influence of too much porn. Geneva was pretty, but not altogether conventionally, with a strong nose and a high forehead, her wavy hair pulled back in a ponytail. She wore a grey sweatshirt, and though he couldn't see her lower body because of the table, he was willing to bet she wasn't wearing a mini-skirt or latex pants. He didn't look at her and think "hooker," which was probably the point.

"Oh, it's good to see her," Bridget said, sad-happily, and Orville felt bad for so frankly thinking about Geneva's body—this woman was a friend of Bridget's, who didn't even know she was dead. "Go over, say hi, and offer to buy her a drink." Bridget made a shoo-go-on motion.

Orville approached, trying to smile—this body seemed to have better teeth than his original had, but he was still habituated to a lifetime of shyness—and said "Hello, Geneva?"

"You must be Orville." She gestured to the chair across from her.

"You, ah, want something to drink?"

"Another coffee if you're going up there." She flashed a smile, and Orville hurried over to the counter, blushing furiously.

"You know, Orville," Bridget said, trailing along, "I wondered, when you told me you were a virgin. You aren't really bad looking—scrawny, and you've got those hangdog eyes, but I think your face has character. But now I see. You're shy."

Orville scowled as he waited in line at the counter. Of course he was shy. Social situations paralyzed him.

"So let me set you at ease a little. Geneva knows what she's doing. Don't leer, don't drool on yourself, look at her face instead of just at her tits—she made that easy with the sweatshirt, considerate of her—and you'll be fine."

Orville bought a coffee for Geneva and one for himself—god, coffee smelled so good, no wonder people liked to drink it so much—and returned to the table.

"So you're Bridget's cousin?"

"Yeah. Grew up just down the road from her in Indiana. We've been through a lot together." Just what Bridget had told him to say.

"Oh, yeah? You guys ever go mountain biking?"

Bridget, who was standing near Orville's right side, laughed. "She knows I hate biking. I got in an accident when I was a teenager and never wanted to ride after that. She's trying to see if you're telling the truth."

"I thought Bridget hated biking?" Orville said, and, at Bridget's prompting: "She tried to teach me to surf once, but all I did was fall off the board a lot and get a sunburn." *This is like* Cyrano de Bergerac, Orville thought. But it was easier, talking to this woman, with Bridget's help.

"Yeah, we used to surf together sometimes, we'd go down to Santa Cruz," Geneva said, seeming more relaxed now. "So how is Bridget? I haven't seen her in months."

"Ask her if she heard about me and Darrin," Bridget said, and Orville did.

Geneva sighed. "I did, she called me a few months ago and told me they'd split up, that she had to work some stuff out. I only met Darrin a couple of times. He seemed nice—maybe like he lived inside his head a little too much, but nice."

"Yeah," Bridget said, a little sadly.

"Yes," Orville said. "I guess she's still trying to figure things out."

"Aren't we all," Geneva said. "I think we can work together, Orville. Would you like to come over to my place?"

"Tell her nothing would please you more," Bridget said.

5

Geneva's apartment was a neat one-bedroom with a spacious living room, on the third floor of an apartment building just a block from the café.

"Have a seat," she said, pointing to a cushiony white sofa. "I'll be right back." She disappeared into the bedroom and shut the door.

Orville glanced over at Bridget, who was perusing Geneva's bookshelves. "Um," he said. "Are you going to be . . . in there . . . with us?"

She looked around, eyebrow raised. "Do you have an exhibitionist streak, Orville? Do you want me to be in there with you? I can stay out here if you go in the bedroom, if that's what you want. It's not far enough away to hurt me."

He didn't know how to answer. The idea of Bridget watching them should have mortified him, but he was also nervous about being away from her.

"I did watch Geneva work once, with a guy who got off on having another girl in the room, just watching. It was easy money. I didn't mind. I wouldn't mind with you, either, if you think you'd need encouragement, or—"

"Please come," Orville said.

"Will do. Oh, offer to pay her when she comes back out. Better if she doesn't have to ask."

Geneva returned a moment later in a short red silk robe, her hair loose. "So, Orville," she said.

"Do you mind, could we settle the, ah, business part, so I'm not thinking about it?"

"Sure." She told him the price, a significant percentage of his poker winnings, but about what Bridget had said to expect. He paid her, and she put the money in a little silver box on the coffee table. She curled up on the couch beside him, and he sat still, so nervous he could barely imagine moving. Geneva leaned over and kissed his cheek, putting her hand on his thigh. "You can touch me," she whispered in his ear. "You can tell me what you want."

But he couldn't. He couldn't possibly. Orville was on the verge of rising and fleeing the apartment.

Then Bridget whispered in his other ear. "Go ahead, Orville. I want to see you touch her. You deserve it. You deserve some happiness." There was no breath in his ear from her voice, but the hairs on his neck stood up anyway. "She'll talk dirty if you want," Bridget said, "or she'll be sweet, whatever you like. Touch her. I'll be with you. I'll be with you all the time."

"Would you like to take your jacket off?" Geneva said, and Orville nodded, shrugging out of it. Geneva knelt on the floor, her body between his legs, and unbuttoned his shirt. He reached out tentatively, caressing her cheek, and she nipped at his fingertip and drew it into her mouth, sucking on it. Then she leaned forward and kissed his chest. Orville trembled.

"Ask her to take off her robe," Bridget said. Her voice was strangely breathy, even though she didn't have breath.

"I'd—could I—I'd like to see you without the robe."

Geneva looked up at him—her face so close to his—and smiled. She stood up. "I didn't know if you liked lingerie, or what kind, so I hope this is all right. I just wore . . . nothing." She let the robe fall.

Orville had never seen a nude woman in the flesh—had always been too afraid to even brave a strip club. He said what he thought: "You're so beautiful."

Geneva smiled, and dimples appeared in her cheeks. "Your turn." She drew him to his feet. She knelt again, and unbuttoned his pants, pulling them down. She caressed his cock through his boxer shorts. "Is this for me?" she said. "How nice." She ran her fingernails up his length, and he gasped.

"Easy now," Bridget said, sitting on the couch. "Don't lose control of yourself. Try thinking about the multiplication tables."

2 x 2 is 4, he thought. *4 x 4 is 16. 16 x 16 is . . .*

Geneva pulled his boxers down, and conjured a condom from somewhere, ripping it open with her teeth. "Sit," she said, and he did gratefully, as his legs were shaking. She leaned forward to roll the condom on, then stopped, and touched his upper thigh. "Oh, I like this tattoo. What is it?"

"Tattoo?" Bridget said. "You never struck me as the tattoo type." She leaned forward, the top of her head nearly touching Geneva's, and the sight of the two women so close together was enough to make Orville moan slightly. "It looks like a bridge, Orville, a little arched footbridge."

"It's a bridge," Orville said, trying to keep his voice calm. He'd known this was a new body—the tastes, the smells, the unbroken legs. But a *tattoo* . . . that was something more. It suggested more than another body; it suggested another *life*, a life he might have had, one that allowed for the possibility of tattoos.

Geneva leaned forward and kissed the tattoo, and Orville gasped—who knew that part of his body could be so sensitive?

She rolled the condom onto him deftly, then closed her hand around his cock. He moaned again, rather less softly.

Geneva took him into her mouth.

Orville sat, his mouth open, his whole body faintly trembling. *I almost killed myself*, he thought. *I almost killed myself without ever feeling this.*

He looked at Bridget, who sat beside him on the couch. She smiled at him beneficently, maybe even proudly. "Don't look at me," she said. "Look at the beautiful woman going down on you. And when you fuck her, ask if you can take her from behind. She told me that's her favourite. And, anyway, I'd like to watch." She grinned, a wicked grin, a grin that made her seem entirely alive.

12 x 4 is 48, Orville thought.

6

"You're sweet," Geneva said later, and patted his cheek. "You can come back sometime if you want. And tell Bridget to call me."

"I wish," Bridget murmured from the office chair across from the bed.

Orville nodded. "I'd like that. I had a nice time." He stole a glance at Bridget. When Geneva had led him into the bedroom, Bridget had followed, watching them with hungry eyes. Watching Geneva, yes, but also watching *Orville*, and her gaze had excited him, almost too much. Orville didn't think he was an exhibitionist. Having anyone watch him wouldn't do. But somehow, because it was Bridget . . .

There was a nude woman beside him in bed, for the first time in Orville's life. And yet, his eyes didn't linger on her skin. His gaze kept shifting to Bridget in the corner, still in her red coat, and even so, he found her more alluring than the naked woman at his side.

"Do you want to shower or something before you go?" Geneva said, rising and putting on a fuzzy blue robe far more modest and comfortable-looking than the short silk one she'd worn earlier.

"Uh, no, no," Orville said, and gathered his own clothes together. The room smelled of sweat and something else—sex, he supposed. Oh, the smells—her hair, her wetness on his fingers, the hollow where her neck met her shoulder. He wondered what Bridget smelled like. As a ghost, she was as odourless as Orville's whole world had been before he swapped bodies. If Bridget hadn't died, Orville would never have met her, but now he would never know her alive. Longing swept through him. Even dead, she'd done so much for him, given him ice cream and winning at cards and sex and a new body with a tattoo . . . and the willingness to live his life. This was better than being dead. In its sensual physicality, he even thought this was better than the light of the other world he'd glimpsed as he fell from the bridge.

Once he was dressed, Geneva walked him to the door. "You've got my cell," she said. "I guess the number Bridget gave you? But for this sort of thing, here's a better number." She passed him a business card, and he mumbled thanks, trying to decide if having a prostitute's card meant he was pathetic or worldly. He decided it didn't matter. He'd had a good night.

Geneva shut the door, leaving him alone in the hall and at a loss for a moment, until Bridget stepped into his vision. "Well, Orville, was it good for you?"

"Very." He set off down the hall, toward the elevator. "It was amazing."

"You looked like you were having a fine time." She seemed sad.

"Are you okay?" A stupid question, in any fundamental sense, but he already trusted her to know what he meant.

She sighed. "I guess it's true that sex is mental. I mean, I've always liked watching, Darrin and I were like a gender-stereotype-reversal that way, he can take or leave porn, but I love it, and I like watching couples too. Seeing you and Geneva was nice. I always thought she was beautiful, and it was hot the way you kept looking over at me—"

Orville blushed, and at the same time, felt aroused.

"—with her not even knowing I was there. So without really thinking about it I reached down to touch myself, and . . . nothing." She waved her hand as Orville pressed the call button for the elevator. "I couldn't even feel myself. I read once about this neurological disorder that destroys your sense of where your arms and legs and hands are? It's like that for me when I try to touch myself. I can affect things in the world, push them around a little, but it's clumsy, like trying to play piano while wearing oven mitts. There's no pressure, no friction. I thought not being able to eat was the worst." Orville got into the elevator, grateful it was empty, and Bridget followed. "But losing my body? It's so much more than just never having a hot fudge sundae again. Once, in the briarpatch, Ismael and I ran into this *thing*, all floating and ragged at the edges, whispering and grabbing at vines and branches, but it couldn't get a grip on anything. Ismael said he didn't know what it was, just that he'd seen them before, and they were harmless, but I wonder if maybe it was something like me, someone who left their body, got lost, and went crazy." She looked at Orville now and said "I don't want that to happen to me, Orville."

"What can we do?" he asked. "We"—as simple as that. They were in this together, not by the necessary association of haunter and haunted, but by his choice. She'd shown him life was worth living. He couldn't give Bridget her life back, but he could pledge himself to help, however possible.

"We have to find Ismael. I can't go where *you* don't, so I need you. Ismael met you, and his aura of fatalism or whatever caught hold in you, so it wouldn't surprise him too much if you tracked him down, asked him for guidance, you know? I think he'd open the door and let you in. He might be able to see me— he's spent so long in the briarpatch, he's attuned to witnessing the weird. If not, you can be my translator, and tell him what I say. I'll make him tell me what happens next, since he failed me. He'll tell me where to go from here. And in the meantime, Orville . . . keep looking at me. Keep paying attention to me. I think that will help hold me together."

The elevator opened on the ground floor, and Orville exited. "What if Ismael won't help you?"

"Where can he run?" Bridget said, with a touch of her earlier zest. "You've seen the light, Orville. You've gone into the briarpatch and brought a new body—a new life—out of it. You can see the paths, if you look, and if he flees, we can follow. He'll help me. He knows what a pain in the ass I can be if I don't get my way."

Orville was glad to hear her sounding resolute—being sad and vague couldn't be good for her cohesion, either. "When do we go?"

"Tomorrow. You need to sleep, after the day you've had."

They left the building and went down the sidewalk to a bus stop bench. Orville sat down. The night was crisp and clear, and he was profoundly satisfied and tired. "Thank you for tonight, Bridget."

She paused in her pacing to flash him a grin, and her smile was somehow wired directly into his heart; he'd never felt as important as he did when she looked at him. "Any time, Mr. Troll." After a moment she stopped in her pacing. "Say, what time is it?"

Orville looked instinctively at his wrist, but he had no watch, having lost it in the jump from the bridge or the aftermath at the hospital. "Um, I saw the clock at Geneva's, it was about nine thirty when we left, so maybe almost ten o'clock now?"

Bridget frowned, a vertical worry line appearing between her eyebrows. "You're shitting me. It's got to be later than that."

Orville shrugged. "We jumped in the morning. I'm not sure what time I woke up, but it couldn't have been too much later. We went through . . . that other place, the briarpatch . . . and back home, and then played poker. It was just getting dark when we left the card club. It's been a long day, and I don't mind going home."

Bridget chewed her lip. Not that she actually *had* a lip, really, but old habits were probably hard to shake. "Would you mind maybe making one more little stop? Something's been bothering me."

Orville nodded, not even needing to hear what she wanted, happy to do anything for her. He wasn't as tired as he should have been. Swapping bodies halfway through the day probably had a rejuvenating effect. "Where to? As long as we can get there by bus. It can be hard to get a cab over here."

"Over near Lake Merritt. Close to the high school."

Orville knew the neighbourhood. "I go to the movies over there sometimes, in that nice old theatre. Probably faster to take the train, though. There's a BART station a couple of blocks back."

Bridget hesitated. "About the trains . . ."

"What?"

"Nothing. I guess it'll be okay, as long as we're careful about which train we get on."

Orville stood and started down the sidewalk, past the closed shops and the teenage punk panhandlers. He didn't much care if people here saw him talking to himself. Around here, you had to start screaming and bothering passers-by to make much of an impression, and even then, people would just walk in a wider arc around you. "I haven't owned a car since I was 17 and rear-ended somebody. Couldn't afford the repairs or the insurance, really. I do mass-transit a lot. Don't worry, I know which train to take."

"That's not what I mean," Bridget said. "You'll see. Once you've been to the briarpatch, once you've had your eyes opened, you see things differently. Down underground, where the trains run . . . it can get a little freaky. Ismael doesn't even know where all the special trains run down there."

Orville wanted to ask what she meant by "special trains," but then she gasped and grabbed his arm (still so strange, her habit of acting as if she had a body, and the lack of pressure from her touch). "Look," she said, lifting her chin, and Orville turned his eyes skyward.

A bridge filled the far quadrant of the sky, a graceful arcing structure with no visible supports, the colour of the moon, more shining with its own light than reflecting. It was beautiful, and Orville suspected it was extremely large and very far away. He couldn't see where it began, or where it ended, just a segment of its length rising from behind the buildings on the left and disappearing beyond the buildings on the right.

"It appears, sometimes," Bridget said. "Ismael thinks it might be important, but he's never been able to reach it, or even come close, though he's chased it dozens of times, he says. It comes and goes like a rainbow."

"Where do you think it leads?" Orville asked, his own voice hushed, more out of respect for Bridget's reverence than because of his own awe.

"I'm not sure it leads anywhere. I think it might be a destination all on its own."

For some reason Orville doubted that, and he wondered if Bridget truly believed it. Bridges only existed to take you from one place to another, right?

"Funny how everything in the whole world, as far as I know, is under that bridge," she said. "You know what kinds of things traditionally live under bridges. Monsters."

"And homeless people and runaways. They're not monsters, usually."

Bridget nodded, still gazing up at the moon-coloured bridge. "But don't you wonder where *our* true home is? What we've run away from? Ismael thinks that bridge leads to the better world, where the light never fades or comes in slantwise."

Orville actually thought light was prettiest when it came in at a slant, passing through clouds, the rays clear in the hazy air, or limning trees in gold with late-afternoon sun. But he knew Bridget had a religion of sorts that sought a purer light. "You don't think so?"

"I don't know. I don't *want* to think so, because then it's just cruel, seeing the bridge, but being unable to reach it, to go to that place. The briarpatch is hard, and strange, but I don't think it's cruel, I don't think there's any intention behind it at all."

"Ah," Orville said. He didn't know much about these matters. His one visit to the briarpatch had been miraculous and terrifying by turns.

The bridge shimmered and faded from view, and Bridget let out a long sigh. "Guess we'd better go. We've got our own world to navigate."

They went down the long escalator into the train station, and Orville used a little of his cash to buy a ticket. They passed through the gates—Bridget jumped it, easy and graceful, and he wondered again if she *would* be able to pass through solid objects if she gave up on the idea of having a body. How much of her current form was just *habit*? Down another escalator, to the platform . . . and now Orville understood what Bridget meant about train stations being strange, now that he had eyes to see.

This station normally had a single platform in the centre, with some benches and a perpetually-broken elevator to the upper level, and train tracks on both sides, one with trains bound for San Francisco, one with trains bound for other points in the East Bay. Orville stood on that platform now . . . but there were other platforms, beyond the tracks, on both sides. The walls were missing—at least to Orville's eyes—and this subterranean space was vast and shadowy now. On both sides, platforms stretched as far as he could see, not connected visibly, tracks between them, so it seemed that in order to reach any one you would have to clamber down onto the tracks and climb up onto a platform on the other side.

"You see?" Bridget said, and Orville nodded, unwilling to speak with so many other people around. A man talking to himself on a train platform wasn't much stranger than a man talking to himself on the street, but it was more noticeable for being in a confined space. "Different trains come to those platforms. Sometimes they come to this platform too, only most people can't see them. Some of them are obvious—there's one that's made of bone, looks like it was carved from the femur of a giant or something, and Ismael says he never quite had the guts to board that one. But there are other trains that pull in here that don't look much different from regular trains. That's what I was worried about, really, seeing a train that looks *almost* right but isn't. Ismael says some of them aren't trains at all, just things that *mimic* trains, and he doesn't know what happens if you board them. Something bad. Ismael once spent six months down here, riding every train he could, hoping to find one that ran to the better world, avoiding the ones that only *looked* like trains."

"How did he avoid them?" Orville spoke out of the side of his mouth, softly, like a convict in an old movie.

"Well, maybe he didn't really avoid them . . . Ismael has this funny power. Only 'power' isn't right, it's not something he can control, so call it a 'quality.' He doesn't die. Whenever death is imminent, whenever something is about to kill him, he just sort of . . . jumps to some other point in the briarpatch, someplace safer."

"Like teleportation?" Like Nightcrawler from the X-Men, he wanted to say, but didn't want to look like any more of a geek in front of Bridget.

Bridget waggled her hand in a "sort of" motion. "Ismael says he thinks it's more complicated than that, that distance and location in the briarpatch don't work the way they do in the mundane world, that it's more like topological crumpling or something, he wasn't very interested in explaining it, so he didn't explain it well. But however it works, when he tried to get on one of those fake trains, he jumped away before he could even step through the doors, which makes him think he would've died as soon as he got inside. But you and me, we don't have that kind of defence mechanism, so we have to be careful. Ismael brought me down here not long after I first met him, to prove to me that the briarpatch really existed. He showed me how to identify the sham-trains, called it 'briarpatch trainspotting.' He has a way of helping you see, by holding your hand, pointing things out, and it's like seeing a hidden picture at first, one of those optical illusions, but pretty soon you can't *stop* seeing it."

A train pulled into the station, with all the customary noise and wind, and it looked normal enough, and like the train Orville wanted. There were people visible through the windows, sleeping or reading newspapers or talking. The doors hissed open. "This one looks okay," Orville said.

"*No.*" Bridget tried to grab his arm again, though it felt more like a hard wind blowing against him than a human touch. "You have to look. No one else is getting on the train, that's the first thing. The wind that came, pushed before the train? It blew your hair, but it didn't move anybody else's. I'm dead, so that explains why the wind didn't touch me, but if this were a regular train, it would have affected other people too. You're susceptible to drafts from another world now, Orville."

"But the people inside the train—" he began.

"There are deep sea predators that have little stalks on their heads with glowing bulbs at the end. Other fish come to the bulb, thinking it must be something good to eat, and then the predator slides out of the shadows and eats them. Those people you're seeing, they aren't real, they're just bait. Look at the sides of the train."

Orville took a step back, as if afraid the train might lunge at him—and maybe it would, for all he knew. The sides were slick with water, he assumed it was condensation, and—

"Shit!" he said, drawing glares and glances from the other people waiting on the platform. Some kid muttered that he was a crazy motherfucker.

But Orville had seen the sides of the train move, expand and then contract, like the train was—

"It's breathing," Bridget said. "Or something like that."

After a moment the doors closed and the train pulled away down the tunnel. For the first few cars it looked the same, like a normal train, but then the far end appeared from where it had been hidden deeper in the tunnel, the train cars darkening, windows disappearing, tapering until the thing no longer resembled a train at all; the end was dark and mottled and looked like nothing so much as the tail of a giant snake, shimmying a little from side to side as it disappeared into the darkness.

Orville sat down hard on an empty bench. He'd almost walked into that *thing*. How could he ever take a train again? How could he come down here without Bridget, if she managed to move on to the better world and leave him unhaunted, unaccompanied? Would this be his life now, filled with terrible miracles? Would he have to tap passers-by and say "Hey, do you see that train?" Were there buses like this too, or cars, or stores, things that tried to eat clueless wanderers? "This is very scary," Orville said.

"It's different. But I don't think it's any scarier than the regular world you know. You just have to learn new rules. There are neighbourhoods you don't walk in after dark, right? And in the briarpatch, or on the edge of the briarpatch, like here, there are certain trains you don't ride. You don't stray from the path in the cavern of trees, and you don't feed the bears, and you don't answer the things that speak from the drains, and a few other rules, and you get by okay."

A moment later another train arrived, and people got on this one. With a glance at Bridget, who nodded, Orville boarded.

Now Orville wanted to ask where they were going. He hadn't before, assuming she would offer an explanation, and then he'd been distracted by the oddness of the train station. Now he couldn't speak to her without looking crazy and making the other riders uncomfortable. Bridget was standing in the middle of the mostly-empty car, anyway, hanging onto a handrail overhead, and didn't look like she wanted to talk. There was something on her mind.

Orville leaned his forehead against the window and looked out. The train passed side-tunnels that didn't conventionally exist, as far as Orville knew, and there were lights in some of them, and through one, he thought he glimpsed an open beach and an ocean under a sapphire-coloured sun, but it passed in a flash. There were wonders in the briarpatch, it seemed, or accessible through it. Unless that ocean was filled with tentacled monsters, or the whole scene was unreal, an illusory projection designed to lure him into something with a mouth the size of a room. . . .

They only had to go a few stops, and soon they exited the train—into the Lake Merritt BART station, which looked utterly normal, to Orville's surprise, no extra platforms. The briarpatch was weird. Bridget walked briskly to the stairs, and Orville followed, figuring she knew the way. "We can wait for a bus," she said. "Or we can walk. It's about two miles, and parts of it are kind of pedestrian-unfriendly, but it's doable. I don't get tired, but . . ."

"I'm okay," Orville said. "Lead on." She set the pace—which was a bit unfair, perhaps, since she didn't have the capacity to get fatigued anymore, but she also knew where they were going, so Orville followed along. They walked along dark sidewalks, down past the courthouse, taking the first few blocks in silence. Finally Orville said "Where are we going, anyway?"

"I . . . have a friend. More than a friend, once. A lover."

Orville frowned. "I thought Ismael was your . . . ?"

She snorted. "God, I never fucked Ismael, or loved him, either. He impressed the hell out of me, and showed me miracles, and I guess I cared for him a lot, but it wasn't *love*. We just made common cause, both of us sick of the world not living up to our dreams, and looking for some unattainable heaven. No, I want to go see Darrin, the man I was with . . . before Ismael."

"You think he'll be able to see you?" Orville wondered why he was jealous of a dead woman's ex-boyfriend, especially when the same dead woman had helped set him up to have sex with a friend of hers. But emotions weren't rational, and he *was* jealous.

"No. I guess not. There's no reason to think he could—he can't see into the briarpatch, no one's ever taught him, so I don't have any reason to believe he's got better perception than anyone else. I just . . . want to see him. It was the strangest thing, this morning on the bridge, just as I jumped, I thought I heard his voice, calling my name. I can't believe he was really there, but I'm afraid . . . I don't suppose you noticed anyone, before you jumped?"

"There were lots of people shouting, leaning over the rail, looking at you fall. Maybe if I saw him I would recognize him. . . ." He shrugged. "So what are we supposed to do when we get to his house? If he can't see you?"

Bridget shook her head. "I hadn't really thought it through. I just wanted to make sure he was okay. Maybe you could knock on the door, ask him if I'm home, say you're a friend of Geneva's, and she was worried about me, or . . . shit, that doesn't make any sense, I don't know. Maybe you can pretend to be a travelling encyclopaedia salesman or something."

"I'll just pretend I have the wrong apartment," Orville said. "How'd that be? Is that enough?" He wanted to help—he owed her—but didn't really care to meet the man who'd lived with her, loved her, made love to her, but had been unable to make her love the world enough to keep her from killing herself. If Orville had been given the chance to make Bridget happy in life . . . well, honestly, he probably would have fucked it up, like he fucked up most things, but he liked to imagine she would have inspired him to better things. He dreaded the prospect of knocking on this stranger's door, with Bridget lingering behind him. He'd never even liked selling candy door-to-door for fundraisers in high school. Orville tended to stammer when forced into awkward conversations with strangers. Still, for Bridget, he'd do it

They hurried through the trickiest part of the walk, following the road beneath an overpass where there were no sidewalks. A little shanty-camp had sprung up beneath the overpass, tarps and pallets and scavenged wood making a shelter for a few homeless people, but none of them bothered him, probably because he was talking to himself and nodding as he went. Sometimes it was good to look crazy; it helped you either blend in or stand out as someone not to be messed with. From there it was a jog across several lanes of thankfully traffic-free asphalt, then a hop over a low barrier into the protected bike lane, and from there onto the sidewalk that curved around the lake. Orville had never spent much time on this side of the lake—the Grand Lake Theater was across, on the other side—but it suddenly became very peaceful as he curved away from the larger street, along the paved multiuse trail, beneath the twinkling fairy lights strung between lampposts. Even this late people were jogging, and a couple sat on a bench looking at the water, talking and holding hands. Orville could smell the water, and the bird shit, and he enjoyed it all.

"I love this lake," Bridget said. "The last couple of springs, Darrin and I came here to see the baby geese. There are Canadian geese here, you know, it's a bird sanctuary, and they're so adorable when they're born, these little fuzzy things, nothing at all like the mean birds they become when they grow up, the ones that try to steal your sandwiches if you have a picnic in the park." She pointed to a crosswalk that led to a small park. "The geese usually trundle across the street here several times a day, leading their flock of babies, and they mostly use the crosswalk, even, though they still cross against the light." She grinned. "Darrin and I would buy some cheap bread from the Merritt Bakery over there, and come sit in this park to feed the goslings. That was . . . really nice. If every day was like that one half-hour, feeding baby birds in the park, I might never have hooked up with Ismael, might never have tried to pass through death into a perfect beautiful place . . . but who am I kidding? I get bored so easily, Orville. I don't know what's wrong with me. Maybe I did too many drugs in high school, and I'm still looking for the next high. Part of what I liked about the idea of reaching a better world was being able to *stop* looking, stop working, to just *be*, and be happy."

Orville didn't answer. He felt like he'd just seen something true and sad about her, a depth of insight he hadn't expected. They'd been through a lot today. Shared trauma could bring people together, even if one of them was already dead, and thus as thoroughly traumatized as it was possible to get. "That sounds nice, about the baby geese," he said at last.

"We should cross here," she said, about a block later, and they cut across the street and went up a steep hill into a residential area. The neighbourhood got nicer as they got farther from the lake, apartment houses replaced by single-family dwellings, mostly. Orville was puffing a little from the hills, which were not insignificant, but he wasn't breathing as heavily as he should have been—the Orville who got his body tattooed also got more exercise, it seemed. He'd have to keep that up, not spoil the gift by sinking back into sedentary habits. He hoped again that he hadn't actually swapped bodies with some other iteration of himself, living some other life, a body snatched from some other possible timeline. There were deep philosophical waters here. With a different body, was he really himself at all? Was the structure of his brain different, or the chemical balance in his body; did those changes affect his mind, make him less depressive, less prone to giving up? Was he even really Orville Troll at all—was the only thing that mattered the continuity of memory? Could he even *trust* his memory? He shied away from the implications. He could consider them later, when things were less in motion.

But he knew one thing: If this body was taken from some other world, then he owed it to that truncated timeline to make his own life a good one, with Bridget's help. For as long as she lasted, anyway.

They passed a church, and Bridget said "Nearly there." They walked toward a big redwood right in the middle of a roundabout in the centre of the street.

"Pretty neighbourhood," Orville said. The air smelled of some sweet night-blooming flower he couldn't possibly identify.

Bridget paused by a stucco wall surrounding the courtyard of a nice-looking group of apartments. "That's the house." She pointed across the street toward a big rambling structure.

Orville whistled. "Darrin must do all right for himself."

"Nah, he doesn't have the whole place. It's busted up into apartments, he's there in the top left. It's nice enough, but not very big, almost too cozy for the two of us. We had to share the spare bedroom as an office and a place to put my craft stuff. We—"

"Evening, mister, do you have the time?" A tall, lanky man spoke, emerging from the driver side of a parked sedan a few feet ahead of them.

"Uh, no, sorry," Orville said. "Before eleven o'clock, I think."

"The night is young," the man said agreeably. "I'm going to need you to give me all your money now."

His voice was so calm and friendly that Orville had trouble comprehending for a moment, but Bridget just said "Shit," in a disgusted voice. "We're getting mugged."

Another man, shorter and less talkative, emerged from the passenger side of the car and took a step toward them. The first man circled around the hood, stepping into a streetlight long enough to illuminate his face—handsome if not for a long-ago-broken nose and pockmarks. "I hate asking for things twice," he said. "Money, now."

Orville didn't back away. He'd never been mugged before, despite living in far worse neighbourhoods than this. Maybe that was the point. There was no reason to mug people in a lousy neighbourhood, because no one there had anything. "Okay," Orville said.

"Oh, to hell with this, I worked hard to get you that money," Bridget said. "Back away from them, just a few steps."

"But—" Orville protested. He knew you were supposed to comply with muggers. Neither man had pulled a gun, yet, but they were drawing closer. They could hurt him if they wanted—the shorter man looked made of muscle. The men drifted apart, probably so they could flank Orville and cut off any line of retreat.

"Do it!" Bridget said, and Orville complied without thinking, holding up his hands in a placating way, taking small steps backward, trapped between the stucco wall and the parked cars on the street, nowhere to run.

"I'm sorry, look, I don't have any money," Orville said, though of course he did, wads of cash in his pants pockets.

"You got shoes," the tall man said meditatively. "We'll take those. And you can get beat for wasting our time if you don't stop walking away from me."

"You can stop now." Bridget circled around behind the tall man. Orville noticed a break in the wall, which was odd, because he hadn't seen it before, but there was an opening in the stucco, leading to a very steep and narrow set of stairs, going down, down, down. Which didn't make much sense, topographically speaking, since the ground was pretty level here, and where were those stairs going down *to*?

Then he figured it out. Those stairs were only conditionally real. They led to the briarpatch.

"Hand him a little of your money, Orville, hold it out to him, and be sure his skin touches yours. Keep contact for as long as you can, don't let go until the last moment. If you touch someone, they can see what you see, the entrances to the briarpatch, they can go *in*. That's how Ismael first took me. I have an idea."

Orville wondered if he would die soon, if Bridget had a real plan or if she was just being careless in a way only the already-dead could be. But he complied, stopping his backward retreat as the muggers drew up alongside the stairway they couldn't see. He fumbled in his pocket, drew out a few bills, and held them out.

"Oh, so you were lying," the tall man said, disapprovingly. He reached for the cash. "We might have to tax you a little for that. Dishonesty tax." Bridget stood behind him. The man touched the money, and Orville reached out and took his wrist, gently encircling it with his fingers. "You want to try some judo shit?" the man said, amused, and then caught sight of the stairs, which he could see now, having touched Orville's hand. "The fuck?" he said, turning to look down the stairs, and trying to pull his hand away. Orville gritted his teeth and held on, and then Bridget hurled herself against the mugger like a football player slamming into a blocking sled. Her shove didn't have the force it would have if she'd been in her original body, but it was enough to knock him off balance. The man gasped and stumbled down a couple of steps, tearing his arm free from Orville—but now he was *in* the passageway, in another world or between them. He tottered on the edge of a step, pinwheeled his arms, and fell, bouncing down the narrow stairs to land on the sandy earth at the bottom. Bridget spat after him. "One down," she said.

Was the man dead? Even if he was alive, without Orville touching him, would he be able to see the way back to this world, or would he be trapped . . . wherever he was now? Orville couldn't decide whether to be exulted or horrified.

The other mugger stared at the wall, clearly unable to see the gap and the stairs. "Marlin?" he said. "Where the fuck did you go?" He looked at Orville, wide-eyed. "Where the fuck did he go?"

Surprised at himself, Orville took a step forward. In a low voice, he said "Do you want me to make you disappear too?"

The man's eyes went even wider, and he backed up, then turned and ran down the block out of view.

"Nicely done, Mr. Troll," Bridget said. "God, I got fucked with so much when I was alive, being a woman in this city, you have no *idea* what it's like sometimes. Glad we got some of our own back."

"What will happen to . . . the other one?"

Bridget shrugged. "If he's still alive you mean? Nothing good. I've been down those stairs, and he's not in such a nice part of the briarpatch. If he can't see any of the passageways out—and there's no reason to think he can—I don't like his chances. There are bears down there. Fuck him. He made his choice, got into that line of work. Don't pity him. Come on. Let's go see Darrin."

Orville closed his eyes. "I can't . . . I just *killed* a man."

"No. You held his hand for a minute, that's all. If anyone killed him, it was me, and I don't mind calling it self-defence." She paused. "Not that he could have hurt me, but he could have hurt you. So call it 'other-defence.' Okay?"

Still shaken, trembling with now-useless adrenaline, Orville followed her around the thug's abandoned car, and across the street. A man came down the steps from the building and paused at the bottom, taking a cell phone from his pocket.

"Wait," Bridget said. "That's Nicholas, Darrin's friend. Didn't expect to see him here. I'm going closer." She slipped up the sidewalk toward him, and Orville tried to look nonchalant, standing on a street that wasn't his own. He was glad of the pause, though. If he'd had to ring Darrin's doorbell so soon after encountering those muggers, he probably wouldn't have been able to get a word out, too nervous to speak.

The man, Nicholas, wasn't talking loudly, but the wind was such that Orville could hear most of the words. "Yeah, I'm still here," he said. "I told him I needed to have a smoke. Relax, he doesn't know I'm calling you. This has been the longest day in the universe. I wish he'd take some sleeping pills or something, I mean, his ex-girlfriend *died* this morning, you'd think he'd be in the mood for sleep, but he's all wound up, I keep pouring drinks in him and hoping he'll pass out. Yeah. What's the plan? Tomorrow . . . shit. No, of course I'm still up for it, as long as you fulfill your end. In the afternoon, though, okay? We're getting pretty smashed here and he's probably going to be hungover. Yeah, of course, he's fucking grieving, man. How're we going to get him out of the house? Oh, hell, her? Whatever. All right. I'll call tomorrow." He flipped the phone closed, took a deep breath, and went back up the stairs.

Bridget came back to Orville, frowning.

"What's up?" he asked.

"I put my ear close to the phone," she said, slowly. "And . . . the voice on the other end was Ismael. I'm sure of it. I don't know what they were talking about, exactly, but I know who. They were talking about Darrin. I don't understand this. What does Ismael care about Darrin? And why would Nicholas be talking to him, how do they even know each other?"

"Do you still want to see Darrin?"

"I . . . not with Nicholas there. Darrin is grieving, he said. He must know I died. Maybe he's still listed as my emergency contact or something, I don't even remember." Her hand strayed to the zipper on the front of her red coat and slid it

halfway down, then up again, then back down, absentmindedly. "If he's drunk . .
. no, this was a bad idea, I don't know enough, something else is going on, Ismael
is doing something I don't understand. But I'll find out." She gritted her teeth.

Orville yawned. "Do you want to go to Ismael's house tonight?"

She considered it, then shook her head. "No. He's too *on* at night, he likes
to stay up and plan, he's at his best after nightfall. I want to go to his house in
the morning and roll him out of bed, put the sun on his face like he's a fucking
vampire." She looked troubled, that line appearing on her forehead. "But what
does he want with Darrin? Does it have something to do with me? I don't get it."

"We'll figure it out," Orville said, and they walked back up the street the way
they came.

7

Arturo leaned against the side of the Wendigo, reading a paperback he'd found in
the depths of the back seat, something by Tim O'Brien. A bunch of pages in the
middle were missing, but he hadn't gotten to that point yet, so he didn't really
mind.

A stocky, muscular man came running down the sidewalk like the devil was
after him, but Arturo didn't see anybody on his heels. The man stopped short,
reached into his pants, and pulled out a gun, a little short-barrelled revolver.
Gasping for air, he said "Give me the fucking keys, man!"

"You don't want to do this." Arturo held his place in the book with his finger.

"Fuck you!" the man shouted. "Why all you motherfuckers gotta be talking
back tonight, shit!"

Arturo held up his hands. This man wasn't going to be dissuaded. "Okay. No
backtalk. The keys are in the car." He backed away.

The man wrenched open the driver's side and slid onto the seat. The door
closed after him, without the man even touching it.

Arturo turned his back on the Wendigo and looked at the apartment building
across the street. It had fake crenellations along the roof, like the turrets on a
castle. Arturo approved of little whimsical touches like that. He didn't go back
to his book yet.

The Wendigo rocked on its shocks, squeaking a little as it moved. There were
no screams, fortunately, and the sound of chewing was brief and seemed far
away. After a while Arturo heard a click, and the driver's side door opened.

Arturo turned and glanced inside. The would-be carjacker was gone, of course, though about sixty dollars in mixed bills lay on the seat, along with a library card and one shoe. Arturo pocketed the money and tossed the shoe and the library card into the back seat, where they would disappear by morning. He sighed. He knew the Wendigo was just protecting itself, and this had only happened a couple of times in the past, but it still bothered him. He wondered if the carjacker was dead, or if the belly of the Wendigo was somehow a world unto itself. Arturo hoped he would never have to know.

He shut the car door and leaned against it again, returning to his book, almost too distracted to read, wondering why the Wendigo had parked itself here and refused to move beyond the neighbourhood. It had something to do with Darrin, probably, but Arturo didn't know what. Ah, well. In time, things would be revealed, or they wouldn't. The Wendigo moved in mysterious ways.

ISMAEL ENTERTAINS VISITORS

1

The morning after Bridget jumped, Darrin sat up in bed and groaned, his head thudding. He dragged himself through the living room, surprised that Nicholas had cleared away the beer bottles and glasses. Nicholas generally didn't bother cleaning up, and the thoughtfulness touched Darrin. The guy really did care—he just didn't know how to show it all the time. Darrin poured a glass of ice water and grimaced as the liquid hit his mouth. He was so dry the water refused to soak into his tissues, but he forced himself to drink it all, swallow some painkillers, and pour another glass. He took a hot shower and felt marginally more human by the time he emerged. Maybe last night hadn't been a good idea. Pouring alcohol into a depressed person was like pouring gasoline on a fire. But seeing Nicholas and looking through the old photo albums had been nice, almost a flashback to college. Nostalgia had done its trick, making the past seem like a beautiful country still possible to visit sometimes.

Once the coffee was brewing, Darrin went downstairs to check his mail, though it was usually nothing but bills these days. There was a white envelope on the floor inside his door, apparently shoved through the crack underneath, and when he picked it up, he saw it bore neither an address nor postage. He ripped it open and withdrew a single sheet of paper, printed text reading:

> If you want to find Ismael Plenty he lives at 357 Beane Street. Bridget used to live there to. Hes a bastard and deserves whatever he gets so good luck.

Was it real? Who could have left it? Who knew he was looking for Ismael, apart from Nicholas and Echo? It *might* be Arturo—he said the Wendigo produced weird notes sometimes.

Darrin looked up 357 Beane Street online, and was somehow unsurprised to find it was only a few miles away, near Emeryville. He'd assumed Ismael lived in San Francisco, and that's where he'd planned to start searching for him, but it seemed Bridget's—what, lover, confidante, cult leader, killer?—preferred the cheaper rents and more convenient parking of the East Bay over the more obvious charms of San Francisco. Assuming the note was real.

After getting dressed, Darrin wrote a brief note for Echo and put it on the kitchen counter, where she was sure to see it—Echo never came over without eating his food or drinking his tea or wine, after all. Her appetites were prodigious. She usually stopped by in the afternoons, and he let her know he was going out for a while, and wasn't sure when he'd be back. He considered signing it "love," but settled on "XOXO" instead.

Darrin went down the steps. It was just after noon, but autumn in Oakland wasn't really too warm or too cold, and the rain probably wouldn't come for another few weeks. The sky was clear, except for a few thin high clouds. Darrin walked along the sidewalk, past the redwood in the centre of the traffic circle, toward the Wendigo. There was no sign of Arturo, which was too bad, because Darrin had planned to ask him for a lift—he'd offered, after all. Darrin didn't know where to find him, or even where to start looking. He glanced inside the car and saw the keys dangling from the ignition, and thought for a moment about just borrowing the car and driving to Beane Street. He remembered the noise the Wendigo's horn had made, though, and Arturo's comment about not wanting to use the high-beams. If Darrin got into this car, there was no telling where it would take him.

To hell with it. He'd start walking, and if he saw a bus going the right way, he'd catch it. He wondered if he should get a weapon, remembering the way Ismael had whipped out that baton and knocked Nicholas down outside the strip club. But Darrin wouldn't know what to do with a weapon if he got one. Besides, he was so pissed, if Ismael came at him with a club, Darrin would take it away and *beat* him with it. Assuming the note was even on the level. Worst case scenario, he wasted an afternoon walking. Big deal. He would've just wasted it on something else, anyway.

As Darrin walked up to Macarthur Boulevard, he felt energy returning to him, an interest in and commitment to life that had been absent these past months. He had a mission, even if he wasn't sure, exactly, what he'd do when he confronted Ismael. Something serious, he suspected. He couldn't be sure what the man had done to Bridget, but he was involved, somehow, in her death, and probably in her departure from Darrin's life. Darrin intended to find out . . . and, if necessary, to make him pay.

Love was a better reason for living than revenge, but revenge would do in a pinch.

And anything was better than that hollow numb ache of loss.

2

Ismael sat in a lawn chair in his sad little back yard, a cup of coffee steaming its warmth away into the cool air on the metal table beside him. He wistfully read *Final Exit*, the practical guide to suicide, though he knew there was nothing inside he hadn't attempted before. If only. He tried not to let himself be hopeful about tonight. The trauma Darrin would undergo this afternoon should push him utterly out of his old life, and such psychological upheaval, combined with Ismael's influence, might be enough to make him rush headlong into undiscovered countries. If Darrin really *was* a child of the briarpatch—born there, or if not exactly born, then coming to life by some spontaneous generation or abiogenesis, the way people once believed mice were born from dirty hay or crocodiles from rotting logs—he could have access to paths Ismael could not reach on his own, just as Harczos had, and perhaps he could lead Ismael to the northwest passage, that overland route to the better world that Harczos claimed to have found—that he had *taunted* Ismael with.

"Oh Izzy," Echo yelled, stomping through his house. "Are you excited? Are you revved up? Are you *game*?" She came through the door, grinning. "You're going to owe me major for this. Darrin's kind of sweet, I don't even mind hooking up with him, but Nicholas is like a frat boy with less charm. He's gonna cost you extra."

Ismael had grown weary of Echo's attempts at humiliation long ago, but she was useful to him, capable of almost any act so long as she was sufficiently entertained. But unless things went badly tonight, he would disappear into the briarpatch with Darrin, in search of the northwest passage, and if he ever emerged again, he would do so somewhere far away, out of Echo's effective range. So why not promise her anything?

"What did you have in mind?" he asked her. "Do you want to shoot me with a flamethrower? Put me in an iron maiden? Perhaps something with piranha?"

"Nah." Echo sat on the back steps, reaching for his coffee, sniffing, and putting it back with disdain. "There's not any whiskey in that. Or even Kahlua."

"It's a little early for me." Ismael glanced skyward. It was still an hour before noon. In the old days, he'd drank beer at all hours, because beer was safer than the frequently-tainted water. But Ismael had changed somewhat with the times.

"Whatever," Echo said. "No, I'm going to have to put some thought into this one, make you do something *seriously* fucked up. I'll let you know later. If it's especially terrible with Nicholas, I'll charge extra too."

"I wait with bated breath. Did you arrange to get Darrin out of the house for a while?"

"Oh, sure." She began picking through the cigarette butts around the bottom of the steps—all her own cigarettes, since Ismael couldn't work up the enthusiasm to smoke anymore—until she found one that wasn't stomped on and that was only half-smoked. She lit it, puffed, made a face, and exhaled.

"Would you eat garbage off the floor?" Ismael asked, genuinely curious.

"I've eaten worse off worse," she said, not very jovially, despite the wide grin she gave him.

"How did you contrive to get Darrin away?"

"Oh, don't worry, he's easy, I can play him like a violin. Nah, violin's too hard, I can play him like a *drum*. He'll be occupied for a few hours, so we can amble over there, and me and Nicholas can get set up. So, what, you're going to hide in the closet or some shit, jump out and say 'boo' at him?"

"No, I'll stay outside," Ismael said. "Lurking, as it were, in the shadows. Until he emerges, a broken man."

"Nicholas called me this morning, trying to be all *nice*." Echo flicked ash off her cigarette. "Like he thought we were going on a date or something. Anyway, we did wonder how mean and nasty we're supposed to be, here. Should we pretend to be all upset when he walks in on us, all 'Oh, honey, this isn't what you think,' or what?"

"Be as cruel as you like," Ismael said. He thought for a moment. "You can even tell him you're working with me, if you wish."

"Because . . . you want him to bash your head in with a rock as soon as he sees you?" The idea seemed to amuse her.

Ismael shrugged. "It doesn't matter. He'll know the truth soon enough. Once he's broken, once he can see the briarpatch clearly, I'll be able to enlist him to my cause."

"Riiiight. Because you know the guy really well. Me, I think it'll be more like the head-bashing scenario, but what do I know? I've only been fucking him and listening to his pillow talk for months, right? Doesn't matter to me either way."

"That indifference is what I value most in you, Echo. When will Darrin be out of the house?"

She shrugged. "I doubt he's even out of bed yet. I'll call in a while and make sure he's gone, then we can head over." She belched. "Mind if I just hang out here until then?"

"You want to pillage the legacy room again, don't you?" He picked up his coffee cup, feeling the remnants of heat through the ceramic.

"It's not like you use that stuff, and I made a killing last time I went to the vintage store to sell some. It's like the '70s died and went to heaven in there. What, did you convince a whole disco to commit mass suicide?"

Ismael didn't answer her. The smell of her cigarette smoke made him crave a few drags of his own. He couldn't remember the last time he'd craved anything other than oblivion. Perhaps the prospect of venturing into the briarpatch again was revitalizing him. Even if his companion this time would be utterly clueless about his own origins and nature, and would view Ismael as a hated enemy besides. No road trip or walking tour or pilgrimage could be perfect, he knew. Once he told Darrin what he wanted to hear most, Darrin would go along with Ismael willingly. He might not know Darrin as well as Echo did—certainly not as *carnally*—but he understood how Darrin felt about Bridget, and that was the only tool he needed. Ismael was capable of far more complex psychological manipulations, but they were seldom necessary. Most people were simple.

"Ransack away," Ismael said. He didn't hold onto material things out of a desire for them—it was just easier to shove it all into a room. The people he helped, the ones he led successfully or unsuccessfully in their search for the light, left all sorts of things with him. They brought the detritus of their lives into his house during their last weeks of existence, and then gradually stopped needing them, and left everything piled on Ismael's floor. After tonight, Echo could have the whole place . . . though she'd probably just burn it down in a fit of pique at losing her chance to make Ismael pay. She had no idea he planned to disappear forever with Darrin tonight. He'd made promises to her. To Nicholas, too, for that matter, though the promises he'd made to Nicholas were ludicrous, and the man was too blind and hopeful to realize it. Nicholas and Echo would both be profoundly disappointed when Ismael vanished. The thought gave him some pleasure. They were vile people. He respected Darrin far more than either of them. At least Darrin knew what he wanted, and wanted something pure—a life with Bridget, in love. Darrin just had the misfortune to have something, to *be* something, that Ismael needed, which meant Ismael had to take away all the things Darrin loved. It was a sad arithmetic, but there was the light of a better world to consider. The touch of that light washed away all doubt and regret, Ismael knew, and he had long since reached the point where he would do anything to reside permanently in its splendour.

He sat in silence for a while, looking at the sky, thinking about the light.

"I'm bored. You're boring." Echo went back into the house, leaving her cigarette burning on the edge of the steps.

He was not sorry to see her go. He continued sitting. Some time passed, as it always did.

"Hey, Ismael, somebody's at your goddamned door," Echo yelled from inside, startling Ismael from his reverie. His reveries were becoming more frequent, and he feared they were approaching catatonia. Unconsciousness was pleasant, yes, but he dreamed of something better than simple coma, and besides, he knew no matter how deeply he slept someday he would wake up again, and be right back where he started. It was good to try a new approach. "The *door*," Echo yelled again. "I'm not your maid."

Perhaps Ismael should have contrived to sleep with Echo. He had many exotic STDs, and if anyone deserved to have her enthusiasm checked a bit, it was Echo. But using his weight of worldly misery as a weapon was distasteful—fundamentally, he wanted to *decrease* the amount of misery in the world. He had an aura of depression about him, true, something that tended to make people dour and reflective in his company, but that was nothing he could control, just the long-accumulated power of a particularly exothermic personality. He wasn't a bad person, just a tired one.

"I'll get it," Ismael said. It might be Nicholas. It might be someone more useless. He would go and see. No outcome would please him. Life was nothing but a million little disappointments punctuated by larger tragedies.

The knock at the door was tentative but constant, and Ismael kicked his way through the debris in the hallway—scattered clothes rejected by Echo, mostly, because she was a walking disaster—and opened the door.

The man on the steps was vaguely familiar, but almost everyone in the world was, after all. There were only so many types of bodies and faces, and Ismael had encountered nearly all of them during his years wandering the Earth. "I can't help you," Ismael said, because saying "May I help you?" only sowed false hope in solicitors and the religious.

"Ah," the man said. "You don't remember me. We met at a little café, it was only a couple of days ago . . ." He trailed off, cocking his head at Ismael, looking at him searchingly. This man was ordinary, but for a certain peculiar intensity that made his eyes shine.

"I meet many people," Ismael said, but he did recognize the man, now. One of his outreach cases, someone who was a near-perfect candidate for letting this world go—someone who didn't have to be convinced as Bridget had. With this man, it had seemed enough to let him step into Ismael's field of resignation and sorrow, and make a few reasonable suggestions. "Did you want something?"

"You told me . . . you told me if my life was so empty, I was better off killing myself."

"And yet you spurned my advice," Ismael said sadly. "I'm afraid I have no other wisdom to offer you." He began to close the door.

"Wait!" the man said, and Ismael paused a moment. "But I did take your advice. I tried, anyway, but I didn't manage to . . . to kill myself."

"I remember you," Ismael said at last. "I thought you manifested a tremendous lack of competence. Might I suggest, next time, leaping headfirst from a great height, perhaps one of the bridges that span the bay. That should prove sufficient to the task. Now, good day."

As Ismael began to close the door, the man said, "When I tried to kill myself, when I almost died, I saw light. It was the most beautiful thing I'd ever seen."

Ismael sighed, opened the door again, and said "I suppose you'd better come in." He stepped aside and gestured, allowing the man to pass. "What's your name?"

"Orville Troll," he said, and when he entered the foyer, he was trailed by faint shimmering apparitions, near-duplicates of his own form wrought in a sort of coloured smoke. Ismael cocked his head, frowning. He'd only seen that particular sort of phenomenon once before, after he'd taken Bridget to the strange hospital in the briarpatch, after she was mauled by the bear. Her new body was trailed for a few days by such ghostly shapes, invisible to all but Ismael. He hadn't mentioned them to her, in part because he liked having secrets, in part because she would want to know what they were, and he had no answer—possible bodies that *hadn't* been drawn up from the depths of potential? A sort of ghost of the old, abandoned body? He had no way of knowing. The briarpatch was more a place of mysteries than a land of revelations. The fact that this man, this Troll, had such a trail meant he was something more than he seemed. Had he been to the strange hospital too, and traded in an old shape for a new one? Or had he undergone some similar but variant experience?

"Since then I've been seeing things," the man said, and Ismael nodded. "Things like hallways, stairs, bridges that lead nowhere . . ."

"Come, sit." Ismael led him past the junk room, where Echo was still opening and closing drawers, but she didn't come out to socialize. He took Orville to the living room and indicated that he should sit on a heap of cushions. Ismael sank into his customary place. "There is a world beyond the world you know," Ismael said. "Your experience has opened your eyes to it. Most are unable to see that world without assistance from men such as myself, but you must be truly prepared to leave this world behind if you saw the light unassisted." It was that fact, that he'd already seen the light, that made Ismael decide to help Orville. A man that close to the better world deserved to be guided. "Most people require a great deal of meditation, ritual, preparation, the careful stripping-away of their egos. When we met, I sensed there was nothing in your life but hollows and darkness, and it seems I was correct. You are a very lucky man."

"That light. What is it?" He leaned forward, expression serious.

"I have every reason to believe it is heaven."

"Harps and halos?" Orville asked.

"Not that, nor a happy hunting ground, nor virgins and a walled garden, though the yearning for all such heavens throughout human history may be a debasement of the just and proper yearning for the light. It is a place where all care, pain, worry, and tension are washed away. To live in the light is to be forever ecstatic. In the better world, there is no disappointment. And you, Mr. Troll, are ready to reach that world. Your soul yearns for it, without reservation. You need only leave this body behind."

"I'll shoot his head off if he wants," Echo said, emerging from the bedroom. "Is that gun still in the backyard, Izzy?"

"Please leave us, Echo. I am trying to help this man."

She snorted. "So am I. You said he's ready to cast off his flesh and so forth, and I'd get a kick out of doing the damage. Everybody wins."

"I—I don't think I want—" Orville stammered.

Ismael waved his hand. "If someone murders you, there will be fear, there will be a clinging to life; it doesn't work. Even if you give consent, the actions of another upon you can make things more difficult. No, it is best if you take your own life. I recommend leaping from a high bridge, headfirst, because that is one of the most certain ways to kill oneself, more sure than drugs, which the body can reject, more sure than bullets, which can graze or ricochet, more sure than strangulation, which can fail. Please leave us, Echo."

"Whatever." She walked off.

Orville nodded. "Headfirst. That makes sense." He looked up at Ismael. "So if I jump from a bridge, I'll go to this other world, this better world you're talking about? For sure?"

"Nothing is sure," Ismael said, thinking of Bridget, and the absence of light beneath her when she fell. "But I believe you will pass through, yes."

"Why don't you tell him what happens if he fails," Bridget said, stepping from a nowhere-space in a corner into the centre of the room. This house was at a nexus of branching corridors leading to various parts of the briarpatch, a sort of magical crossroads, quite convenient for Ismael's comings and goings—but it did have the potential for the occasional adept and traveller to come wandering in. He hadn't expected to see *Bridget*, though.

Ismael gazed at her, and felt something he had not felt in a very long time: the cold weight of fear in his gut. But he would not reveal that fear to this ghost of the woman he'd once tried to help. "Hello, Bridget. I'm sorry you couldn't reach the light."

"You're *sorry*? You son of a bitch. I wondered if you'd be able to see me."

Ismael shrugged. "Anyone who can see the pathways in the briarpatch can also see things like you." He paused. "Alas, such people are few, so it will not expand your social circle much." He nodded to Orville. "Now, to answer you more fully: If you were to undergo certain preparations which I generally advise, you could loosen your spirit from your body. If you followed this path, and leapt from a bridge in hopes of finding a land of peace and wonders beyond this one, your last act before hitting the water would be to let your spirit leave your body, so that it might pass into the light of a better world. But if you had not properly released all the hungers, needs, and desires of this world, your spirit would be unable to make the transition. *Your* spirit, Orville, is already unburdened, and would pass to the better world naturally, without all that tiresome study and preparation. But if, for some reason, you failed . . ." Now he turned his eyes to Bridget, still in the shape of a body, the poor girl, still in the ghost of the *clothes* she'd died in, how sad. He went on. "In that case, your soul might be trapped between worlds, lost, angry, hopeless, and worthy of pity. Inhabiting the memory of a body, walking around in a trite human shape, a poor imitation of life—"

Bridget slapped him. Ismael let her. Being touched by a dead woman's hand was peculiar, but not really painful. Her hand moved, and there was pressure, but the impact was minimal. The dead could do more dangerous things—wield knives clumsily, or throw crockery, that was always a favourite—but their attacks were generally easy to avoid if they didn't catch you unawares. They were clumsy because they didn't really have bodies, just the persistent memories of bodies. Orville—who was somehow bound to Bridget, it seemed; ghosts sometimes got entangled that way—stared at them with wide eyes.

"I'm sorry, Bridget," Ismael said. "I truly thought you were ready. You were serious, and fearless in the briarpatch, and always striving for what came next, but I failed you. I should have held you back. You did not divest yourself of all your worldly wants and wishes, loves and hates. I should have realized, but you convinced me you were prepared. I'm sure you even convinced yourself. But you were not ready."

"You're saying this is my fault?" Bridget clenched her non-existent fists.

Ismael shook his head. "Quite the opposite. I should have been a better teacher."

Bridget seemed at a loss, as if she'd expected resistance, or defiance, or some other strong response. He'd thought she knew him better than that.

"If you're so sorry, you can fix this," Bridget said.

"Of course," Ismael said. "I can take you where you need to go right away." He didn't have much time before he needed to deal with Darrin, but the place Bridget should go was on the way. Harczos had shown him the path long ago, and though it was worthless to Ismael, he still remembered how to get there.

Bridget frowned, that pretty line appearing in her forehead. "What's the deal, Ismael? You can show me the way to the light now that I've permanently departed my body?"

Ismael understood. "Oh, Bridget, no. You cannot reach the light. I can only show you the passage to the land of the dead, the place where only ghosts can go. I have never seen the other side, but I trust there is some peace or oblivion there, if not the utter pleasure of living forever in the light."

"Fuck that," Bridget said. "I'm not giving up that easily. I want to get to the better world you promised me, Ismael. There has to be a way."

"It is impossible," Ismael said. "I can show you the passage to the land of the dead, but that is all. If you refuse, I must ask you to leave."

"I'm not going anywhere."

"Hmm," Ismael said, glancing at Orville. "You, Troll—she haunts you? Her spirit is somehow tangled with yours?"

"Ah, I guess so," Orville said, and Bridget shushed him.

"I see," Ismael said. "I give you one last chance, Bridget—you can go to your resting place, or you can leave me forever, but those are the only options."

She stepped closer to him. "Tell me what's going on with you and Nicholas. Tell me what Darrin has to do with all this. You're going to give me answers, Ismael."

That cold fear returned. What did she know? Not much, apparently, or she wouldn't be asking. But how did she know *anything*?

Of course. She was a spirit. Tethered to this Troll, but still able to move invisibly and listen. She might have been watching Darrin or Nicholas or Echo all day yesterday, since her unfortunate death.

Troubling, but no cause for fear. He still had the power here. "Echo!"

"Yeah, babe?" she shouted.

"Would you still like to kill Mr. Troll?"

"No!" Bridget shouted.

Orville stood and said "We'd better go, Bridget."

"You can't do this, Ismael," Bridget said. "You failed me, and now you threaten my friend?"

"I offered you all the help I could," Ismael said, not without sadness. "But I don't have time for your drama or complications. You're a ghost, and I think you're haunting this man, which means his immediate death might jostle you loose from this world, or at least restrict your mobility." He stepped closer to her, and said, "Also, you're bothering me."

"Sorry." Echo came into the living room, cradling the chrome-plated shotgun in her arms. "Would've come sooner, but I was on the phone. Nicky called from his hiding place in the bushes, and the birdy has flown the coop, the fish has taken the bait, whatever you want to call it, the house is empty, so we can get over there and set things up." She glanced at Orville. "You want me to shoot him in here, or should we take him to the laundry room or something where the spatter won't get on the pillows?"

"Back off, bitch," Bridget spat, getting up in Echo's face, but Echo failed to notice she couldn't see Bridget. Echo was not as sensitive as Ismael was, could not even enter the briarpatch without his help, despite several excursions which should have opened her eyes. Echo was firmly and happily part of this world, and her preference for living in a perpetual now of entertainment and sensation made her unsuitable for solo otherworldly excursions.

"She can't see you, Bridget," Ismael said.

Echo perked up. "Bridget? The dead girl Darrin used to fuck? She's here?" She looked around. "What, like her ghost or something?"

"Essentially," Ismael said. "Anyway, you can shoot Orville here, we've got plenty of extra pillows."

Orville dove sideways, probably just leaping instinctively away, but he managed to pass into one of the cross-corridors of the briarpatch that converged in the room. Bridget gave a whimper, as if suddenly in pain, and then leapt after him.

"No fair!" Echo shouted.

Ismael nodded. He could pursue them, try to put Orville down, but he couldn't quite muster the enthusiasm. Wandering in the briarpatch with only Bridget as his guide would very likely prove to be fatal for Orville anyway. "I guess Mr. Troll wasn't so eager to die after all," Ismael said. "Perhaps Bridget has given him something to live for."

Echo growled. "Are we going idiot hunting?"

"No. If Darrin is out of his house, we should join Nicholas and prepare. If we run into Orville again, however, you needn't hesitate to kill him. You're sure Darrin will be gone for some time?"

"Sure as I can be."

"We'll go through the briarpatch to meet Nicholas. It will be faster. Lock the front door. I'll get the back."

They met in the living room. Ismael took Echo's hand—she couldn't even glimpse the briarpatch without his help, much less enter it. Fortunately, once inside, he didn't have to keep holding her hand—touching Echo was like holding a sleeping rattlesnake. The sense of imminent danger was constant. She couldn't find her way *out* of the briarpatch without help either, and if she ever became too problematic, he might strand her there, though that was dangerous, too. Long exposure to the briarpatch could change people, as anyone who encountered one of the bears knew. He didn't like the idea of encountering a wandering, half-mad Echo in the briarpatch at some future date.

They stepped through space, into a dank, dripping stone hallway, which would lead them by and by to Darrin's neighbourhood, and from there to the next phase of Ismael's search for a world of beautiful light.

3

"I'm sorry I ran away," Orville said. He sat with his back against a smooth black boulder, the only feature on an otherwise perfectly level salt flat that stretched as far as he could see in all directions. The sky was a sort of perpetual dusk, but even without direct sunlight, the whiteness all around was almost too bright to look upon. When he'd fled headlong into the briarpatch, this was where he'd ended up, in the lee of a black rock. "That woman was going to shoot me."

"No, you did the right thing." Bridget lay sprawled on her back, her coat appearing redder than ever against the white, like something freshly killed. "I don't know who that woman is, but she didn't look like the type to shy away from killing."

"Ismael was . . . different than I expected. He seemed almost sad for you, until he tried to have me killed."

"I think he *was* sad for me, but he didn't want to help me. I'm the past to him. He considers me a failure, and now he's moved on. But I can't move on."

"What do you think he meant, about the land of the dead?"

"Don't know. Probably a landfill for ghosts, some little pocket hell for uneasy spirits. Doesn't sound like a place I'd want to visit. I've stood in the reflected radiance of the light of a better world, and I'm not going anywhere but there."

"Okay. But . . . what do we do now?"

"They're planning to do something to Darrin. I don't know what, or why, but I intend to find out. We should go over to his house, I think. So we can warn him. Or so you can, since I have no idea if he'll be able to see me or not."

Orville nodded. "What Ismael said, about how you hadn't let go of the real world sufficiently to enter the better world . . . do you think that's true?"

"I never know what to think about what Ismael says. He doesn't always lie, but he doesn't always tell the truth, either. I guess it's possible, sure. I thought I'd let everything go, turned my back on my old life, but maybe I'm not as good at letting go as I thought. Anyway, I'll find another way. We'll find another way. We'll make it to the light."

Orville wondered, if he killed himself, would he still see the light? Or had this past day and a half spent with Bridget changed him, made him more attached to this world? Certainly smell and taste and sex were still new pleasures that overwhelmed him with delight. And there was more, too. He wanted to help Bridget. He felt needed. That was new, and Ismael would probably consider it a terrible chain, binding him to the world. But Orville was happy for the connection.

"Let's get out of here," she said, sitting up. "Darrin needs our help."

Orville considered saying no. This wasn't his fight, and he was already so fond of Bridget that he didn't relish the thought of going to see her ex-boyfriend, especially with shotgun-wielding maniacs in the equation. But he wouldn't even *have* this life without her, so he owed her—and she could probably make his life unpleasant if he didn't do as she asked. Being followed at all times of the day and night by a furious woman no one else could see or hear would be miserable.

And if he helped her, she might be grateful.

4

Darrin stood outside the house. It was one of the many rundown residences in the area, white paint peeling, roof shingles askew, grass half-dead, overgrown. Ismael Plenty didn't strike Darrin as the type to care much about lawn maintenance, so maybe this was his place. There was no name on the mailbox, and when Darrin opened it, there were no envelopes inside, either, so he couldn't be sure this was the right place. Nothing for it but to knock on the door, and if Ismael answered . . . he would improvise.

Darrin banged on the door a few times, to no avail. Either nobody was home, or nobody was answering. He touched the doorknob, hesitant, then gave it a turn. To his surprise, the door opened. This wasn't a neighbourhood where people generally left their doors unlocked. Darrin paused on the threshold, called "Hello?" a few times, then sighed and stepped inside. He'd come this far.

The dim foyer smelled of dust and old sweat. Dozens of coats hung on the hooks inside the door, and dozens of shoes lay piled on the floor. He went through the living room, where cushions lay scattered all around a big hookah. Darrin went down a hallway strewn with old clothes. Pushing open a creaking door, he entered a room lined with dressers and sea-chests, all filled with more clothes, in a variety of sizes and styles from the past few decades—it was like a thrift-store graveyard. Eyes watering from the dust, he started snooping.

Darrin tried to do a reasonably meticulous search to uncover some evidence of the nature of Ismael's relationship with Bridget. Letters, pictures, a date planner, anything at all would have helped, but it was dispiriting work. Every drawer seemed stuffed with jangling tangles of junk, from paperclips to strings of fake pearls. He pulled down dusty shoeboxes from closet shelves only to find them full of ancient parking citations and the presumably losing tickets from long-ago horse races. The chests mostly held mothballs and clothing so old it was neither fashionable nor unfashionable, just dusty and threadbare. He spent fifteen minutes poking around, finding nothing of interest, before deciding he had to move on—he couldn't spend forever searching.

He moved on to the master bedroom. The bed was an impressive four-poster, but swaybacked, sagging in the middle. A desk, heaped with papers, stood against one wall, and Darrin picked through the contents. Old bills, letters in French, and faded postcards. He pulled out the drawers, rifling through the old paperclips and dried-up inkwells. He was about to give it up as another room full of useless detritus—but then he found a drawer full of photos. These weren't yellowed photos from some long-forgotten family's album—they weren't even actually photographs at all—but printouts of digital pictures, printed in black-and-white on low-quality paper.

They were photos of Darrin and Bridget, taken last year. Darrin even remembered the day, a picnic by the lake, but there had been no one there taking pictures—at least, no one they'd seen. Darrin's face was circled in red, and written on the back, rather cryptically, the words "Another brother?" Darrin dug through the desk further, but didn't find anything else about himself. Why did Ismael have photos of him? Could there be more to this than just seducing Bridget away and brainwashing her?

The invasion of privacy implied by these photos—the *stalkerness* of it—was profoundly unsettling. Darrin had often felt, in recent months, as if events were conspiring against him, but maybe it was more than that. Maybe a *person* was conspiring against him. The numbness he'd felt after seeing Bridget die was increasingly replaced by confusion and anger, hot feelings superseding the cold, and he wondered, if he got angry enough, would he be able to avoid feeling grief entirely? He'd always coped with his problems by throwing himself into some project or hobby⊠from urban exploring to geocaching⊠maybe he could turn some of that capacity for obsession to a useful task: finding out what the hell was going on here. Who was Ismael Plenty? What did he have to do with Bridget's death?

And the question that photo brought up: what did he want with Darrin?

He considered waiting around for Ismael to show up, but after a few minutes of pacing in the man's filthy bedroom, he became uncomfortable. What if Ismael found him here? He'd be perfectly within his rights to call the police, or even to *shoot* Darrin. So what if the front door had been unlocked? It was still breaking and entering. Better to sit on Ismael's front steps and wait there. He went back to the living room, and stepped on something half-hidden by the cushions. He slipped and almost fell, then caught sight of the gleaming shotgun on the floor. He bent down to look at it and reached out, almost touching it before coming to his senses—he didn't want to leave his fingerprints on some stranger's weapon. What kind of nutcase left a gun on the floor in a room where they also did drugs?

A cross-breeze ruffled his hair, and Darrin looked up, heart thudding, sure the front door had opened—where else could the breeze have come from in this claustrophobic place?

But the front door wasn't open. Instead, he saw corridors all around him, five tunnels branching off from this room, passages that had been invisible—or, at least, unnoticed—a moment before. They must be paths into the place Arturo called the briarpatch, which meant—what? That Ismael had something to do with that place too?

Darrin was out of his depth here. He was no detective. He didn't even like mystery novels. He had a good mind for systems—chess, coding, music, cooking—but he faltered when it came to matters of art and intuition, which was why so many of his photographs were technically proficient but lacked that indefinable aspect that made light and shapes into art.

So . . . was the briarpatch a system, or an art? Could it be deciphered, or must it be interpreted?

He took a step toward the nearest corridor, and his perspective shifted—he was looking down, as if from a great height, onto a salt-white plain, marred by a speck of black and speck of red. There was no sense of scale, so he couldn't tell if the black and red were bits of blood and pepper on a tablecloth, or mountains on a salt flat. The vertigo of standing upright and looking down was too much, so he retreated to the centre of the living room again. Those passageways had an allure, but he remembered the beast from the bone pit, and his curiosity was dampened.

He'd come here to find evidence of Ismael's complicity in Bridget's death, and had instead found intimations of something more vast. Darrin had never been one to rush into things without sufficient information—he was a researcher, a devotee, a student by nature. He preferred to be prepared, and now he needed guidance. When he got home, he'd look for Arturo, and ask for his help. If he encountered Ismael now, what would he say, what would he do?

Darrin eased past the twisting passageways, toward the front door, and out into the brightness of the ordinary world.

NICHOLAS GETS CAUGHT WITH HIS PANTS DOWN

1

"Oh, fuck me *sideways*." Ismael stopped dead on the sidewalk and leaned heavily against the stucco wall of an apartment building.

"What are you on about?" Echo said, frowning. Ismael was usually placid, infuriatingly so, but now he was almost shivering. They were less than a block from Darrin's house, and Nicholas was already there, waiting for them.

Ismael extended his arm and pointed at a car parked by the curb. It was an off-white, battered four-door giant of a sedan with curiously bulging tail lights, and Echo had a vague recollection of seeing it around here before. Somebody had probably abandoned it.

"What about it?" she asked, walking toward it. She reached out and touched the trunk, and Ismael sucked in a breath suddenly, as if he'd just watched her plunge her hand into fire. She looked at him curiously, wondering if his face was paler than usual or if it was just a trick of the light.

"Wendigo." She frowned at the name on the trunk. She'd been stealing cars since she got her learner's permit, and she'd never heard of a Wendigo, but then, she never bothered to steal anything this old. She walked around the side and looked in the window, and saw the back seat was filled completely with papers. The passenger seat up front was filled with papers that spilled over into the driver's side. She jiggled the door handle, but it was locked.

"Don't touch it," Ismael said, hoarsely, as if just finding his voice. "I know you don't have a death wish, Echo, so get away from that thing."

"Thing? It's called a car, Ismael." She rejoined him on the sidewalk. "They invented 'em about a hundred years ago. Detroit rolling iron, and it'd be a real bitch to parallel park, but I bet it's a smooth ride, assuming the suspension isn't shot."

"That is not a car," Ismael said. "At least, that's not *all* it is. It's a fucking *apport*. The biggest one I've ever seen. So big it makes my head ache." He levered himself off the wall and stood upright, but only to take a step away from the Wendigo. "That car is from some other Detroit, where ghouls work the night shift in the auto plants and there are alien graveyards on the *moon*."

"Oh yeah?" Echo said, somewhat interested. "So it's briarpatch shit, is what you're saying? A really *unlikely* car? If it bothers you so much, we can set it on fire. Smash a window, spray some accelerant on all those papers in the back, and light a match. Whoosh. No more scary car."

"Echo, I don't even think it would burn." Ismael backed up farther, then started across the street toward the opposite sidewalk.

Echo sighed and followed. "It's not going to bite you, Ismael."

He paused for a moment, clearly still uncomfortable, even with the width of the street between himself and the Wendigo. "You actually have no idea whether or not that is true," he said, then continued up the street, hurrying as she'd never seen him hurry. Not quite running—he didn't strike her as much of a runner— but coming awfully close. She glanced back at the Wendigo. From the front, it looked stranger, with pop-eyed headlights and a great chrome grille that seemed caught halfway between a smile and a snarl.

Echo grinned back at it.

"All right," Ismael said a minute later. He glanced back down the block. "We're out of that car . . . that *Wendigo's* sightlines, assuming it can see. This will do."

"What will do?" Echo asked. They were almost directly across from Darrin's house, near the walled courtyard of a small apartment complex.

Ismael took her hand and pointed. With him touching her, she could see the briarpatch, and there was an entry point here, a set of steep, narrow stairs leading down to a bush-lined path. She grunted. "There's blood on the steps." A splash of red marked the concrete halfway down.

"Does that bother you? I was under the impression you rather liked blood."

He let go of her hand, and the steps vanished from sight. That irked Echo, as always. Ismael said that most people, once shown the briarpatch, could see it by themselves forever after, or at the very least catch glimpses. It was an effort for them *not* to see the secret corridors into the liminal world, he said. But no matter how many times Ismael showed her that world, or how many times she ventured into it even, it was closed to her without help. Ismael said it was because she was too much a creature of the physical, the present, the here-and-now—too much a woman of flesh and appetites. Echo didn't disagree with that assessment, but it pissed her off that things she considered her signal virtues kept her from exploring that other world on her own. When Echo was pissed off, she tried to hurt the things that pissed her off, but in this case, that meant somehow hurting the fundamental substructure of the world, and she wasn't sure yet how to go about that. She was confident that she'd figure it out eventually though. "So you'll hide on the steps, then, and wait for Darrin?"

"That is the plan. Just make sure he has good reason to flee."

"Oh, he'll run off. Believe me. He loves Nicholas like a brother, and he'll be more sad than pissed off, I bet. I doubt it's going to turn into a crime of passion in there. But what if he, you know, sees you on the steps? He can see into the other world and all that shit, right?"

"It's possible," Ismael admitted. "But the stairs are steep, and I'm good at being inconspicuous."

"Whatever," Echo said. "I don't see why all this emotional trauma is necessary, if he can already see the briarpatch."

"I need him to be broken," Ismael said simply, "so that I can convince him only I can put him back together again. He must have nothing left holding him to this world, so that nothing will prevent him from entering another for as long as it takes."

"Ah," Echo said. "Okay. I think you just like fucking with people's heads. That's all right. I can respect that. So after you talk to Darrin, assuming he doesn't bash your brains out on the curb because of what happened with Bridget, we'll meet you later on, back at your house?"

"Yes. I'll determine whether or not Darrin needs another . . . jolt to his system, to fully loosen his ties to this world."

"Cool," Echo said. "Because, like I said, you owe me big time for this, and I mean to collect."

"I can't wait. Now, go. Don't keep Nicholas waiting."

Echo sniffed. Ismael vanished from sight, stepping down onto a stairway she couldn't see. She really needed to do something about her inability to navigate the briarpatch, but if it meant cultivating a Zen-like detachment from, or even a burning hatred for, this world, it probably wasn't worth it.

She went to Darrin's door and let herself in.

2

"How's this?" Echo emerged from the bathroom dressed in an outfit that consisted of little more than black leather straps held in place with metal o-rings, a narrow leather collar around her throat, and a metal leash dangling down her front. She wore knee-high black boots with spike heels. She'd stolen the boots from a stripper she knew, and they fit perfectly, because Echo was lucky like that.

Nicholas stared at her. "Whoa. Wow. That's . . . wow." He was sitting on the low couch by the front windows in the living room, keeping a lookout for Darrin's return, but now he was staring at her, of course. Echo said, "I thought wearing something elaborate was best. I don't want Darrin thinking this was some temporary indiscretion, some momentary lapse of judgment. It has to look *planned*, you know? Like we've been getting together for a while, probably. Nothing says premeditation like a leather harness." She'd also made a point of refusing to be even a little bit kinky with Darrin, though he liked a little spanking and scarves-on-the-headboard light bondage, as so many men did. She'd demurred, saying such things turned her off, and they'd had a straightforward if vigorous sex life instead. Seeing Nicholas get what he wasn't permitted would make Darrin feel even more betrayed, she reasoned.

"That makes sense," Nicholas said, staring at her breasts. That was okay. That's what she wanted him to do. "Uh, does Darrin have condoms? I didn't bring any."

Gotcha, she thought. Echo crossed her arms. "Excuse me? What do you need a condom for?"

Nicholas looked away. "Shit, don't get all offended, it's not like I think you're diseased or something, I just take precautions, hell, you don't know where *I've* been—"

"You misunderstand, Nicky. You don't need a condom because you're not putting your dick in me. Please. You're such an idiot."

He scowled. "What are you talking about? That's the whole reason we're here, so Darrin can catch us fucking and feel betrayed or whatever it is Ismael wants. You even *said* we'd be screwing—"

Echo sat in the armchair across the room and crossed her legs almost demurely. She twirled the end of the leash around her finger. "Have you never seen a movie, Nicholas? I don't mean a porno, but just a regular movie, with a sex scene? You think the actors are really fucking each other? When Darrin comes in and sees me dressed like this, on my knees, with you sitting on the couch with your pants down, and this leash in your fist, he's not going to come over and make sure I've actually got your dick in my mouth. When I look over at him, and lick my lips, and wipe my mouth with the back of my hand, and say, 'Hi, hon, I didn't think you'd be home so early,' he's going to feel plenty betrayed. I don't need to let any part of you touch any part of me. I've never had a taste for aging frat boys, Nicky."

Nicholas threw up his hands. "Whatever, shit, it's not like I'm dying to tap Darrin and Ismael's sloppy seconds."

"Some days, I fuck them both in one afternoon," Echo said, though it wasn't true. "But not you."

He turned around, rather violently, and looked out the window again, watching the front walk. Echo grinned, pleased with herself. If Nicholas had suggested they just pretend to fuck, or expressed discomfort at the idea of actually sleeping with her, she would have insisted they do the deed, to make sure it was as realistic as possible, etc. Nicholas was so easy. She could jerk him around in any direction she wanted.

Echo didn't figure Darrin would be along too soon, not with Ismael's whole house to ransack, so she went into the kitchen, got a glass, and opened a bottle of red wine. She read the note Darrin had left on the counter and nodded. Better and better. Now she could plausibly say she hadn't expected him home so early. Beautiful.

She stood sipping by the sink, looking out the window into the neighbour's back yard. The Cambodian man who lived there was working in his garden, and when he glanced in her direction, Echo waved merrily. He didn't react, just went back to work, and Echo pouted. There was probably a glare from the sun on the window, hiding her from view. Too bad.

Echo leaned back against the counter and wondered if she should get something to eat. She tugged at the leather strap running up through the middle of her ass like the world's most uncomfortable thong. She did kinky stuff, sometimes, for fun, but she was pretty much always the dominant party. She much preferred making other people uncomfortable to being uncomfortable herself. Seeing her in the submissive role would hurt Darrin more, though, she figured. It was too bad. She liked the guy okay—he didn't seem to want anything from her, and he went along with her so easily she almost never felt the need to needle him.

She was on her fourth glass of wine, and feeling good, when Nicholas called out, "He's coming!"

"You won't be," she muttered, put the glass down, and headed into the living room.

Nicholas was tugging his pants down, revealing a nice-enough looking dick, semi-erect, bigger than Darrin's. Why did the assholes so often have nice cocks? "He's just coming down the block, he'll be here in a couple of minutes."

"So sit yourself down." Echo put her hand against his chest and gave him a little push to make him sit on the couch, his pants and underwear still pooled around his ankles. She took a pillow from the couch and knelt on it between his legs. His erection grew, and she smiled—it was so easy, but Echo took satisfaction in the easy things, too. She handed him the end of the leash, and Nicholas tugged it, experimentally, but a bit hard. "Don't get any ideas," she said. "Try to put that thing in my mouth, and you'll lose as much of it as I can bite off." The erection wilted a bit at that, and Echo laughed.

"Fuck you," Nicholas muttered. "Let's just get this over with."

Echo exhaled gently over his cock, not touching it, and when Nicholas cursed her, she giggled. The leather outfit was better when she knelt. It pulled tight through her crotch, but in a good way. Nicholas didn't turn her on particularly, but the idea of playing a scene like this did, and she wiggled a little against the harness, letting the leather rub her right.

They stayed like that for a minute, waiting for the door to open, and for Darrin to come up the stairs.

3

Darrin walked along the sidewalk, with the persistent sense of another world so close to this one: sometimes shimmering at the edges of his vision, and other times so natural he couldn't tell the entry points to the briarpatch from ordinary streets. He needed answers, and hoped Arturo could provide them. But if he couldn't, Darrin would still confront Ismael. He would go back tomorrow, with a backpack and some food and water, and simply wait on the front steps all day if Ismael wasn't there when Darrin arrived. His life had been upended in the past six months, almost everything he had known and trusted torn away from him, and he believed Ismael was at the root of it.

Walking with his head down, Darrin almost passed his own front steps. Sighing, trying to bring himself back into the present, he walked briskly up the steps, checked the mailbox—just bills, which he didn't want to deal with now, so he left them in the box—and to the door. He put his key in, but the door was unlocked, which meant Echo was here, probably. He did *not* want to deal with Echo just now. If he tried to talk to her about these things, she would think he was crazy, maybe rightly so.

"Echo?" he called, trying to sound happy about her presence. Maybe she could take his mind off things for a while. She was good at that.

He came up the stairs, and into the living room, and saw his girlfriend on her knees, giving his best friend a blowjob.

The feeling was like being hit in the back of the head with a brick, and simultaneously kicked in the stomach. He wanted to fold up on himself, but he stood unmoving in the doorway instead. Nicholas leapt from the couch, trying to untangle his legs from his pants, eyes wide, face horrified. Echo, in contrast, simply leaned back, turned half-around, and gave him an annoyed look. She was dressed in the sort of outfit Darrin usually only saw on certain websites, the kind of outfit he would have sworn she would never wear.

"Shit, Darrin, it's not what you think, she, she seduced me—"

"Oh, shut up." Echo turned her look of annoyance on Nicholas. "Maybe the first time I seduced you, but this time *you* called *me*." She turned back to Darrin and gave him a look of pity. "I didn't expect you home so soon, hon. I'm sorry you had to see this. I didn't want you to find out this way."

Nicholas pulled up his pants, trying to get his belt buckled. He looked sweaty and miserable and Darrin almost felt sorry for him, somewhere down deep below the ice in his belly. "Get out," he said. "Both of you, get out."

Nicholas and Echo exchanged glances, and then Echo laughed. "Sorry, no dice, try again, Darrin. I know for a fact you had to borrow money from Nicholas to pay your rent for the past two months, and *I* paid your last fucking power bill. People who depend on the kindness of strangers shouldn't be so high and mighty. So how about *you* leave instead? We're not finished yet."

Darrin wanted to hit Nicholas, who was just looking at him stupidly now, not speaking. He wanted to curse at Echo, who was staring at him with open contempt. But he was just too tired, too withered inside, too beaten-up. *It's too much*, he thought. Losing Bridget, losing his job, seeing Bridget die, fearing for his sanity, and now *this*, his oldest friend sleeping with a woman he'd started to trust, the two people closest to him having an affair right under his nose, and now reminding him of all his insufficiencies as a man.

"Beat it, Darrin." Echo made a shooing-away gesture. "Come back in a couple of hours. You can have the place once Nicholas is done with me. I'll let you have a turn then, if you're good."

"I never want to see you again," he said, and then looked at Nicholas. "Or you."

"Darrin," Nicholas said. "Please, I didn't mean . . ." He looked genuinely anguished, but there were no more words forthcoming, just a mute gesture of helplessness.

"So you never want to see us again. So we'll fucking *blindfold* you when you get back," Echo said. "Just get lost for a while. Maybe go out and look for a *job* for a change, how'd that be?"

Darrin turned and went down the stairs, half running, half falling, tears starting to well up in his eyes, rage and sadness all mixed together. He'd come back, all right, he'd change the locks on his doors, he'd have them arrested for trespassing, it was still his name on the lease, the cops wouldn't care if Nicholas had helped him with the rent. Shit, there was nothing holding him here anymore, he wouldn't renew his lease next month, he'd get his security deposit back and he'd take off, fuck Ismael, fuck finding out what happened to Bridget, fuck *all* of it, he'd just get *away*, anything was better than this, anywhere, just *away*—

Someone shouted his name. Echo, probably. To hell with her. He sped up.

When Darrin rushed across the street, Ismael Plenty was there, stepping from a patch of nowhere, opening his mouth to say something, but Darrin didn't wait for him to speak, just launched himself at the man, letting all his rage and desperation out in a single shout, reaching for Ismael, intending to shake either answers or the life out of him.

Ismael sidestepped neatly as Darrin passed by, unable to halt his own movement.

A steep stairway appeared before Darrin's eyes—though really it was more like it had always been there, and he'd just *noticed* it now. Darrin nearly fell down the stairs, grabbing onto the iron handrail at the last moment to arrest his fall. Darrin turned around, eyes wide, gasping, and Ismael stood at the head of the stairs, looking down on him. "Darrin. You don't want to hurt me. If you do, you'll never see Bridget again. And you *do* want to see her again, don't you?"

Darrin stared at him, swallowed hard, and said, "Yes, you son of a bitch. Yes, I want to see her again."

BRIARPATCH

"I'll take you to her," Ismael said simply. "Come along." He went down the stairs and into the briarpatch. After a moment, Darrin followed, because he couldn't think of any reason to refuse.

TWO
INTO THE BRIARPATCH

ARTURO GETS CARJACKED

1

Orville crouched by the edge of the rooftop, looking down at the lake below. "This is really the quickest way? I mean, the house is only about a mile from here, we could just walk."

"The more you travel in the briarpatch, the easier it gets," Bridget said. "The more connections you can make out. I think you can get from anywhere to anywhere if you just know the right route. Though not everyone can go everywhere, or see the same passageways. Ismael says the briarpatch is a subjective place." She stood on the edge of the high apartment building, with its view of Lake Merritt. Orville supposed that, being dead, she didn't fear falling. He was not so comfortable. Being this high up reminded him of his jump from the Golden Gate Bridge. He could still remember the sense of enormous, lurking pain beneath the fog of morphine in the hospital, before Bridget found him a new body. And now she was telling him they *had* to jump. He supposed there was no choice, really. The doorway on the roof was locked, so they couldn't go down the building's stairs. The route they'd taken through the briarpatch to get here— along a mouldy hallway with a low ceiling of roots—was apparently a one-way street, because he couldn't see the way back, either. The only exit in sight was hovering just a foot or so away from the edge of the roof, and perhaps eighteen inches below the roofline. It was a sort of shimmering blue oval, and Bridget assured him she'd been that way before.

"I used to take this shortcut from Ismael's house to my—to Darrin's apartment all the time. Just go for it, Orville. You trust me, don't you?"

Orville nodded mutely. He took a breath, stood up, and looked at the shimmering oval. He'd never had the greatest hand-eye coordination, and could easily see himself tripping on the roof's edge, tumbling like a rag doll to land on the edge of the lake with a splat. But this new body seemed smarter—or at least more used to being used—than his old one had been. He bent his legs, tensed, and jumped out.

This new body really was stronger than his old one, and he nearly overshot his mark, and came within a handsbreadth of sailing above the entry to the briarpatch. Bridget cried out, a wordless sound of anguish, and Orville put his legs together, trying to make himself into an arrow that would fall straight down. The blue shimmered beneath him—not as inviting as the light he'd glimpsed on his fall from the Golden Gate Bridge, but still pretty, the rich blue he'd seen in pictures of tropical waters.

His fall ended abruptly when he landed in an enormous heap of straw. Orville laughed aloud, staring up at a late afternoon sky the same blue as the shimmering portal, with a huge full moon—not, he was sure, the moon he was used to, though he couldn't have said exactly how it differed—hanging above his head. The air smelled wonderful, and Orville took great deep gulps. "God, what is that, those smells?" Having his sense of smell was like learning the world all over again, and he'd been making Bridget identify odours all morning.

Bridget, who'd landed beside him, or tagged along, or transitioned in whatever bodiless way she had, spoke from some other part of the haystack. "Apples. Fresh-mown hay. Just a whiff of distant fires. I haven't explored this place much, because the exit to my old neighbourhood is so nearby, but it's always autumn here. A good thing, too, or otherwise this heap of straw might be gone one of these times, and we wouldn't have that nice soft landing. I think time works differently in this place. I don't think the moon has moved more than a few degrees across the sky in all the times I've come this way."

Orville struggled to sit up, which, in the mass of straw, was a bit like trying to do jumping jacks in quicksand. He finally got his head high enough to look around, and saw a vast field, dotted with heaps of straw, and in the far distance, against a backdrop of brown hills, a lodge of timbers and sod that looked too gigantic to be real. The straw pile he rested in seemed impossibly high—not quite as high as the building he'd jumped from, but a close contender. He sat back before vertigo could make him sick. "How do we get down from here, Bridget?"

"Well—" Bridget began, and then there was a sound, a slow creak from the direction of the timbered lodge. Orville struggled to his knees again, the straw shifting beneath him, and looked out across the field. One whole wall of the lodge was slowly, ponderously swinging open, and he realized the wall was merely a door, built into the side of one of the brown hills. And now, with incredible slowness, that door was opening, and if they waited long enough, they would see the denizens of this autumn land begin gradually to emerge.

Orville wondered if they would be horrible, or wonderful, or merely strange. But he didn't really want to find out.

"We dig down," Bridget said, and there was fear in her voice. If the dead woman was afraid, that was motivation enough for Orville. "Just dig down into the haystack, Orville, make a hole and *wiggle*."

Orville did so, diving in, pulling handfuls of straw aside and burrowing down, letting gravity help as much as possible. He heard small squeaks and felt mice scurrying away from his touch, but that didn't make any sense, if the larger creatures of this world and the moon moved so slowly, shouldn't the small creatures, too? Bridget was descending near him, and once he was deep in the dark, itchy depths of the haystack, he actually ran into her, and the contact was like bumping into a tiny windstorm.

"Here," Bridget said, "hollow out a cavity," and Orville threw his weight around, pushing back the walls of straw. It was totally black, and then there was another creak—like the ongoing creak of the door in the hill opening, but quieter, and more brief—and light came in.

"Shit, my hands, I can't get a grip, I *hate* this. . . ." Bridget pointed to a wooden trap door. "Can you open that?"

Orville did—it wasn't that heavy—and light spilled up from the passageway it revealed.

A peal of thunder shook the air. Bridget stared at him, eyes wide in the light coming up from the trapdoor. "I think that was the sound of the big door hitting the hill when it opened all the way. Let's go." Orville dropped down into the opening, and reality did one of its disorienting, vertiginous flips—he'd fallen down, but now he was standing in a passageway, and the trapdoor was in the wall behind him, not in the roof, like it should have been. He leaned against a concrete wall, water-stained but dry, and steadied himself. Bridget came after him, the trapdoor closing. "That door never opened before, Orville. I wonder what's coming *through* it?" She sounded shaken. "Come on." She hurried down the passageway, toward the bright light at the end, and Orville followed.

They emerged, blinking in the afternoon sun, from the side of Darrin's building. Orville looked behind him, confused, and the passageway they'd followed was gone—there was a dirty storage room there now, with a furnace and some yard tools leaning against the dank walls. Bridget followed the path that went toward the front of the house, and Orville went with her. "It's later than it should be." She shaded her eyes against the sun. "I think something went funny with time in that place with the haystack, usually it seems to cut time off the trip, that's why it's such a good shortcut, but I guess that's not a constant, because by the sun it looks like hours have gone by. Shit. We'd better—"

A man came barrelling down the stairs from Darrin's house, head down, talking to himself. He stalked across the street.

"Darrin!" Bridget shouted, but he didn't hear her—even if he *could* have heard a ghost, he was probably too far away. "What's wrong with him?" Bridget said, anguish and distress in her voice, and before Orville could answer, Darrin shouted something. They looked across the street, and saw—

"That's Ismael," Bridget said. "What is going on?"

Darrin lunged at Ismael, who stepped out of the way easily, and touched Darrin as he passed by. Bridget made her way toward them, Orville following, though he was loath to approach Ismael again. They were halfway across the street when Darrin and Ismael disappeared down the same not-quite-real stairs they'd shoved the mugger onto. Bridget let out a wordless cry and rushed after them, Orville close behind, but Darrin and Ismael were nowhere to be seen. They'd taken some branching side path and disappeared into the greater depths of the briarpatch. Bridget stood at the base of the stairs, looking first in one direction, then in another, at all the shimmering potentialities in the air, all the possible paths to follow. "Ismael took him away. What happened? What does Ismael want with him?"

"I don't know," Orville said, wishing he knew how to comfort her. "Maybe we should go back to Darrin's house, and try to find out what upset him so much? Unless you want to go looking for them in the briarpatch?"

"I wouldn't know where to begin." Bridget slumped. "It would be like trying to find a particular grain of sand on the beach. Maybe if we wait at his house, he'll come back?"

Unless Ismael is convincing him to kill himself, Orville thought, but didn't say. "Sure. Let's try that."

2

"I thought that went well." Echo stripped off the collar and the leather harness. "I was surprised when he told us to get out, but it was easy to fix. I guess having your whole world destroyed helps you grow a backbone or something."

"I'm a worthless piece of shit." Nicholas sat in the armchair now, head in his hands. "Christ, I can't believe I did that to him. Fuck. Me and Darrin, we go *back*."

"Yeah, you suck. You never did tell me why you did it, what Ismael offered you."

"I'm not supposed to talk about it," he mumbled.

"I'm trying to think what a guy like you cares about. Money? Sure. Women? Sure. But enough to get your best friend fired, to hide the information about where his one true love was living, to sleep with his new girlfriend? How much money, how many women, could Ismael possibly offer you? I know the guy has hidden resources, but—"

"He offered me life," Nicholas said, and that seemed to buck him up, somehow. He wiped at his eyes and nodded. "And that's worth anything."

Echo rolled her eyes. "I told you I don't believe Ismael threatened your life."

"He didn't. He promised to make my life last forever. He's going to teach me the secret of immortality."

Echo looked at him for a minute. Yep, he was serious. She might have laughed, but instead she said, very calmly, "You got scammed, Nicky."

"Bullshit." He stood up from the couch, balling his fists. "Ismael has been alive for centuries, I've seen those old photos, the coins he has, that ancient shit. He knows the secret of eternal life."

"Don't you know he only wants to *die*?" Echo said, still naked, but unselfconscious as usual.

"That's his damage," Nicholas said. "He grew up in the Dark Ages or whatever, he's seen some bad shit, it's understandable. Me, I've already got some money put away, I'm going to live the good life, forever. So what if Ismael doesn't know how to turn off eternal life? That's the whole point, if you ask me. It's eternal."

"I'm guessing Ismael hasn't told you much about his history," Echo said, sitting in the armchair. She almost didn't want to spoil Ismael's game, but Nicholas was going to find out the truth sooner or later, and it was amusing to be the bearer of such catastrophically bad news. "He didn't *do* something to make himself immortal, he just *is* immortal. That doesn't mean he can teach you how to be. Just because the guy's got a full head of hair doesn't mean he knows how to cure baldness."

But Nicholas didn't look shattered. He looked smug. "Ismael didn't tell you about it, psycho, because he said the last thing the world needed was for *you* to live forever. But he found something in the briarpatch that can impart immortality, like a magical fountain. It's not something he's in the habit of leading people to, since he thinks most people should aspire to death, but he told *me* because I laughed in his face when he started going on about transcendence and leading me to heaven and shit. I don't care about any of that. I like this world—I just want *more* of it. Every man in my family for the last four generations has died young, some of them in their thirties, because of bad hearts. I'm not going to let that shit happen to me. And Ismael promised, after I did this, he'd take me into the briarpatch with him, and give me eternal life. I figure I'll have forever to make it up to Darrin. And I will, too. Bet you wish you'd made a better deal, huh, you nutcase?"

Echo didn't answer. Could it be true? It was more likely Ismael was just stringing Nicholas along, wasn't it? Could he really have the secret of eternal life? Would Echo want it if he did?

Well, of course she would. Whether damnation or oblivion awaited her after life, she wasn't interested in either.

"I'm going to have a talk with Mr. Ismael Plenty," Echo said finally. "A long, *hard* talk."

The front door opened with a creak, and footsteps began climbing the stairs. Echo frowned. Was Darrin back?

"Oh, hell," Nicholas said, apparently having the same thought, and rising to his feet.

But it wasn't Darrin. It was that little guy from Ismael's house, the Troll. He gaped at them, and Echo smirked. "Did you decide you wanted me to kill you after all?" she asked.

But Nicholas wasn't reacting as calmly. He was whimpering, and backing away. "No," he said. "No, no, no, you're dead, Bridget, you're *dead*."

"Oh, fuck," Echo said, irritated. "Why is it everybody else can see this ghost bitch but *me*?"

3

Orville moved to put the other man—Nicholas, Bridget called him—between himself and Echo, in case she did decide to attack him. "Bridget, he can see you."

"That's interesting," Bridget said. "Has Ismael been teaching you things, Nicholas? How to see beyond the normal world?"

"He showed me all kinds of shit," Nicholas said, backing away. "Took me into the briarpatch. Down hallways that don't go anywhere, through tunnels in the clouds, to the edge of bottomless pits in the middle of sidewalks. But I never saw any *dead* people before."

"I want answers, Nicholas," Bridget said. "Or I'll haunt you for the rest of your miserable life."

"Bridget, I—" he began.

"This is bullshit," Echo said irritably. "There's somebody in here talking, and I can't even *hear* her? That pisses me off. I never could see any of that crap Ismael talked about, he said I was too firmly grounded in myself or whatever—"

"Or just because you're about as sensitive as a block of wood," Nicholas said.

"Fuck you, frat boy, I'll—"

"Shut her up, Nicholas," Bridget said, and there was something in her voice that chilled even Orville.

"Be quiet, Echo," Nicholas said, trying to regain his composure.

"You don't tell me—"

"SHUT UP!" he roared, turning on her. "For god's sake, some things aren't about you, nutcase! Piss off!"

Echo stared at him, then, slowly, smiled. "Nicky's got some balls after all. Of course, after that little outburst, I'm going to have to cut them off sometime, when you least expect it. But, sure, go on and have a nice talk with miss thin air over there. I'll just fix myself a drink. Want to come, Mr. Troll? No? Okay, suit yourself." She went toward the kitchen.

"Bridget," Nicholas said. "Ah, shit, I thought you were gone." He'd backed up as far as he could, against the wall.

"Tell me what Ismael wants with Darrin," she said.

"Uh, see, it's complicated, really, and—"

"I'm a smart woman, Nicholas. I can understand complicated things." She took a step toward him, and he held up his hands.

"Okay, okay! Ismael's trying to find this place, in the briarpatch, some place where everything's beautiful and perfect, you know?"

"I know. What does Darrin have to do with it?"

"Can I sit down?"

"Yes, fine, just talk."

Nicholas sat on the couch, ran a hand through his hair, and sighed. "Ismael says Darrin is like him. A briarpatch baby. Someone who was never born, exactly, but just, like, *grew* in the briarpatch. That they both just came into existence, no mother or father."

"That's the stupidest thing I've ever heard," Bridget said, chilled by the thought. For Darrin to be like Ismael, in that fundamental way? Someone who could cross the mortal bridge behind Ismael's shed and find no familiar corpse waiting on the far side? A living apport?

Nicholas shrugged. "Darrin doesn't know who his parents are. He was found wandering the streets in North Carolina when he was three years old, right? He doesn't have any memories before that. He went to the orphanage, then foster homes, yadda yadda. Even his last name is just one he picked out because he thought it sounded cool. I mean, it's not like there's any proof *against* what Ismael says. He says people like Darrin are rare, that he—Ismael—has only met a couple of them, and that they all have access to different parts of the briarpatch, they can see paths other people can't. Ismael wants Darrin to help him explore, to show him paths Ismael can't find on his own."

Bridget had known Darrin was an orphan, but hadn't considered the implications—that he was like *Ismael*? "Oh, god," Bridget said. "He wants Darrin to help him find the northwest passage."

"Yeah, that's what he said .But, see, Darrin wasn't even aware of the briarpatch, you know? I mean, maybe he saw glimpses sometimes, but he didn't go into it. Ismael said sometimes there needs to be a, what do you call it, a 'triggering event.' Like a really rough emotional jolt, or even physical trauma, the kind of thing that changes your perception of the world. Literally, in this case. Ismael said *he* couldn't see the entryways into the briarpatch clearly until he saw the family he was living with get murdered by barbarians or whatever, and that when he'd lost everything else, he fled, and wound up in the briarpatch."

"He told me that story too," Bridget said.

"So, in order to get Darrin into the briarpatch to start looking for this overland route or northwest passage or whatever you want to call it, the path to this better world Ismael's always talking about . . . Darrin needed a little shove."

Bridget sat down in Darrin's worn armchair. "Shit. How long has Ismael been planning this? Did he find out about Darrin when he met me, or . . ."

Nicholas shook his head. "He's known about Darrin for a while. You were step one, Bridget." His voice was gentle. "Ismael said you were a good candidate anyway, but he chose you in particular because he wanted to take you away from Darrin, and start breaking Darrin down. Ismael didn't plan for Darrin to see you die, but—"

"So he *was* there," Bridget said. "I never meant for him to see that."

"Yeah, he was supposed to be having lunch with me that morning, but Ismael says sometimes there's a gravity to events, weird shit happens when you start messing with briar-patch babies, and maybe Darrin was somehow drawn to the bridge that morning. Or maybe it was just straight-up coincidence, who knows? He was on the bridge taking pictures, and got there just in time to see you go over the edge. I was, ah, real sorry to hear you didn't make it, you know, through the portal or whatever."

"What was your part in all this?" Bridget asked.

"Ismael told me about it, he wanted my help, and eventually he convinced me this was the best thing for Darrin, you know, Darrin's always been looking for a purpose in his life, and if this was the only way to help him find the briarpatch, shit, it was the least I could do for the guy, you know—"

"I call bullshit." Echo reappeared in the doorway, dressed now, and crunching on an apple. "Dead girl is asking what Nicky had to do with all this, yeah? I'll tell her. Is she listening, Troll?"

"She can hear you." Orville scooted around the room to put more distance between Echo and himself.

"Shut up, Echo, I swear—" Nicholas said.

"Let her talk," Bridget said, and Nicholas went silent.

"Go on, she's listening," Orville said, thinking that he'd never expected to be the translator between a ghost and a sociopath.

Echo grinned—showing bits of apple caught in her teeth—chewed, swallowed, and said, "Nicholas sold out Darrin for the promise of eternal life. After you disappeared, dead girl, Nicholas told Darrin's boss he was looking for another job with a rival company, and Darrin got canned—they told him it was because of 'resource reallocation' or some shit, but it was all Nicholas. Then Nicholas introduced Darrin to me—and that sucked, because me and Nicky had to pretend to be *friends*, and he hates me almost as much as I laugh at him. So me and Darrin got together, and I fucked him until he thought he loved me—we had all kinds of fun in your bed, dead girl—but even that was all just a setup for the *big* betrayal. Ismael thought Darrin needed a little extra push, so we arranged to have Darrin walk in on me and Nicky having sex right in his own living room. And that happened, oh, just a few minutes ago. You missed all the fun, ghostface! We could've had a crazy ectoplasmic four-way or something."

Bridget didn't look at Echo at all while she talked, just kept her eyes focused on Nicholas. "Is all that true, Nicholas?"

"She put it in the nastiest possible way," Nicholas said miserably, "but, yeah, that's pretty much how it went down. I mean, I thought it would be good for Darrin, fuck, it's a great adventure, right? It's not my kind of thing, but he used to dig crawling around storm drains or whatever, so I thought exploring the briarpatch would be awesome for him, and he'd quit whining about not knowing what to do with his life. Hell, Bridget, he thought you *were* his life, and when you ditched him, he was *broken*. You betrayed him just as much as I did."

"That might be true." Bridget sounded sad rather than angry. "I thought he'd be okay. I knew I'd disappoint him eventually, that we couldn't have the little picket fence life he dreamed of. I thought he'd find another girl. But *I* didn't know I was being used, Nicholas. You went into this with your eyes open."

"Split hairs all you want," Nicholas said. "We both fucked with Darrin's life for our own reasons. At least I was trying to help give his life some meaning, at the cost of our friendship, no less. You think he'll ever forgive me, even if I explain why I did that shit? Hell, no. I wouldn't."

"This is like listening to one side of the world's most boring phone conversation," Echo said. "I'm going to wait for Ismael at his house. Have fun rotting, dead girl."

Bridget burst out laughing.

"What are you laughing at?" Nicholas said.

"She's laughing?" Echo looked at Orville, who only nodded, not understanding her reaction himself.

"You idiots think Ismael is coming *back*?" Bridget said. "Translate for me, Orville, this is too funny."

Orville dutifully repeated what she'd said for Echo's benefit.

"Why wouldn't he come back?" Echo demanded.

"Why would he? He's got Darrin, who he thinks is his key to finding a physical passageway to the one place he's been trying desperately to reach for maybe *centuries*. Why would Ismael come back out of the briarpatch again? They're just going to stay in there until they find the pathway, or until they give up, and that could take a long time. Darrin can be just as stubborn as Ismael, under the right circumstances."

"That's bullshit," Nicholas said. "Ismael *owes* me. He's supposed to show me how to live forever."

"Somebody better tell me what the dead girl said," Echo demanded.

Orville hurriedly translated Bridget's words, and Echo curled her hands into fists. "That fucker. He owes me too. He can't do this to us."

"Ismael doesn't bother to pay his debts," Bridget said. "He just outlives them. I feel bad about letting Ismael trick me, but at least he tricked you two idiots as well. Yeah, go to his house, hang out and wait for him. You'll be waiting until you die of old age." She shook her head while Orville relayed her words to Echo.

"She's right," Nicholas said, looking gobsmacked. "Why would he come back? I just assumed, he comes and goes all the time, but . . . he's over there now. He's searching. He doesn't need anything else."

Bridget rose. "Come on, Orville. We're going into the briarpatch to find them. Once Darrin finds out how Ismael fucked with his life, that he had a part in my death, he won't help him anymore. Revenge isn't much, but it's all I've got right now."

"Darrin already knows Ismael is involved," Nicholas said. "He saw Ismael on the bridge when you jumped, and they'd met once before, so he knew you guys were spending time together. It's not going to be a big crushing revelation."

Bridget blinked. "But . . . why would Darrin help him, if he knew Ismael had a hand in my death?"

That's got to hurt, Orville thought.

Nicholas shrugged. "I think he was going to tell Darrin he could find you, like your spirit, in the briarpatch. Or tell him you'd gone to the better world, and that if Darrin helped him find the pathway there, you'd be waiting for him. Darrin loves you a lot more than he hates Ismael."

"Then I'm definitely going to find him," Bridget said. "Darrin's been lied to long enough."

"I'll go with you," Nicholas said, standing up.

"Who's going where?" Echo demanded.

"No," Bridget said. "Fuck you, Nicholas. I don't need you *or* want you with us."

"Please, Bridget, he's my friend, I didn't mean for it to go down this way—"

"No," she said. "Orville, let's go."

Orville nodded. This was all very confusing, but it was a lot more interesting than working the phones at his old job, so he couldn't complain. Bridget went down the stairs, and Orville followed. The last sound he heard before closing the front door behind him was Echo and Nicholas arguing.

4

"Sure, I can see the briarpatch," Nicholas said. "Not well, I haven't been there often, but yeah, Ismael took me enough times that I got a sense of it. But what do I want to go in there by myself for? Or with you? I'd get eaten by fucking bears or fall down a bottomless pit or something. With a guide, sure, somebody like Bridget who's been there a lot, I'd have a shot, but by myself?" He punched his own thigh, hard. "Fuck. I can't believe Ismael did this to me. But no, I won't take you in there."

"I can't go by myself, Nicky," Echo said, trying to keep her cool. "I need you."

"Go to hell, psycho. We're done."

"I will kill you if you don't help me," Echo said. She'd never actually killed anyone, but Nicholas probably believed she had. She was certainly capable of killing someone, but so far the risks had always seemed to outweigh the rewards.

Nicholas just stared at her. "You can try it, but you don't have the element of surprise with me, Echo. I know what you are. And I won't hesitate to put you down myself if I get the chance."

They stared at each other for a moment, until finally Echo spat on the floor. "Shit. You'd be worthless in there anyway." She'd suddenly had a better idea. Nicholas might be able to get into the briarpatch, but he'd stumble around blindly for a while and then get lost. She needed a guide with more experience, someone who knew the secret byways of that strange world. And, because luck was always on Echo's side, she had an idea where to find just such a guide. "Take care, Nicky. See you around."

"Not if I see you first," he muttered.

Echo went into the kitchen, took Darrin's biggest, sharpest butcher knife, slipped it into her purse so only the handle was showing, and went down the back stairs.

5

Arturo strolled back up Park Boulevard, hoping the Wendigo would see fit to cough up a little cash again tonight. Since getting thrown out of the bar with the mutton-chopped bartender, he'd been reduced to spending most of his waking hours at a bar a few blocks down, by the Parkway theatre, and they demanded real money in exchange for booze, as opposed to a pinprick of blood like the other place had taken.

When Arturo reached the corner, he saw right away the Wendigo had turned itself around—the headlights were pointed toward him. Arturo swore. The Wendigo was known to drive itself, so maybe it had just executed a neat three-point-turn in the wide residential street and re-parked itself, but Arturo didn't think so. He wasn't particularly prone to the metaphysical, and had always been reckoned a practical, hard-headed man by his friends and family, but he understood the Wendigo was more than just a car—being a car was a convenience for it. Arturo didn't think it bothered with the brute business of moving around on the street. He thought it just reversed direction, quick as a blink, modifying reality to suit its needs.

Anyway, *how* was less important than *why*. The Wendigo was finally pointed away from Darrin's house, and at the street—pointed *out*, which meant maybe they were ready to go. Arturo didn't know what had changed, but he put his trust in the Wendigo. It had never steered him wrong.

He reached the car and put his hand on the door. Suddenly something cold pressed against his throat, just below his chin, and he went still. Unless Arturo was very much mistaken, someone had a knife to his throat.

"I'm Echo," said a pleasant female voice right in his ear. "What's your name?"

"Arturo," he said, trying not to open his mouth too wide when he spoke, afraid of getting cut. Then, because politeness was a reflex, he mumbled "Pleasedtomeetcha."

"Likewise."

Arturo wondered if she was going to cut him. Slashing a throat was harder than most people realized—there were a lot of tough muscles in the neck—but death was still pretty likely if she left him bleeding.

"You're going to take me for a ride," Echo said, and Arturo almost laughed, he was so relieved. "Go around and open the passenger door." The knife left his throat, only to prod him between the shoulder blades. "I won't hurt you if you behave, but I'm still close enough to bury this in your kidneys."

Maybe one kidney, Arturo thought. Anatomy probably wasn't her strong point. He walked around the back of the car, his unseen carjacker staying close behind. He didn't even think about running, or fighting back. If she wanted to get into the Wendigo, he wouldn't stop her. The Wendigo had its own ways of dealing with unwelcome passengers. "Open the door," she said, and Arturo did. "Empty the crap out." He pulled on the tottering pile of paper that filled the passenger seat, sending reams of brightly coloured paper spilling out onto the street. He felt a twinge of guilt, but knew the Wendigo's papers would disappear before they could get stuck in gutters or tangled among tree branches.

Eventually the seat was clear—mostly—and Echo told him to get in and scoot across the seat to the driver's side. He did, and got his first glimpse of her, though she kept the knife angled so she could slice out his eye with a single thrust. "You're Darrin's girl," he said. "Well, hell, I didn't realize he was datin' the criminal element."

"Quiet, walrus." She slid into the seat beside him, keeping her knife handy.

Arturo frowned. Was that a crack about his moustache, or his weight?

Echo glanced around, then reached for the door handle.

That's it, Arturo thought. *Shut the door*. Once she was closed in, the Wendigo would do . . . whatever it did to unwelcome passengers. He turned his face away, closed his eyes, and listened to the door click shut.

Silence. Then "I said be quiet, not avert your eyes." She sounded more amused than angry.

Arturo looked at her. She still had the knife held at the ready. The Wendigo wasn't eating her, which meant the Wendigo *wanted* her to be here. Which meant Arturo did too, whether he liked it or not.

"You don't need the knife. You're welcome here."

"Oh, really? Look, walrus, I'd just leave you in a ditch somewhere, but I'm guessing it takes more than a key and a full tank of gas to get the most out of this car."

"True enough. And my name is Arturo, not walrus. Where do you want to go?" He turned the key and the Wendigo growled to itself as the engine turned over.

"Into the briarpatch." She said it with great relish, as if delivering the scene-ending line in a movie.

"Well, yeah," Arturo said. "But *where* in the briarpatch?"

For a moment, the pretty woman beside him lost her sly, self-satisfied expression, and revealed a face of total bafflement. "I need to find Ismael."

"Don't know him."

"He's . . . did you say you know Darrin? Ismael is with Darrin."

The Wendigo's engine revved, though Arturo hadn't pressed the accelerator. "All right, then." He shifted the car from park to drive. "Let's see what we can do." He reached out for the radio.

"Did I tell you to touch that?"

Arturo looked at her. "Miss, if I'm drivin', I'm listenin' to the radio. If you object, you can stick that knife in my belly and drive yourself into the briarpatch. If you think the Wendigo will let you."

For just a moment, he thought he'd miscalculated, and that she *was* going to stab him. He wondered what the Wendigo would do to stop her, if anything. Maybe he was meant to die at her hands, and take the direct route of death to find Marjorie.

But instead she just said, "Whatever. Get moving."

He turned on the radio, and it was Willie, singing "On the Road Again." The Wendigo always got the best stations on the radio, except when it didn't get any radio stations at all. Arturo pulled away from the curb, easing down this rational road, looking for an on-ramp into the briarpatch. It felt so good to be driving again, even at knifepoint, that he started singing along with the radio.

After a moment, Echo started singing too, her voice off-key but enthusiastic.

Could be this won't be so bad, Arturo thought. Road trips were always more fun with company.

DARRIN AND ISMAEL TAKE A WALK

1

From the stairway, Ismael led Darrin down a gravel path between high hedges, and whenever Darrin demanded to know where they were going, Ismael would only say, "Into the briarpatch, to find Bridget."

Finally, after what seemed an hour spent trudging through an English hedge-maze, Ismael stopped. "There's a house up ahead, through there." He pointed to an iron gate at the end of the hedgerow. "Follow my lead. Once we get inside, don't go into any of the doorways we pass, no matter what you see there, even if you think you see Bridget. It's a house of mirrors, in a way, and you see what you want to see—it's nothing real. But we need to pass through it. We should rest first."

He unslung his shoulder bag and reached inside, withdrawing a bottle of water. He offered it to Darrin, who scowled, thinking, *Poison.*

Ismael sighed, uncapped the bottle, took a swig, and said "See? No cyanide. I'm not your enemy, Darrin." He sat cross-legged on the gravel and began rolling his head around, as if working out kinks in his neck.

Darrin sank to the ground across from him, their knees almost touching in the narrowness of the hedgerow, and took the water bottle. He wasn't tired from their long walk—he'd been well-conditioned over the past few months, having spent most of his days walking—but it was important to stay hydrated. He hadn't come prepared for a long trip, though at least he was wearing decent hiking boots. His greatest regret was that he hadn't brought his camera. The long walk, looking at the back of Ismael's head, had helped drain away some of his rage toward Nicholas and Echo, though the opportunity for contemplation had brought a lot of questions too. He was no longer overwhelmed by the very idea of the briarpatch, though he was still a little unclear on what it *was*, exactly, and why he was able to enter it when other people couldn't. But he had other questions.

"I'm not going any farther with you until I get some answers," Darrin said.

Ismael sighed. "I can help you find Bridget. It is a long and arduous trek, but it can be done."

"Listen. The first time I saw you, you cracked Nicholas in the knee with a club. The second time I saw you, you were standing in the crowd when Bridget jumped to her death. The third time I saw you, you promised to *lead* me to Bridget. I think you need to fill in some fucking *gaps*."

Ismael looked upward, meditatively. "Agreed," he said at last. "We are not precisely on a schedule, and I can see how this might set your mind at ease. Let me tell you how I met Bridget." He gestured for Darrin to give him back the water bottle, took a sip, and then began to speak.

2

The day I met Bridget, I was travelling from my home in Oakland to a place in San Francisco, near the park, where I had a meeting with an associate. The briarpatch is many things, but one of its baser attributes is a series of shortcuts. If one is experienced in walking its pathways, one can use it to travel quickly from one point to another in the narrower world, with the added advantage of avoiding the press of humanity on trains and buses. It is a trivial journey, as I can enter the shed in my back yard, pass into the briarpatch, take a relatively safe ten minute walk along a lonely dirt track in a place where the air is sweet and fields of red blossoms sway in the breeze, and emerge behind one of the many statues hidden in Golden Gate Park. The man who designed the park despised statues, and whenever the city forced one upon him, he planted densely around it, often hiding the monument completely from view, which made my spot a convenient exit point. Because of the vagaries of time, which does not flow evenly everywhere in the briarpatch, I sometimes arrive in the park shortly before even leaving my home. Efficient, hmm?

But one day last year, I emerged from the briarpatch to find a woman sitting cross-legged—much as we are sitting now—at the base of the statue, smoking a joint. She stared up at me, and did not seem particularly startled by my emergence from empty air. "Want a drag?" she asked.

I nearly said no and hurried away. But I am always looking for . . . prospects, people who can be guided and saved . . . and I have come to develop a sense for these things. Some people are willing to consider the mysteries that lie at the heart of the world, and I thought this woman might be one. Either that or she was sufficiently stoned that seeing a man appear from nowhere didn't merit comment. So I sat with her, and we passed the joint back and forth in companionable silence, looking at the legs of the forgotten statue. Finally she said, "How did you do that? Just . . . appear like that?"

I answered her honestly, which is generally my policy, because most people don't believe me, and those who *do* can sometimes be useful to me. I said, "There is a world—there are *worlds*—behind and beyond this world, and some people can travel those worlds at will. I am one of those people."

She pinched closed the end of the joint and put it away in her pocket, then said, "Prove it."

"I'm not a magician. I don't do shows."

"I don't believe you," she said.

"I don't care."

Then she said, more softly: "I *want* to believe you."

I have a hard heart. I have endured much in the way of suffering, and little in the way of joy, and I discovered long ago that compassion is just a winding path to greater misery, because when you allow yourself to care for someone, they can hurt you far more than any stranger ever could. But I felt compassion for this woman, and the longing in her voice.

"Take my hand," I said, and she did. "Now look." I nodded to the left of the statue, and she gasped, because she could see it then, as clearly as I could, a wooden archway hung with boughs of white flowers, and beyond the arch, a path that led off into a place that was not the park.

"It's beautiful," she said, seeing the red flowers in the distance, and I agreed that some parts of it were beautiful, but other parts were ugly, or dangerous, or simply incredibly strange. I let go of her hand, and she made a noise of disappointment, because she could not see it anymore. "If you spent enough time in the briarpatch, you wouldn't need my help to see it anymore."

"Why do you call it the briarpatch?"

"It's just what a friend of mine used to call it," I told her. "His name was Harczos, and he used to say he was born and raised in the briarpatch, and there was nowhere he would rather be. Though since then I have heard others call it the same thing. Harczos was a talkative man. I suppose his term for the place spread. Before I met Harczos, I called it the dark wood, or sometimes the wild garden, but the briarpatch seemed more fitting."

She surprised me with her next question. She said "What is it *for*?"

Most people, made aware of the briarpatch's existence, don't think to question its utility. I had to think for a moment before I answered her. "There is a better world, a place where there is no pain or suffering, where everything is made luminous. But it is difficult to reach. It is almost impossible to even glimpse from this world, though sometimes—through sex, through music, meditation, drugs—it is possible. From the briarpatch, you can more directly sense the existence of that better world. It is . . . a step closer to the sublime. There are places where you can glimpse the light, indirectly, without its true potency, but enough to get a sense of its power. There may even be an overland route, a way to walk to that better world from the briarpatch, but I have not found it yet. The briarpatch provides encouragement, reassurance that there are other worlds than this, and other options besides drudgery and empty death."

She nodded as if this all made sense, but then said, "That's what it means to you, the purpose it serves for you. Okay. But what is it, really?"

A fair question, and—forgive me—a thorny one. Harczos used to go on and on about the true nature of the briarpatch, and I tossed off one of his favourite quips: "It is the fleeting memory of a dream had by God." The sort of answer that says nothing much and may or may not mean something, but that certainly sounds meaningful, in a kōan sort of way. But she looked at me with this terrible ferocity that I came to know so well—a look that said this was a serious talk we were having, that even though she was high enough to take the discovery of the briarpatch in stride, she wasn't anywhere near high enough to take it lightly. I suspect you saw the same look on her face many times during your relationship. I certainly saw it many times while I knew her.

"Tell me," she said, and I sighed and replied, "It is a mystery. It is an impenetrable thicket of miracles. I have never been a philosopher, but for a while my friend Harczos believed the briarpatch was a dumping ground for worlds too implausible to exist. He said it was God's storehouse, the place where the creator put away worlds half-made and then abandoned because they did not fit into the greater scheme of the universe, or because they were poorly made, or because they displeased Him. I have met scientist-shamans who talk on and on about quantum mechanics, convinced the briarpatch is a garden of forking paths, *possible* worlds that have not quite resolved into proper existence. I have met people who believe the briarpatch is Fairyland, and people who believe it is the access tunnels to the workings of the universe, where gods and their minions can make adjustments to reality, and people who believe it is the medicine lands, or the Dreamtime, or the outer boroughs of Hell. No one knows what it is. But it is full of wonders."

That seemed to satisfy her, and I thought more highly of her then, because she was happier with a messy, incomplete, truthful answer than with a neat complete one. "I'd like to go there," she said. "Will you show me?"

3

"Enough." Darrin stared down at his knees. He believed Ismael, all too easily. Bridget had always longed for something more, something important, and she'd dabbled in drugs, and religions both mainstream and alternative, and extreme activities of all kinds. How could she have passed up an opportunity like that, to see a world beyond the world she knew? How had he not realized? In the months before Bridget left him, Darrin had been busy, routinely working seventy-hour weeks. Bridget had professed not to mind, and she'd certainly always been an independent person with friends and a life of her own. They'd kept their Sundays together, their walks and brunches, their time spent sipping margaritas in the back yard, and those days had kept Darrin sane. But maybe they'd just been habit—or, worse, obligation—for Bridget. Now he had some idea of what she'd been doing the other six days of the week.

"She did love you, you know," Ismael said.

"Then why didn't she tell me about . . . all this?" He looked up into Ismael's long, placid face.

"She planned to, for a while," Ismael said. "Until she decided to kill herself. She didn't think you would go along with it."

Darrin stood up then, wobbling a bit, one of his legs having fallen asleep during Ismael's story. "Yes. Right. *That.* Why did she kill herself? What did you have to do with that?"

Ismael didn't even bother to look at him when he answered. "Death is one path to the better world. You've heard of suicide cults. They believe that by casting aside their bodies, their souls could go to a better place. They are correct in theory, but woefully inadequate in practice. The soul and the body are tightly wound together, nearly inseparable, and it takes months of preparation to unbind them. While Bridget still lived with you, she took trips with me, here, into the briarpatch. She learned her way around, learned to see the same paths

I could see, and, eventually, I took her to a place where she could see the light of the better world. Not reach its source, no—I've never found a direct path—but *see* it, as you can see the skyline of San Francisco from the shores of Oakland. After seeing the light, she decided to leave you, and dedicate herself to preparing for the journey there."

Darrin sat back down, his anger draining away. It was exhausting, being angry. "What kind of preparation did that involve? Brainwashing her? Sleeping with her?"

"The pleasures of the flesh no longer interest me," Ismael said. "I have had a surfeit of them, and they all grow tedious in time. No, Darrin. She meditated. She fasted. She studied. She drank preparations developed over the centuries by certain shamans, though I suspect they work more as placebo than true magic. She ritually destroyed most of her possessions, and gave the rest away. Leaving you was the most difficult step for her, because you were symbolic of everything she was leaving behind, of the total abandonment of her life. She needed to turn her back completely on this world, to carry nothing from her old life with her, until she felt she could leave this world without regret. And then, once she felt she was ready, I went with her to Golden Gate Bridge, and she jumped. As she fell, she saw a light appear beneath her, a pinprick at first, growing to a portal. When people give up everything of this world, even their bodies, a door to the better world opens before them. The body cannot pass through that door, but the *spirit* can, and with her study, and her willingness to give up everything, she was able to separate her spirit and her body. Her physical form died when it hit the water, but her spirit lived on, and passed through the portal, into the light of a better world." He spread his hands. "She transitioned. She is a blessed one. She dwells forever in the light."

"You said you could take me to her. But if you can't get to this place with the light unless you die, how are we supposed to do that?"

"We are going to find a northwest passage. We will search for an overland route to the better world, a way to reach it physically, and once we get there, you will find Bridget. I believe that once you see the light, you will choose to stay there forever. As will I."

"If you're so keen to find this place, why don't you just kill yourself? Instead of trying to find some path that might not even exist?"

"The path *does* exist. I know, because my old friend Harczos found it. He did not take me with him, because we had a . . . difference of opinion. But he went away, into the light, and came out again to tell me he'd found it. Because of our falling out, he would not take me there." Ismael shook his head. "It is a cruelty on his part that I have never been able to forgive; we have not spoken for many decades."

"Decades?" Darrin said. "What are you talking about? You don't look more than maybe thirty-five."

"I am at least 800 years old," Ismael said. "I stopped aging before I was forty, as near as I can tell. If I could die, I would, but I will live forever, Darrin. The overland route is my only hope for transcending the essential misery of existence."

"You're crazy," Darrin said, though he knew saying something like that, in a place like this, was folly—how could he know what was possible and impossible anymore?

"Not crazy, Darrin. Just born and raised in the briarpatch. I have no father, no mother. Neither did Harczos. We are implausible creatures, people who might have been, and we came into existence in the briarpatch independent of any creation, just like these hedges, just like that fence. There are a dozen of us, children of the briarpatch, possibly a score, though Harczos is the only one I've spent any amount of time with." He paused. "Before you, that is. You are a child of the briarpatch too, Darrin."

"Bullshit," Darrin said, but his heart was pounding.

"You were found wandering the streets as a toddler. You came out of the briarpatch, and you suffered from years of blindness, until the devastation of your life opened your eyes to other passages in the world again. No one held your hand or showed you the way. You can see paths that I cannot, just as Harczos could. I have explored as far as I can alone, but with your help, I can access whole other regions of the briarpatch, and together we may be able to find our northwest passage."

"What makes you think I can find it?"

Ismael shrugged. "I know I cannot find it on my own. With your help, I can cover so much more ground. I *know* it exists, somewhere, in the tangles of the briarpatch. We may fail, I suppose, but I have all the time in the world, so why not try? Hope is very important, Darrin. It's something I haven't felt for a long time."

"You used Bridget to get to me," Darrin said. "You took her away from me, so the grief would tear me up, and make me find the briarpatch. *Didn't you?*" He shouted the last two words, and the sound was shocking in this quiet place.

"No. I took on Bridget in good faith, and it was only as she told me about you that I began to suspect. When I encountered you in San Francisco, after your friend Nicholas attacked me, you chased me partway down a path into this world, and I knew then what you truly were."

That was it. Ismael was lying. Darrin knew for sure, now. Ismael was unaware Darrin had been inside his house, had seen proof of Ismael's meddling in his life.

Ismael was trying to use him. But Darrin knew he was being used, and that gave him some power. What else was Ismael lying about, though? About Darrin being a child of the briarpatch⬚what would that even mean? That *he* would live for centuries? The idea was ridiculous. About the light of a better world? About Bridget? Maybe she was simply dead, tricked into suicide in order to make Darrin fall apart. That seemed most likely. But lately, Darrin had been forced to accept lots of unlikely things. If there was any possibility Ismael was telling the truth, that Bridget still existed, in some form, and could be reached . . . how could Darrin give up the chance to find her? He had to go along with this, at least until he knew for sure, or found the leverage to make Ismael tell him the truth.

"If we don't find Bridget, I will kill you," Darrin said. "I know you think you're immortal, but I bet the truth is that nobody's ever really *tried* hard enough."

"Understood," Ismael said. "Shall we go? I have some ideas about where we can start our search."

"Lead the way."

4

When they left the hedgerow, swinging open the black iron gate, they didn't enter the English garden Darrin had expected, but a desert landscape of chalky white dunes, with the sun a bright flash in vaulted blue. The soil crunched underfoot, and Darrin knelt to sift a handful in his fingers. The powdery earth was mixed with fragile chunks, like beetle carapaces, all the same bone-white—almost the colour of the Wendigo, actually.

"Be thankful there's no wind, or the air would be thick with white dust, worse than any fog," Ismael said. "I think this used to be a sea. We're walking on the powdered bodies of ancient trilobites and the like."

Darrin rose, shaking the dust off his hand. Ismael led the way up, over a dune, sinking almost ankle-deep in the white in places. Despite the blanket of whiteness, it wasn't much at all like walking through snow; more like walking through ashes. At the top of the dune, Ismael pointed. "There."

When Ismael had said they were going to a house, Darrin hadn't envisioned this: something like an abandoned Depression-era farmhouse, boards weathered colourless by wind and grit, a sagging porch, and a screen door dangling from one hinge. Ismael approached the house, put his foot tentatively on the step, and pushed down with his heel. The board splintered under the impact, and Ismael sighed, lifting his foot from the hole. "It decays a little more each time. I don't know what I'll do if it ever falls down completely. There is another way to the place we're going, but it is the long way, the scenic route, useful for impressing new visitors to the briarpatch, but not as efficient. Still, perhaps I will never have to pass this way again." He climbed onto the porch carefully, without using the steps, and gestured for Darrin to follow.

"Look, can't we go around? This place looks like a death trap." Darrin wondered if it *was* a trap, if Ismael had brought him into the briarpatch to kill him, and leave him where his body would never be discovered. He couldn't think of any reason why Ismael might do that, but he knew the man had lied to him about many things.

"There is no around," Ismael said. "The only way out is through. Pathways in the briarpatch are conditional. You must approach them from the right direction. Think of it as a series of one-way streets, only it's physically *impossible* to go the wrong way. Come, it's not as bad inside." He continued on, swinging aside the broken screen door and pushing open the inner door. Darrin followed his lead, and stepped into the house.

Inside, it was a mansion—like a movie set of a mansion, really, so ostentatious as to seem unreal, with a marble floor, a diamond-bright chandelier, staircases swooping up on either side of the room, and a stone-and-gold fountain bubbling in the centre of the space. There wasn't a speck of dust anywhere.

Ismael went to a small door under one of the staircases. "Through here." He ducked inside, and Darrin followed, into a long dim corridor that gradually widened out into a residential hotel sort of hallway, lit by low-watt bulbs and lined with identical red doors. Some of the doors were open, and when Darrin looked toward one Ismael said, "Eyes front. There's nothing you need in these rooms." Darrin bristled a bit against the command, but he was new to this place, and perhaps it was better to do as he was told. Lights flickered in some of the rooms, and he heard harpsichord and cello music from another, and from one door the smell of fresh buttered popcorn was strong and almost supernaturally inviting.

"We're almost through," Ismael said, and Darrin saw the fire door at the end of the hall, with its utterly prosaic glowing red "Exit" sign above.

"Darrin," Bridget said, leaning casually in the doorway of the last room on the left. She wore an oversized t-shirt, and her hair was mussed, as if she'd just gotten out of bed. "Baby, I missed you. Come here."

He stared at her, eyes abruptly welling up with tears.

"That's not Bridget," Ismael said sharply. "I see my wife, Mirari, who died two hundred years ago, and it isn't *her* either." The Bridget looked at Ismael, perplexed, and then turned her soft smile back to Darrin.

"Shit." Darrin wiped at his eyes and stumbled toward the exit door. "I know it's not her, I'm not stupid, damn it."

"Ah," Ismael said. "Of course. I'm . . . sorry. Your loss is still very fresh. But we will find Bridget, the real Bridget. You can join her in the light."

"Just open the fucking door, Ismael," Darrin said, thinking *your fault your fault your* fault.

Ismael pushed open the door, and they stepped out together. The door swung shut behind them, silently, and they were standing on a bridge.

"This isn't funny," Darrin said. "You bring me to a bridge? Do you want me to jump now?"

The bridge was nothing like the Golden Gate. It was made of blackened steel, a rust-belt monstrosity never meant for foot traffic, and it jutted out over a bubbling tar pit, the petroleum stink roiling in the air.

"The briarpatch is full of bridges, Darrin. Bridges, and hallways, and rope ladders, and staircases." Ismael walked to the railing and looked down into the steaming tar below. Darrin glanced back, and was not surprised to see there was no fire door, no wall at all, just a pitted blacktop road stretching back in a straight line through a desolate scrubland. One of Ismael's one-way streets.

Darrin thought about charging at Ismael while his back was turned, shoving him over the rail to sink in the tar like the mammoths at La Brea, but then he'd be lost here . . . and he would give up his chance of finding Bridget, the chance that was probably a lie but might not be.

"I do not think they are really bridges," Ismael went on, leaning forward to rest on the rail. "That is, I do not think anyone actually mined this steel, or shaped these rivets, or designed this ugly bridge, or erected it on this spot."

"It looks like a pretty plausible bridge to me," Darrin said, remembering Arturo's word. He joined Ismael at the rail.

Ismael smiled, slightly. "Indeed. We are passing through worlds of greater and lesser likelihood, yes, indeed, and some of those likelihoods involve bridges, certainly. But *some* bridges, *some* hallways, are more than what they seem—

they are passages from one world to another. When you walk in the open in the briarpatch, through fields, through forests, you never pass into another world; it's not like crossing a property line. There is always some liminal space, you see— often a bridge, though sometimes only a shadow. In the woods, the bridges are made of rough logs and lashed with vines. In ruins, the bridges might be made of tumbled rubble. Here, it is a thing of black steel. But I believe we are simply seeing a bridge because we are incapable of seeing the reality of our passage from one unlikely world to another. Back behind us, there is one world—a bleak place full of underground caves populated by plague rats, and the ruins of old military bases littered with the wreckage of crashed flying saucers. On the other side of this bridge, we'll enter another world, one of great sadness and beauty. But while we are on the bridge, we are in neither world, though in the centre we can reach both."

"So . . . this isn't really a bridge? And that hallway we walked through, it's not a real hallway?"

"I think the spaces between worlds are so strange and terrible and lonely that human eyes cannot look upon them. And so we perceive the spaces as methods of passage: bridges, ladders, hallways, doors, tunnels. It is something I think about when I cross such bridges. I wonder what I'm really walking through. Every bridge is a walkway to a new possibility."

"Like the moon bridge," Darrin said.

"The what?"

Darrin shrugged. "That first night, when you attacked Nicholas in San Francisco, I saw a bridge, high in the sky, beautiful silver, luminous like the moon. I saw it another time too, when I was riding in a car. It was one of the prettiest things I've ever seen. Where does it go?"

Ismael shook his head. "I do not know. But perhaps it leads to the light. If you see it again, you must take my hand, so that I might see it too."

"The times I saw it, it looked impossibly far away," Darrin warned. "I'd have about as much chance of reaching the *real* moon as getting to it."

"You would be surprised at the avenues of approach the briarpatch affords. Would you stop at anything to reach that bridge, if there was a chance you might find Bridget waiting on the other side?"

"I'm here with you, aren't I? That should give you some idea of the lengths I'm willing to go to."

"Indeed. Come. We're nearly there."

"Nearly where? Another desert? Another petroleum swamp?"

"I do not think you understand the nature of the better world. How could you? My description . . . it is too abstract. So I'm going to take you to a place where you can see the light." He reached out a hand as if to touch Darrin's arm, then thought better of it. "If you see the light, you might understand why Bridget was willing to leave you for it. That might make you feel better."

"You care about how I feel now?" Darrin crossed his arms over his chest. "I'm not convinced."

"I am a compassionate man," he said, and Darrin realized Ismael actually believed that. He'd loathed the man before, but now, for the first time, Darrin feared Ismael, because people who would do horrible things for the sake of compassion were dangerous, like the madmen who killed their own families to spare them the pain of a sinful world. Now Ismael did clap Darrin on the shoulder, a companionable gesture that Darrin resisted the urge to flinch away from. "Come," Ismael said. "Soon you'll see the light."

Off in the distance, something broke the surface of the tar, a serpentine shape dripping blackness, coil after coil rising up and falling down again. Darrin shivered, and, at the same time, wished he had his camera so he could photograph the thing, though it would be tricky, getting the settings right, so it would appear as something other than blackness against blackness. He'd have to take the pictures in his mind now.

"I've often thought of bringing a torch here," Ismael said, "and throwing it into the tar. If it didn't snuff out immediately, it would burn ferociously, I think, and I wonder what would rise up to escape the flames? Think of the creatures that must live beneath this blackness, and their suffering, their miserable unlikely lives. It would be a mercy, I think, to burn them. But it might destroy this bridge, and so I have always refrained." He set off across the bridge.

Darrin looked at his back for a moment before following. *A compassionate man*, he thought, and then hurried to catch up.

BRIDGET BAITS A BEAR

1

"You said before you didn't have any idea where they were going," Orville said between mouthfuls of hummus and pita. God, *hummus*. How could something that looked like mush be so delicious? He sat with Bridget in the far corner of a little Middle Eastern restaurant near Lake Merritt, far enough away from the customers that he could talk to her unheard, probably. "So where do we start?"

Bridget didn't seem to hear him. She'd been staring off into the distance for a while now, though whether she was lost in deep thought or simply overwhelmed by recent revelations, Orville didn't know. She'd wanted to go charging into the briarpatch the moment they left Darrin's house, but Orville had needed food before setting off on a trek like that. This new body seemed to need more fuel than the old one ever had . . . or, maybe, he just felt like he needed to eat more often, since food was now more pleasure than chore. Bridget had slowed down a bit as they walked to the restaurant, melancholy creeping over her when she didn't have immediate action to distract herself.

"Bridget?" he said, and she looked at him, cocked her head, and nodded.

"If Ismael is taking Darrin into the briarpatch in hopes of finding a direct route to the better world, I think I know the first place they'll go. He'll want to show Darrin what he's looking for. There's a kind of . . . scenic overlook, I guess . . . a place where you can glimpse the light of the better world. I think they'll go there. I don't know how long they'll *stay* there, though, and if we miss them . . ."

"Well, let's go." Orville mopped up the last of his food and shoved a wad of pita into his mouth. He chewed and swallowed as he stood up, leaving some cash from his poker winnings on the table.

Bridget nodded. "Just let me think . . . We could have gone directly from Darrin's house if I'd thought about it, down the stairs where we shoved that mugger—that leads to the same world, branch, or whatever, that we need to pass through. Hmm. There might be a better way though—I know a shortcut from the lakeshore to Ismael's neighbourhood, and from there we can go through his back shed. It's still kind of a long journey that way, but time moves funny in the briarpatch, so maybe we'll get to the scenic overlook before they leave." Bridget seemed livelier now, with a plan of action in mind.

They crossed the street, went over a freeway overpass, and were soon within sight of the water. Bridget led him toward the ornamental pillars that decorated this end of the lake, and the air shimmered, revealing a passageway between two pillars that led into a place of green mist. "Hold your breath, and squint your eyes," Bridget said. "The air in there isn't good, but it's only a few steps across, just follow me straight in, okay?"

Orville nodded, wondering if the green mist was poison gas, if it would burn his skin, if Bridget would be so sanguine about rushing through there if she still had a body of her own. But that was unfair. Bridget did care about him. At first she'd wanted to keep him safe out of simple expedience, because she was tied to his body, but he believed she'd grown to care about him for less selfish reasons. She hadn't given him a reason to stop trusting her yet. So he took a deep breath, squinted his eyes, and plunged into the green darkness.

2

They made it to Ismael's living room in less than five minutes, passing first through the choking green mist—which hadn't burned him, but had given his sight a strange greenish tinge for a while afterward—and then through what seemed to be a giant's playground, with jungle gyms as high as skyscrapers, titanic slides, and a filthy merry-go-round with carved wooden animals straight out of undersea-themed nightmares. Bridget led him beneath a swing-set the size of an auditorium, through a shadow that was also a door, and from there into Ismael's remarkable living room, a nexus of branching pathways into the briarpatch. "Where to now?" he said.

"First, we pack a bag for the trek." Bridget showed him Ismael's supply room, selecting a backpack for him, and filling it from Ismael's cupboard, stocked well with water bottles, jerky, trail mix, bandages, and other travelling necessities, including a can of red spray paint in case they deviated from the path and needed to leave markings to follow back. "Want a walking stick?" She opened a closet filled with them. Orville selected one, a Victorian-style walking stick with a heavy brass ball on top. Then he paused and nodded at the chrome-plated shotgun lying on the pillows. "Ah, do you think . . . ? You said there are dangerous things in the briarpatch."

Bridget shrugged. "If you want to carry it, it couldn't hurt. It might stop a bear, I guess. Have you ever used a gun before?"

Orville had—his stepfather had tried to make a man of him in a variety of ways, and marksmanship being one approach. "It's been a while, but yes." They looked around for shells, but couldn't find any, so Orville opened the breech on the shotgun and took the two shells out, pocketing them. He remembered enough about basic gun safety to know carrying around a loaded shotgun wasn't the smartest idea, and he hadn't survived a leap from a bridge to accidentally shoot himself now. The backpack was equipped with a number of rings and snaps for securing gear to the outside, so Orville rigged it sufficiently to hold the shotgun in place, barrel pointed skyward, then slung the whole thing on his back. It wasn't too heavy, and the weight was well-distributed. "Lay on, MacBridget," he said.

They went into the backyard to the sagging wooden shed. "When we go through here, into the briarpatch," Bridget said, "there's a bridge, and . . . Ismael liked to surprise people with it, but I'll just tell you. You'll see your own corpse there. I probably won't, since I'm not alive anymore, but you'll see a dead body that looks just like your own. After that, there's not too much to worry about, until we get to this dense wood full of weird trees. You can't leave the path there, no matter what you see, and you mustn't climb the trees. I tried to climb one once, and Ismael had to pull me down. I'd rather not have to do the same thing for you, okay?"

"Got it," Orville said. "Dead body, evil trees. I'll be careful."

He didn't think it would be so bad, seeing his own corpse. It was just some trick of the briarpatch, after all, and he was prepared for it. But when they walked through the shed and out again, onto the long bridge, the thing at the other end didn't even look like a person at all. Orville only made it halfway across before the wind shifted, and the smell—rot and salt—hit him like a wet rag in the face. Having a sense of smell had seemed like a great gift, until now. He leaned over the side of the swaying bridge and vomited up his hummus and pita, setting the bridge to swinging sickeningly, and he sank down, holding onto the sides, trying to steady himself, breathing through his mouth.

"I'm so sorry," Bridget whispered. "It wasn't so bad for me."

"That's what would have happened if I'd hit headfirst and really died," Orville gasped, squeezing his eyes shut. "If that boat hadn't found me and pulled me out of the water." The corpse at the far end of the bridge was wet, shattered, spilling open. Orville abruptly rose and rushed across the bridge, jumping over his corpse, and continuing down the path without looking back. He was shaking, and his knees were weak, but with every step he put between himself and the corpse, he felt better. What had he been thinking? His life had been hard, yes, and miserable, and it might have continued that way indefinitely, but had he really believed that being a broken pile of meat would be better?

"You wanted oblivion," Bridget said, walking behind him now as they followed the narrow path and passed through a cleft of rock. "It's nothing to be ashamed of. Life is hard."

Orville nodded. That was true. But seeing that body back there made him wonder if, maybe, death wasn't harder still.

3

After the path under the lake, after the cavern with the deadly trees (which Orville had avoided by staring at his feet during the walk), they finally reached a rock-strewn plain beneath a sky so grey it hurt to look upon. Orville swung his pack off his back, sat on a flattish rock, and took out a water bottle. "I'm assuming this is a safe-ish place?"

"It was boring as hell the last time I walked this way," Bridget said. "This is the longest part of the walk, and it's hard to find the path. Ismael marked some of the rocks with spray paint so we can find the way." She pointed to a rock splashed with red. "There's this big boulder, and you crawl under it, and come out in the scenic overlook."

"Is this place actually in the briarpatch, or is it just, like, some badlands somewhere, on a really overcast day?"

Bridget shook her head. "I've never been here when the sky wasn't just like that, but I've only been here a couple of times, so I can't be sure. The air smells stale, though, don't you think?"

Orville sniffed obligingly. He didn't have a lot of experience smelling air, fresh or stale or otherwise, but he thought he knew what she meant—the place did have a stifling, closed-in feel, despite its evident vastness. The sky seemed too close to the earth. He took another swig of water and started to repack his bag.

"Shit," Bridget said softly. "Orville, is that shotgun loaded? I see a fucking bear."

Orville looked around, startled, and after a moment saw a shape far off on the horizon, brown, shaggy, shambling. He supposed it could be a bear, though as he watched, it disappeared behind some rocks. He took the shells from his pocket and loaded the shotgun, trying to keep his hands steady. "Can't we just, like, go wide? Try to avoid it?"

"We can try. But in the briarpatch, bears often travel in packs. Besides, we can't stray too far from the marked rocks, or we'll get lost."

He tied his walking stick onto the backpack where the shotgun had been, and they moved off, Bridget silently pointing out red-daubed rocks. Orville started to speak, to ask how much farther, but Bridget shushed him. "Sound can carry a long way out here," she whispered, and Orville wondered if the bears could hear her, or if, being a ghost, she would be outside their observable experience. Either way, he kept his mouth shut, and the only noise was the crunch of small rocks underfoot. The shotgun, cradled in his arms, felt very heavy. After an interminable time, Bridget whispered, "We're nearly there. It's that big rock ahead."

"One more step, motherfucker, and I'll air-hole you."

Something hard and pointed pressed into the small of Orville's back, and Bridget spun to face Orville, her eyes narrowing. "Shit," she said. "It's that guy who tried to mug us, the tall one that we shoved into the briarpatch."

Orville closed his eyes. The mugger. Of course it was. Hadn't Orville learned in junior high that standing up to bullies didn't do any good? The teachers, the books, they all said if you stood up to a bully, he'd leave you alone in the future, because they preferred easy prey. But the one time Orville had stood up for himself, had shoved Bobby Cavalier back when he tried to steal Orville's lunch money in seventh grade, it hadn't worked out so well. Bobby and two of his friends had jumped Orville in the bathroom the next day and dunked his head in the toilet, and that had been just the beginning. Orville had let Bridget convince him to fight back, and now these were the consequences, and they would probably be more deadly than a toilet-dunking. But the lead ball of dread in his belly was lightened a bit by the knowledge that the man wasn't dead; Orville hadn't helped kill a man after all. That was something. It would be a great comfort when the mugger shot him in the head.

"I don't know what you're doing here," the mugger said, voice rough like he'd been screaming for hours, "but I know what I'm going to do *about* it."

Bridget waved her arms around, and then grunted. "I guess getting knocked down the stairs hasn't made him any more perceptive than he was before—he still can't see me. This place is part of the same world you can reach from the stairs down by Darrin's house, where we shoved him, but it's miles and miles and *miles* away, that's why I didn't bring us by that route. He looks really bad, like he's been here way more than a day. I think time must have slipped a gear for him or something." She circled around. "He's got a pistol pointed at your back, Orville. You probably figured that out. He—"

"Drop the gun." The mugger jabbed Orville harder. He let the shotgun fall to the rocks. "You got anything to drink?" the mugger said, and now the fear-roar in Orville's head subsided enough that he could hear the mugger's desperation.

"Sure," Orville said. "In the bag."

"I could probably manage to hit him in the head with a rock," Bridget said. "But I don't know how hard, and if it's not hard enough, he might shoot you. You know I'm not thrilled at the idea of risking your life. You have any better ideas?"

The gun left Orville's back. "Turn around," the mugger said.

Orville did, and what he saw shocked him. Bridget had said he looked bad, but that hadn't conveyed the magnitude. The mugger's clothes were ragged and torn, and his sallow, pockmarked face was filthy. His hair was wild, with leaves stuck among the strands, and he had a ragged beard. "I knew it was you," the mugger said, keeping the gun aimed in Orville's general direction. He grinned— it was the kind of crazy smile Orville sometimes saw on the faces of homeless people in the Mission district in San Francisco. "Damn it, I knew it was you. We weren't going to hurt you, we just wanted to get paid, and then you had to . . . to . . ." The smile disappeared. "What did you do? You drugged me, dragged me out into the desert, some shit like that? And then you came back to see if I was dead yet?"

"Goddamn briarpatch," Bridget said. "Ismael says he thinks the place has a sense of humour, sometimes, the kind of stuff that happens, people get flung together against all odds. I mean, there must be millions of miles of space out here in the back forty of the world, and we run into this guy again."

"Answer me!" the man shouted.

Orville flinched. "I've got water for you," he said, because it seemed like something the man might appreciate.

"I been drinking out of puddles," the man said. "There's places around here that aren't the desert, exactly, I walked and walked and never got anywhere, I been eating berries and raw fish and shit, I'm lucky I didn't die."

"Beef jerky too," Orville said. "If you just let me take off my bag." He glanced down at the shotgun by his feet. The mugger hadn't told him to throw it aside, or kick it—

"Kick that gun over here," the mugger said, and Orville suppressed a sigh. Did thinking make it so? He gave the shotgun a kick, terrified it would go off and blast his shins, but it just spun a couple of feet closer to the mugger.

"Good. Now dump it out," the man said. "The whole bag, dump it out."

"Do what he says, Orville," Bridget said. "I'll be right back."

Orville opened the backpack and poured its contents on the ground. The mugger let out a low moan when he saw the pouches of granola, the bottles of water, the strips of jerky. "Sit down," he said. "Sit on your hands." Orville complied, small stones cutting into the backs of his hands.

The mugger crouched and pawed at the pile with his free hand, keeping the pistol on Orville, and pulled out a water bottle with a twist top. For a moment he looked bewildered, then gripped the lid in his teeth and twisted it open, spitting the cap out when he was done, and tipping the bottle back to drink.

For a moment, the mugger's eyes closed as water ran down his chin, and Orville slid the walking stick away from the bag. The wood made small clicks against the stones on the ground, and Orville tensed up, expecting the mugger to hear, but he seemed utterly focused on drinking. Orville slid the stick behind his back. The mugger's eyes stayed closed for a while longer—long enough, almost, for Orville to decide to try to knock the gun out of his hand. But then his eyes opened, and fixed on Orville.

Somewhere off in the distance, Bridget was shouting, but Orville couldn't make out the words. She hadn't gone this far away from him before—she said it started to hurt and made her mind go fuzzy if she got more than a dozen yards away—which meant she was probably doing something she thought was worth the pain.

"You're going to take me out of here," the mugger said, very reasonably, and then gnawed on his thumbnail. His fingernails were ragged, bitten beyond the quick, his fingers bleeding in places and scabbed in others. "I been out here for a long time, days, weeks, sometimes I think forever, sometimes I think I was *raised* by bears, you know? But I'm not all the way gone yet, I can get back, you can take me. You put me here, you can get me out, and if you don't, I'll . . . I'll eat your *heart*." The man gnawed at his fingernail again, and this time blood trickled, and ran into his beard.

When he said he would eat Orville's heart, Orville did not think he was speaking figuratively.

"Of course," Orville said. In truth, he felt horribly guilty about this man's circumstances. He was a mugger, yes, he'd swaggered and threatened Orville like a thousand bullies before him, but he'd been lost in the briarpatch, and it was driving him insane. That was Orville's fault. He'd sent the man here.

"I killed people before," the man said. "Shot them, and even cut up that one woman, I did, you know I did, but it was nothing like this, nothing as terrible as this. The shit I've seen over here, it'd make your hair turn white." He reached for another water bottle, and Orville stared at him. Hadn't there been something on the news, about a rash of muggings near Lake Merritt, one of them fatal, another involving a rape? Something about a pair of muggers who liked to lie in wait . . .

"That was you?" Orville said. "You were the ones who got that woman coming home from work, dragged her into her own house and . . . and did those things? And her boyfriend found her?"

"I don't know who the fuck *found* her." The man chewed off another lid. "I just know how we *left* her."

Any sympathy Orville had felt melted away. Muggers driven to theft by poverty, desperation, even drug addiction, they might be excused, but this man and his friend had terrorized a community, and Orville didn't owe him anything. Bullies were one thing. Murderers were another. Orville had a deep understanding now, about the preciousness of life. While the mugger sucked at the water bottle, Orville reached carefully behind him and felt the brass ball of the walking stick. If he whipped the stick around fast enough . . .

"BEAR!" Bridget shouted. The mugger didn't hear her, of course, and if he noticed Orville flinch, be probably assumed it was because of his threats. Bridget came running, pursued by a bear, a great brown grizzly loping after her with its head low. Its fur was damp and matted, sticking up in little curlicues and corkscrews of darker hair, and it made a strange low whuffing sound as it ran.

The mugger must have heard it too, because he turned his head, then leapt to his feet and staggered backward. "No!" he shouted. "Not you, no, not you, I'm *out*, I'm getting *out*, I won't be that way again!"

Orville sat, shocked into stillness. The bear was chasing Bridget, who was running straight at the mugger. The bear could see Bridget. Orville pulled the walking stick into his lap.

The mugger started running, veering off at an angle, and Bridget pursued him, with the happy effect of leading the bear *away* from Orville. The mugger was weeping and shouting as he ran.

Then Bridget fell to her knees, gasping, hugging herself, and shivering. She'd gone as far away from Orville as she could stand, and the bear loped toward her. Bridget crouched, protecting her head. The bear was upon her in moments, reaching out with a great paw to swipe at her—

—and though Bridget flinched, the paw didn't seem to hit her. It passed close to her, but she didn't go flying, didn't scream, didn't bleed. The bear grumbled and swiped again, with the same effect, and Bridget stopped huddling. She stood up, wincing as she moved, and stepped aside. The bear sniffed at her, shook its great head, and then seemed to catch sight of the mugger for the first time, and set off in pursuit of him. The mugger, who by now had put some good distance between them, looked back over his shoulder, staggered, and fell—probably tripped on a rock, Orville thought. The bear bounded after him, running like an exuberant puppy, and Orville approached Bridget.

"Shit," she said. "Funny how I forgot I was a *ghost* for a minute. You can get used to anything." Her cheeks were flushed red, as if from exertion, and Orville thought that was strange, since she didn't have blood vessels.

"Wait," Bridget said. "What . . . what's happening?" She pointed to the place where the mugger had fallen. The bear wasn't attacking him; it was merely sniffing around on the ground, occasionally pawing at the dirt, while the mugger . . . The mugger was growing. Changing. He was forty or fifty yards away, just a shape on the ground, but he was visibly changing shape, his crouched form on the ground turning darker, swelling in all directions.

"He's becoming a bear," Bridget said. "Shit. He must have gotten scratched, or bitten . . . Orville, we have to go."

"He's becoming a bear? I don't understand. What—"

Where the mugger had been, a bear stood now, with darker fur than the bear Bridget had lured over to save Orville. They bumped their heads together, as if in greeting, and then both turned to face Bridget and Orville.

The mugger was a bear, which was far worse than him being a mugger. So much for Bridget's plan.

"Run!" Bridget said, and tore off in the direction of their original goal, the passageway to a different part of the briarpatch. Orville came after her, knowing the bears were pursuing, knowing things were far more strange and dangerous here than he'd realized. The mugger they'd shoved into this world had been changed by it, and become some kind of shape-shifting lunatic. Orville ran past the scattered contents of his pack, the shining shotgun left lying in the dirt, and it was ten steps later before he realized he should have tried to grab the gun—but being chased by a bear was a pretty big distraction. At least he still had the walking stick in hand. It wasn't much of a weapon, but it was better than bare hands. Bridget paused by the shadow of a great rock, beckoning him frantically, and Orville put on an extra push of speed, the way he'd run in Junior High when a particularly dangerous bunch of bullies was after him, though he'd never truly believed any of *them* would kill him. He ran into the shadow by the rock, a shadow that was also a door, and darkness engulfed him.

ARTURO HITS AND RUNS

1

"So, Echo," Arturo said. "Have you always been a psycho carjackin' liar?"

"People don't usually talk to me like that when I have a knife," Echo said.

Arturo shrugged and twisted the wheel to veer around the ruins of a pagoda in the middle of the wide slate avenue the Wendigo was bombing down. Not that the Wendigo couldn't steer itself, if necessary, but Arturo liked to feel like he was involved, and the Wendigo went along with that. "So stab me to death. Then you'll be stuck in a car in the middle of the briarpatch."

"Or maybe I'll just save up my stabbiness until you've taken me where I need to go, and then let it all out in one long rush."

Arturo shrugged again. "Whatever the Wendigo wills, honey. I'm just curious. You're the one who told me the story, I'm just doing a, what do you call it, follow-up question."

"I get bored on road trips. When the radio gave out, I had to talk about *something*. That doesn't give you the right to quiz me. I just need you to take me to Ismael, so I can teach him not to fuck with me."

"I'm thinkin' that's a good lesson." Arturo braced himself as the road ahead turned into washed-out ruts deep enough to challenge even the Wendigo's supernatural suspension. He bounced and jostled in his seat, and Echo bounced around too, gripping the door handle with one hand. She wasn't wearing a seatbelt, and Arturo figured, if all else failed, he could jam the brake pedal to the floor and send her flying headfirst into the windshield. He hadn't tried it, though, because if the Wendigo wanted to get rid of Echo it would have, and

Arturo had been putting his trust in the Wendigo for years now. Somehow, he believed, this would help him find Marjorie.

"It's just, not to be rude or nothin', but I'm wonderin', have you had any professional help? I mean, is this an off-your-meds type situation?? The pathological lyin', the attempted murder, that stuff isn't so great."

"I'm not a pathological liar," Echo said, which almost made Arturo laugh, because what else would such a person say? "I'm a strategic liar," she went on. "Mostly. I tell lies when it furthers my purpose, or when it's funny. It's not like I can't help myself. I'm hardly compulsive. As for trying to kill people, it's only *Ismael*, and he doesn't die. Not that I'd mind killing other people. But, really, I think most people have murder in their hearts, don't you?"

Marjorie did, Arturo thought, *Probably. But the only one she murdered was herself*. But that wasn't something he could say to *this* one. "A lot of people have some dark stuff in them, it's true. But part of bein' a good person is keepin' that stuff under control."

"Most people lie to themselves," Echo said. "I've had a couple of therapists. One of them, the one I went to see when I was fifteen, I fucked him, and after that, he was so scared I'd tell my parents that he said I was totally well-adjusted, and everything they were worried about was just a phase. The other one, the one I had to see because of the court order, he eventually told me he liked paying homeless people to beat each other up and have sex with each other and shit. I got along with that guy pretty good. We understood each other. I do keep stuff under control, Arturo. If I didn't, I'd be dead or in jail."

"So you weren't beat as a child or raised in poverty or nothin' like that, then?" Arturo said. The rutted road abruptly vanished, and they were riding along smooth asphalt, a nice normal country road lined by fields overgrown with kudzu, but instead of yellow or white lines drawn down the middle of the road, the lines were electric blue. "Because that stuff, it's not an excuse, but it's at least an explanation."

"I don't need excuses. I take responsibility for myself. And I don't need *explanations*. I'm a self-made woman. I am what I want to be. I have *fun*."

"You're havin' fun now?" Arturo asked.

Echo rapped her knuckles against the passenger window, staring out at the green passing by. "Well," she said after a moment. "Right now I'm mostly pissed off. But if I don't teach Ismael a lesson, it'll weigh on my mind, and I won't be able to have as much fun again in the future. So I have to see this through."

"So you don't have, like, a purpose? Some goal for yourself?" Arturo was thinking of the note he'd found in the Wendigo, all those years ago—*A man needs a purpose like a car needs a driver.* The Wendigo had saved Arturo's life. He wondered if maybe it would be possible to save Echo's life, or, at least, her soul.

"I could die any time. My purpose is staying alive and keeping myself occupied. That's it."

"There's somethin' to be said for livin' in the moment, I guess. But sometimes it's gotta be hard to get up in the mornin'."

Echo snorted. "I've got good brain chemistry, Arturo. I like my life."

"You don't ever feel bad? You don't feel remorse for the things you've done? What's that word for the kind of crazy where you don't think anybody but you is real?"

"Sociopathic. But believe me, I know other people are real. It wouldn't be *nearly* as much fun fucking with them if they weren't."

"I guess I'm not cut out for this psychology stuff," Arturo said. "Because it seems to me like you're just plain messed up."

"Everybody's messed up, Artie. You drive around in a car from another world, for whatever fucked-up reason. You're messed up too. I just don't lie to myself. Anybody else in the world, yeah, absolutely, but never myself."

"I think you'd feel better, if you had a purpose," Arturo said, knowing it was the best sort of outreach he could provide, knowing it wasn't nearly enough for someone like this.

"Maybe so. Right now my purpose is ripping Ismael a new one, and I feel pretty good about that."

The Wendigo transitioned again, in that seamless way it had, and rattled calamitously over a wide plain scattered with rocks and boulders, under a flat grey sky.

The bumpy ride dislodged the pile of paper rising in the back seat, and a few glossy pages from lingerie catalogues—normally kind of a nice present for Arturo, but not much good to him now—came cascading down into the front seat. Echo brushed them off onto the floor and said, "What's with all the paper in here, anyway?"

"I'm not sure. The Wendigo provides. I don't question it, and I wouldn't get an answer if I did. Most of it seems like junk, but sometimes useful stuff turns up." He was thinking of the fragments of Darrin's imaginary journal, though how "useful" those had been he wasn't sure, since they'd mostly led him to hanging around too long and getting carjacked.

"So if you throw it out, more just appears?"

"That's the way it goes."

"The paper fills up the whole backseat?"

"Front seat, too. And the glove compartment."

"What about the trunk?"

"The trunk doesn't open," Arturo lied.

Echo reached out and twisted the little silver plastic knob on the glove compartment. That was where money showed up, usually—Arturo figured the Wendigo was smart enough not to leave money lying around on the seats in plain view of passersby—and he hoped that, if Echo ripped him off, the Wendigo would replenish his supply. The car was like an absent-minded parent doling out irregular allowances, though Arturo had never really suffered during the dry spells when no money was forthcoming. There was always something to eat—if only because of freebie restaurant coupons the Wendigo coughed up—and he could sleep in the car.

But money didn't spill from the glove compartment. When it popped open under the pressure of its contents, a flurry of thin strips of paper confettied out over Echo's legs. She picked one up, frowned, and said "They're fortunes. Like from fortune cookies."

"I know a game you can play with those fortunes," Arturo said. "You read the fortune out loud and add the words 'in bed' to the end."

"Everybody knows that game," Echo said. She picked up a fortune and said "Let them eat cake. In bed." She tossed that fortune aside and took another from the pile on her lap. "Off with her head. In bed."

"Not really my idea of a good time," Arturo said. "Though the cake didn't sound bad. I like a good piece of cake."

"These aren't even real fortunes. They aren't even the sort of stupid-non-fortunes you usually get. How is 'off with her head' a fortune?" She read another: "All strange and terrible events are welcome, but comforts we despise."

"In bed," Arturo said helpfully.

Echo ignored him, and read more in quick succession: "'In my end is my beginning. I am one of the people who love the why of things. All my possessions for a moment of time. Fools are more to be feared than the wicked. We are never tired, and we all love hospitals. In praising Antony I have dispraised Caesar. Great events make me quiet and calm; it is only trifles that irritate my nerves.' What the fuck are these?"

"Huh," Arturo said. "That one about the cake, that's somethin' Marie

Antoinette supposedly said, when they told her the peasants didn't have enough bread. And the 'off with her head' thing is from Alice in Wonderland, it's what the Red Queen said to Alice."

"It was the Queen of Hearts, not the Red Queen, idiot," Echo said. "And everybody knows Marie Antoinette said that other thing."

Arturo didn't take offence at being called an idiot. He'd been called worse by better for less reason. "What I'm tryin' to say is, maybe they're all quotes from queens. They seem kinda queenly. That one about Antony and Caesar, that's probably somethin' Cleopatra said, right? In the Shakespeare play, anyway? So maybe the others are from queens, too."

"Queens," Echo said thoughtfully. "Empresses. Sure. But why would there be fortune cookies about queens?"

"One time the glove compartment was full of programs for productions of David Mamet plays. I didn't think that meant much, and I don't think this does either." Though in truth he wondered. The Wendigo had a way of communicating obliquely, but what was it trying to say to Echo? Or to Arturo, about her?

Echo rolled down the window and let some of the fortunes go fluttering out into the wind. Arturo winced. Litter offended him—he saw too much of it on the roadsides he drove past. And while, in the real world, the Wendigo's freight of paper tended to vanish after a little while, like fairy money, he wasn't sure the same would be true here, in the briarpatch, where reality was more bendable.

"What's that in the road up there?" Echo said.

Arturo looked where she pointed. There was something on the ground, something other than rocks, but he couldn't tell what. Trash, it looked like.

"Stop the car there," Echo said.

"Okay." Opportunities for escape were fine by him. After another minute he reached the pile, and stopped the Wendigo.

"Turn off the car, and then get out," Echo said.

So much for driving off when she got out. Arturo did as she said. She scooted across the seat and got out on his side, keeping her knife in plain sight. He could've taken off across the plain, but he was no good at getting around in the briarpatch without the Wendigo. Besides, Echo would probably have chased him. So he stood by, hands clasped before him, as Echo slammed the door.

"Okay, let's check it out." They walked around to the front of the Wendigo, and Echo gasped. "My shotgun!" She rushed to the weapon, an ostentatious chrome-plated job, and scooped it up in her arms. "How the hell did it get out here?"

"Mind if I pick up some of that water and beef jerky?" Arturo said. "I got some coupons for El Pollo Loco in the car, but I don't think we're gonna find a drive-through out here."

"Sure, fine." Echo pulled the backpack toward her and began rifling through it. "Damn it. No shells."

"It makes a pretty club, though." Arturo filled his pockets with jerky and picked up a couple of water bottles.

Echo opened the gun and laughed. "Oh, it's loaded. Two shells, just like I left it. So don't go thinking I'm defenceless."

"That's damn near the last thing you are."

"I do wonder how it got here, though. Maybe Ismael took it, and dropped it here? So it's a clue, right? But why drop it here? What—"

"Um," Arturo said. "There's bears out here." A trio of grizzlies was approaching, still some distance away, but he knew bears could move fast if they wanted to. One of the bears had dozens of little blue ribbons woven into its fur, which undid any hope Arturo had that these were *ordinary* bears. These were the other kind of bear. He began backing toward the Wendigo.

"I didn't tell you to move," Echo snapped. "You listened to me when all I had was a knife, you'd damn sure better listen when I've got a gun."

"Can you threaten me later? Bears! Get in the car!"

Echo finally looked around and saw the approaching animals. "Fuck. How can anything live in this desert?" She hurried to the passenger side.

Arturo got into the car and shut his door, and as soon as Echo was inside, he pressed the button that locked all the doors. The bears couldn't work a door handle in this shape . . . but bears in the briarpatch had a distressing tendency to shapeshift. Arturo started up the Wendigo, put it in reverse, and glanced up to the rearview mirror.

There were five bears behind them, two big grizzlies, two smaller black bears, and one by-god polar bear, a variety Arturo had never encountered in the briarpatch before. "Oh, shit," he said. "There's a whole goddamn herd of bears back there, too."

"A group of bears is called a sloth," Echo said, twisting in her seat to look behind. "I heard that on a nature show. So what do we do?"

The bears ahead of them stopped at the pile of food and began nosing the contents around. Arturo wished he hadn't picked up that jerky. "We try to get away," Arturo said. More bears were ambling in from both directions, and there were over a dozen now, a bigger congregation of the creatures than he'd ever seen in one place before. The Wendigo was fairly well boxed-in, and while it was possible the grizzlies would scatter if he drove toward them, it was also possible they'd decide to attack. They wouldn't be able to break into the Wendigo, but being stuck in a car with Echo, surrounded by ravening monsters pounding on the glass, wouldn't be fun. And if they managed to flip the car over, Arturo and Echo might *really* be stuck here.

One of the grizzlies behind them rose up and put its forepaws on the trunk of the Wendigo, making the whole car rock back.

"Fuck!" Echo said, sounding genuinely alarmed for the first time.

"Cover your ears," Arturo said. Echo just looked at him, frowning. "Suit yourself," Arturo said, and slammed his hand down on the Wendigo's horn.

The roar was loud, vast, bowel-churning, and Arturo squeezed his eyes to slits and gritted his teeth. Echo had her palms pressed flat to her ears.

The effect on the bears was instantaneous. Most bolted away from the Wendigo, and the grizzly leaning on the trunk staggered back. Arturo would have gunned the engine . . . but the polar bear wasn't acting scared. The polar bear was acting *pissed*, and it charged toward the Wendigo, mouth open in a roar Arturo couldn't hear over the Wendigo's horn.

Before the bear quite reached the Wendigo, it changed into an enormously fat, naked albino man. All the bears around them began changing too, transformations so abrupt it was a bit like watching balloons pop, larger volumes suddenly reduced to human proportions.

"This is fucked up!" Echo shouted, hands still held to her ears. The albino man ran and flung himself onto the hood of the Wendigo, face twisted in a snarl, and began pounding on the windshield.

Arturo stopped pressing the horn. It was good for scaring away animals and the occasional not-quite-animal, but it wasn't much good on bears in human form—they might be crazy, but they were smart enough to know the noise was coming from a car, and not some gargantuan apex predator. Arturo hit the gas, and the Wendigo shot backward, sending the polar man sliding off the hood, but Arturo couldn't continue his high-speed reverse, because a boulder loomed up in the rearview mirror. He hit the brakes, and the Wendigo lurched to a stop. The now-human bears approached the Wendigo from the front, and some of them stopped to pick up chunks of rock from the ground.

"I doubt I can shoot them all," Echo said. "Even if they were grouped up nicely, I've only got two shells in this gun."

Arturo sighed. "I'd rather keep the murderin' to a minimum if that's okay with you. I've got one more thing I can try. Get the sunglasses out of the glove compartment."

"What are you talking about? The glove compartment is full of fortune cookie—"

"Just look, would you?" The bears were getting closer, and while the Wendigo was tough, enough guys bashing the glass with rocks would get in eventually. And then Arturo and Echo would die. Or, worse, they *wouldn't* die, and would, instead, be changed.

Echo dug into the fortunes in the glove compartment and came out with two pairs of oversized aviator sunglasses.

"Give me a pair, and put yours on," Arturo said, and added "Trust me," when she hesitated. She handed him the sunglasses, and donned her own.

Once he put them on, the sunglasses blocked Arturo's vision almost completely—they were much darker than ordinary sunglasses. The Wendigo owner's manual was only intermittently available, but it was very clear about the necessity of protective eyewear before turning on the high beams. Arturo had only used the bright headlights a couple of times in all the years he'd been driving the Wendigo, but if this wasn't an emergency, he didn't know what was.

"Let there be headlights." He pulled the lever by the steering wheel.

Even through the heavily smoked glasses, the light was bright, twin expanding cones of intense brightness that threw the bear-people before them into stark relief. They didn't try to shield their eyes, though—they just stopped moving, and stared.

"So pretty," Echo murmured, and started to reach up to take off her sunglasses.

Without thinking, Arturo grabbed her wrist. "No," he said. "That light is like heroin or something, okay? Once you start looking, it's hard to stop."

"It's the light of a better world, isn't it," Echo said, but when he let go of her hand, she didn't try to take her glasses off. "What Ismael's been looking for."

Arturo sighed. "No, it's like an imitation of that light, okay? The same way the horn sounds like the roar of a big scary animal, but *isn't*. This light, it's just a trick." Arturo wasn't certain of that, actually, but even if the light pouring forth from his high beams was somehow imported from the supposed heaven so many briarpatch pilgrims were searching for, it wouldn't do them any good. The high beams couldn't stay on forever, and if they could, the pilgrims would just starve to death while basking in the light.

"Those bears might not stay subdued for long. The light has funny effects on them, maybe because they're crazy, I don't know, but it's like red kryptonite to

Superman, you never know how they'll react. Sometimes they just sit and enjoy it, and other times they try to kill each other, like the light is a limited resource and they're afraid the other bears will eat it all up." He nosed the Wendigo forward a bit, to put some space between them and the boulder behind. The bears were swaying and weeping and laughing not far from the Wendigo's front end, but if he could rock the car back and forth in a seven- or nine-point turn, he should be able to get a gap big enough to drive through.

"Pretty pretty pretty," Echo murmured. Arturo backed, filled, backed, filled; and then the headlights flickered briefly. Echo let out a low moan at the instant of darkness before the lights returned.

Arturo glanced at the dash, and the glowing red "low battery" light was on. Shit shit shit. He'd never left the brights on for this long, and if the battery died, they were well and truly screwed, because they couldn't get a jump out here, and Triple A didn't service the briarpatch.

He finally got the Wendigo turned so there was no one directly in front, though the bears outside the cone of the lights began shaking and thrashing and keening horribly in withdrawal. The brights flickered again, and Arturo shut them off and put the Wendigo in drive, pulling his sunglasses low on his nose so he could see.

The fat albino man lurched to the front of the car and screamed "Bring back the light! Bring it back!" He pounded on the hood with his fists.

Arturo froze. If he turned the brights back on, the man would just stand there, and Arturo would have to spend more time—time the battery probably didn't have—to back up and get around him.

Then Echo stomped on his foot with her own, driving his foot down on the accelerator, and the Wendigo's engine roared. The car shot forward, the fat albino rolling up onto the hood and then bouncing off, hard, when Arturo jerked the wheel around. Echo kept pressing on his foot with hers and the Wendigo's speedometer ratcheted up and up, putting distance between them and the bears. A glance at the rearview mirror showed them pursuing, changing into bears again, but they couldn't catch the Wendigo.

Finally Echo took her foot away, and Arturo was able to ease up on the speed a little. "I did *not* like the way that light made me feel."

"You seemed to like it a lot." Arturo felt almost friendly toward her, flush with the giddiness of survival, riding high on the Wendigo's power.

"I liked it the way I like high doses of painkillers, and I *disliked* it for the same reason. I don't like losing control."

"I guess you won't be joinin' Ismael in his search for the better world, then," Arturo said.

"Hell, no. Though I can see why he wants it. He just wants to hide from the mean old world that hurt him so bad, boo-fucking-hoo. Whereas me, I want to hurt the world *back*."

Arturo was reminded, then, that Echo was crazy. But, still. "That was some good drivin' back there."

Echo took off her sunglasses, tossed them onto the floor, and looked at him. She grinned. "You too, old man."

The landscape flickered, the vastness suddenly replaced by grassy hills strewn with bits of classical-looking ruins, tilted pillars and broken arches. The clouds were dark against the blue sky, their edges limned with brightness from the concealed sun. The Wendigo climbed up to the top of a high hill, and Arturo stopped it. From this vantage, they could see, off in the distance, a sort of crack in the sky, with honey-coloured light filtering down, illuminating a valley as if with a spotlight.

"That looks like the light that came from the headlights," Echo said. "But weaker, like it's shining through dirty glass."

"Yeah, I been here before. It's a place where you can sorta glimpse that better world Ismael told you about, stand in the reflection of a reflection of its light, filtered and indirect. Lotta skeletons down there of people who starved to death starin' up at the light. Supposedly if you can make it to the land of light, you don't starve to death, or else you don't need your body, or somethin'. I've heard different stories."

"Fuck it," Echo said. "Let's keep moving."

But the Wendigo's engine suddenly shut off, and Arturo couldn't get her started again. He was afraid the battery was dead, but, no, the radio and dash lights and dome light all still came on. The Wendigo had just decided to stop here.

"What's this?" Echo reached into the glove compartment and drew out what looked like a hand-drawn treasure map. She showed it to Arturo, and there was a little kid's drawing of a car, with a dotted line leading in a winding path through little cartoon pillars and hills toward an X—marking who knew what kind of spot.

"I guess we're walkin' from here," Arturo said.

"This will lead us to Ismael?"

Arturo shrugged. "This will lead us wherever the Wendigo wants us to go."

"You better not be fucking with me, car," she said. "I'll slash your tires and rip out your spark plugs. I know a lot about cars, and I can make it so nobody could even rebuild your engine, got it?"

Arturo managed not to laugh, which was probably for the best, since Echo seemed totally sincere in threatening the Wendigo. "Let's go." She unlocked her door and climbed out, shotgun in hand.

Not quite daring to hope, Arturo tried to start the Wendigo, because escaping from Echo before she found Ismael would be nice. But the car didn't respond. It wanted him to accompany Echo a little farther, it seemed. Ah, well. Arturo had trusted the Wendigo this far. He got out of the car and joined Echo at the summit of the hill, and together they looked at the distant pool of honeyed light.

DARRIN GETS JUMPED

1

Darrin followed Ismael into a horrible dark nothing place that stank of hot asphalt. The only feature in the black sky was distant threads of a different and glistening quality of darkness.

"This way!" Ismael shouted, and grabbed Darrin by the wrist, dragging him through the empty place. The stench was so overwhelming Darrin stopped breathing in self-defence. Each step was heavy, as if the air itself were thickening. The dark threads grew larger and wider, and after a moment of confused staring Darrin realized they were coming *toward* him, somehow, that what he'd taken as some nightmarish dark-energy aurora was actually something else, a phenomenon with physical substance. There was a sound like a clatter of ball bearings falling into a metal bucket.

They blundered through a side-passage and into cooler air, and though this new place was in twilight, it seemed positively incandescent compared to the place they'd just been. Darrin looked around at the field where they'd landed, covered by shifting mists, more like something from a horror movie than any real fog he'd ever encountered. He sank down onto the tough, wiry grass, sucking gulps of damp air. Ismael sat beside him, hugging his arms around himself. "What was that?" Darrin said.

"We were in no danger," Ismael said. "Not . . . immediate danger. If we'd lingered, perhaps . . . well."

Darrin waited a moment and then sighed. "When human beings have conversations, Ismael, often one human asks a question, and the other one *answers*."

"I am not certain I am human," Ismael said. "Nor you. But, yes. *That* was supposed to be our last stop before the scenic overlook I want to show you. It used to be a sandy beach, with a profusion of tiny cobalt blue crabs, and the flash of mermaid tails off in the blue-green water. It was a pleasant place, but . . . not very plausible. I fear it has dissolved. It happens, sometimes, in the briarpatch. Worlds rise and fall. Most of the places I visit are stable, but others have only a tentative existence, and it can be difficult to tell ahead of time if a particular area is in danger of fading away. Unravelling."

"Those things in the sky, the dark threads, that noise . . ."

"The sound of a world being unmade," Ismael said. "A probability wave collapsing. The act of God forgetting. A few moments later, and we would not have been able to enter that place at all. As it is, we did not pass through to the place I expected." Ismael rose and brushed grass off his pants. "But I do know this place. Come. The overlook is not far from here either."

Darrin stood up. He still had a lot to learn about life in the briarpatch. But it was extraordinary, wasn't it? He'd never hungered for frontiers quite as desperately as Bridget, but he'd always enjoyed discovery, and seeing places no one else had ever seen, or at least, hadn't seen for a very long time. Ismael wasn't an ideal travelling companion, but in a place like this, confronted with these shifting wonders, there was no chance of sleepwalking through his life, and that was a welcome change from the slough of despond he'd been slogging through these past months.

"This way." Ismael set off through the horror-movie mist. They crested a hill, and the mists swirled away as they reached higher ground. Darrin gasped at the spectacle before them. A dark chasm stretched below, so wide he couldn't see the far side, spanned by a massive suspension bridge with black metal support towers the size of skyscrapers. Twinkling green lights dotted the structure, revealing the graceful arcs of its shape. But there was something wrong. . . .

"That bridge," Darrin said. "It doesn't have a deck. There are towers, and dangling cables, but there's nothing to walk or drive across."

"Yes," Ismael said.

"I've seen photos of the Bay Bridge when it was being constructed, before they built the deck, and it was like this. But . . . who's building this? Will it ever be finished?"

"That bridge *is* finished," Ismael said. "It is all that it will ever be. It is simply not a bridge the likes of you or I are permitted to cross." He sounded sad. He always sounded sad, but this seemed deeper, less weary, more profound.

"Ismael—" Darrin began. He didn't know what he was going to say. Ismael didn't give him a chance to say anything.

"Come, let us go. This is a dark place." Ismael beckoned, and started down the far side of the hill. Darrin looked at the strange dark span of the bridge—a bridge he could never cross, as far as he could imagine; and where would it lead, if he could? Then he went after Ismael, into a hole in the base of a hill, and into yet another world.

2

Perhaps an hour later, if time could be trusted in the briarpatch, Ismael said "Here. We're here."

"Here" was pleasant enough, green grass and marble ruins, hills and a deep blue sky. "There," Ismael pointed, and Darrin saw something like a spotlight shining from the sky, a beautiful golden light pouring down onto some blessed bit of earth.

"It looks like the light we get in summer afternoons, in the living room," Darrin said. "Bridget used to curl up on the couch by the window and look out at the light. She said it even made dirty rainwater in the gutters look beautiful."

"She went into that light," Ismael said. "Come, we'll go closer, and you can stand in it, and understand why she felt it was worth giving up everything to reach."

Mesmerized even from afar, Darrin followed as Ismael picked his way down the slope, past chunks of marble. Then something glistened, among the clouds, and Darrin stopped. "Wait, what's that?" He gestured, and a cloud moved, and there it was, the perfect arc of the moon-coloured bridge Darrin had first glimpsed in San Francisco all those months ago. It began somewhere beyond the horizon, and its far end disappeared into the golden light seeping from the sky.

"What?" Ismael shaded his eyes, looking up. "I don't see—"

Darrin reached out and touched Ismael on the back of the neck. Ismael gasped, and reached up to clasp Darrin's hand to his neck, as if afraid he would take it away. "What a lovely bridge," Ismael said, voice shaking. "Do you see how it stretches to the light?"

Darrin eased his hand away, and left Ismael blinking and staring. "I hope that, in time, I will be able to see paths only you can see," Ismael said after a moment. "I have always been able to pass my gift for sight on to others. The way, in fairy stories, the fairies can give second sight to mortals, and allow them to see the secret world. My old friend Harczos, he believed fairy stories were told about people like us, visitors from the briarpatch, and this may be true. But Harczos was never able to grant me his vision. When he touched me, I could see the corridors and stairways he perceived, and when I touched him, vice-versa, but neither was contagious in the usual sense. We saw many of the same things, but we each perceived passages the other did not. Perhaps you and I will, hmm, rub off on one another? You will see what I see, and I will see what you see? I can hope. Until then, we will hold hands for the difficult crossings, yes?"

"Sure," Darrin said, amazed to hear hope in Ismael's voice. The world-weary immortal, burdened by centuries, finally had something to hope for. "Whatever helps me find Bridget."

Ismael seemed to sag a little, at that. "We will find her there, ahead of us, in the light, perhaps across that silver bridge of yours."

"Or maybe he'll find me right here." Bridget stepped with another man from behind a cracked marble half-dome. "And then he'll find out what a lying sack of shit you are."

"Bridget?" Darrin said. It looked like her, in her red coat, her expression fierce and serious. But that thing in the hotel had looked like her too, hadn't it, and—

But no. Ismael was backing away, scowling, and muttering under his breath. Darrin didn't hear most of it—something about spoiling things, something about the light—but he wasn't interested in anything Ismael had to say now. He was interested in *Bridget*, here, right here before him. All the anger, all the sadness, all the acid in his gut and pounding in his head, faded away, and he only wanted to go to her. So he did, closing the distance between them in a few steps, and threw out his arms to embrace her—

—and she just slipped away, out of his arms, so smoothly he couldn't even feel her, and he fell to his knees from the momentum.

"I'm so sorry, Darrin," Bridget said, kneeling beside him and putting her hand against his cheek—but instead of warm flesh he felt only something like the brush of wind. "I wish I could hold your hand, feel your touch, but I can't, I . . ."

"She's dead," Ismael said. "She doesn't have a true physical form anymore, just . . . a very persistent psyche. She set her soul free and threw away her body in an attempt to reach the better world, but she failed. She did not let *everything* go. I never thought of it before, but it's right here in front of me. She's wearing that red coat. You gave her that coat, didn't you, Darrin? I told her to dispose of all her meaningful possessions, but she went to the bridge, to her death, wearing a gift from you. That was what held her back, I think, or rather, it is emblematic of what held her back. *You.* You are the reason she is a lost thing now, Darrin, haunting that idiot Orville Troll." He lifted his chin toward the man Bridget had appeared with.

"You were supposed to help me find her." Darrin turned toward Ismael. "But you knew where she was all along. Fuck you. I'll never help you find your way to the light."

Ismael shrugged. "Yes, well, it's all ruined now. But it's not the first time my plans have failed. I am nothing if not patient. And there is always another plan, isn't there? I had hopes for this one, but I've grown used to disappointment, and moving on. I've got my eye on a nice piece of property outside the city. I could stand to spend a little time in the country, perhaps with a few like-minded seekers. I already have some good prospects in mind, and a new approach that may prove fruitful—"

Darrin's fury at Ismael overcame his interlaced joy and grief at seeing Bridget again. "There is no plan B." He stalked toward Ismael. "Not for you. I'm going to make ruining your life *my* life's work. I—"

Darrin froze when he heard the unmistakable ratcheting sound of a shotgun being pumped, and they all looked up the hill. "Sorry to break up the party," Echo said, standing entirely too close to them, with a chrome-plated shotgun in her hands. "But I really think it's time to talk about *my* problems."

Arturo was there with her, improbably, standing just a few feet behind her, and Darrin was trying to wrap his head around that—was Arturo in on this, somehow, too? And what was Echo doing here?

"Darrin, honey, Ismael hired me to fuck you," Echo said. "Is your dead girlfriend ghosting around here somewhere? She should hear this. Ismael recruited me, told me where to find you, and sent me to turn on the charm. It wasn't hard—you were so broken up about miss blondie being gone that you just needed some comfort, and I can be good at comforting. Besides, it wasn't too bad—I've been with worse."

Darrin's eyes stung, but he was damned if he was going to cry now. Any affection he'd had for Echo had vanished when he found her going down on Nicholas in his living room. "Did he get to Nicholas, too?"

Echo nodded. "Sure." She gestured in Ismael's direction with the shotgun. "He promised Nicholas eternal life, if you can believe *that* bullshit. At least, it better be bullshit, because if he has access to that kind of shit and didn't tell *me*—"

"So what did he promise you, Echo?" Darrin said. Arturo was creeping closer to her, a look halfway between terror and concentration on his face, and Darrin thought maybe he wasn't a willing travelling companion.

"He promised me entertainment," Echo said. "That I wouldn't be *bored*. There's nothing in the world worse than being bored. Just ask Ismael—that's why he wants to go live in magical la-la land, because it's all just too fucking tedious. And then he tried to take off without paying me."

"Don't be so tiresome, Echo," Ismael said, with his full weight of weariness. "Just shoot me and have done with it."

Arturo made a grab for her shotgun, but Echo must have sensed his approach, because she pivoted smoothly on her heel and drove the gun stock hard into his gut. Arturo gasped and folded up, falling to the ground and rolling partway down the hill. Echo didn't even look at him, just turned back to Ismael. She walked down the hill, coming within killing range . . . for those who could be killed. "You want me to shoot you, Ismael? So you can pop out of here and land someplace safe and warm? No, I got bored trying to kill you a couple of days ago. But there are *other* ways to hurt you. Like taking away your latest playmate."

Echo swung the gun up, aimed it point-blank at Darrin's chest, and pulled the trigger.

The last thing Darrin heard wasn't the gunshot, but Bridget screaming "No!"

3

At first, Orville thought the gunshot had somehow *disintegrated* Darrin, because he disappeared instantly when Echo fired. But there was no wounded body, no body at all, and Echo said "God damn it!" and stalked toward Ismael, who was backing away again.

Bridget went to the place where Darrin's body should have been and began pawing at the ground, as if looking for some sign of him, making a long low keening noise.

"*All* you fucking briar-patch babies can do that? You never *told* me Darrin was unkillable!" Echo pumped the slide on the shotgun again, ejecting the spent shell. "Damn you, Ismael, I'm tired of shooting things I can't kill."

"Do it," Ismael said. "Do it, do it, *shoot* me!"

"Oh, you'd like that, wouldn't you, your get-out-of-shit free card," Echo said. "No way. I think I'll run you down and tie you up and see how much I can hurt you without triggering your flight mechanism."

Ismael turned and ran past a tumble of broken columns. Echo cursed and gave chase.

The middle-aged man with the walrus moustache limped toward Orville, wincing with each step. Orville had never been good at processing lots of new information quickly, but since Echo had hit this guy in the stomach and left him on the ground, he was probably no friend of hers, right? "Hey," the man said. "While she's chasin' him, what do you say you and me and your ghostly friend get out of here?"

Bridget looked up from her study of the ground. "Who . . . who are you?"

"Name's Arturo. Me and Darrin were drinkin' buddies."

"You were with Echo," Bridget said, rising.

"Yeah, and I'd rather *not* be with Echo again, so maybe we should get a move on, huh?"

Bridget looked at Orville, and after a second he realized she was looking to him for guidance—seeing Darrin shot (or shot *at*, anyway), and watching him disappear, had unhinged her a little, it seemed, and done something to her usual forward-charging confidence. "I don't know who to trust," Bridget said.

Orville had never considered himself a good judge of character. He tended to think the worst of people, and was generally not disappointed. But this man—Arturo—wanted to take them away from the crazy woman with the gun, and that seemed fairly trustworthy to Orville. Maybe there was some complex conspiracy afoot, the kind that Ismael and Echo had worked on Darrin, but Orville had a hard time imagining that someone would expend that kind of energy to fuck with *his* head. "Okay," he said. "I think we should go with him, Bridget." To Arturo: "Do you know a quick way out of this place?"

"The Wendigo knows," Arturo said. "Come on, my car is this way."

"You've got a car?" Bridget said, incredulous.

"It's sort of a car," Arturo said, setting off away from the direction Echo had gone. "It's a car that drives through the briarpatch. I can't find my way around this place worth a damn on foot, I get lost every time."

Orville looked back over his shoulder, toward the shining light in the sky, the oval of illuminated ground in the distance. He'd been looking forward to another look at that light, but staying alive was better than standing in the reflection of something beautiful. He hurried along after Arturo. "How did you know Bridget was a ghost?"

"Darrin told me Bridget was dead. Which means, if she's still here, she must be a ghost, or somethin' like that." He paused. "Or else Darrin was wrong. Funny how that didn't occur to me right away, even though it makes more sense. Not that this place makes sense, necessarily."

"No, I'm dead," Bridget said. "It just didn't stick."

"What happened to Darrin?" Orville asked, expecting it to be a rhetorical question, and was surprised when both Arturo and Bridget started to speak. They both stopped, and Arturo laughed. "You take this one," he said.

"Ismael is immortal," Bridget said. "Which you knew. But it's more than a matter of not getting cancer or aging or whatever. He's protected from death by murder or accident, too. If he's about to die, some sort of self-defence mechanism kicks in, and he's transported instantly to somewhere else in the briarpatch, somewhere safe. And, I guess, Darrin is the same way." She shook her head. "All the time I was with him, I had no idea he was a . . . a *magical* person."

Arturo grunted. "He seemed like a pretty good guy to me. Ismael seems like an asshole. Those are more important than whether they're magical. They're briarpatch babies, people who were just plausible enough to exist at all."

A gunshot sounded far behind them, and they all hunched instinctively, even Bridget, who had nothing to fear from a shotgun. "Do you think Echo tried to shoot Ismael?" Orville whispered. "Or did Ismael get the gun away from her?"

"Who knows?" Arturo said. "She only had two shells, though, so she's all out of ammo now. But even if she can't come over here and shoot us, I don't much want to see her again. Let's hustle." They went on, toward a series of gradually rising hills.

"Are you a briarpatch baby, too?" Bridget asked.

"Nah. I'm just a poor slob who used to be a mechanic." He puffed a little as he spoke, out of breath. "A little while after my wife died, I found the Wendigo, and I've been drivin' around with it ever since."

"Just driving around?" Bridget asked. "Or trying to get somewhere?" She glanced back, toward the receding oval of light.

"I'm not lookin' for that place with the light. Don't worry about that. I do have a purpose, though."

"What's that?"

"Lookin' for my Marjorie."

"Your wife?" Orville asked. "The one who died?"

"Yup. But just because she's dead doesn't mean I can't find her again." He inclined his head toward Bridget.

"How did she die?" Bridget asked.

"It was a car thing," Arturo replied.

They walked in silence for a moment. Then Orville said "What does *that* mean?"

Arturo looked over his shoulder at Orville, his shaggy eyebrows raised. "Well. I found her in the garage, in the car, with the motor runnin'. Dead from the carbon monoxide."

"Suicide," Bridget said.

Arturo stopped, turned to face her, and said, "I don't *know*." His hands were balled into fists, and Orville instinctively took a step forward, as if to protect Bridget, but of course Arturo couldn't hurt her. Arturo relaxed, took a step back, and sighed. "Marjorie wasn't always as careful as she could've been. Maybe she just started the car to run some errands and got distracted, looked for somethin' in her purse, dropped somethin' on the floor, started listenin' to somethin' on the radio—she had this funny thing, she wouldn't listen to the radio when she drove, said it was too dangerous, because she might get distracted while drivin', so sometimes she'd sit and listen to the end of a program before she drove off. So maybe she just didn't think about being in the closed garage, and passed out and died. There wasn't a note or nothin', so I can't know for sure."

"Unless you can find her and ask," Bridget said.

"We were happy," Arturo said. "I want to be happy again. And I won't be until I see her." He walked off again, faster, leaving them behind, and Orville exchanged a glance with Bridget. She shrugged. They went after him, up the hill, and there was a big boat of a car parked on the grass, improbable as a cherry on top of a cheeseburger.

"Meet the Wendigo," Arturo said, leaning against the side of the car.

"This car . . . it can go anywhere?" Bridget asked.

"All over the briarpatch and beyond." He patted the hood. "I'll drop you guys off wherever you want." He paused. "Well, anywhere the Wendigo wants, I guess, but it sometimes takes requests."

"If you're going looking for Marjorie," Bridget said slowly. "Do you think we could . . . tag along? Darrin is out there somewhere, lost, and he doesn't know his way around like Ismael does. If you're searching for someone anyway . . ."

Arturo rubbed his chin and chewed his moustache. "Look," he said finally. "The Wendigo goes where it wants. It has its own, whatcha call them, search protocols, I guess. If you guys want to tag along, I don't see any reason why not. It gets lonely on the road. But the briarpatch is a big place. So . . . don't get your hopes up, okay?"

"Okay," Bridget said. She turned to Orville. "Is that okay with you? I thought this would be over by now, Orville, that you'd have your life back. I'm so sorry I still need you. But I'm afraid for Darrin. I need to find him, I need to *explain*. Seeing him, it was like getting hit in the chest by a truck. I need to talk to him, and try to make things right."

Orville thought about it. What could he say? He couldn't say no, because Bridget couldn't go anywhere without him, and if he tried to have a normal life with a mournful ghost following him around, what luck would he have?

"Count me in."

"Okay," Arturo said. He looked at the Wendigo and sighed. "I guess we're goin' to have to clean out the back seat, though. It would probably feel kinda weird having a ghost sit in your lap." He opened the rear door, and a mountain of white and yellow paper cascaded onto the grass.

4

Echo pursued Ismael through the ruins. After a couple of minutes spent running over hill and through pillars, she realized she'd left her ride out of the briarpatch behind. If Arturo had any sense—and he struck her as a fairly sensible guy— he was long gone by now. Which meant Ismael was Echo's only way out of this place. "Stop," she shouted. "Come on, Ismael, let's just talk, we've got some shit to work out!"

Up ahead, Ismael stopped running and stood still in a little clearing, before a still-standing marble arch. Elated—but thinking, *How could he be so stupid?*— Echo raced toward him.

And stopped a few feet behind him, when she saw the bears.

There were twice as many bears as there had been in the rocky desert, with the same mixture of black bears, grizzlies, and that one towering polar bear in the lead. Shit⊠Even the *animals* around here could navigate the briarpatch? Life was so unfair. The bears spread out to flank Ismael, and Echo turned to run back the way she'd come, hoping she was upwind and as-yet-unnoticed.

But no.

Bears were closing in from behind her, hemming them both in.

"So, Ismael," Echo said. "I hope you've got some fancy bear-charming tricks to get us out of this mess."

Ismael turned to look at her. His eyes were furious and cold. "You are a spoiled, petulant woman, and I hope you die a painful death, with nothing but darkness waiting for you on the other side."

"Save the sweet nothings for later." The bears were still closing in. "We've got a situation here."

"Yes," Ismael said. He ran toward the polar bear—its shoulder was almost as high as he was tall—and punched it, hard, between the eyes. Echo gasped—was that some kind of Vulcan nerve-pinch for bears, was it like punching a shark in the snout, something that hurt bad enough to send the animal running? She didn't really know shit about bears, except what she'd seen on a couple of nature documentaries, which was how she'd known a bunch of them was called a "sloth." These didn't seem slothful.

The polar bear roared and reared up on its hind legs, and Echo shrank back, her bowels clenching.

Ismael looked back at her and, improbably, grinned.

Then the polar bear fell upon him, enormous paw swinging down to strike.

Ismael, of course, disappeared, and the polar bear fell forward comically, then shook its head, and roared again in frustration.

"Oh, fuck *him*," Echo said, which brought her to the polar bear's attention again. It flickered and became the albino man.

"You," he said. "You tricked us, you hurt us, you hurt me." The other bears around him flickered, becoming people again, some men, some women, some tattooed, some mud-streaked, some with thick body hair woven with ribbons.

"You must not *hurt*—" the albino began, but Echo just lifted the shotgun and pulled the trigger. The gun kicked satisfyingly, and the bear-man's head turned into a red cloud, blood and tissue spattering the people gathered around him. God, that felt *good*, after all those failed shootings, those people who didn't even get hurt, she'd finally blown a motherfucker away.

Killing the polar bear didn't exactly solve her problems—the shotgun was empty now—but it gave her the confidence needed to *deal* with her problem. The bear-people were just staring at her, and at their dead leader's pretty-much-headless corpse, all of them stunned into silence. Echo laid the shotgun across her shoulder and put her other hand on her hip. "So," she said. "Let me tell you how it's going to be." She was out of ammunition, but she'd bluffed her way through a lot of bad situations. Maybe not *this* bad, but it was worth a try.

The bear-people stared at her, but none of them moved to attack, and Echo knew she was going to be all right. People were the same all over.

DARRIN HITS THE ROAD

1

Darrin woke up in a tree. If "woke up" was the right term for emerging from a brief interval of swirling blackness streaked by flashes of light. He reached out and grabbed onto some small branches—he was seated on a broader branch—and looked about him. Nothing but leaves and branches as far as he could see, above, below, and around him, and the sharp smell of eucalyptus, though these rough-barked trees didn't look like eucalyptus.

What the hell had happened? Had Echo shot at him with some kind of magical gun, some briarpatch weapon that teleported people? And where was he now? There were plenty of branches for climbing, and Darrin began easing his way down, glad again that he'd started walking so much all those months ago.

After he'd climbed down about fifteen feet, a rough plank platform appeared. A probe with his foot proved it stable, so he dropped to the platform, into an area cleared of branches. At first he thought it was just a platform for deer hunting or something, but then he saw the rope-and-board bridges radiating away from it to other platforms in other trees. This was like some Swiss Family Robinson treetop village, complete with lean-tos built against trees, but he didn't see anyone around. Darrin tried one of the bridges, found it solid, and ventured halfway across. Below the bridge there was a clear view, and he looked down at the forest floor, far enough away to give him a surge of vertigo and make him grab onto the rope guiderails.

Something came trundling out of the brush below, a low-slung scaly thing with a horned crest around its head and a great bony club on the end of its tail. It looked like a dinosaur, and as it disappeared into another clump of bushes—which were actually probably small trees, given how far away the ground seemed—Darrin realized he was still in the briarpatch, in one of those improbable little worlds Ismael had talked about. He couldn't decide if being stuck in the briarpatch, lost and alone, was better or worse than being up a tree in South America or somewhere.

He went on, toward a large central platform built across the trunks of several trees. There was a barrel filled to the top with clear water, and after sniffing it, Darrin cupped his hands and drank, hoping he wasn't ingesting otherworldly parasites but too thirsty to worry about it much. He walked across the creaking boards, looking for some sign of habitation—preferably human—and saw, at the far edge of the platform, a man sitting on a bench, holding what looked like a fishing pole.

While Darrin was trying to decide what to do—call out, sneak away, find a weapon—the man gave a joyful shout and began reeling in his line. Something small and furry and distinctly rabbit-like kicked at the end of the wire, which appeared to be some sort of a looped snare rather than a baited hook. The man, who was short but broad-shouldered and compactly built, with a messy shag of brown hair, stood and drew a long knife from his belt. He lashed out at the still-kicking thing (which wasn't quite a rabbit—the legs were right, but the ears were wrong), sending a gout of blood spraying over the edge of the platform. The animal stopped struggling, and the man removed its body from the line and set the fishing pole aside.

"Well?" he called without turning around, his voice tinged with a slight Eastern European flavour. "Come on, then, if you're hungry. You can put the pot on to boil while I skin Br'er Rabbit here."

"Ah, okay." Darrin approached cautiously, and the man looked at him now. He was clean-shaven, and his grin was boyish.

"English! Good, good. I hoped I would get it on my first try. I hate spending time trying to find a common language—it means less time to talk!"

"So I guess you aren't, ah, a native here," Darrin said.

"On the contrary! I was born and raised in the briarpatch." He beckoned, and Darrin followed him across a short bridge to another platform, this one with a stone-lined firepit in the centre, a few embers glowing. At the man's direction, Darrin put a few pieces of dry wood from a nearby pile onto the flames and got them burning. He scooped water into the pot from another barrel—"Good clean rainwater!" the man said—and hung the pot on a hook over the fire to boil. Meanwhile, the man skinned the animal on a low stone table. "Rabbit stew. Not quite rabbit, but very much stew. I have some potatoes in my pack there, if you'd care to cut them up. There's a knife in there too, if you don't have one."

"You'll just let me have a knife?" Darrin said, incredulous.

The man looked up and laughed. "What, you would kill me to steal my rabbit, which I will share with you anyway? You would kill me to steal my fishing pole, perhaps, which I will give you freely if you ask? Go on then, try to kill me with my paring knife! I will wait! Take your time!"

Darrin laughed. "No, no, I just . . . thank you."

"It is no problem. Company is rare here, and so many of the people I encounter—the wanderers, like you and me, yes?—they are crazy, so deep inside their minds that they have no room left to talk with me. But you do not seem mad, or a poet, so I think you are like me, yes, a child of the briarpatch?"

"I guess so." Darrin found the potatoes—small, slightly withered, but he was hungry enough to look forward to them—and began cutting them up into chunks and tossing them into the pot. "I just found that out recently, though. My name's Darrin."

"It is a pleasure to meet you. My name is Harczos."

Darrin stopped cutting the potatoes, and gripped the knife more tightly. "Harczos. Ismael told me about you."

Harczos grunted. He took a handful of rabbit meat, cubed, and dropped it into the pot. "Ahhh. And how do you know Ismael?" He spat. "May the bears eat him and shit him out again. Forgive me. I hope you aren't *friends*."

Darrin considered what to say. "He cozied up to my girlfriend, convinced her to kill herself, then convinced my best friend and my *new* girlfriend to betray me, so I'd go crazy with grief and escape into the briarpatch, and he could trick me into helping him. He wants to find an overland route to this better world he's always talking about."

"I see." Harczos sighed. "It sounds like he has not changed much, then."

"This is just . . . I don't believe this is coincidence. You're in on this, aren't you?"

"And how could I be in on anything?" Harczos said. "You found *me*. It is improbable, I grant you that, but the briarpatch is an improbable place. "

"I didn't find you. Something sent me here. Someone shot at me, and, and I was just *here*."

"You *are* new to the briarpatch. Our kind—you, and me, and Ismael, and some others I have met—we are protected by this place. If we are attacked, if death is imminent, the briarpatch gathers us to her bosom and takes us away to safety. We cannot control where we go, but going anywhere is better than dying, yes?"

Darrin mulled that over. It made sense, sort of—it explained that sudden movement when Echo tried to shoot him. He couldn't quite think through the implications of being unable to *die*, though. "Okay, if you say so. But what are the odds that I'd run into *you*?"

"Absolutely astronomical," Harczos said cheerfully. "Like finding a grain of gold dust on a beach of golden sand. And yet, here we are. Ismael and I met in a similar way, actually. I've often wondered if there are gods here, toying with us—if there are, I've never met them, but sometimes I think I see evidence of their meddling. Ismael thought there was just an affinity among those of us who wander the briarpatch, some force that brings us together on occasion. Maybe we're iron filings drawn together by our personal magnetism?" He paused. "I, myself, am exceedingly magnetic."

Darrin rubbed his forehead. Life was giving him a headache lately. "Shit. Okay. So now I'm lost here?"

"We are deep in the briarpatch, but I am not lost. I can show you around, if you like. Or I can show you the way out."

Darrin opened his mouth to say yes, please, show me the way out, and then didn't say anything. Why go home? What if Echo came and tried to kill him again? What if Ismael came after him? What did he have to return to? Bridget was dead. Seeing her earlier had lit up hope in his chest, but he hadn't even been able to touch her. She was dead, and the sooner he accepted that, the better he'd feel. His hope of finding Bridget, of repairing their love—it was truly an impossible dream.

"When I was seventeen, I left my foster parents and moved to California," Darrin said. "I went off to college with nothing but a suitcase, and I didn't know anybody. I was trying to start a new life. For a while, it was good—I had friends, and hobbies, and a good job, and then I fell in love with Bridget. But . . . everything fell apart. It all went to shit. I was trying to stick it out, trying not to run away from my problems, but . . ."

"There is a difference between running from your problems and starting a new life," Harczos said. He stirred the pot with a long wooden spoon, and the smell that rose up was savoury and warm. He crumbled a handful of crushed herbs into the water. "I am doing what I always do, travelling, and you are welcome to join me. Or not."

"Can you tell me about this place, about Ismael, about the better world? There's still so much I don't understand."

"Of course," Harczos said. "This place is the briarpatch. Ismael was my best friend and my travelling companion, until I discovered some of his true nature. And as for the better world . . ." Harczos shrugged. "It isn't all that great." He dipped the spoon again, and tasted, and smiled. "I'll elaborate over dinner."

2

Two days later—if "days" could be defined as "periods of time punctuated by intervals of sleep"—they leaned together on the rail of a low-slung ferry, skimming across the surface of a golden sea, toward a city that appeared made entirely of pearl. Darrin had thought of the briarpatch as a largely barren place, but Harczos told him there *were* people, whole societies, some of them aware of the briarpatch, some not. "But they are all *deep*," he said. "Ismael was never willing to go very deep, especially alone. He became horribly lost, once, and had terrible experiences, and he could never let go of that fear. Helplessness frightens him more than anything. He is always unhappy, but he is *most* unhappy when he is not in control. He liked to be no more than five or six steps from the 'real' world—though it would be better to call it the most *plausible* world. Here, we are thirty or forty steps in, and it would take a few days to walk out again." The air that blew against their faces smelled not of salt but of sweetness. "The people in this city are all very old, and no child has been born to them in a long time. They have golden eyes and teeth of pearls. I think they are not people at all, but intelligent automatons, built by some long-dead race. But do not mention this theory to them. The idea is embraced only by a radical segment of the population, and the others find it offensive in the extreme."

Darrin nodded.

Harczos was beloved in that city. That night they feasted on fish that tasted like apricots. As he ate and drank beneath the peculiar stars, his most recurring thought was: *Bridget would have loved this.*

3

A week later they huddled beneath Harczos's oversized poncho, sitting on a rocky outcropping. "Waiting for a train," Harczos sang. "Just sitting here in the rain, waiting for a train." The "train" was a mobile passage to the next world, a swarm of black flies that had near-human intelligence and, coincidentally, acted as a moving portal. "The swarm is obsessive-compulsive," Harczos had explained. "It moves on the same route every day. I brought it some sweets from the market in the black-glass city, and it will gladly give us passage for that."

Darrin sang with him, in the rain.

4

"The last time I had a drink was in a vampire bar," Darrin said, sitting at a table on a patio by the sea with Harczos, sipping a mai tai.

Harczos had a lava flow—a piña colada laced with strawberry juice—and munched a coconut shrimp. "There are some nice vampire bars," Harczos said. "Though they don't usually have anything I like on tap."

"So what world is this?" Darrin asked, looking around at the very normal-looking people having lunch.

"This would be Maui, in Hawai'i," Harczos said. "Welcome home. For a given value of 'home.'"

Darrin laughed and raised his glass. He looked out at the water. "You know, Bridget and I used to talk about coming here. She wanted to learn to scuba dive, swim around Molokai, but we never did."

"Just as well," Harczos said. "Isn't that where they have a leper colony?"

"We would've skipped that part," Darrin said. He stretched. "Being around people makes me feel human again. A dirty dishevelled human, but still."

"We can buy you some razors, if you want to get rid of that beard." Harczos rubbed his own stubble—he'd lost his straight razor in the throat of a shaggy drooling monster several worlds back. "After we stop by to see a jeweller I know. I have some black coral to sell him. It's much easier to get in some other worlds than it is here, and it's nice to have a little money."

"I kind of like the beard," Darrin said. He'd never grown one before. It made him feel a little bit like a new man. If he couldn't quite forget Bridget, then maybe the new man he became would be able to.

"Suit yourself," Harczos said.

5

"It is very odd." Harczos chewed meditatively on some nuts while Darrin sat on a stump with a sketchbook on his lap, trying to start a map of the places he'd seen in the briarpatch. He thought maybe this place *was* a system, at least as much as it was an art. "But I have not seen a bear in all the time we've been together."

"Ismael mentioned bears," Darrin said, scribbling out some lines that weren't right. Trying to map the briarpatch, even crudely, was like trying to think in eleven dimensions. "What's so special about bears?"

"Some people become lost in the briarpatch and, for whatever reason, become shapeshifters. They change from people to bears and back again. Perhaps it is transmitted by a bite, or a cut, or perhaps it happens to those who drink from a particular stream—people used to believe you could become a werewolf if you drank from water touched by a wolf. Maybe it's caused by some strange radiation. For whatever reason, there are always bears, wandering in groups or alone, and while they are animals, they are no more dangerous than any animal. But when they become human, they are dangerous as only an insane human can be."

"Guess it's lucky we haven't run into any, then."

"Yes," Harczos said, perhaps a trifle doubtfully. "Very lucky."

6

"Ismael brought me here." Darrin looked at the great chasm, the deckless bridge, the swirling mist. "We passed by, anyway. What is it?"

"A bottomless pit, there," Harczos said. "Ismael jumped into it once, expecting oblivion. He fell for three days, and when he was about to die of thirst, the briarpatch flung him into a fountain."

"But the bridge. Where does it go? I mean, I guess it doesn't go anywhere, but . . ."

"I think it goes to the land of the dead," Harczos said. "Or so I have been told, by those older than me. We cannot cross the bridge, because there is nothing for the living to walk on. But for the dead, there is something solid underfoot, and they can cross. I have seen ghosts walk over the chasm."

"It's the real land of the dead?"

"For some people, at least. Maybe there are many lands of the dead. Perhaps some go into the light, and lose themselves. Some others cross this bridge, and go into who knows what world?"

"Do you think this is where Bridget is supposed to go?"

Harczos shrugged. "I'm not sure anyone is *supposed* to go anywhere. We go where we go. Come. I want to show you a place I know, where all the children have wings, which wither and fall off when they grow up. Such a beautiful place and sad."

7

After many weeks together, Darrin felt comfortable enough to ask about the details of Harczos and Ismael's falling out. They swung in hammocks strung from trees in an orchard, below pendulous orbs of hallucinogenic fruit.

"Ah, that is a tale," Harczos said. "Ismael and I travelled together for many years. For a time, in the early part of the 20th century, we lived in France. I was bored with wandering around the outskirts of the briarpatch, and Ismael was reluctant to go deeper, so we decided instead to embrace life in the plausible world. I took a wife and had children. I did not know it at the time, but Ismael passed the time by finding suicidal people and goading them toward death. He had become obsessed with finding the better world, and I understand why—it is a very plausible heaven, quite stable, and I was as entranced by the occasional glimpses of the place as anyone. Ismael discovered, quite by accident, that he could glimpse the light when people died, sometimes, and he developed a theory that by letting go of life completely, and meditating to loosen your soul, and killing yourself, you might reach the light. There is reason to believe his theory is correct, by the way."

"But why did he get so obsessed?" Darrin said. "I mean, you're not."

Harczos swayed in the hammock silently for a moment, then said, "Ismael's life in the plausible world was always harder than my own, because for many years he tried to live among people as an ordinary man, while I had always been willing to slip away into the safety of the briarpatch when things became too unpleasant. Ismael saw plagues, and pogroms, terrible things. He was set upon by dogs, and attacked by swordsmen, and rode down by mounted warriors. He was a peasant and a slave and a victim. He nearly died a number of times, and was flung into the briarpatch again and again. He suffered, and went hungry, thirsty, and got sick, but didn't die, because our bodies do not seem to die. What do men crave most, Darrin?"

"What they can't have."

"Precisely. Ismael craved death. He came to believe life was all suffering—

and, for most people, for most of history, that has been true, yes? He wanted to give people the gift of death, a gift he could never receive himself. And so he made suicide pacts with people, promised to die with them. They would both jump from, a bridge say, and Ismael's friends would die, while Ismael himself was shunted to safety somewhere in the briarpatch. I did not find out about this habit of his until later. He discovered that those ordinary suicides seldom led to the light, and in time, he started telling people the truth, convincing them to strive for the light with him. Ismael has a forceful personality. He is able to make others feel what he feels—usually his pain and depression. He considered himself a shepherd. He meant well, I believe—he helped people reach the light, but he never asked himself if the light was *worth* reaching. He believes that the best imaginable life is one in which there is no pain, only ceaseless pleasure. I do not agree. A little pain adds savour, and makes the pleasure more potent."

"So you stopped being his friend when you found out he was convincing people to kill themselves?"

"It is more complicated than that," Harczos said. "I was happy enough, as I said, in France, with my wife and our children. Ismael grew restless, and wanted me to join him in his search for the better world. He became convinced there must be an overland route, and that he could not find it himself. Since all children of the briarpatch have access to different pathways, he wanted me to help him. I refused, and he left in anger. Some months later, there was a terrible fire, and my wife . . . my children . . ." He fell silent.

"I'm so sorry," Darrin said.

"It was long ago. My wife would be dead now anyway, perhaps my children as well. I did not, at first, suspect Ismael. I joined him and we entered into the briarpatch. But my grief was great, and Ismael tried to comfort me, telling me my wife and children were surely in a better place, perhaps *the* better place, that we might find them in the light, and he let slip something, some comment about how they did not suffer, perhaps, and I grew suspicious. Eventually, I confronted him, and Ismael confessed he'd killed my family—though he said he 'set them free.' He killed them so I'd have nothing holding me back, of course, so I would come with him like he wanted. In my unthinking rage I attacked him, and he was swept away into the briarpatch. I saw him again, years later. I told him I'd found an overland route to the land of perfect light, and that, since I could not kill him, my only revenge was in withholding the route to that light. Oh, how he begged, but I just laughed at him. It was very satisfying."

"You lied to him, then?" Darrin said. "You fucked with his head?"

"Oh, no, I did find the land of light. Would you like to see it? We can go there next."

"You found it?" Darrin frowned. "And you didn't show him the way?"

"I could not kill Ismael for the crime he committed against my family. But I could punish him that way, and I did."

"He killed Bridget to get to me," Darrin said. "So I could help him find the light. If you'd just let him go there, into the light, Bridget would still be alive."

Harczos bowed his head, sighed, and said, "I am sorry for your loss, Darrin. But I did not goad Bridget to her death. Ismael did. Save your anger for him."

"If you'd just—"

"Bridget would have died eventually." Harczos looked up to meet Darrin's eyes. "I am sorry, but it is something you must face. This pain you feel now, for her loss, you would have felt it eventually. Hate Ismael for cutting your time with her short, but remember, you will live forever. Every mortal you allow yourself to care for will wither beneath your gaze."

"Fuck you, Harczos." Darrin stormed off into the trees. If not for Harczos's need for revenge, Bridget would still be *alive*, he'd never have met Ismael, he wouldn't even know he was a child of the briarpatch. How many people had died at Ismael's urging? How many people had leapt for the light and failed to reach it in the decades since their falling out? Harczos had lived too long. He might miss his wife and children in the abstract, but he didn't really care about *people* anymore. And why would he? Their lifespans were too short. It would be like Darrin fretting over a butterfly's quality of life. Would that happen to Darrin, now that he knew he was a child of briarpatch? Would he become capable of such epic cruelty and caprice? He hated Ismael for urging Bridget to kill herself . . . but if sending Ismael into the light would save the world from his influence, Darrin wouldn't hesitate.

After a while, he returned to the hammocks. Harczos was still there, gazing at the sky.

"Forgive me?" Harczos said.

"I want to see the light," Darrin said.

"Okay." Harczos closed his eyes.

8

Three days later they stood together on the moon-coloured bridge, a structure so broad and smoothly shining it was like a bridge from a dream. He'd seen it before, always a distant gleam in the sky, and it was just as gleaming up close. The glow of the better world rose up before them, swallowing the end of the bridge, and it was a mesmerizing, soothing light.

"Is that really where the gods live?" Darrin asked, straining toward the light, pulling against the rope Harczos had tied around his waist and secured to the railing of the bridge.

"I don't know about gods," Harczos said. "I believe the briarpatch *itself* is God, the body and mind of God. But the light . . . it is a place of no pain. A place of great peace and tranquility. A place, ultimately, to dissolve. There are religions that believe God is a state of being, a transcendent experience that absorbs you and strips away your personality, returning you wholly to godhood. That is what happens there. I found the light, and was entranced by its beauty, and entered. My mind remained my own, for a time, and I floated there, feeling at one with the universe, but my memories began . . . not slipping away, exactly, but fading, becoming less important, less connected to me. I realized, after a while, that I didn't care that my wife and children were dead, because what was flesh but grass? What was life but an obstacle to the beauty of the light?" Harczos shuddered. "When I lost that kernel of grief at the centre of myself, I knew I could not stay in the light. It was difficult to leave. More difficult than you can imagine. But I do not want to dissolve. I love my *self*, my ego, my particular memories. I do not seek an end to pain. Pain is the price I pay for all the joys in life. I do not think ill of those who wish to enter the light and lose themselves, but . . . it is not my path. Would you like me to cut the rope, Darrin, and let you go?"

The light was seductive. "Why don't you want to return? How can you stand it?"

"Because I remember. Having been exposed to the pure light, I am more resistant to its charms. I know what waits for me there. Oblivion is not for me. Someday, perhaps, when I have lived too long, and want no longer to continue, but not yet. Do you want to go in?"

"I . . . no," he said. "No. I don't want to go." *Not yet*, he thought. *Someday, maybe, if I become like Ismael, and death seems like the only hope. Because that light is death, however beautiful its aspect.*

Harczos slipped a dark cloth bag over Darrin's head, and that blocked the light enough that Harczos could lead him away.

9

"How long have I been with you?" Darrin asked, many, many worlds later.

"I'm not sure," Harczos said. "Time is strange here, and the suns do not always rise and set in a predictable way. A little more than half a year, as time is reckoned in the plausible world?"

They ambled along a worn path by a creek. "I feel like I've figured out a lot of things," Darrin said. "I don't know when I've had this much time to think before."

"It is a good life," Harczos said agreeably. "What have you figured out?"

"That I like walking. And drawing maps." His pack bulged with papers, his attempt to chart the strange interconnections of the worlds they visited.

"Useful things to know."

"I think I understand why Bridget left me, too."

"Ah. I know that has troubled you."

"She's always wanted to find the *next* thing, you know? Whenever she had a new experience—whether it was going scuba diving with me, or driving up to wine country, or going caving, or urban exploration, or whatever—she'd enjoy it, for a little while, but she didn't usually want to repeat it. It was like she . . . sucked every experience dry. Like she was looking up to the next mountain even when she reached the peak of the one she was climbing."

"Sounds exhausting."

"Maybe. But I kind of admire it. That striving. I was silly to think she'd be happy with me, the way we used to be, indefinitely. It felt like a safe, steady place to me, but for her, I think it was a rut. When she discovered the briarpatch with Ismael, I'm sure she thought it was magical . . . for a little while. But then she wanted the next level, and that was the next *world*. Though, you know, I think she would have hated it, if she'd really understood. The idea of dissolving . . . I don't think she'd like that."

"Ismael probably misrepresented things a bit. He was always good at telling people what they wanted to hear."

"Bridget must be miserable now, a ghost, no body, so limited, stuck haunting some guy she hardly knows . . ." He shook his head. "I wish I could help her."

"Perhaps you could help, if you could find her."

Darrin grunted. "Tell me about this place we're going. You said it was a city of bees?"

"Oh, yes." Harczos brightened. "One of my favourite places. I do not know its whole history, but it was once a city of beekeepers, with enormous hives, fruit trees everywhere, and more honey than you can imagine. At some point something changed, and the bees developed intelligence—at least, their queen did. Now, grown huge, she lives in the centre of the city, in the middle of her vast hive. Her bees fly everywhere, and they have lost their stingers—it's remarkable. The human inhabitants, or their descendants, have been incorporated into the new society, and are essentially drones, still dressed in their faded, ancestral beekeeping garb, which is more ceremonial than protective at this point. The people don't seem to have individual personalities anymore—they are extensions of the queen's will. It is amazing and strange. They pay me no attention, just go about their business as I walk through their buildings. And oh, the honey, Darrin, it has extraordinary properties, and gives vivid waking dreams. I suppose if we attacked the queen, they would fight us, but if we are peaceful, they will let us pass."

It sounded horrible to Darrin, like slavery, and he said so. Harczos nodded. "You are not wrong. But the people seem no different from the queen's other drones. Perhaps they even entered into the relationship voluntarily, long ago? Or perhaps their minds are controlled. I don't know. I only know the honey is delicious, and it seems like a very implausible place, so I visit it as often as I can, since it could disappear at any time." He pointed. "There, the city's towers." The spires were dark and oddly organic-looking, with twisted curves rather than mathematical angles. Harczos inhaled, then frowned. "It's odd. Usually, I can smell the flowers from the fruit trees by now, but all I smell is . . . smoke?"

They emerged from the trees with the city before them, into a field of stumps littered by the ashes of bonfires. "Something terrible has happened here," Harczos said.

"What's that white thing over there?" Darrin asked, pointing. They walked around the burned field, and the glimpse of white that Darrin had seen was revealed as a huge patchwork pavilion, opaque in places, mesh in others, erected on the outskirts of the city's lumpy buildings.

"That cloth, it looks like it's made of beekeeper uniforms," Harczos said. "But where are the people who should be wearing them? Where are the bees? They should be buzzing everywhere, the sound should be as constant as the sea, but . . ." He went still, and touched Darrin's arm. "Bears. There are bears approaching." Darrin saw them, ambling brown shapes in the streets of the city, coming toward them. "We'd better go," Harczos said, grimmer than Darrin had ever heard him before. They turned back the way they'd come, and there were more bears moving silently out of the trees, blocking their way. There were people in among the bears, naked, armed with spears and hoes and axes and hedge clippers. Once they had Harczos and Darrin hemmed in, they stopped moving, and stared at them, bear and human alike, expressionless and patient.

"If they attack us, and we are separated when we escape, we should meet again at the bridge to the land of the dead," Harczos said. "You have travelled widely enough now that if you find yourself in a strange place, you should be able to reach some familiar area in a few days."

"Okay," Darrin said, but he hoped it wouldn't come to that. He knew he was immortal, that if the bears attacked him the briarpatch would whisk him away to safety, but he didn't really *believe* it. It was hard to shake a lifetime of reasonable fears.

"She comes!" shouted one of the bear-people, and the other people cheered, while the bears roared. Darrin looked back at the pavilion, and the flaps in front were pulled apart by bear people. Three bears emerged, the one in the lead an enormous grizzly, with a woman riding on its back, her hands sunk into the fur around its neck. Her unbound hair blew in the breeze behind her, and Darrin knew who it was even before she got close enough to prove him right.

"Echo," he said when she reached him. The bear she rode cocked its head at him. Echo leaned forward, looking down on Darrin and Harczos. She wore a crown woven of twigs and white flowers, and her chrome shotgun hung across her back on a homemade strap.

"Hey, lover," she said. "I like the beard. Who's your friend?"

"His name is Harczos."

"Oh, really? Ismael told me about you. You guys used to be butt-buddies, right?"

Harczos frowned. "We were lovers for a time, yes."

Darrin glanced at him, surprised. Harczos had left out that detail of their relationship.

"But ol' Izzy screwed you over, am I right?"

Harczos nodded.

"Well, hell, then. The enemy of my enemy is my friend and shit. Guys," she said to the bear people, "you can take off. I've got these two covered." The bears and bear people wandered away, except for the one Echo was riding. She looked back down at them. "You want to come in, have a seat, eat some honey?"

"Ah," Harczos said. "What happened to the people of this city?"

Echo shrugged. "Victims of conquest, you know how it is. After the bears here made me their queen, I got sick of the living-in-caves thing *real* quick. This was the first city we found, and I figured, hey, bears like honey. Besides, it was a fucked up situation, people made into slaves for the queen bee, she was like something out of that movie *Aliens* . . ." Echo shook her head. "I was hoping to make the beekeeper guys into bears, but when my boys killed the queen bee, all the bees and beekeepers died too. Some kind of enforced loyalty thing. Wish I could manage that trick. Anyway, we made a big tent out of the beekeeper outfits, because it's hot inside those buildings. You want to come in?"

"Echo," Darrin said carefully. "The last time I saw you, you tried to shoot me."

"Yeah, but it didn't work, did it? I've moved on. I hope you can too. Bygones and all that. We had some good times, didn't we?" She dismounted the bear in a smooth motion, patted its flank, and sent it on its way.

"You united the bears?" Harczos said.

"Yup. It's been pretty great."

"It's keeping you entertained, then?" Darrin couldn't keep the bitterness out of his voice, even though pissing off Echo could be dangerous.

"It's doing more than keeping me entertained," Echo said. "It's given my life a purpose. And a person needs a purpose like a car needs a driver."

Darrin frowned. "Arturo said something like that to me once."

Echo nodded. "I thought it sounded like one of his greatest hits. Good advice, though."

"Arturo is the man you met, the driver of the Wendigo?" Harczos said. Darrin nodded, and then Harczos shivered, as he always did when the subject of the Wendigo came up, though it was a shiver more of awe than fear. He'd told Darrin stories, myths, and legends about the car, which had not always been a car, and probably would not always remain so. The Wendigo was older than Harczos and Ismael combined. Possibly as old as the whole briarpatch itself. If there *were* gods of the briarpatch, then the Wendigo was probably one of them.

"Arturo helped Echo track me and Ismael down," said Darrin.

"Only at knifepoint, and gunpoint, later," Echo said. "And he didn't know I was going to shoot you, Darrin. He's kinda dumb, and he's on one of those big-time hopeless quests, but he liked you." Echo sounded almost like she was trying to reassure him.

Has Echo become a queen, Darrin wondered, *or is she just a sociopath pretending to be a queen? Does it even matter?*

"After I shot you, and you disappeared, I went after Ismael and we blundered into a bunch of bears. Ismael threw himself at one of them, and it took a swipe at him, so *he* escaped, while I got stuck facing them. I showed them who was boss, and I've been boss ever since. Bears are hierarchical creatures, and people are *totally* hierarchical creatures, and these guys are both. They just needed a strong leader."

"Are you like them?" Harczos asked. "Do you transform?"

"Hell, no," Echo said. "I'm *me*. I've always been me, and I always will be. I don't need to change into anything else. But we help each other. I still can't navigate this stupid place on my own, but the bears can, so I ride them where I need to go. Riding a bear's more comfortable than riding in the Wendigo. That thing had like no shocks. You sure you don't want some honey?"

"I think we'd better move on," Darrin said. "Unless that would . . . upset you."

"I don't get upset as easily as I used to. You never did anything to wrong me, Darrin. You don't have to worry. If you run into Ismael, though, tell him I've got an army at my back now, and that I *remember* what he did. I'll find him, sometime, and when I do, he'll be in trouble. I won't kill him—I know I can't. But I can make him wish he was dead, even more than he wishes that *anyway*."

She smiled. How had he ever thought, even for a moment, blinded by sex and grief, that it was a pretty smile?

"Sure," he said. "I'll pass the word along if I see him." Echo waved and walked off, back toward her pavilion.

"You used to have sex with her?" Harczos said after a moment, and Darrin nodded as Harczos went on. "I used to think the Wendigo was the scariest thing I'd ever heard of in the briarpatch, but she makes me reconsider. We should count ourselves very lucky she isn't immortal."

"You've got that right."

10

"I can't change your mind?" Harczos asked. It was a week or so after they'd encountered Echo, and Darrin had come to a decision. They sat in the back of a wrecked convertible in a junkyard that seemed to stretch for miles in every direction, beneath a sky the colour of old engine grease, lit by a sun as dull as a dirty penny.

"No, I'm going. You sure you won't come with me?"

Harczos shook his head. "I understand your desire to find Bridget. But I am happy with my travels. There are countless places in the briarpatch I have never seen. You should see them with me."

"I'll never be able to get my head straight if I don't find Bridget. I'll feel like I've shirked my duty. I want to move on with my life, but there's too much holding me back." He thought of Bridget, and her attempt to cast off her old life and leap headfirst into the light. She hadn't been able to let everything go, and neither could he, and Darrin didn't think that was a bad thing. He hadn't told Harczos his *other* reason for leaving, because Harczos wouldn't help him, and might even try to stop him.

"I will visit the bridge to the land of the dead from time to time, so if you'd like to rejoin me, you can find me there. Yes?"

"Okay," Darrin said. "Do you really think I'll be able to find the Wendigo?"

"No. But if you give yourself up to the will of the briarpatch, the Wendigo might find *you*, if it so wills. I think it knows everything that happens here." He got out of the car and lifted the sledgehammer from where it leaned against the rear fender. "Last chance to change your mind."

"Go for it," Darrin said. Harczos grunted, lifted the hammer, and swung it at Darrin's head.

Before the hammer could strike, the briarpatch scooped Darrin up and carried him out of harm's way.

11

Arturo opened up the Wendigo's trunk and lifted out a heavy wicker picnic basket. Orville sprawled on a blanket in the sunshine nearby, and Bridget was singing a song about smoking pot, one of the many things she vocally missed about being alive. Arturo slammed the car hood and carried the basket over to the blanket. "Let's see what the Wendigo provided today," he said, and opened it up. "Sandwiches." He unwrapped one portion and sniffed it. "Tuna fish." He handed it over to Orville. "And bottles of black cherry soda. Unmarked bottles, natch. Courtesy of Wendigo Beverage Imports, I guess." He frowned. "That's weird, though. Three bottles of pop, and three sandwiches, instead of just two."

"That's just cruel," Bridget said. "Reminding me I can't *eat*."

"The Wendigo ain't usually that bitchy." Arturo shrugged and tucked into his lunch. This was a pleasant place, very pastoral—much nicer than the beach where they'd camped a couple of nights ago, beside an ocean the colour of piss. Arturo wondered if this was a field in the real world somewhere, Kansas or something maybe. It was pretty enough, and the sun looked right, so maybe. He settled down, relaxing. He'd been a little wary of travelling with Orville and Bridget initially, but they'd proven themselves good company. Bridget's brittleness and tension had settled down after a few days, and Arturo's continuous reminders that Darrin was okay, that he *couldn't* die, finally sank in, and she seemed to accept that finding him was merely a matter of time. They were seemingly no closer to finding Marjorie *or* Darrin, but Arturo was used to being patient. And the Wendigo provided. When they couldn't find something to eat, they could always open the trunk and find food. When it rained, they could open the trunk and find raingear. When it was cold, they could open the trunk and find blankets. The things the Wendigo provided had a tendency to disappear if you stopped paying attention to them, but that was okay.

Orville was surprisingly good company too, with a streak of self-deprecating humour, and countless stories of misery and misfortune that he managed to make funny. He was clearly head-over-heels in love with a dead girl, but Arturo could relate. At least Orville got to spend time with Bridget, even if he couldn't touch her. Things could've been worse for all of them. They kept going, and they found hints of Darrin's passage, occasionally encountering people who claimed to have seen him, often as recently as a few days or weeks ago. But looking for someone in the briarpatch was difficult. You couldn't ask around and find out what direction they'd been going, because every direction was fractal with possible destinations. Still, Arturo was confident. They'd find him. And, if not, at least looking for him gave a shape and direction to Bridget's and Orville's existence, and that was just as important.

Arturo broke out a deck of cards. Orville was a fiend for poker, and Bridget liked playing too. Her manual dexterity wasn't the greatest when it came to manipulating such small items—"Ever try doing card tricks while wearing boxing gloves?"—so they propped the cards up with a rock where she could see them and nobody else could. He was shuffling when a banging noise erupted from the Wendigo, and they all jumped.

"What the hell?" Arturo muttered, hurrying over to the car. He'd never heard it make a noise like *that* before. The banging was coming from inside the trunk, and Arturo had a horrible vision of some terrible monster jumping out. But, hell, this was the *Wendigo*. Monsters were afraid of *it*. Orville and Bridget joined him, looking down at the trunk, which thumped and shuddered.

"Better open it," Bridget said.

Arturo nodded. He touched the trunk, and it popped open, without need for a key. Arturo was the key.

Darrin—a tanned Darrin, with a beard—sat up from inside the trunk. "Hey, guys," he said.

Bridget burst out crying, and Arturo just grinned. "Hey," he said. "You want a sandwich and a bottle of pop, old buddy?"

ISMAEL HAS A PLAN

1

"So that's it," Darrin said, sitting on the grass with his dead lover, the man she was haunting, and Arturo. "I think Ismael has to be stopped. Who knows how many more people he'll hurt?"

Bridget nodded. "But how?"

Darrin shrugged and took a sip of his soda. "We'll give him what he wants. We'll take him to the better world."

"You *found* it?" Orville said.

"Sure," Darrin said. "And it's not that great." He told them what Harczos had told him, about dissolving into the light, becoming one with it, and losing yourself.

"A year ago, that would have sounded great to me," Orville said. "But I'm a little more attached to myself now. I never thought the search for transcendence was a moving target."

"I didn't know it was like that," Bridget said, worry line visible on her forehead. "I'm . . . not sure it's what I want either."

"I'll take you there if you like," Darrin said. He had trouble looking at her. Even beyond the fact of her death, they'd both changed so much in the past several months, he wasn't sure who he was looking at—or who was doing the looking. "But I don't think it would appeal to you."

"Let me think about it," Bridget said. Orville looked at her with hopeless longing, and Darrin felt a pang on his behalf, though he didn't know the man at all. Orville had feelings for Bridget, clearly, but Bridget was just with the guy because she was *haunting* him, right? Darrin found that his own feelings for

Bridget existed mostly in the past tense—the passionate feelings, at least. At some point during his travels with Harczos, he'd come to terms with Bridget's death, and more importantly, he'd accepted that she was lost to him. She still cared about him—she'd said so a dozen times already, and he believed her, and told her so. He still cared about her, in that he wanted to see her safe, and happy, whatever those words meant for a bodiless spirit. But he was no longer the Darrin who had loved her, and she was no longer the person he'd loved— assuming she ever really *had* been that person. He'd never understood her true nature until she was no longer in his life. That was sad, but such sadness was part of life, and he accepted it. They'd . . . grown apart. It happened.

"So you'll help me?" he said. "And I'll help you, if I can?"

"Sure," Arturo said. "Where do we start?"

"With Echo otherwise occupied, there's only one person I can think of," Darrin said. "Let's go see my old friend Nicholas."

2

Nicholas came into his apartment, hung his jacket on a coat hook, and walked, humming, into the dim living room. As he reached out to turn on the lamp, Darrin said, "Working late tonight, Nicholas?"

"Oh, hell," Nicholas said, and switched on the lamp. He turned to face Darrin, who sat in the far corner of the room on a barstool, his back against the wall. "I thought you were lost forever, bro. Ismael said you were probably so deep inside the briarpatch you'd never find your way out again."

"Ismael's full of shit about a lot of things," Darrin said. He looked at his old friend, his betrayer, and still didn't know how to feel about him—it was nothing so simple as hatred, because he could still remember the good times he and Nicholas had shared. But hatred was a large part of it.

"That beard looks stupid on you," Nicholas said. "No offense, but with the raggedy hair, you've got a real crazy woodsman thing going on." He went to the liquor cabinet and poured himself a drink, scotch neat, and took a sip. "Want something to drink?"

"I need to know where to find Ismael, Nicholas."

Nicholas set his glass down. "Sorry, bro. You remember non-disclosure agreements. It's pretty much like that."

"But you are still working for him? Still hoping he'll make you immortal?"

Nicholas waved a hand and grinned. "Hell, that ship has sailed. I am immortal. Ismael took me to the fountain of youth months ago, and dipped me in the waters."

Darrin had no doubt that Ismael had taken him *somewhere* and dipped him in *something*, but he doubted it was the water of eternal life. "How do you know he wasn't lying to you?"

"Aw, I feel better than I ever have, like I can wrestle mountain lions and fuck ten chicks a night. It's gotta be immortality."

Or a placebo effect, Darrin thought. The problem with immortality was that there was no way to test it without risking the death of the subject. Nicholas would only realize he'd been tricked when he died, and by then, it would be too late by definition.

"So you don't work for Ismael anymore? That's smart, at least."

"Nah, we still have a business relationship." Nicholas dropped into an overstuffed armchair and kicked one leg over the side, like a boy king lounging on a throne. "I do all kinds of things for Ismael, shit he doesn't have time for, real estate deals, helping out with legal arrangements, stuff like that. I'm no lawyer, but I know the guys to hire. He can't be bothered to do all that stuff himself. He's got all his spiritual shit to deal with, so I help with the practicalities."

Darrin shook his head. "Why are you working for him? Jesus, Nicholas, you fucked me over because you thought you'd get to live forever, and while I can't forgive you, I can understand it. But what's in it for you now? What can he possibly be offering you?"

"You would not *believe* the heaps of cash Ismael has." Nicholas shook his head. "I guess when you live forever and you hardly buy anything and most of your friends wind up killing themselves and leaving you their whole estates, the cash starts to pile up. Anyway, he pays me well for my services."

"I thought you were making good money?"

"You can never be too rich. Especially if I'm going to live forever, I don't want to spend any of that time poor. It takes a lot of money to keep up quality of life over the long haul. Anyway, the stuff he's asking me to do now, it's not all psychologically complicated like that thing with you. That tore me up, Darrin. You gotta know that. And really, it was for your own good, right? You were in a rut, just spinning your wheels, and Bridget was going to leave you sooner or later, no doubt. And now, look at you. You've practically got fucking *superpowers*. You can walk around in a whole secret magical world. Pretty sweet deal. It's gotta beat the hell out of checking out old subway tunnels and abandoned train stations, or doing those little treasure hunt things you used to like. So, I know it seems like I shafted you, but I really think I helped you out. I understand if we can't be tight anymore, and I'm bummed about that, but everything worked out okay."

"Except Bridget is dead," Darrin said.

Nicholas didn't answer, just swirled the liquor in his glass. After a while, he sighed. "Yeah, but she made her choice. Ismael doesn't force people to do anything. He just helps them out."

That wasn't quite true, Darrin knew—Harczos had told him about Ismael's ability to project his emotions, and about his occasional acts of outright murder. "What is Ismael doing now?" Darrin said. "I know he's got some kind of plan, a plan B, since things with me fell through."

"Sorry. I told you, that's NDA territory. I didn't sign anything, but let's just say, me and him have an understanding."

"Okay," he said. "Now, Arturo."

Arturo and Orville stepped in from the hallway, where they'd been lurking and listening, and crept up behind Nicholas's chair. Arturo threw a rope around Nicholas and leaned back, pulling it tight, pinning Nicholas into the seat. Darrin walked over, avoiding Nicholas's kicking feet, and he and Orville grabbed the arms of the chair and dragged it into the kitchen, where there was an entryway to the briarpatch Darrin had found after days of searching.

They dragged the chair through a shadow beside the refrigerator and on into the briarpatch. This place was close to the edge of a rocky promontory, beneath a black starless sky lit only by an aurora the colour of rainbows in an oil slick, and by the ruby glow of fires pulsing far below. The air reeked of something that wasn't quite sulphur. Arturo tied the rope, throwing a few more loops around Nicholas to secure him in place. At first, Nicholas cursed at them, then went silent as Arturo, Darrin, and Orville all formed a semicircle before him. Bridget loomed up from the darkness, scowling at him. She'd never liked Nicholas, and he hadn't given her a reason to change her mind.

"What, is this some Mafia-style bullshit?" Nicholas said, his face mostly shadowed. "I told you, I'm immortal now. You don't scare me."

"Let's say you are immortal," Darrin said. "Do you think it would hurt if we kicked your chair off this rock, to bounce down into that chasm, into the fire?"

"You wouldn't do it in a million years," Nicholas said, but his voice was fake-confident, a flavour of bravado Darrin had heard often over the years of their friendship.

"You conspired against me with Ismael. You fucked Echo in front of me. You knew she was a lying psychopath, and you didn't tell me. The fact that you got me fired from my job is actually at the bottom of the list of bad shit you did to me. If I ever owed you anything, Nicholas, from friendship to brotherhood to goodwill, you burned through it. These are my friends now, Arturo and Orville and Bridget, and you're my enemy. I will push you over if you don't tell me everything you know about Ismael, about what he's doing, and about where I can find him. Do you understand?"

Nicholas didn't answer. Darrin went to the chair and put his foot against the base, shoving the chair a few inches closer to the precipice. Orville gasped, and Arturo shushed him. "I asked if you understood, Nicholas," Darrin said. "Answer me, *bro*."

"Yeah, shit, yeah, quit it!" Nicholas said. "Hell, I don't owe Ismael anything now, I'll help you out. Me and you go back, Darrin, there's no need for this kind of crap."

"Right," Darrin said. "Now talk."

Nicholas swallowed, then began. "These past months, while you've been gone, Ismael's been making new friends. Taking on new students. Like, a few dozen of them. I mean . . . I guess you'd call it a cult. Ismael gave them all the same spiel he did Bridget—come to the briarpatch, get a glimpse of heaven, and all you have to do to live there forever is *die*. They're all hard-core, true believers. They're going to march out to the Golden Gate Bridge one morning and then jump, all at once, like massive tandem base-jumping, but with no parachutes."

"Why?" Darrin said. "Is he just trying to, what, mass-produce transcendence?"

"Ismael has this idea. A theory. He thinks that so many souls tearing free of their bodies all at once might make, like, pinpricks in reality. See, imagine if a portal to the better world opens up underneath all of them at the same time. That's a lot of passages all at once, like punching holes in a piece of construction paper with the tip of a pen. If you punch enough holes, you don't have a piece of paper anymore, so much as a bunch of empty space with scraps of paper *around* it. Ismael thinks if he opens enough holes to the better world all at once, it'll loosen reality so he'll be able to pass through bodily. So he'll jump from the bridge a moment after his followers do, and, he hopes, fall into the light after them."

"And if it doesn't work, he'll just bounce away to safety in the briarpatch," Darrin said.

"Pretty much," Nicholas agreed.

Darrin pushed for more details, and Nicholas seemed genuinely eager to provide what he could. "Okay," Darrin said at last. "One more thing. I need you to give a message to Ismael."

3

"Ismael won't believe us," Bridget said. They were all lying belly-down on the ridge of a hill overlooking the compound below, trying to stay out of sight. Even Bridget had to keep a low profile; if Ismael had taught any of his new pupils to travel to and from the briarpatch, to perceive the hidden pathways of the world, then they might be able to see her, and a horde of angry cultists running up the hill toward them would really spoil their reconnaissance mission.

"Probably not." Darrin peered through binoculars at the property below—Ismael's "place in the country." Darrin had sent Nicholas with a message: if Ismael would meet him peacefully, Darrin would take him to the better world. But Ismael would probably think it was a trick, even though Darrin meant it sincerely. Darrin hadn't told Harczos his plan, for fear Harczos would try to stop him. That might still be a problem, but Darrin would deal with it when the time came.

Ismael had been a busy man during the months Darrin and the others had wandered the briarpatch. Having failed to get Darrin's help achieving his goal, he was well on his way to enacting his backup plan. Darrin passed the binoculars to Arturo.

"I see maybe twenty-five, thirty people down there. Probably more in the buildings." The old farm below was only a few miles from the Golden Gate Bridge, on the Marin side, where—if you had enough money—you could experience rural peacefulness within sight of the lights of San Francisco.

"That could have been me," Orville said, lying on his back and staring up at the sky. "If Ismael had been that organized when I first talked to him, I'd be down there getting excited about jumping off a bridge."

"You gotta admit he has a good schtick," Arturo said. "Most cult leaders have to get by on charisma and psychological tricks. Ismael can take his people by the hand and lead them to a no-shit, magical, other world. It must be pretty easy for him to convince them. And now he's got them all down there, with their heads shaved, dressed in white. . . ."

"Taking away their individuality." Bridget ran the zipper of her red coat up and down, up and down. "Making sure they've given up on their old lives. Brainwashing them. He doesn't want a repeat of what happened with me."

"You'd think the cops would do somethin' about it," Arturo said.

Bridget shook her head. "They might start paying attention if he had hundreds of followers instead of fifty, or if they were selling drugs of stockpiling weapons. But California's full of little communes and cults and compounds. Lots of new age types and hippies, and plenty of fringe religious groups too. It's not illegal to be a weirdo, and cops around here tend to be careful about not trampling on religious rights. I doubt Ismael is talking about mass suicide in public, anyway. As far as anybody knows, they're just looking for meaning in their lives. Like I was."

"Even if Ismael *does* believe me, I'm not sure he'd leave these people behind," Darrin said. Without the binoculars, Ismael's cultists were just a handful of white specks moving around the ugly, functional buildings of the compound. They looked like sheep. "He thinks he's helping them, taking them to the better world." He shook his head. "I don't even think his plan will work though. It's crazy, right?"

Orville rolled over. "I don't know. When I jumped from the bridge, and saw the light below me, it really did look like a portal opening up that I would pass through, you know? Multiply that by fifty or so. . . ."

Darrin grunted.

He had his doubts. His glimpse of the light had been an issue of perception, not a physical process at all. Maybe the force of dozens of people jumping all at once would tear apart reality more seriously, but it seemed like a long shot. But then, what did Ismael care? He'd spent months getting the group together, and he'd send them all to their deaths, but if it didn't work the way he hoped, so what? He'd only wasted time, and time was one thing he had in ample measure. He wouldn't regret the deaths of his followers . . . and neither would they, assuming they all made it safely through to the light. But it would still be a tragedy, as much as Jonestown, as much as Heaven's Gate, a bunch of deluded people led away from their best interests at a madman's behest.

"I doubt I could even get in to see him," Darrin said.

"Nah," Arturo said. "He's got a couple guys at the gate, watchin' the road. Maybe you could find a path through the briarpatch into the place, get to his inner sanctum or whatever, but who knows if those guys are armed? All it takes is one bullet and, bam, you bounce out to someplace in the briarpatch, who knows how deep?"

Darrin nodded. "But we know where he's going, and when. Nicholas told us that much, and I doubt Ismael would change his plans just because we know about them. He's got a brainwashed army down there, so what can we do to stop them?"

Ismael intended to march his people to the bridge in eight days, once the last of them was properly prepared. Nicholas had finally admitted that if Ismael succeeded in passing on to the better world, all the estates of the people committing suicide would be willed to Nicholas in a few months through a series of blind trusts. Nicholas was no better than a grave robber, and perilously close to an accessory to mass murder.

"Well, exactly," Bridget said. "What *can* we do? Park the Wendigo outside their gates so they can't get out? There are only four of us, and I'm not much good in a fight. You want to run up to Ismael when he leads the march and try to convince him you're on the level, ask him to leave those people behind?"

Darrin sighed. "No. I have an idea. It sucks, and it'll take just about all the time we have left to even try, but I can't think of anything else."

4

"So that's the plan," Darrin said after a few days of travel into the briarpatch. He sat uncomfortably on a rough wooden stool at the base of an equally rough wooden throne on a raised dais. A breeze blew through the white pavilion, carrying with it the smell of smoke and bears.

Echo sprawled in her high seat. "Huh. I'm not so clear on what's in it for *me*. Things are pretty cushy here. Why leave?"

"Do you still hate Ismael?"

Echo laughed. "Does a bear shit in my throne room?"

Darrin glanced and sniffed around. The answer was definitively yes. "So help me for that reason. To ruin his plans. To get back at him."

Echo looked at the ceiling and hummed thoughtfully. "But you want to let him go to the better world, right? I don't *want* him to fulfil his life's dream."

"No, no," Darrin said. He'd hated lying to Harczos, but had no qualms about doing so with Echo. "We're going to *tell* him we're taking him to the better world. But it's a trick. We'll tie him up and take him as deep in the briarpatch as we can and we'll dump him. We'll give him a fake map to the light of a better world and let him waste a few decades looking for it." Darrin rooted around in his pack and came up with one of his thick sheaves of maps. "See? I already made the map."

Echo clapped her hands. "Sounds fun, Darrin. When you can't kill somebody or even really torture them much without them disappearing, I guess psychological torment's the best you can do. I never knew you had this perverse streak. I would've made things between us a lot kinkier if I had. Okay. Me and the bears will be there. It'll take us a few days to make the trip anyway. You mind if we take a few of the cultists back with us when we're done? We can always use more recruits."

Darrin hesitated. "What if I *do* mind?"

Echo shrugged. "I'll do it anyway. I just won't expect applause."

He shook his head. "I won't let you take people against their will. If that's your price, I'll find another way." He stood up.

She rolled her eyes. "Sit down, Darrin. Don't be a drama queen. Some of these people are ready to jump off a bridge from what you told me. I'm not looking for hostages. I'm looking for converts. If they want to come with me, willingly, what do you care?"

Darrin rubbed his eyes. "Echo, if you hurt them—"

She shook her head. "Why would I hurt them? I'm the mama bear here, Darrin. Any of my people can leave any time they want. But they like being here. They just want someone to be the leader. Just like Ismael's little cultists do. At least I won't convince them it's a good idea to jump off a bridge."

Darrin sighed. Echo seemed less sadistic since joining up with the bears, certainly, but he was under no illusions. He was dealing with a devil but she was his best chance to stop Ismael, who was a worse devil, if only by virtue of the fact that he'd be around causing trouble for centuries. Giving up a few people to Echo's cult in order to save them from *Ismael's* cult was hardly a clear win, but the alternative was worse. "Fine," he said and had the surreal experience of shaking the hand of his old lover, the queen of the bears.

5

Ismael woke on the morning of the great leap with more than his usual amount of trepidation. *I have allowed myself to hope*, he thought. *Thus, I am sure to be disappointed*. He'd allowed himself to hope about Darrin too, and that had ended as badly as anything ever had.

Ismael emerged from his room and went down the stairs into his private dining room. His followers ate together in a converted barn, but Ismael preferred privacy. Nicholas was waiting for him at the table, wearing a suit of all things, even though they had a three mile hike in the pre-dawn air ahead of them. Ismael sat and took one of the croissants from the box Nicholas had brought.

"You think Darrin and his merry men are going to try to stop us?" Nicholas said.

Ismael shrugged. "We have them outnumbered. And you have your pistol. If Darrin approaches, shoot him in the chest. The briarpatch will lift him out of our way."

Nicholas grimaced. "Sure. I hope it doesn't come to that. I don't want to shoot at Darrin."

"Mmm," Ismael said, nibbling the pastry he didn't have much of an appetite for. "Are my people gathered in the yard?"

"Yeah. Doing spontaneous calisthenics to clear their minds."

"Good," Ismael said. He'd always worried that trying to teach many people at once would be more difficult than single prospects, like Bridget and many others before her, but the opposite had proven true. Once you had a group of dedicated people, they created a normalizing atmosphere, and new recruits could be assimilated quickly. Limiting their food intake, reinforcing their places as part of a group—not as individuals—all the tried-and-true approaches of cult leaders worked well for him. But unlike Jim Jones or David Koresh or Marshall Applewhite, Ismael *did* have a true revelation, and could offer real salvation.

All these desperate people—runaways, recent divorcees and widows, disillusioned hippies, all the types susceptible to cults like this—wanted someone to show them miracles, and take responsibility for their lives. They'd all been across the bridge behind his shed, and seen their own corpses. They'd all been to the scenic overlook, and seen the light. They knew what they were going toward. They were 47 empty vessels, waiting to be filled with light.

And, with luck, Ismael would be able to go with them. He imagined a serene pool of light appearing below him when they all jumped from the bridge, and Ismael himself falling down, and through, and finally into the light he'd so longed for.

And if it didn't work, well, he'd try again, with a bigger group.

Ismael put down the pastry and rose. "It's time." Out in the courtyard, lit only by the light of the moon and stars, his people were gathered, dressed in their white clothes—no colours, and nothing they'd owned before—wearing simple walking shoes. "My people!" he shouted. "What will you do this morning?"

"Leap!" they shouted back, in one thunderous voice.

"How will you leap?"

"Headfirst!"

"Where will you land?"

"In a better world!"

"Let us go." He began walking, with Nicholas by his side. The followers mostly didn't like Nicholas, seeing him rightly as an outsider, but they understood he was the caretaker of worldly necessities, helping to keep them insulated from the miseries and indignities of the wider world. They'd signed all their possessions and estates over to a trust, which Nicholas administered, keeping the farm running. Someone had to tend to worldly matters, at least until they managed to leave that world behind. . . .

The electric gates swung open, and Ismael led his people up the compound's long driveway toward the road to the bridge. The lights of San Francisco twinkled in the distance like earthbound stars.

"ISMAEL!"

The voice was loud, amplified, and seemed to come from everywhere. Nicholas was startled, spinning around, and the followers made confused noises, but Ismael was calm. "It's only Darrin," he said, then raised his voice "Keep walking, my people!"

"Ismael!" Darrin's voice on the megaphone went on. "You don't have to do this! I found Harczos! He showed me the path to the light! I can show you! Spare these people!"

Ismael gritted his teeth and walked on. Lies. Nicholas had brought the same message days ago, and he hadn't believed it then, either. Besides, he wasn't endangering these people. He was saving them.

"I can't let you do this, Ismael!" the voice boomed.

"He cannot stop us!" Ismael shouted, for the benefit of his followers. "We are many! We go in search of a better world!"

"A better world!" his followers shouted, louder than Darrin's amplified voice.

But then, out of the gloom ahead of them, the bears emerged. At least a score of them, blocking the dirt road completely.

"Oh, fuck me," Nicholas said.

Ismael cursed. One of his followers screamed, and that set off a general panic of voices and confused milling at his back. He'd warned them all about bears, in very strenuous terms, when they entered the briarpatch to see miracles, so naturally they were afraid, faced with them now. Ismael wasn't afraid the way his people were—the bears couldn't hurt him—but he was confused about their presence. Had Darrin somehow led them here? But how could anyone get the bears to do anything?

One of the bears, a huge grizzly, came forward. A woman rode on its back.

"Echo," Ismael said. "Nicholas, shoot her for me, would you?"

"Fuck that," Nicholas said. "She's got an army of motherfucking bears, Ismael!"

"Coward." Ismael reached out to take the gun from Nicholas's jacket. He didn't reach it in time. The bear Echo was riding roared and surged forward, rising up, and lifted a paw. Nicholas fell backwards, whimpering, and scampered away on all fours. Ismael watched him run with disgust. Apparently he didn't *really* believe he was immortal, despite the fine story Ismael had spun to convince him. Echo cooed at the bear, and it sank back down on all fours again.

"Be calm, my people!" Ismael said, but it didn't seem to have much of an affect. The neat row of followers behind him dissolved. People were running back to the compound. Not all of them, but some, and the others would follow soon if he couldn't seize control.

"Izzy," Echo said. "You know how you never settled that outstanding balance you owe me? Well, don't worry. I think this is *plenty* entertaining. We're square now."

"Ismael." Darrin emerged from the shadows beside the road. He looked older, more serious somehow, and not just because of the beard. "I just want to save these people. Tell them to go back to the compound, and I'll take you to the better world."

"Of course you will," Ismael said. "Why wouldn't you? How have I ever wronged you?"

"It's true," Darrin said. "I can take you there in one jump. Just take my hand. I'll show you."

Ismael shook his head.

"What can it hurt?" Darrin asked. "Let me touch you, and you'll see." He held out his hand.

Reluctantly, but plagued as ever by the shadow of hope, Ismael extended his hand.

Darrin clutched it, and a passageway did appear to Ismael's eyes, not far from the place where Darrin had emerged, a ragged opening in the air that led somewhere else. And in that space . . . there was light.

Tears sprang to Ismael's eyes. It was not the pitiful light of the scenic overlook. It was the pure soft cleansing light he sometimes glimpsed when watching people leap to their welcome deaths. It was truly the light of a better world.

Darrin pulled his hand away, and the light vanished. Ismael cried out and tried to clutch him, but Echo's bear shouldered into the way. "Please," Ismael said. "Please, please, please." How had he ever doubted? Darrin meant him no ill. Darrin would help him.

"Tell them to go back, Ismael."

Ismael whirled. He wanted to save these people from their misery, but if the choice was a slim chance of reaching the light through their deaths, or the *certainty* of reaching the light by leaving them to their suffering, the choice was clear. "The omens are bad today!" he shouted. "There are bears and voices from the darkness! Return to the compound, and continue your meditations, and we will try again tomorrow! Nicholas will give you further instructions!"

The people muttered, but they obeyed, as they'd been taught to obey, and they dispersed.

"Take me," Ismael said. "I'm sorry I doubted you, please, take me."

"Yeah, take him," Echo said. "Get him out of my sight."

Darrin nodded, and took Ismael's hand. The passageway to the light appeared before them, and Darrin gestured to let Ismael lead the way.

6

"I hope we can trust Echo to do her part," Arturo said, sitting behind the wheel of the Wendigo with his dark glasses on. They were parked in a little nothing place, a barely there weedy lot of a spot on the outskirts of the briarpatch. The Wendigo's headlights—the high beams—were on, shining toward the passage to Marin, in the plausible world, mimicking the light of Ismael's hoped-for salvation.

It was a dirty trick, but whatever got the job done.

"There they are," Orville said. He was standing outside the car, holding a rag that reeked of chemicals.

"Don't hold it over his nose too long," Bridget said. "We don't want to risk giving him a lethal dose and losing him."

Ismael walked into the headlights, his arms held before him, eyes open wide to the brightness. He looked incandescently happy.

Orville, wearing dark sunglasses, circled around, crept up behind Ismael, and clamped the chloroformed rag over his nose. Ismael struggled, but only weakly—the lights were a great soporific. Once Ismael slumped, unconscious, held up by Orville and Darrin, Arturo flipped off the headlights. Orville took a roll of duct tape and started binding Ismael's hands and feet.

Arturo opened the back seat and swept out the recent accumulation of receipts, menus, and ticket stubs. They needed the whole car clear to fit everyone.

Bridget could technically sit in somebody's lap, but it was like having a dust devil pressed up against you, and nobody enjoyed the sensation. Orville and Darrin manhandled the unconscious Ismael into the back seat.

"Getting in, Darrin?" Bridget asked.

"I need to check on something first," Darrin said. "Take the long way, would you, Arturo? I'll meet you on the bridge."

"Sure thing," Arturo said, and started the car.

7

Nicholas lay in a ditch by the road, hidden by bushes, and listened for the approach of bears. It was quiet out there, but bears could be quiet. His pants were wet with urine, and he wondered if the bears could smell it.

The bushes rustled. Nicholas took the pistol Ismael had given him—a square-bodied, round barrelled old Luger—from its shoulder holster and held it out awkwardly before him.

"Hi Nicholas," Darrin said. "I thought you should know. You aren't immortal. Ismael lied to you."

"Fuck you, Darrin," Nicholas whispered. "Ismael knows secrets."

Darrin sighed. "Okay. Suit yourself. Just be careful. Don't do stupid things because you think you can't die. I've got . . . mixed feelings about this whole immortality business myself."

"Be quiet," Nicholas hissed. "What if those bears hear you?"

"Nicholas, I *brought* the bears. Now give me your gun."

"No."

"Give me the gun, or I'll call the bears."

"You wouldn't. Me and you, we—"

"Please," Darrin said. "Don't try me."

Nicholas whimpered. "What, are you going to shoot me?" He threw the gun at Darrin's feet. "Shit, go on, I deserve it, right? I don't care, I'm *immortal*." Nicholas started crying, tears dripping from his face into the dirt, and he didn't even know why.

"I won't shoot you, Nicholas," Darrin said. "I just need to check on something." He picked up the Luger, and left without another word.

EVERYBODY GETS WHAT'S COMING TO THEM

1

"I'm scared," one of Ismael's liberated cultists said on their long walk through the woods, on the far edge of the territories Echo had claimed for her own. "I want to go back to my cot."

"You don't need a cot," Echo said, riding her bear, once a common street mugger, who preferred now to stay in bear form all the time. "You haven't known comfort 'til you've spent a cold night curled up with a bunch of bears. It doesn't get any warmer than that."

"I guess." The woman trudged along with the half dozen others Echo had convinced to join her.

Echo grinned. They'd all get used to it. The dead queen bee's hypnagogic honey would help them adjust. Even with all the bees dead, there was enough honey to last for years, and it was better than any drug Echo had ever tried. Being the queen of bears would keep her occupied for a long time, probably, and if she ever got bored, hell—there was a whole wide world out there to fuck with, right? And maybe she'd encounter Ismael, wandering around with his stupid fake map, and get to mess with him, too.

Maybe she could even figure out a way to invade Ismael's beloved better world, and put out those lights for good. If she could get some sunglasses like the ones Arturo had, and get them fitted on the bears. . . .

The future was bright. Echo had never been happier than she was right then, and she'd spent most of her life being pretty happy indeed.

2

Nicholas groaned when his phone rang. He'd come home from the bear-related disaster, having spent an hour cowering in the bushes, and collapsed into bed. Everything had gone to shit, and now someone was calling him. He looked at the clock. Jesus, he'd slept all day. It was nearly twilight. He fumbled for the phone. "Yeah, who is it?"

"Mr. Cloke," said a worried-sounding voice. "This is Martin, with building security. There are, ah, some people here to see you. They're not on your list, but they're very insistent."

"Tell 'em to fuck off," Nicholas growled. "I don't pay to live in a secure building to deal with shit like this."

"Ah, Mr. Cloke, we'd really like you to come speak to them. They refuse to leave."

"Who are they?"

"There are about forty people downstairs, Mr. Cloke," Martin said, and Nicholas finally heard the fear in his voice. "They're all wearing white, and they have shaved heads. They're saying something about bears, that bears kidnapped some of their friends? And other things, sir. They say you have all their money? The police are on their way, but they'll need to talk to you as well—"

Nicholas hung up the phone and sank back into bed. He covered his face with his hands.

Five floors below him people began shouting his name. They sounded pissed. His phone rang again.

3

Harczos sat on the moon-coloured bridge, near the light, wearing sunglasses and holding a crossbow in his lap. Darrin wore a pair of shades from the Wendigo, so he could see Harczos clearly, though he would have been lost in the glare to anyone with unshaded eyes.

"Harczos," Darrin said, standing a dozen feet away from the man. "I wondered if I'd find you here."

Harczos nodded. "Darrin. Did you think I wouldn't know? The way you reacted in the orchard, when I told you I'd denied Ismael the light? I knew you'd try to bring that monster here, and give him peace. And when you do, I will shoot him with this crossbow, and he will be lifted away to safety, and feel the pain of his salvation denied. It's what he deserv—"

Darrin drew the Luger and fired at Harczos's chest. Harczos didn't even have time to look startled. He just vanished, crossbow and all. Darrin tossed the pistol off the side of the bridge. He sighed. Harczos might have shot Darrin as soon as he arrived, but Darrin had counted on the man's love for talk. "Sorry, friend," Darrin said. He had just made an enemy, he knew, one who would travel in the same circles with him forever. But Darrin didn't have a choice—he had to save the world from Ismael's influence while he was still human enough to care.

Darrin turned his back on the light and waited for the Wendigo to arrive.

4

"We had to trick you," Orville said. "Because you wouldn't believe we were telling the truth."

"You weren't telling the truth," Ismael said. He'd stopped trying to fight his way out of the moving car, at least. "And now you've got me inside this *thing*, this Wendigo. You people don't know what this thing is. It's so wrong it makes my teeth ache."

"It's okay, Ismael," Bridget said. "You'll be out of the car soon. My own temptation was to put you in a hole in the ground with plenty of water and a year's supply of dog food to eat, but you've probably suffered worse. Hurting you isn't any good. So we're going to give you what you want."

"And why would you do that?"

"To get rid of you!" Arturo said.

Ismael subsided, and stared past Orville, out the window.

"It's the bridge," Orville said.

Ismael looked. "So it is." The silver bridge appeared below them, at the base of a long low hill, and the Wendigo rolled down and smoothly onto the moon-coloured expanse. They crested the top of the bridge, and Arturo put on the brakes, and turned off the engine.

"There you go." Orville gestured at the light. "We're here, on a bridge, between one thing and another. It's your better world. Just walk there."

"It's a trick," Ismael said. "You'll let me get halfway and then you'll shoot me in the back, you'll send me *away*, you won't let me reach it, just like Harczos did, he taunted me—"

"Just go." Orville opened his door.

Ismael twisted, and slipped his legs out, and Orville cut the tape binding his ankles. Ismael tried to kick him, and Orville stepped back, frowning. "You don't have to do that."

Ismael was crying, his hands still taped in front of him. "It's a trick. You're going to take it away from me."

Darrin walked toward them from the light, and seeing him, Ismael hissed. "Liar."

Darrin looked at Ismael's face, twisted with hate and longing, and managed to feel pity for him.

Bridget went to Ismael. "Let us untie your wrists. We'll let you go in with your hands free."

"I meant you no harm, Bridget," Ismael said. "I only tried to give you what you wanted. Why are you part of this charade?"

"It's okay." she said.

Orville came over, warily, and cut the tape on Ismael's wrists. He didn't try to strike this time, just stared at his feet, not even looking at the light.

Bridget leaned over, and whispered in his ear. He lifted his head, eyes wet and hopeful. "I did," he said. "I really did mean well. I just wanted to spare you all the pain I suffered."

She whispered something else. It hurt Darrin's heart to see her being tender with this man, and reminded him of the way she'd left him for Ismael's promises.

"Yes," Ismael said. "I'll go, if you go with me."

"Bridget!" Orville said, and Darrin stepped forward. She'd looked for the light for so long. If she went in, would she ever come out again?

She looked back at them. "It's okay, guys." She walked toward the light, Ismael shuffling along beside her. A moment before they disappeared into the light, Ismael lifted his head and looked at the splendour before him.

"It's truly beautiful."

And then they were gone. Orville sat down on the hood of the Wendigo. "Is . . . is she going to come back? Or do you think she'll stay in there, in the light?"

"It's not like it's a bad place," Arturo said, chewing the ends of his moustache. "I mean, it's not my idea of heaven, but . . ."

Darrin stared at the light. Having turned his back on it once, it was easier for him to look at now. Orville said it was the same way for him, and Arturo had seen the Wendigo's high beams often enough to develop a degree of immunity to the light's considerable charms.

In his heart, Darrin had finally let Bridget go. He felt ten pounds lighter, and though there was sadness at his core, it was a manageable sadness, at last.

And then Bridget emerged, first the red of her jacket visible. She came back alone, and her eyes were wet. She was a ghost, and she was crying. "It was beautiful in there," she said. "But I couldn't bear the thought of spending eternity melting into Ismael, and having him melt into me." She shook her head. "There at the end . . . he said to tell you 'Thank you.' He said to tell you he was sorry."

"Let's go," Darrin said.

"Where to?" Orville said.

"Um," Arturo said. "There's an envelope on the Wendigo's dashboard. It wasn't there a minute ago." Arturo lifted it out. "It's addressed to you, Darrin."

Darrin took the envelope from Arturo's outstretched hand. There was a single sheet of paper inside, with a few typewritten lines. Darrin nodded, and crumpled the letter in his hand. "Let's go," he said. "I'll drive."

"I don't think that's a good idea," Arturo said.

Darrin shrugged. "It's what the note said I should do." Arturo looked worried. "It's okay, man," Darrin said. "I really think it's okay. Come on."

5

"It's the bridge to the land of the dead," Darrin said.

"Yeah. I can see that." Bridget was standing beside him. "Did that note from the Wendigo tell you to bring me here?"

Darrin shook his head. "It didn't mention you at all. But I thought you should see it. You were always looking for the next thing, you know? The next horizon, the undiscovered country." He gestured toward the deckless bridge in the mist. "There you go. It's there. I just wanted you to know the way."

"I . . . don't know if I'm ready to cross that yet," Bridget said. She looked over at Orville, something well beyond friendship and tenderness in her gaze, and for the first time Darrin realized that Orville's love for her might be reciprocated. In which case, they weren't doomed after all, just . . . very unconventional. "I think I'd like to hang out in the world a little while longer. Orville here's never had the vanilla challah French toast with caramelized bananas at the Blackberry Bistro, and I want to be there the first time he eats them. I want to see him try for the world series of poker, too, even if he says he won't let me cheat for him."

"Sure," Darrin said. "But you know where this place is, if the time ever comes."

"I can find it again, anytime you want, Bridget," Orville said, and the kindness in his voice was enough for Darrin to feel a surge of warmth in sympathy.

"I need to talk to Arturo," Darrin said. "You guys . . . thank you for your help. I couldn't have done it without you. I . . . maybe I'll see you around?"

"Definitely," Bridget said.

Darrin reached into his pocket and withdrew a folded piece of paper. "Here you go, Orville. It's a map. Three steps back to the wider world. It should work for your current emotional state—I assume you guys are pretty happy at the moment, anyway. You'll come out near the duck pond in Montclair, near Highway 13. It's the closest I could get you in the shortest distance."

Orville looked over the map, nodding. "Thanks, Darrin. It was . . . real weird meeting you."

"Yeah," he said, and, after a moment's pause, "Be good to her, would you?"

Orville blushed, and Bridget smiled. Orville embraced Arturo, Bridget said her goodbyes, and then the dead woman and her boyfriend set off together into the mist.

"So," Arturo said. "What's the deal with tryin' to hijack my ride?"

"The note said I was supposed to drive you here, and then tell you to look in the trunk." Darrin shrugged. "I'm just doing what the Wendigo wills."

Arturo grunted and went around to the trunk. Darrin didn't go with him—he wasn't sure he was supposed to. Maybe it was private. The trunk creaked open. Silence.

Then Arturo started laughing. "Come here, Darrin."

Darrin went over and looked. The trunk was full of climbing gear. Ropes, carabiners, an illustrated book on climbing, a harness, and weird discs with handles and buttons on them. Darrin picked one up, pushed the button, and the disc nearly jumped out of his hand, adhering to the lid of the trunk. He let the button go, and the disc released. "Electromagnets," he said. "For climbing on metal, I guess."

"So that's the bridge to the land of the dead, huh?" Arturo said. "So there's a chance, you think, that my Marjorie is over there?"

"It could be," Darrin said. "But . . . hell, Arturo. Are you really going to do this? Try to cross the bridge by climbing on the struts?"

He shrugged. "I'm middle-aged, overweight, and I never climbed anythin' but a *ladder*. What do you think my chances are of making it across?"

"Probably not that good," Darrin said. The equipment looked high-quality, but Arturo didn't know what he was doing.

"Nothin' ventured," Arturo said. "The Wendigo brought me this far. And, hell, worst case scenario, I die. And if I'm lucky, then I wind up crossing this bridge anyway, right?"

"Good luck, Arturo. I hope you find her."

"Even if I don't, I had a pretty interestin' time lookin'. But me and her sure would have a lot to talk about. The stories I could tell. The stories she could tell *me*." He took the climbing equipment out of the trunk and closed the lid. He held out his hand, and Darrin shook it.

"Thanks for taking me out for that drink," Darrin said.

"Thanks for being a great drinkin' buddy. Wish we could've lifted a few more brews together."

"Me too. Kind of funny how the Wendigo went through all this to get you here. I mean, it could have just *driven* you to this bridge in the first place."

Arturo shrugged. "Mysterious ways. The Wendigo has her reasons. Anyway. I'd rather not have you around when I start this. I'd get nervous at you watching and miss my first foothold, you know?"

"Yeah. Okay. Be safe."

"Same to you. If you wind up riding around with the Wendigo, be good to her."

Darrin got into the car, turned the key, and drove away. Though, really, the car drove itself. The note had also said that, after Arturo was gone, Darrin should drive the Wendigo away, park it, and look in the trunk again.

He did, stopping in a wooded area with mushrooms the size of palm trees. He went to the trunk, and it popped open as he approached.

Inside, there was a compass, some surveying equipment, and loads of graph paper. Mapmaking tools. Darrin took everything out. He went to the back door, opened it, took out his pack, and put the new supplies in with his others.

The back door shut itself. Darrin frowned, reached out, and jiggled the handle. It didn't open.

"Ah," Darrin said. "Got it. A person needs a purpose, and I guess I've got mine." Having a car would be useful, but you saw the world more clearly when you were walking in it, instead of looking out from behind glass. If he was going to map the briarpatch, he'd do it one pace at a time.

The Wendigo purred to life and rolled away, down some road Darrin couldn't see.

Darrin looked at the compass in his hand. The needle spun crazily, unable to find any semblance of true north. Darrin laughed, shook his head, and set off again into the briarpatch.

ACKNOWLEDGEMENTS

I'd like to thank the participants of the 2006 Blue Heaven novel writing workshop for their insight and advice: Tobias S. Buckell, Brenda Cooper, Charles Coleman Finlay, Sandra McDonald, Paul Melko, Catherine M. Morrison, Sarah Prineas, William Shunn, Mary Turzillo, and Greg van Eekhout. Their critiques were invaluable. Thanks also to Jenn Reese; my agent Ginger Clark; ChiZine publishers Brett Savory and Sandra Kasturi for giving this novel a home; my editor Chris Edwards for making me make it better; my wife Heather Shaw, who ensures this is the best of all worlds; and my son River, who gave me a whole new set of reasons to live.

ABOUT THE AUTHOR

Tim Pratt's fiction has won a Hugo Award, and he's been a finalist for Sturgeon, Stoker, World Fantasy, Mythopoeic, and Nebula Awards. His other books include two short story collections; a volume of poems; a contemporary fantasy novel called *The Strange Adventures of Rangergirl*; and, as T. A. Pratt, six books (and counting) about sorcerer Marla Mason. He works as a senior editor for *Locus Magazine*, and lives in Berkeley, CA with his wife, Heather Shaw, and their son, River. Find him online at timpratt.org.

EMB
RACE
THE
ODD

PICKING UP THE GHOST
TONE MILAZZO

AVAILABLE AUGUST 15, 2011
FROM CHIZINE PUBLICATIONS

978-1-926851-35-8

ISLES OF THE FORSAKEN
CAROLYN IVES GILMAN

AVAILABLE SEPTEMBER 15, 2011
FROM CHIZINE PUBLICATIONS

978-1-926851-43-3

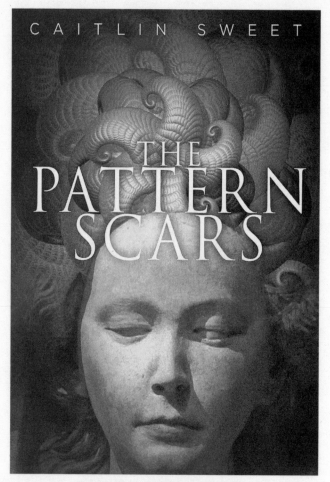

THE PATTERN SCARS
CAITLIN SWEET

AVAILABLE SEPTEMBER 15, 2011
FROM CHIZINE PUBLICATIONS

978-1-926851-43-3

BEARDED WOMEN: STORIES

TERESA MILBRODT

AVAILABLE OCTOBER 15, 2011
FROM CHIZINE PUBLICATIONS

978-1-926851-46-4

ENTER, NIGHT
MICHAEL ROWE

AVAILABLE OCTOBER 15, 2011
FROM CHIZINE PUBLICATIONS

978-1-926851-45-7

978-1-926851-10-5

TOM PICCIRILLI

EVERY SHALLOW CUT

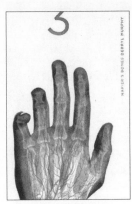

978-1-926851-09-9

DERRYL MURPHY

NAPIER'S BONES

978-1-926851-11-2

DAVID NICKLE

EUTOPIA

978-1-926851-12-9

CLAUDE LALUMIÈRE

***THE DOOR TO
LOST PAGES***

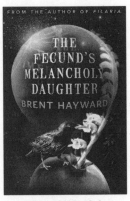

978-1-926851-13-6

BRENT HAYWARD

***THE FECUND'S
MELANCHOLY
DAUGHTER***

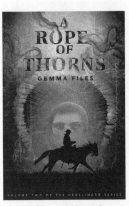

978-1-926851-14-3

GEMMA FILES

A ROPE OF THORNS

978-0-9813746-6-6

GORD ZAJAC

MAJOR KARNAGE

978-0-9813746-8-0

ROBERT BOYCZUK

NEXUS: ASCENSION

978-1-926851-00-6

CRAIG DAVIDSON

SARAH COURT

978-1-926851-06-8

PAUL TREMBLAY

**IN THE
MEAN TIME**

978-1-926851-02-0

HALLI VILLEGAS

**THE HAIR WREATH
AND OTHER STORIES**

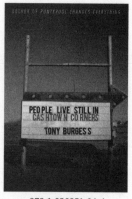

978-1-926851-04-4

TONY BURGESS

**PEOPLE LIVE STILL
IN CASHTOWN
CORNERS**

"IF I COULD SUBSCRIBE TO A PUBLISHER LIKE A MAGAZINE OR A BOOK CLUB—ONE FLAT ANNUAL FEE TO GET EVERYTHING THEY PUBLISH—I WOULD SUBSCRIBE TO CHIZINE PUBLICATIONS."

—ROSE FOX, *PUBLISHERS WEEKLY*

ALSO AVAILABLE FROM CHIZINE PUBLICATIONS

978-0-9812978-9-7

TIM LEBBON

**THE THIEF OF
BROKEN TOYS**

978-0-9812978-8-0

PHILIP NUTMAN

CITIES OF NIGHT

978-0-9812978-7-3

SIMON LOGAN

**KATJA FROM THE
PUNK BAND**

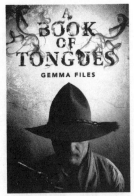

978-0-9812978-6-6

GEMMA FILES

**A BOOK OF
TONGUES**

978-0-9812978-5-9

DOUGLAS SMITH

CHIMERASCOPE

978-0-9812978-4-2

NICHOLAS KAUFMANN

**CHASING THE
DRAGON**

"IF YOUR TASTE IN FICTION RUNS TO THE DISTURBING, DARK, AND AT LEAST PAR-
TIALLY WEIRD, CHANCES ARE YOU'VE HEARD OF CHIZINE PUBLICATIONS—CZP—A
YOUNG IMPRINT THAT IS NONETHELESS PRODUCING STARTLINGLY BEAUTIFUL
BOOKS OF STARKLY, DARKLY LITERARY QUALITY."
—DAVID MIDDLETON, JANUARY MAGAZINE